P9-CBF-222

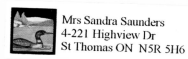
Mrs Sandra Saunders
4-221 Highview Dr
St Thomas ON N5R 5H6

NOW YOU SEE HER

NOW YOU SEE HER

A Novel

JOY FIELDING

Doubleday Canada

Library and Archives of Canada

ISBN: 978-0-385-66671-8

Fielding, Joy

     Now you see her / Joy Fielding.

ISBN 978-0-385-66671-8

     I. Title.

PS8561.I52N69 2011   C813'.54   C2010-905252-8

Printed and bound in the USA

Published in Canada by Doubleday Canada, a division of Random House of Canada Limited

Visit Random House of Canada Limited's website: www.randomhouse.ca

10 9 8 7 6 5 4 3 2 1

For my two gorgeous girls,
Shannon and Annie.
I love you more than words could ever say.

ACKNOWLEDGMENTS

As always, my thanks to Larry Mirkin, Beverley Slopen, Tracy Fisher, Emily Bestler, Sarah Branham, Judith Curr, Louise Burke, David Brown, Brad Martin, Maya Mavjee, Kristin Cochrane, Val Gow, Adria Iwasutiak, and Corinne Assayag. Thanks as well to some recent recruits—Pauline Post, Carole Schwindeller, Lynn Henry, and Nita Pronovost. It's a pleasure to have you aboard.

Thank you also to my various publishers, agents, and translators around the world for the magnificent job you're doing.

Special thanks to my wonderful family—my husband, Warren, and daughters Shannon and Annie, Annie's husband, Courtney, and my beautiful new grandson, Hayden, who makes me smile every time I picture his sweet little face. Thanks also to my sister Renee and to Aurora for her continuing efforts to make me as comfortable as possible.

And finally, I raise a pint of beer to the magnificent country of Ireland. I look forward to returning there again soon.

NOW YOU SEE HER

ONE

"O KAY, IF YOU'LL ALL just gather around me for a few seconds, I'll give you a wee bit of information about this glorious building in front of you." The guide smiled encouragingly at the group of tired and somewhat bedraggled-looking tourists milling around the front of St. Anne's Shandon Church. "That's it, darlin'," he cajoled in his exaggerated Irish lilt, the emerald-green scarf in his hand waving impatient circles around his portly frame. "Move in a little closer, young lady. I won't bite you." His smile widened, revealing a bottom row of spectacularly stained and crooked teeth.

Good thing her husband hadn't made the trip to Ireland after all, Marcy Taggart thought, taking several reluctant steps forward. He'd have interpreted the poor man's lack of a perfect smile as a personal affront. *People spend all this money on facelifts and designer clothes, and they forget about the most important thing of all—their teeth,* he often fumed. Peter was an orthodontist and therefore prone to such pronouncements. Hadn't he once told her that the first thing that had attracted him to her wasn't her slim figure or her large, dark brown eyes but rather her obvious regard for oral hygiene, as evidenced by her straight, flawlessly white teeth? To think she'd once found such statements flattering, even romantic; Marcy marveled at it now.

"Can I have your full attention, please?" the tour guide asked with only a hint of reproach in his voice. He was clearly used to the casual rudeness of those in his charge and had ceased to take offense. Even though the largely middle-aged group of twenty-four men and women had paid a lot of money for the day's excursion to Cork, the Republic of Ireland's second-largest city, with a population of approximately 120,000, only a handful of those in attendance had actually been paying attention to anything the man had been saying since leaving Dublin.

Marcy had tried, she really had. She'd repeatedly instructed herself to focus as the guide educated them on the history of Cork during the seemingly interminable bus ride, 168 miles of severely congested highway and narrow country roads. She'd learned that the name Cork was derived from the Irish word *"corcach,"* pronounced "kar-kax," meaning "marshy place," because of its situation on the river Lee; that it had been founded in the sixth century AD and now served as the administrative center of county Cork, and that it was the largest city in the province of Munster. Corkorians, as they were known, often referred to Cork as "the real capital of Ireland." Its nickname was "the Rebel County," the town's reputation for rebelliousness having something to do with its support of the English pretender Perkin Warbeck back in 1491, following the War of the Roses. Today it was better known as the heart of industry in the south of Ireland, the chief industry being pharmaceuticals, its most famous product none other than Viagra.

At least that's what Marcy thought their guide had said. She couldn't be sure. Her imagination had an unfortunate tendency to get the better of her these days, and at fifty, her once prodigious memory for facts both useful and otherwise was no longer what it used to be. But then, she thought, grit-filled eyes surreptitiously scanning the glazed faces of her fellow travelers, all clearly years past their "best before" date, what was?

"As you can see, because of its envious hilltop position, the tower of St. Anne's Shandon Church dominates the entire north side of the city," the guide was saying now, his voice rising to be heard over the other competing tour groups that had suddenly materialized and were jockeying for position on the busy street corner. "St. Anne's is Cork's prime landmark, and its giant pepper-pot steeple, which was built in 1722, is widely regarded as a symbol of the city. No matter where you are in the downtown area, you can see the marvelous stone tower, on whose top sits a gilt ball and a unique fish weather vane. Two sides of the tower are faced with red sandstone, the other two with white limestone, from which the colors of the Cork hurling and football teams are taken." He pointed toward the large, round, black-and-gold clock in the middle of the bottom tier of the four-tiered steeple. "Corkorians depend on Shandon clock for their time and its weather vane for their weather forecast." A gentle chorus of bells suddenly drifted down the hill from the church, bringing forth oohs and aahs from those nearby. "That's our famous peal of eight bells," the guide said proudly. "As you've probably already noticed, you can hear them all over the city all day long. And if you choose to climb the belfry, you can even play the bells yourself. Any tune you want, although most people seem to pick either 'Danny Boy' or 'Ave Maria.'" He took a deep breath. "Okay, you have thirty minutes to visit the inside of the church, then we'll head over to Patrick's Hill, so you can get a feel for its steepness. Americans say it rivals the notorious streets of San Francisco."

"What if we're not up to the climb?" an elderly woman asked from the back of the crowd.

"I think I'm all churched out," the man beside her muttered. "I don't know about the rest of you, but I could use a pint of Guinness."

"For those of you who have seen enough and would prefer to enjoy a bit of rest and relaxation before heading back to the bus, there's no shortage of pubs in the area. Although you're more likely to find the locals drinking Murphy's or Beamish, two stouts that are brewed right here in Cork."

"Sounds good to me," someone said.

"We'll meet back at Parnell Place Bus Station in one hour," the guide announced. "Please be prompt or we might not have enough time to visit the famous Blarney Castle on our way back to Dublin. And you don't want to miss out on kissing the legendary Blarney Stone, do you?"

No, we certainly wouldn't want to miss out on that, Marcy thought, recalling Peter's revulsion at the idea of being held by his feet and suspended backward and upside down like a bat in order to kiss "some dirty piece of bacteria-soaked gray rock coated with other people's saliva," as he'd so memorably phrased it when she'd first shown him the brochures. "Who in their right mind would want to do such a thing?" he'd asked accusingly.

Marcy had smiled and said nothing. Peter had ceased believing she was in her right mind some time ago.

Wasn't that why she'd agreed to go on this trip in the first place? Hadn't everyone been telling her that it was important—some said crucial—for both her mental health and her marriage that she and Peter spend more time together, time in which they could come to terms with what had happened, *as a unit*? Wasn't that the term her psychiatrist had used?

So when her sister had first floated the idea of a second honeymoon in honor of their twenty-fifth wedding anniversary, Marcy had thrown herself into its planning with every fiber of her being. It had been Peter's suggestion to go to Ireland, his mother having been born in Limerick. He'd been talking for years of making a pilgrimage to the land of his ancestors. Marcy initially argued in favor of somewhere more exotic, like Tahiti or Bali, someplace where the average July temperature was substantially more than sixty-six degrees, where she could sip mai tais on the beach and wear flowers in her hair instead of a place where Guinness was the order of the day and the humidity would pretty much guarantee she'd always look as if a clump of unruly moss had just landed on her head. But what difference did it make where they went, she'd reasoned, as long as they went there *as a unit*?

So Peter's choice it was.

And ultimately, Peter had chosen someone else.

Did one person still qualify as a unit? Marcy wondered now, recognizing that as much as she loved the often-spectacular scenery and the much-vaunted forty shades of green of the Irish countryside, she hated its dull, rain-filled skies and the pervasive dampness that clung to her like a second skin.

He couldn't take any more drama, he'd said when he told her he was leaving. *It's better this way. We'll both be better off. You'll see, you'll be much happier. Hopefully, eventually, we can be friends.* The cowardly clichés of the deserter.

"We still have a son together," he'd told her, as if she needed reminding.

No mention of their daughter.

Marcy shivered, gathering the sides of her trench coat together, and decided to join the ranks of those opting for a brief respite and a pint of beer. They'd been on the go since their bus had pulled out of Dublin at eight thirty that morning. A quick lunch at a traditional Irish pub when they'd first arrived in Cork had been followed by a three-hour walking tour of the city, a tour that included such landmarks as the Cork city jail, spelled "gaol"; the Cork Quay Market, pronounced "Kay"; the opera house; and St. Fin Barre's Cathedral, as well as a stroll down St. Patrick's Street, the city's main shopping thoroughfare. It was now concluding with this visit to St. Anne's Shandon Church and a proposed hike up the steep slope of Patrick's Hill. Since Cork's center was located on an island lying between two branches of the river Lee, the city naturally divided into three main sections: the downtown core known as the "flat of the city," the North Bank, and the South Bank. Marcy had spent the entire afternoon crossing one bridge after another. It was time to sit down.

Ten minutes later, she found herself alone at a tiny table for two inside another traditional Irish pub overlooking the river Lee. It was dark inside, which suited the mood that was rapidly overtaking her. She was crazy to have come to Ireland, she was thinking. Only a crazy woman goes on her second honeymoon by herself, even if the trip had already been paid for in advance, even if most of the money was nonrefundable. It wasn't as if she couldn't afford the loss of a few thousand dollars. Peter had been more than generous in his settlement offer. Clearly he'd wanted to get away from her as quickly and with as little effort as possible. Marcy found herself chuckling. Why should he put any more effort into their divorce than he'd put into their marriage?

"You find something amusing, do you?" a voice asked from somewhere above her head.

Marcy looked up to see a roguishly handsome young man with enviably straight black hair falling into luminous, dark green eyes. She thought he had the longest eyelashes she'd ever seen.

"What can I get you, darlin'?" the young man said, notepad and pencil poised to take her order.

"Would it be too ridiculous to order a cup of tea?" Marcy surprised herself by asking. She'd been planning on having a Beamish, as the tour guide had suggested. She could almost hear Peter admonish her: *It's just like you to be so contrary.*

"Not ridiculous at all," the waiter said, managing to sound as if he meant it.

"Tea sounds wonderful," she heard someone say. "Could you make that two?" Beside her, a chair scraped the wood planks of the floor. "Do you mind if I join you?" The man sat down before Marcy had a chance to respond.

Marcy recognized him as a member of her tour group, although she couldn't remember his name. Something Italian, she thought, placing him in the window seat three rows from the front of the bus. He'd smiled at her as she'd made her way to the back. *Nice teeth,* she'd heard Peter whisper in her ear.

"Vic Sorvino," he said now, extending his hand.

"Marcy Taggart," Marcy said without taking it. Instead she gave a little wave she hoped would satisfy him. Why was he here? There were other tables he could have chosen to sit at.

"Taggart? So you're Irish?"

"My husband is."

Vic looked toward the long bar that ran the entire length of the room. "I'm sorry, I didn't realize you were with anyone," he said, although he made no move to relinquish his chair.

"He's not here."

"Doesn't like bus tours?"

"Doesn't like being married," Marcy heard herself say. "At least to me."

Vic looked vaguely stunned. "You're not big on small talk, are you?"

Marcy laughed in spite of her desire not to and pushed at the mop of curls falling into her narrow face.

So much hair, she thought in her mother's voice, for such a tiny face.

"I'm sorry," she said now. "I guess that falls under the category of too much information."

"Nonsense. I'm of the school that believes information is always useful."

"Stick around," Marcy said, immediately regretting her choice of words. The last thing she wanted to do was encourage him.

The waiter approached with their teas.

"He probably thinks we're crazy, ordering tea in a pub," Marcy said, following the handsome young man with her eyes as he returned to the bar, watching him flirt with several of the women clustered on high stools around him. She watched him fill half a dozen mugs of draft beer and slide them with a flick of his wrist across the dark polished wood of the bar toward a group of noisy young men at the far end. His female admirers broke into a round of admiring applause. He can have any woman he wants, she thought absently, estimating his age as early thirties and wondering if her daughter would have found him attractive.

"Actually, Americans have the wrong idea about Irish pubs," Vic was saying, his easy baritone pulling her back into the conversation. "They're not bars, and they're as much about socializing as drinking. People come here to see their friends and neighbors, and lots of them choose tea or soft drinks over alcohol. I've been reading the guidebooks," he admitted sheepishly, then, when Marcy remained silent, "Where are you from?"

"Toronto," she answered obligingly.

"Toronto's a lovely city," he said immediately. "I was there a few times on business." He paused, obviously waiting for her to ask: When? What business? When she didn't, he told her anyway. "It was a few years back. I was in the manufacturing business. Widgets," he said.

"You manufacture midgets?" Marcy asked, realizing she'd been listening with only half an ear.

Vic laughed and corrected her gently. "Widgets. Small, mechanical devices whose names you usually can't remember. Gadgets," he said, explaining further.

Marcy sipped her tea and said nothing. I'm an idiot, she thought.

"I sold the business and retired last year," he continued. Then, when no further questions were forthcoming, "I'm from Chicago."

Marcy managed a tepid smile. She'd always liked Chicago. She should have gone there, she was thinking as her cell phone began ringing in her purse. Chicago had wonderful architecture and interesting neighborhoods. It didn't rain almost every day.

"Is that your phone?" Vic asked.

"Hmm? Oh. *Oh,*" she said, locating it at the bottom of her purse and lifting it to her ear. "Hello?"

"Where the hell are you?" her sister demanded angrily.

"Judith?"

"Where have you been? I haven't heard from you in over a week. What's going on?"

"Is everything all right? Has something happened to Darren?"

"Your son's fine, Marcy," her sister said, not bothering to mask her impatience. "It's you I'm worried about. Why haven't you returned any of my calls?"

"I haven't checked my messages."

"Why the hell not?"

Because I didn't want to speak to you, Marcy thought, but decided not to say. Judith was obviously upset enough already. Marcy pictured her sister, older by two years, pacing the marbled floor of her new luxury condominium. She was undoubtedly dressed in her standard uniform of black yoga pants and matching tank top, because she'd either just finished working out or was just about to start. Judith spent at least half the day exercising—a thirty-minute swim first thing in the morning, followed by an hour or two of spin classes, then an hour and a half of "hot yoga" in the afternoon. Occasionally, if time allowed and she was in the mood, she'd throw in an additional Pilates class, "for my core," she insisted, although her stomach was already as hard and flat as steel. Possibly she was munching on a piece of raw carrot, Marcy thought; her sister's diet consisted solely of sushi, raw vegetables, and the occasional spoonful of peanut butter. Judith was on husband number five. She'd had her tubes tied when she was eighteen, having decided when she and Marcy were still children never to have any of her own. "You really want to take that chance?" she'd asked.

"Something's not right," she said now. "I'm coming over."

"You can't." Marcy allowed her gaze to drift toward the pub's large front window.

"Why not?"

"Because I'm not there."

"Where are you?"

A long pause. "Ireland."

"What?"

"I'm in Ireland," Marcy repeated, knowing full well Judith had heard her the first time and holding the phone away from her ear in preparation for Judith's shriek.

"Please tell me you're joking."

"I'm not joking."

"Is someone with you?"

"I'm fine, Judith." Marcy saw a shadow fall across the front window. The shadow stopped and waved at the bartender. The bartender acknowledged the shadow's wave with a sly smile.

"You aren't fine. You're off your rocker. I demand you come home instantly."

"I can't do that." The shadow stepped into a cone of light, then turned and disappeared. "Oh, my God." Marcy gasped, jumping to her feet.

"What is it?" Vic and Judith asked simultaneously.

"What's going on?" her sister added.

"My God, it's Devon!" Marcy said, slamming her hip into a nearby table as she raced for the door.

"What?"

"I just saw her. She's here."

"Marcy, calm down. You're talking crazy."

"I'm not crazy." Marcy pushed open the pub's heavy front door, tears stinging her eyes as her head swiveled up and down the tourist-clogged street. A light drizzle had started to fall. "Devon!" she called out, running east along the river Lee. "Where are you? Come back. Please come back."

"Marcy, please," Judith urged in Marcy's ear. "It's not Devon. You know it's not her."

"I know what I saw." Marcy stopped at St. Patrick's Bridge, debating whether or not to cross it. "I'm telling you. She's here. I saw her."

"No, you didn't," Judith said gently. "Devon is dead, Marcy."

"You're wrong. She's here."

"Your daughter is dead," Judith repeated, tears clinging to each word.

"Go to hell," Marcy cried. Then she tossed the phone into the river and crossed over the bridge.

TWO

WITHIN MINUTES, SHE WAS lost in the labyrinth of lane-ways that twisted around the river Lee. Normally Marcy would have found the narrow streets with their collection of small specialty shops engaging, the Old World asserting its presence in the middle of the bustling new city, but their charm quickly gave way to frustration.

"Devon!" Marcy cried, her eyes pushing through the ubiquitous crowds, straining to see over the tops of black umbrellas that were sprouting up everywhere around her. Two teenage boys walked aimlessly in front of her, laughing and punching at each others' arms, in the way of teenage boys everywhere, seemingly oblivious to the raindrops grazing the tops of their shoulders.

One of the boys turned around at the sound of her voice, his gaze flitting absently in her direction for several seconds before he returned his attention to his friends. Marcy was neither surprised nor offended by his lack of interest. She understood she was no longer on the radar of teenage boys, having seen that same vague look on the faces of her son's friends more times than she cared to remember. For them she existed, if she existed at all, as a necessary pair of hands to make them a sandwich at lunchtime or a human answering machine to relay urgent messages to her son. Sometimes she served as an excuse—"I can't come out tonight; my mom's not feeling well." More often, a complaint—"I can't come out tonight; my mom's on the warpath."

"Mom, mom, mom," Marcy repeated in a whisper, straining to remember the sound of the word on Devon's lips and picturing her own mother when she was young and full of life. She marveled that such a simple three-letter word could mean so much, wield such power, be so *fraught*.

"Devon!" she called again, although not as loudly as the first time, and then again, "Devon," this time the name barely escaping her mouth. Her eyes filled with tears as she circled back to the main road, wet curls clinging to her forehead. Seconds later she found herself at the busy intersection of St. Patrick's Street and Merchant's Quay.

In front of her stood the hulking Merchant's Quay Shopping Centre, an enclosed shopping complex that served as the city's main mall. Marcy stood staring at it, thinking she should probably go inside, if only to escape the rain, but she was unable to move. Had Devon taken refuge there? Was she wandering through the various stores—or shops, as they were always called here—waiting for the sudden downpour to stop? Was she searching for racy underwear at Marks and Spencer or hunting for an old-fashioned, paisley-print blouse in Laura Ashley?

What do I do now? Marcy wondered, deciding against going inside. Large shopping malls tended to make her anxious, even in the best of times.

And this was definitely not the best of times.

Instead, she found herself running down St. Patrick's Street, her eyes darting back and forth, trying to see between the raindrops, to fit her daughter's delicate features on the face of each young woman who hurried by. As she approached Paul's Lane, she heard a tour guide explaining to a bunch of wet, fidgety tourists that until recently the lane had been a wonderful antiques quarter, but that virtually all the shops that had made the street unique were now closed due to high rents and the young population's lack of interest in anything older than itself. In today's world, he said, tut-tutting beneath his bright green umbrella, it was all about the new.

St. Patrick's Street curved gently, like a shy grin, into Grand Parade, a spacious thoroughfare where shops and offices mingled with charming eighteenth-century houses and the remains of the old city walls. Marcy continued south, her eyes scanning the now-empty benches inside Bishop Lucey Park. She proceeded to the South Mall, a wide tree-lined street that was Cork's financial center, its Georgian-style architecture housing what seemed like an endless succession of banks, law offices, and insurance companies. No chance Devon would be here, Marcy decided. Her daughter had never been very good with formal institutions of any kind. She'd been even less good with money.

Marcy shuddered, remembering the time she'd berated Devon for taking forty dollars from her purse. Such a paltry sum and she'd made such a fuss. You'd have thought Devon had stolen the crown jewels, for God's sake, the way she'd carried on.

"I was just borrowing it," Devon had insisted stubbornly. "I was going to pay it back."

Marcy had protested in turn. "It's not that. It's a matter of trust."

"You're saying you don't trust me?"

"I'm saying I don't like it when you take things without asking."

"I just borrowed it."

"Without asking."

"I'm sorry. I didn't think it was such a big deal."

"Well, it *is* a big deal."

"I apologized, didn't I? God, what's your problem?"

What *was* her problem? Marcy wondered now, her eyelashes so heavy with rain—or was that tears?—that she could barely see the sidewalk in front of her. Why had she made such a nothing incident into such a huge issue? Didn't all teenage girls occasionally steal money from their mothers' purses? So what if Devon had been almost twenty-one at the time? She was still a child, still living at home, still under her mother's protection.

Her mother's protection. Marcy scoffed silently. Had Devon ever felt protected in her mother's house?

Had Marcy in hers?

Everything that happened is my fault, Marcy told herself silently, slipping on a patch of slippery pavement and collapsing to the sidewalk like a discarded piece of crumpled paper. Immediately the wetness from the concrete seeped into her trench coat and right through her navy slacks, but she made no move to get up. Serves me right, she was thinking, recalling that awful afternoon when the police had shown up at her door to tell her Devon was dead.

Except she wasn't dead.

She was here.

Right here, Marcy realized with a start, her head shooting

toward a young woman exiting a two-story gray brick building directly across the street. Not only was Devon still alive, she was here in Cork. She was standing right in front of her.

Marcy pushed herself to her feet, ignoring the concerned whispers of several passersby who'd stopped to help her up. Unmindful of the traffic that was coming at her in both directions, she darted across the street, forgetting that cars drove on the opposite side of the road from those in North America and almost colliding with a speeding motor scooter. The driver swore at her, a good Anglo-Saxon four-letter word that exploded up and down the street, drawing the attention of everyone in the vicinity, including Devon, whose head snapped toward the angry expletive.

Except it wasn't Devon.

Marcy could see immediately that this wasn't the same young woman she'd been chasing after. This girl was at least three inches taller than Devon, who'd always complained that, at five feet, four and a half inches, she was too short for the current vogue. "Why'd I have to get your legs and not Judith's?" she'd asked Marcy accusingly, as if such things were in Marcy's control.

Marcy had sympathized. "I always wished I had her legs, too," she said, seeking common ground.

"Marcy!" she heard a voice calling faintly in the distance, her name sounding strange, even meaningless, to her ears. "Marcy Taggart," she heard again, the name expanding like a sponge, gaining weight, becoming more solid, if not more familiar. Someone was suddenly beside her, touching her arm. "Marcy, are you all right?"

A man's face snapped into focus. He was deeply tanned and his dark hair was graying at the temples. A nice face, Marcy thought, saved from blandness by a pair of unsettlingly blue eyes. Why hadn't she noticed them before?

"It's Vic Sorvino," the man said, his hand lingering on her arm, as if afraid she might bolt again at any second.

"I know who you are," Marcy said impatiently. "I'm not crazy."

"I'm sorry. I didn't mean to imply—"

"I didn't just lose my memory all of a sudden."

"I'm sorry," he said again. "I was just worried about you."

"Why?"

"Well, the way you took off . . ." He paused, glanced up and down the street, as if looking for someone. "I take it you didn't find her."

"What are you talking about?"

"The girl you went chasing after. Devon, I think you called her."

"Did you see her?" Marcy demanded. "Did she come back?" Why hadn't she thought to go back to the pub instead of stumbling down a bunch of blind alleys, chasing uselessly after her own tail?

"No. I didn't see anyone," Vic said. "All I know is that one minute you were sitting beside me, sipping your tea and talking on the phone, and the next you were running down the street, shouting, 'Devon.'"

"So you followed me?"

"I tried, but I lost you in the crowd after you crossed the bridge."

"Why?"

"Why did I lose you?"

"Why did you follow me?" Marcy asked.

"To be honest, I really don't know. I guess I was worried. You looked as if you'd seen a ghost."

Marcy stared at him. Was that what had happened? Had the girl she'd seen been nothing but an apparition, a figment of her desperate imagination? That's what Judith obviously thought. Was she right?

It wouldn't have been the first time she'd chased after ghosts.

How many times in the last twenty months had she stopped strangers on the street, certain each girl with a passing resemblance to Devon was the daughter she'd lost? And each time, she'd been so sure, so certain that the young woman waiting in line at the grocery checkout counter, the girl hugging her boyfriend on a street corner, the woman laughing with her friends on the outside patio of a local restaurant, was her child.

And each time she'd been wrong.

Was she wrong this time as well? Did it make any sense—any sense at all—that her daughter could be here?

It wasn't that far-fetched a possibility, Marcy quickly assured herself. How often had Devon heard her father extolling the imagined glories of Ireland? The most beautiful country in the world, he'd proclaimed repeatedly, promising to take her there as soon as his busy schedule permitted. Devon had worshipped her father, so it wasn't that surprising she would choose Ireland as her place of refuge.

Was that why Marcy had really come here? Had she somehow known she'd find Devon?

"I guess I did see a ghost," she said when she realized Vic was waiting for some kind of response.

"It happens."

Marcy nodded, wondering what he knew of ghosts. "We should get back to our bus."

He took her elbow, gently led her along South Mall toward Parnell Place. By the time they saw the pinched face of their guide as he paced impatiently outside their waiting bus, the rain had slowed to a weak drizzle. "I'm so sorry we're late," Marcy said as the guide hurried them inside the coach.

"Please take your seats," he urged, instructing the driver to start the bus's engine.

Marcy felt the unabashed animosity of her fellow tourists pushing her toward her seat as the coach pulled out of the station. She lost her balance and lurched forward.

"Careful," Vic said, grabbing the back of her coat to steady her.

What was he still doing here? Marcy wondered, shaking free of his sturdy grip. She was too old for a babysitter, and she no longer believed in knights in shining armor. Shiny armor had a way of rusting pretty quickly, especially in the rain.

"Would you please get settled as quickly as possible?" the guide said as Marcy crawled into her seat at the back and Vic sat down beside her. "In a few minutes we'll be passing through Blarney, which boasts one of the most impressive castles in all of Ireland," he announced in the next breath, "although all that remains of it today is a massive square tower, its parapet rising to a height of twenty-five meters, or eighty-two feet. The Blarney Stone is wedged underneath the battlements. Those who kiss it are said to be granted the gift of gab. Clearly, I've kissed it many times." He paused for the chuckles that dutifully followed. "Blarney Castle also boasts a beautiful garden and a lovely dell beside Blarney Lake. Someday I hope you'll take a tour of the dungeons that were built right into the rock at the base of the castle, and also Badger Cave, for those of you who aren't too claustrophobic. Unfortunately, we won't be able to do any of those things today." A loud groan swept through the bus. The guide continued. "I'm sorry, but I did warn you about being late. You can register your complaints with the tour company when we arrive back in Dublin. Perhaps they'll reimburse you a portion of the fare, or maybe you'll be able to make arrangements to return some other time. Despite the crowds,

Blarney Castle is well worth the trip." He glared at Marcy, as if blaming her in advance for whatever tips he wouldn't collect. Several angry heads swiveled in her direction.

"I'm very sorry," she whispered to no one in particular, then turned to stare out the window, seeing only her own reflection staring back. I used to be considered beautiful, she thought, wondering when she'd become so tired looking and old. People were always telling her she looked at least a decade younger than she was, and maybe she had at one time. Before, Marcy thought. Before her life had changed forever. Before that awful October afternoon when she'd watched a police car pull to a stop outside her sprawling bungalow in Hogg's Hollow, her eyes following the two officers slowly up her front walk, her breath catching painfully in her lungs at the sight of their crisp blue uniforms.

She'd always hated uniforms.

"Aren't you going to answer that?" Peter had called as the doorbell rang. He was in the den, watching some sporting event on TV. "Marcy," he'd called again. "Aren't you going to get that? Marcy?" he'd repeated as the doorbell rang a second, then a third time. "Where are you? Why aren't you answering the door?"

"It's the police," Marcy managed to croak out, although her feet had turned to lead and she lacked the strength to move them. She was suddenly fifteen years old again, standing beside her sister in the principal's office.

"The police?" Peter marched into the foyer and pulled open the front door. "Officers?" he asked, the word suspended ominously in the air as he ushered the two men inside.

"Are you Dr. Peter Taggart?"

"I am."

"We understand you have a cottage on Georgian Bay," one

of the officers said as Marcy felt her body go numb. She looked away, not wanting to see their faces. If she didn't see their faces, she reasoned irrationally, she wouldn't have to hear what they'd come to say.

"Yes. That's right," Peter answered. "Our daughter is up there for the weekend with some friends. Why? Has something happened? Did she set off the alarm again?"

"Your daughter is Devon Taggart?"

"Yes, that's right. Is she in some sort of trouble?"

"I'm afraid there's been an accident," the policeman said. "Perhaps you'd like to sit down."

"Perhaps you'd like to tell me what's happened."

Out of the corner of her eye, Marcy saw the police officer nod, then look toward the floor. "Neighbors saw your daughter climb into a canoe at around ten o'clock this morning. The water was pretty rough and they noted she wasn't wearing a life jacket. When they saw she still hadn't returned some three hours later, they called the police. I'm afraid they found her overturned canoe in the middle of the bay."

"And Devon?" Peter asked quietly, his skin turning the color of parchment paper.

"They're still searching."

"So you haven't found her," Marcy interrupted forcefully, still refusing to look their way.

"Not yet."

"Well, that's good. It means she probably swam to shore."

"I'm afraid there's little chance of that," the officer told her, his voice so low it was almost inaudible. "The canoe was miles from anywhere."

"It could have drifted," Marcy said stubbornly.

"Yes," he acknowledged. "I guess that's possible."

"Devon's a very strong swimmer."

"The water is extremely cold," the second officer stated. "It's doubtful—"

"You said she went to the cottage with friends?" the first officer interrupted to ask Peter.

"Yes," Peter said. "Carrie and Michelle. I can't remember their last names," he added helplessly, looking to Marcy.

Because you never knew them, Marcy thought angrily. When did you ever take the time to learn the last names of any of your daughter's friends? You were always so damn busy with work or golf. Although that never seemed to matter to Devon. "Stafford and Harvey," Marcy informed the officers. "I'm sure they'll be able to tell you where Devon is."

"According to your neighbors, your daughter was at the cottage alone."

"That's not possible. She told us she was going up there with Carrie and Michelle. Why would she lie?"

Why did she usually lie? Marcy thought now, brushing aside a tear.

"Are you all right?" Vic asked immediately, as if he'd been watching her every move.

Marcy didn't answer. She burrowed down in her seat and closed her eyes, pretending to be asleep.

"Do you know if your daughter has been depressed lately?" she heard one of the policemen ask.

"You're saying you don't think this was an accident?" Peter said, avoiding the officer's question. Marcy had to grab her hands to keep from slapping him, twist her fingers to keep from scratching out his eyes. How dare he even entertain such a suggestion, let alone say it out loud?

"I have to ask: Do you think it's possible your daughter took her own life?"

"No, it's not possible," Marcy said adamantly, fleeing the

room and racing down the hall before Peter could contradict her. She flung open the door to Devon's bedroom, swallowing the room in a single glance.

The note was propped up against Devon's pillow.

"Despite our not being able to visit Blarney Castle," the guide was saying now, "I hope you have enjoyed our little tour today." Marcy opened her eyes to see that they had arrived at Dublin's city limits. "As you no doubt observed from our brief visit, you really need more than one day to fully appreciate Cork. The library is well worth a visit, as is Cork's Butter Museum and the Crawford Art Gallery. And don't forget the wonderful university, whose campus is home to more than seventeen thousand students from all over the world."

Over seventeen thousand students from all over the world, Marcy repeated silently, thinking how easy it would be for someone like Devon to blend in. To disappear.

"Have you ever just wanted to disappear?" Devon had asked Marcy one day not long before her overturned canoe was found in the frigid waters of Georgian Bay. "Just go somewhere and start all over again as someone else?"

"Please don't talk that way, sweetheart," Marcy had said. "You have everything."

What a stupid thing to say, she thought now. She, of all people, should have known that having everything guaranteed nothing.

They'd never recovered Devon's body.

"That *was* you I saw," Marcy whispered under her breath.

"Sorry, did you say something?" Vic asked.

Marcy shook her head. "No," she said out loud. But inside a voice was screaming, "You aren't dead, are you, Devon? You're here. I know you are. And whatever it takes, however long it takes, I'm going to find you."

THREE

THE MESSAGE LIGHT ON her phone was flashing ominously when Marcy returned to her hotel.

It must be a mistake, she thought, letting her stained and still-damp coat fall to the thick oatmeal-colored carpet and kicking off her shoes, normally reliable black flats that had lost all credibility sometime around two o'clock that afternoon. She balanced on the side of her king-size bed, watching the phone's red light flash on and off, wondering who could have called. Nobody knew she was here.

Probably the tour bus company, she decided. They're holding me responsible for the missed excursion to Blarney Castle and expecting me to cover whatever extra cost they incurred as a result. Fine, it's the least I can do, she thought, deciding not to listen to the message until later. She leaned back against the stack of fancy lace pillows at the head of the bed and lifted her feet to rest on the down-filled comforter, sleep already tugging at her eyelids. She hadn't realized how utterly exhausted she was. She closed her eyes. Almost immediately, the phone started ringing.

Marcy's eyes popped open, her head swiveling toward the sound, a new thought piercing her brain, like an ice pick to the back of her skull.

Could it be Devon? she was thinking as she stared at the ringing black telephone. Was it possible she'd been aware of her mother's presence all along, that she'd spied Marcy through the pub's window at the precise moment Marcy had spotted her? Had she watched her mother's frantic search from a safe distance, and had she been thinking of coming forward when Vic Sorvino suddenly appeared? Had she followed them to the bus terminal, watched them board the bus back to Dublin, then started calling every first-class hotel in the city in a desperate effort to track her mother down? Was it possible?

Slowly, carefully, her heart careening wildly between her chest and her throat, Marcy removed the receiver from its carriage and lifted it to her ear.

"Marcy? Marcy, are you there?" Peter's voice filled the large, elegant room. "Marcy? I can hear you breathing. Answer me."

Tears of disappointment filled Marcy's eyes. "Hello, Peter," she said. It was all she could think of to say to the man with whom she'd shared the last twenty-five years of her life. "How are you?"

"*How am I?*" he asked incredulously. "*I'm* fine. It's *you* I'm worried about. I've called half a dozen times, left messages. . . ."

"How did you know where to find me?"

"Your sister called," he told her. "She's frantic, says you've

gone off to Ireland by yourself, that you think you've seen—"
He broke off, took a second to regroup. "I remembered the
name of the hotel in Dublin where we . . ."

"Were supposed to stay together?" Marcy finished for him.

A second's silence, then, slowly, cautiously, almost lovingly, "You have to come home, Marcy. You have to come home
now."

"Why?"

"*Why?*"

"I saw her, Peter. I saw Devon."

He sighed. "This is crazy talk, Marcy. You know that."

"I know what I saw."

"You only *think* you saw Devon," Peter told her gently, the
hint of impatience in his voice tempered by his obvious concern. Marcy could almost feel him shaking his head.

Poor Peter, she thought. After all these years, he still had no
idea what to make of her. "I *did* see her."

"You saw a girl who looked like her. . . ."

"No."

"A pretty girl with long dark hair and high cheekbones,
who maybe walked the way Devon walked and held her cigarette the same way. . . ."

"I saw Devon."

"Just like you saw her all those other times you were so
convinced?"

"This time is different."

"This time is exactly the same," Peter insisted. "Marcy,
please. I thought we got past this."

"No, *you* got past it."

"Because I had to. Because there was no other choice. Our
daughter is dead, Marcy."

"They never found her body."

Another silence. Another sigh. "So, you're saying . . . what? That she faked her own death . . . ?"

"Maybe. Or maybe it was an accident and she saw an opportunity . . ."

"An opportunity for what, for God's sake? Why would she do something like this? Why would she let us think she was dead?"

"You know why!" Marcy shouted, silencing him. She imagined Peter hanging his head, closing his eyes.

"How did she get there?" he asked quietly.

"What?"

"She didn't have a passport. She didn't have any money. . . ."

Marcy brushed aside these new questions with an impatient wave of her hand. "She could have had money put away. She could have arranged for a passport. She had friends, Peter, friends we knew nothing about. . . ."

"Think about what you're saying, Marcy."

"I don't have to think about it," Marcy insisted, refusing to be swayed. "Our daughter is alive, Peter. She's here in Ireland."

"And you just happened to run into her."

"She walked right by the pub where I was sitting."

"You were drinking?" he asked, almost hopefully.

"I was drinking tea."

"And Devon walked by," he said.

"Yes."

"Dublin has, what . . . a population of a million and a half?"

"I know. It's quite a coincidence," Marcy said before Peter had the chance, deciding not to tell him the sighting had taken place in Cork.

Another moment's silence, then, "Did you talk to her?"

"What?"

"Did she see you? Did you talk to her?"

"No. I tried following her but I lost her in the crowd." Again she felt him shaking his head. "Just because she didn't see *me* doesn't mean I didn't see *her*."

He sighed. The sigh said he'd given it his best shot. There was nothing more to talk about. "Come home, Marcy. Your sister is half out of her mind. . . ."

"Good-bye, Peter. Please tell Judith not to worry."

"Marcy—"

She hung up the phone before he could say anything else.

The phone rang again almost immediately. This time Marcy let it go directly to voice mail. If it wasn't Peter, it was Judith, and she didn't have the strength to have the same conversation a second time. If they wanted to think she was crazy, so be it. They were probably right.

But that didn't mean she was wrong about Devon.

She'd leave for Cork first thing the next morning, she decided, a renewed burst of energy pushing her to her feet. She retrieved her suitcase from the closet, placing it on the cream-colored ottoman at the foot of the bed. Within minutes, it was packed, shoes and nightgowns at the bottom, shirts and dresses laid neatly over the top, followed by a few T-shirts and her favorite jeans, along with a nice pair of black pants and a couple of sweaters, her underwear stuffed into every available crevice and corner. The travel agent had advised layers. You never knew what the weather in Ireland would be like. Even mid-July could sometimes feel more like the middle of October, she'd warned Marcy. And make sure to pack an umbrella.

Yeah, sure, Marcy thought, picking her dirt-stained coat off the floor and hanging it over the back of the mahogany chair that sat in front of the sleek, modern desk. The travel agent had highly recommended the five-star luxury hotel, perfectly situated on the cusp of the historic old city and the somewhat bohemian district of Temple Bar. Her room was spacious and sophisticated and warm. Probably she didn't need the rather grand king-size bed, but what the hell? At least she had plenty of room to thrash around without worrying about someone poking her in the ribs, telling her to be still.

She walked to the large window that overlooked College Green, across from Trinity College. The street was filling up with people, all of whom seemed to know exactly where they were going and what they were doing. She glanced at the clock beside her bed. It was almost eight o'clock. She hadn't had anything to eat since lunch. She thought she should probably call room service, ask them to send something up. Or maybe she should go out, let the night breeze blow Peter's doubts out of her head.

Except that Peter didn't have any doubts. He never had. Wasn't that one of the things that had drawn her to him in the first place? That he'd always been so sure of himself, so certain of everything? Hadn't that been exactly what she was looking for?

He was right about one thing: It would have been too much of a coincidence for her to have spotted Devon here. If their daughter had settled in Dublin, and not in Cork, the odds were that Marcy never would have found her. Dublin was an amazingly young city. An astounding half its inhabitants were under the age of thirty, she remembered reading as she watched a young woman fly toward her boyfriend's extended arms on the street below. The kiss that followed was long and deep. After about thirty seconds, they broke apart, the girl laughing giddily, the boy gazing dreamily up toward her hotel room. Immediately Marcy backed away from the window, although she was on the third floor and it was highly doubtful he could have seen her.

Had Peter ever kissed her with such passion? she wondered. Had she ever responded with such unbridled joy?

Marcy crossed back to the closet and opened the safe deposit box, her hand brushing against the pair of gold hoop earrings Judith had given her for her fiftieth birthday as she reached for the midsize envelope at the very back of the black-velvet-lined box.

Returning to the bed, Marcy opened the envelope and removed the half-dozen photographs, careful to avoid the smaller second envelope inside it, the single word "MOMMY" scrawled across its front. She laid the pictures across the white comforter, studied each one carefully: Devon as a round little baby in her mother's arms, one happy face mimicking the other, both with the same huge brown eyes, the same cupid's-bow mouth; Devon as a child of five, wearing a fluffy pink tutu, balancing on chubby little legs and smiling proudly toward the ballet slippers on her feet; Devon on her twelfth birthday, meticulously straightened bangs completely covering her forehead and falling into her eyes, her mouth stretched wide open to show off her newly installed porcelain braces; Devon and Marcy celebrating Devon's sweet sixteen, arms circling each other's waists as they leaned over the flower-covered cake to blow out the candles; Devon at eighteen, hovering on the edge of beauty, staring straight at the camera, straggly dark curls falling past her shoulders, her smile timid, unsure. Marcy noted the sadness that was already creeping into the corners of her daughter's eyes, although there was still a hint of defiance in the set of her chin, as if she were daring the photographer to get too close; and finally, Devon, only weeks before her overturned canoe was found floating in the middle of the bay, wearing an old blue sweater and smoking her now omnipresent cigarette, her once expressive dark eyes blank and rimmed with red, her cupid's-bow lips now a thin, flat line, carrying not even the pretense of a smile.

Marcy sat staring at the pictures, wondering at Devon's transformation from giddy toddler to morose young woman. My fault, she thought. Everything, my fault.

There was yet another photograph inside the envelope and Marcy pulled it out. It was a black-and-white picture of her mother, taken around the time she'd turned twenty-one. She was standing in front of a large mirror, her regal profile reflected in the glass at her back. Her eyes were downcast and her long brown hair was pulled off her forehead and away from her face. She was wearing a dress of pale organza, a dark velvet bow at her breast. Her left hand held a gardenia that she pressed coyly to her chin.

Only the slightest hint of madness in her eyes.

The person who'd taken that picture had been desperately in love with her, as her mother had been fond of recounting. Theirs had been an exciting, wild affair, full of fights and reconciliations, of tantrums and ultimatums and declarations of undying devotion, a whirlwind of constantly shifting emotions. And yet, in the end, her mother had opted for safety and security over whirlwinds and excitement. She'd married George Fraser, a man whose name said it all. He was uncomplicated, straightforward, and too sane for his own good.

A man much like Peter in so many ways, Marcy acknowledged reluctantly. Both men never knew what hit them.

Marcy stuffed the pictures back inside their envelope, quickly returning the envelope to the safe deposit box. Then she grabbed her coat and purse and headed out the door, unexpectedly coming face-to-face with her image in the full-length mirror beside the elevators and seeing the faces of both her mother and her daughter staring back, their dark eyes filled with reproach. "I'm so sorry," she whispered as the elevator door opened.

The elegant lobby was lined with marble columns and decorated with magnificent plasterwork. To one side was a hall whose walls were completely covered with mirrors. Marcy made her way to the reception desk, the reflections of her mother and daughter mimicking each step.

"Where do I go to rent a car?" she asked a middle-aged woman behind the counter. The woman had sleek black hair pulled into a bun.

"Oh, I wouldn't advise renting a car in Dublin," the woman, whose name tag identified her as Lynette, said cheerily in her thick Irish brogue. "It's much easier getting around the city without one."

"I'm thinking of taking a drive into the countryside."

"Have you driven on Irish roadways before?"

"No, but—"

"They're a little tricky, especially for people who are used to driving on the other side of the road."

Marcy smiled, trying not to feel insulted by the woman's concern. It's my hair, Marcy was thinking. If I had straight, manageable hair like she has, she wouldn't be questioning my competence. "I'm sure I'll be fine."

Lynette smiled indulgently as she handed Marcy a map of the city, drawing a big red circle over the area where the major car rental offices were located. "It's a shame you didn't think to rent a car in advance," she said. "You'd have gotten a much better rate."

First Peter expected her to think about what she was saying, and now a total stranger expected her to think *in advance,* Marcy thought in amazement, taking the map from Lynette's hand and deciding to walk the few blocks, to get all the paperwork taken care of tonight so she'd be ready to leave for Cork first thing in the morning.

"Of course they're all closed at this hour," Lynette said.

"Of course." Now she'd have to waste a valuable chunk of the morning just getting organized. So much for advance thinking. Her stomach growled, as if underlining her displeasure. "Do you happen to know a nice restaurant in the area, nothing too fancy . . . ?"

"There's Flannery's over on O'Connell Street. The food's good. Simple, but good." Lynette took back the map from Marcy's hand and circled the spot.

"Thanks. I'll give it a try." Marcy was walking through the lobby when she heard a now-familiar voice call out her name. What was he doing here? she wondered, pretending she hadn't heard him and continuing toward the front entrance.

"Marcy?" he called again.

She spun around, the suddenness of her movement obviously catching him by surprise, so that his hand, which had been reaching for her elbow, grazed the side of her breast. His touch sent a spasm of electricity charging through her body. It had been a very long time since anyone had touched her breast, however inadvertently. In the waning years of their marriage, Peter hadn't even tried. When Devon left them, she'd taken with her whatever intimacy still existed between them.

"Vic." Marcy acknowledged him now, noting that he smelled of soap and shampoo and that he'd changed his clothes since she'd seen him less than an hour ago. He was wearing a black turtleneck sweater that emphasized the intense blueness of his eyes. "I didn't realize you were staying at this hotel."

"I'm not. I'm at the Morgan, just down the block."

"Why are you here?" she heard herself ask.

He laughed. "That's right, I almost forgot. You're not much for small talk."

"Sorry. I don't mean to be rude. You just surprised me." You touched my breast, she thought, dismayed to find her flesh still tingling. "I didn't expect to see you again. How did you know where to find me?"

"The bus let you off at your hotel," Vic said with a shrug. "Not exactly Sherlock Holmes."

Of course, Marcy thought, remembering that she'd rushed off in such a hurry, she hadn't even said good-bye.

He continued. "I thought I'd take a chance you might be free for dinner."

"You want to have dinner with me?"

"I tried calling your room, but I got your message machine, so I thought I'd just drop by."

"You're asking me out?"

"I'm sorry if I'm not very good at it. I haven't had a lot of practice lately."

"I can't," Marcy said.

"You have other plans?"

"No."

"Oh. Oh," he said again. "I'm sorry. I didn't mean to bother you."

Marcy continued unprompted. "It's just that I'm a mess. I mean, look at me. I haven't showered or changed. My hair's a disaster."

"You look gorgeous."

Marcy released a long, deep breath. When was the last time a man had been so nice to her? When was the last time *anyone* had been so nice to her? "I can't," she said again.

"I understand," he said, although he clearly didn't.

"I just don't think I'd be very good company."

"No need to explain."

"I haven't even thanked you for all your help this afternoon."

"No thanks necessary." He began backing away.

"Vic," she said, stopping him, wondering what she was doing now.

He stared at her expectantly, as if he was wondering the same thing.

"I hear there's this very nice restaurant over on O'Connell Street. Good food. Not fancy, but good."

"Are you asking me out?" he said with a smile.

"I'm sorry if I'm not very good at it," she parroted.

"On the contrary. You're doing just fine. It sounds wonderful."

"Would you give me a few minutes to shower and change my clothes?"

"As long as you don't change your mind."

"I won't."

"Then I'll wait right here."

FOUR

"I THINK I'LL TRY THE shepherd's pie." Marcy handed her big, unwieldy menu back to the waiter, who was tall, bald, and wearing a large white apron over skinny black pants.

"Sounds good," Vic said. "I'll have the same. And a glass of Irish whiskey to start." He smiled at Marcy expectantly.

"What the hell? Why not?" Marcy said, although she'd never been much of a drinker. But why not celebrate? She'd seen Devon. The daughter she'd feared dead was very much alive. Improbable as it might seem—impossible as it *did* seem to Peter and Judith—Devon was living less than a three-hour drive away. Tomorrow morning, Marcy would rent a car and drive back to Cork. It was a relatively small city. Once she was settled, it shouldn't take her too long to find her daughter. Not that it mattered. She'd stay as long as necessary. Marcy had no intention of leaving Cork without her.

"What is it they call it? The water of life?" Vic asked, answering his own question.

"What?"

"The Irish call their whiskey the water of life."

"The Irish have a nice way of looking at things."

"And speaking of nice ways of looking," Vic said, "have I told you how lovely you look?"

"Yes, I believe you did. Thank you. Again." Marcy fingered the collar of her cotton shirt self-consciously, wondering if she should have done up the top button. She'd had to unpack her suitcase to get at her white blouse and gray pants, not to mention her heels and some fresh underwear, but the change had made her feel better. Even her hair seemed calmer.

The waiter approached with their drinks.

"To a holiday that gets better every day," Vic said, lifting his glass and clinking it against hers.

"I'll drink to that." Marcy took a sip, feeling the liquid burn the back of her throat. "Wow. That's pretty strong stuff."

"Good, though."

"Getting better every sip." She looked around the noisy, brightly lit restaurant, slightly more formal than the pubs they'd visited earlier in the day, although not much. A large bar in the very center of the room was its dominant feature. Approximately thirty people were sitting or standing around it, all of whom seemed to be talking at the same time, their hands punching at the air, punctuating whatever point they were trying to make. Around the bar were small oak tables, all of them occupied. There wasn't an empty seat in the place. They'd been lucky to get in.

"So what did you think of 'the Stiletto in the Ghetto'?" Vic was asking.

Had she heard him correctly? She didn't want a repeat of the widget/midget fiasco. "The what?"

"The Millennium Spire," he said, then, when that didn't seem to register, "The monument we passed on the way over? The tall, stainless steel needle in the middle of the road?" he said, clarifying further. "The one that replaced the statue of Admiral Nelson erected by the British and blown up by the IRA. It's pretty hard to miss. You missed it," he said.

"I guess I was pretty focused on finding this place."

"You seem to have a habit of doing that. Focusing on finding things," he said by way of explanation, although there'd been no need. Marcy understood he was referring to the events of earlier in the day.

"You called it 'the Stiletto in the Ghetto'?" she asked, returning to safer ground.

"Also known simply as 'the Spike.' The Irish seem to get a kick out of giving rather colorful nicknames to their public monuments. You remember Molly Malone?"

"The one who wheeled her wheelbarrow through streets broad and narrow?"

"That's the one. Apparently the statue of her on the corner of Grafton and Nassau is rather well endowed, and so the natives have taken to calling her 'the Tart with the Cart.'"

"Cute." For sure she should have done up her top button, Marcy was thinking.

"There was also 'the Floozy in the Jacuzzi' right on this very street, across from the post office, but apparently she was extremely ugly, aesthetically speaking, and everybody hated her, so she got torn down."

"The Irish like their tarts but they're not big on floozies."

Vic laughed. "And then there's my favorite, the statue of one of Ireland's greatest patriots, Wolfe Tone."

Marcy's eyes narrowed. She'd never even heard of Wolfe Tone. So much she didn't know, she thought.

"Have you been to St. Stephen's Green yet?" Vic was asking.

Marcy shook her head, downing the remaining contents of her glass in one extended gulp. Truthfully, she didn't know whether or not she'd been to St. Stephen's Green. Since arriving in Dublin five days ago, she'd done little but walk around the city in a daze. Today had been her first real outing.

"Well, on the park's north side," Vic said, "you'll find a semicircle of very rough-looking columns in Tone's honor. The locals call it 'Tonehenge.'"

It was Marcy's turn to laugh.

"I'd be happy to show it to you. If you're free tomorrow . . ."

"I'm not."

A flash of disappointment registered in his eyes, although his quick smile disguised it. "You've booked another tour?"

"No. I think that's it for me and tour groups."

"I'm with you. Or not, as it turns out."

"It's just that I've already made other plans for tomorrow." Marcy felt the need to explain.

"Well, if you should find yourself with some extra time on your hands, feel free to give me a call." Vic reached into his pocket, pulled out a business card, and handed it across the small wood table. "Sold the business, kept the cell phone number."

Marcy slipped the card into her purse without looking at it. "Actually I'm leaving Dublin tomorrow."

"Oh. I'm sorry to hear that. Where are you off to?"

"I'm meeting my sister in Paris for a few days," she lied. Hell, it was just easier that way.

"Paris is a beautiful city."

"Yes, it is."

"I started my trip there a few weeks ago. Paris, then London," he said without prompting. "Then Scotland. Now here. Next stop, Italy."

"That's quite the trip."

"Well, I want to see the village where my great-grandfather was born, and I figured if I wait too long, I might not make it." He paused, as if waiting for her to ask the logical follow-up, then continued when she didn't. "My father died of a heart attack when he was fifty-nine. My mother died of cancer at sixty-two, my first wife at fifty-three, also cancer. I just turned fifty-seven. I figure I might not have a whole lot of time left."

Marcy nodded, held up her empty glass. "In that case, do you think we could have another one of these?"

"I think that could be arranged." He signaled the waiter for another round. "And thank you."

"For what?"

"Most people tell me I'm being foolish when I tell them my philosophy of life. Or death, as the case may be."

"Sounds quite logical to me."

"Sounds to me as if you also lost a loved one at too young an age."

"Actually my father was almost eighty when he died."

"And your mother?"

Marcy extended her hand toward the approaching waiter, smiled when she felt the weight of the glass in her hand. "Forty-six." She took a swallow. "You said your *first* wife. How many have there been?"

Vic smiled. "Just two."

"What happened to the second?"

"We divorced a year ago."

"I'm sorry."

"Don't be. It was a disaster from the word go."

Marcy took another sip of her drink and waited for him to continue.

"I was married to my first wife for almost thirty-three years," he said, obliging her. "She was my high school sweetheart. We got married right out of college. We were the quintessential all-American couple. And then we were the quintessential all-American family, with three sons, a house in Lake Forest with a four-car garage, and everything you could possibly ask for. And then one day Kathy said she was feeling kind of funny—those were her exact words, she was feeling 'kind of funny'—and we went to the doctor, and he said she had pancreatic cancer, and three months later she was dead."

Marcy lowered her glass, stared at the table.

"And I was just reeling. Worse than reeling. I was off the wall. I mean, Kathy was it for me, you know? I'd never even been with another woman. And suddenly there I was, all alone. Well, I had my sons, of course, but they had their own lives to deal with. David and Mark are married, with small children, and Tony is twenty-three and finishing up his master's degree in music. They had enough on their plate. And I'm acting like a total lunatic. One minute I'm holed up in the house, refusing to go anywhere, and the next minute I'm out on the town, staying out all night, bedding anything that moves. I mean I'm suddenly the new guy in town, right? And I don't have any unsightly warts and rashes, so I've got all these women basically throwing themselves at me."

"Floozies in Jacuzzis," Marcy said, looking up, relieved when she saw Vic smile.

"Tony called them 'the Brisket Brigade.'"

Marcy laughed.

"Anyway, one day I decided it was time to sell the house. I mean, Kathy and I had been talking about it for years. The kids were pretty much on their own, what did we need such a big house for, the usual discussions, right? And now that Kathy was dead, it was just me and seven empty bedrooms. It was time to move on."

"Don't the experts usually advise not making any big moves for at least a year after the death of a spouse?"

"If they don't, they should. But it's hard to listen to reason when you're not being rational. And real estate agents aren't exactly big on periods of reflection."

"So you sold your house?"

"No. I married my realtor."

"What?"

"Yup, you heard correctly. Good old reliable, once-sane Victor Sorvino up and marries a woman twenty-five years his junior, a woman he's known for less than three months, barely six months after his beloved first wife passed away, and he flies off to Las Vegas and marries her without telling anyone, without even a prenup, and the marriage is a total fiasco from the moment he says 'I do,' and she basically says, 'I don't, at least not with you,' and six months later, we agree to a divorce, and among other things, she gets the house, which, incidentally, she now has up for sale."

"What some agents won't do to secure a listing." Everybody has a story, Marcy was thinking, marveling at what he'd just told her.

"Grief makes us do funny things," he said.

Marcy agreed silently. "I'm sorry. I didn't mean to be glib. Are you all right?"

"Let's say I'm recovering. Like an alcoholic, I guess. I don't think we ever fully get over the death of someone we love. We just learn to live with their absence."

"Do we?"

"Do we have a choice?"

Marcy turned her head, grateful to see the waiter approaching with their food.

"Careful, it's hot," the waiter warned as he lowered their dishes to the table.

"Looks good," Vic said, inhaling the steam rising from his plate.

Marcy immediately tore into her shepherd's pie. "It's delicious," she said.

"I think I should apologize," Vic said.

"For what?"

"For monopolizing the conversation all night."

"It's been fascinating."

Vic shrugged. "Tell me more about you."

"Not much to tell. My husband left me for one of the golf pros at our country club. Her handicap was lower than mine," she added, feeling the smile she tried to muster wobble precariously on her mouth.

"How long were you married?" Vic asked.

"Going on twenty-five years. This trip was supposed to be a second honeymoon to celebrate our anniversary. Didn't quite work out that way."

"So you came by yourself. That's very . . ."

"Stupid?"

"I was going to say brave."

"I don't think that's a word too many people would use to describe me."

"Then it's amazing how wrong people can be."

"Yes." Marcy agreed. It *was* amazing how wrong people could be.

"Do you have any children?" he asked.

"Yes. Two."

"Boys? Girls?"

"One of each. Darren's nineteen, very tall and handsome, thinking of going into dentistry, like his dad. He's working as a camp counselor for the summer."

"Sounds like fun. And your daughter? What's she up to?"

"Devon is twenty-one, or no, actually, she'd be almost twenty-three now," Marcy said, correcting herself immediately.

Vic cocked his head to one side, smiling to mask his obvious confusion. "Devon is the girl you thought you saw this afternoon?"

"I *did* see her."

"Your daughter is here in Ireland?" This time there was no attempt to hide his confusion.

"She's traveling through Europe for the summer," Marcy said. "I didn't realize we'd both be here at the same time, not until I saw her this afternoon. I guess she must have changed her plans at the last minute. That's a lie," she added in the next breath.

"I kind of figured."

"I'm sorry."

"That's all right. You don't owe me any explanations."

"My daughter supposedly drowned in a canoeing accident about two years ago," Marcy said, watching Vic's brow furrow and his eyes narrow. "Twenty-one months ago, to be precise. Except they never found her body. And I know, I *know*, she's still alive, that for whatever reason, she faked her death."

"Why would she do that?" Vic asked, as Peter had asked earlier.

"To get away. To start a new life. Start over."

"Why would she want to start over?"

"Because she was so unhappy. Because she'd gotten herself into some trouble . . . I'm sorry. Can we not talk about this anymore?"

"We can not talk about whatever you'd like."

Marcy continued, unable to stop herself. "Everybody else is so positive she's dead. But I know what I saw. I saw my daughter. You think I'm crazy, don't you?"

"I think a mother knows her own child."

Relief washed across Marcy's face like a cool breeze. "God, you're a nice man," she said.

"And you've had a very eventful day. Come on. Finish up. I'll take you back to your hotel."

Marcy reached across the table, took Vic's hand in hers. "I have a better idea," she said.

FIVE

HER SISTER WAS RIGHT about one thing, Marcy thought, sitting up in bed and gazing through the darkness at the man snoring softly beside her: Sex was like riding a bicycle. Once you knew how to do it, you never really forgot the mechanics, no matter how long it had been since the last time you did it. And it didn't matter what kind of bike it was or how many speeds it had or how many embellishments had been added, the basic operating premise remained the same: You mounted; you worked the pedals; you got off.

And her sister would know. As Judith herself admitted, she'd ridden a lot of bicycles.

Marcy climbed out of bed and walked to the window overlooking Fleet Street. It was quiet, although surprisingly, even at almost two in the morning, there were still people out walking.

The trendy area of Temple Bar never really shut down, according to Vic, who'd pointed out several scantily dressed fashion models draped like fur stoles around the shoulders of some music industry bigwigs at the boutique hotel's crowded bar.

They'd gone to his room at her suggestion.

"Are you sure?" he'd asked when they first entered the elegantly underfurnished lobby of his hotel.

"I'm sure."

They'd undressed each other quickly and expertly, made love easily and effortlessly. And repeatedly, she thought now, feeling the pleasant soreness between her legs. When was the last time she and Peter had made love more than once in a single night? Not in at least a decade, she thought, then immediately amended that to two decades.

She grabbed her blouse off a nearby chair and wrapped it around her, the soft cotton teasing her nipple, mimicking Vic's earlier touch. At first she thought it would be strange to have another man's hands exploring her so intimately. After almost a quarter of a century of being with the same man, she was used to a certain way of doing things, a clearly defined order of what went where and when and for how long. She and Peter had long ago fallen into a familiar rhythm—satisfying and pleasant, if no longer terribly exciting. But good nonetheless, she'd always thought. Dependable. Reliable.

She'd had no desire to change things.

And then Devon had paddled her canoe into the middle of Georgian Bay one brilliant October morning—the air cold, the dying leaves a miraculous succession of red, orange, and gold—and nothing was ever the same again.

Marcy shook thoughts of Devon from her head and looked around the room, which was sparsely decorated in various neutral shades: cream-colored walls, crisp white bedspreads, light beechwood furniture. The only real color came from several exuberant paintings by Irish artists, one on the far wall, another over the bed. The effect was at once understated and luxurious, a heady mix of old-school restraint and modern decadence.

Rather like the man lying on his back in the middle of the queen-size bed, a white sheet wrapped lazily around his still-slender torso, Marcy thought, watching the steady rise and fall of Vic's chest as he slept. She'd always liked a man with hair on his chest, had never really understood what today's women found attractive about someone who'd been shaved and waxed to within an inch of his life. Hairy chests were like English gardens, unruly and vaguely chaotic, yet strong and stubbornly resilient. There was just something so reassuringly grown-up about a hairy chest, she thought, returning to the bed and perching on its edge.

But then there were all sorts of areas where she and other women parted company on what constituted sex appeal. For one thing, she wasn't overly fond of muscles. A well-defined pair of biceps tended to make her more anxious than aroused. As did men in uniforms of any kind, including the mailman. *You're worse than my poodle,* Judith had once said, chastising her. And how many women could say they actually enjoyed the sound of a man snoring? How many found such a sound not only comforting but life affirming? When she was a child, there were nights when she would tiptoe into her parents' bedroom during one of her mother's unexplained and extended absences, and she would lie down on the floor at the foot of their bed, soaking up her father's prodigious snores, which filled the room like a lullaby, assuring her of his continuing presence as she reluctantly gave herself over to sleep.

Peter never snored, although he claimed *she* did. "Why do you have to sleep on your back?" he'd say accusingly, as if her snoring was something she was doing deliberately to provoke him. And then increasingly, as the years passed and more grievances surfaced: "Do you have to move around so much?" "Do you know you talk in your sleep?" "Can't you ever just lie still?" Until one morning about a year after Devon's accident she woke up to find Peter's side of the bed empty, and when she'd gone to look for him, she'd found him asleep in the guest bedroom.

He never came back.

Five months later, he moved out altogether.

All he'd taken were his clothes and his golf clubs.

Marcy sighed, reaching her hand out to touch Vic's cheek, then withdrawing it before she made contact, returning it to her lap. What on earth had possessed her to sleep with a man she barely knew, a man she'd met on a bus, for God's sake, a man who was still grieving the death of his first wife even after divorcing his second? *Grief makes us do funny things,* he'd said.

Was it grief that had brought her to his bed?

Or was it gratitude?

I think a mother knows her own child, he'd said, and she'd actually had to hold herself back from leaping across the table, crawling into his lap, and smothering his face with kisses. Yes, thank you, you believe me!

At last, somebody believes me.

Was that all it took?

Or maybe it was hope that had brought her here. Hope that had let a virtual stranger undress and caress her, hope that had allowed her to respond so eagerly to his touch, hope that because Devon was alive, so too was she, that two people hadn't drowned on that horrible, cold October day, and that she could finally spit out the water that had been trapped in her lungs for far too long, inhale and exhale without feeling a knife plunging into her chest.

Devon was alive, which meant Marcy had been given a second chance, a chance to make things right, a chance for both of them to be happy again.

Had they ever truly been happy?

"What's the matter, sweetheart?" she remembered asking one July night almost exactly five years ago. The night when everything changed. The night she had to stop pretending they were a normal family, that everything would be okay.

It was after midnight. Devon had been out partying with friends. Marcy was lying in bed, Peter asleep beside her. She'd been drifting in and out of consciousness, having never been fully able to give in to sleep until she knew Devon was home safe, and now she waited for Devon to tiptoe by her room, possibly stick her head in the door to see if she was still up so she could kiss her good night. Instead Marcy heard her moving around in the kitchen, restlessly opening and closing the cupboard doors. Open, close, open, close. First one, then another. Open, close, open, close.

Then a crash. The sound of glass breaking.

Marcy had jumped out of bed, grabbed a bathrobe, and run from the bedroom, telling herself she was overreacting, that there was no need to be alarmed. Devon was hungry; she'd been searching for something to snack on and had knocked something over in the dark. It was an accident. She was probably down on her hands and knees at this very moment trying to clean up the mess.

Except that when Marcy entered the kitchen, she discovered Devon standing ramrod straight beside the granite counter, her mouth open, her jaw slack, her eyes blank and filled with tears.

"What's the matter, sweetheart?" Marcy asked, drawing closer.

"Don't," Devon warned.

Marcy noted the pieces of glass that were scattered around Devon's feet and the tulips that were lying half in, half out of what remained of their crystal vase. Water was splashed across the top of Devon's open-toed sandals, the red polish of her toe-nails wet and shiny in the moonlight. Her hands were curled into tight fists at her sides, white granules squeezing out from between her clenched fingers and falling toward the floor like snow.

"What is that, sweetheart?" Marcy asked, flipping on the overhead light, seeing a familiar cardboard box lying on its side on the counter. "What are you doing with the salt?"

In response, Devon raised her fists to her face, began shoveling the salt into her mouth.

Marcy was instantly at her side, tearing Devon's hands away from her face. "Devon, for God's sake, what are you doing? Stop that. You'll make yourself sick."

Devon's eyes suddenly snapped into focus, as if she were seeing her mother for the first time. "Mom?" she said, opening her palms and letting the remaining salt spill free.

Marcy felt the avalanche of tiny, hard crystals as they landed on the tops of her bare feet. "Are you all right?" She began frantically brushing her daughter's hair away from her face, trying to wipe away the salt still stubbornly clinging to her lips and chin.

Devon looked from her mother to the floor. "Oh, God, I'm so sorry."

"What is it, sweetheart? What happened?"

"I don't know. I was reaching for a bag of potato chips and I stopped to admire the flowers. You know how they say you have to stop and smell the roses? Even though these are tulips and they don't smell. Only I knocked over the vase and I couldn't find the potato chips. Do you remember Vicki? Vicki Enquist? She's really tall, almost six feet, her nose is a little crooked? She was like my best friend in the seventh grade, do you remember her?" she said, all in the same breath.

Marcy was about to answer that no, she had no memory of anyone named Vicki Enquist and could Devon please slow down, that she wasn't making any sense, but her daughter had already moved on.

"Her mother was like this famous gardener or something. She had, like, her own TV show or something in Vancouver. Anyway, she was there tonight. Vicki, I mean, not her mother. At the party over at Ashleigh's. And she looked so pretty," Devon said, suddenly bursting into tears. "Her nose didn't look too crooked at all. And I felt really bad about all the times we teased her. I was really mean to her, Mom."

"Sweetheart, please. You're scaring me. Why don't we sit down?"

"I don't want to sit down. I want to go dancing." Devon pushed herself onto her toes and did a clumsy pirouette. "But everybody else just wants to sit around and get high," she said, losing her balance and tumbling into her mother's arms.

"Is that it?" Marcy asked, holding her daughter at arm's length, forcing Devon's eyes to hers. "Are you high, Devon? Have you been doing drugs?"

"I'm so thirsty," Devon said, ignoring the question and extricating herself from Marcy's grip.

"I'll get you a glass of water."

"There's water on the floor," Devon said, as if noticing it for the first time.

"I'll clean it up in a minute."

Devon suddenly sank to her knees, began moving the water and salt around the large sand-colored squares of the ceramic tile floor with the palms of her hands, as if she were a child who'd just discovered the joys of finger-painting.

"Devon, please, sweetheart, be careful of the glass. No, don't put that in your mouth. Please let me help you up."

"I don't want to get up."

"You need to let me help you." Marcy succeeded in dragging her daughter to her feet and sitting her down in one of the four kitchen chairs clustered around the large oval-shaped pine table. "I'll get you some water. Please, baby. Tell me what you've taken."

"I'm just so thirsty," Devon said again. "Why am I so thirsty? Did I tell you that Bobby Saunders was at the party tonight? He's like this big-shot hockey player or something. I think he plays with the Maple Leafs. All the girls are crazy about him, although personally I don't think he's all that hot. I think he looks kind of stupid. He has this big, goofy grin, and he's missing a couple of teeth. Anyway, he was coming on to all the girls, saying things like, 'Are we going to have sex tonight?' even though he supposedly has this gorgeous fiancée who's some kind of supermodel. It was disgusting. Do you even know who I'm talking about? You don't know anything about hockey. I bet Dad would know. Dad's very into sports." She started crying again.

Marcy's hands were shaking as she went to the sink and poured a glass of water for Devon, letting the sound of the water gushing from the tap temporarily drown out Devon's insane chatter.

"Devon," she said, turning off the tap and swiveling toward her. Except that Devon was no longer sitting on the chair. She was curled up on the floor in a semi-fetal position, her knees pressed tight against her blue T-shirt, her face half-submerged in a mound of soggy salt, a large shard of glass pressed against her cheek, mere inches from her eye. "Devon?" Marcy said again, her voice lost between a cry and a whisper.

She collapsed to her knees beside her daughter. Immediately a piece of crystal pierced her skin and she cried out. It was then that she heard a faint sigh escape Devon's parted lips and realized that her daughter had fallen asleep. Sound asleep, Marcy realized when she tried to rouse her.

She thought of waking Peter but decided against it. There was no reason for both of them to be up. It took her almost fifteen minutes to get Devon out of the kitchen, down the hall, and into her bedroom, another twenty to get her undressed and cleaned up, five more to maneuver her into bed, and then another fifteen to go back and clean up the mess in the kitchen. By the time Marcy returned to her room, she was bathed in sweat, and blood was dripping in a series of straggly lines from her knee to her ankle. She took a shower, applied a Band-Aid to her knee, and climbed back into bed.

"Can't you stay still?" Peter muttered, flipping over onto his side.

"What are you doing sitting there?" Vic asked now, his eyes finding hers in the dark hotel room. "Are you all right?"

"I'm fine."

"Are you crying?"

Marcy immediately swiped at the tears in the corners of her eyes. "No. Of course not. Well . . . maybe a little."

Vic pushed himself onto his elbows, reached for her hand. "Are you sorry that we . . . ?"

"What? Oh, no. No. Honestly. I promise that's not it."

"You were thinking about Devon," he said, the name sounding comfortable, even familiar, on his tongue, almost as if he knew her.

"Yes."

"Have you decided what you're going to do?"

"No."

"Would you like me to go with you?" he asked with a smile. The smile said, *Don't even try to lie to me.* "I'm serious. I'd be happy to go back with you to Cork."

It was certainly tempting, Marcy thought. It would be nice to have company. "No," she said after a moment's pause. It would only complicate things. "I think this is something I need to do alone."

He nodded, as if he weren't surprised. "Promise you'll keep me posted."

"I have your card," she said.

"You'll call the minute you find Devon?" Again the easy use of her daughter's name. Had Marcy ever felt such ease where her daughter was concerned?

"You think I'll find her?" Marcy was suddenly very much in need of his assurance.

"I know you will."

"How do you know?"

"Because I know you."

"But you *don't* know me. Not really."

"I know how determined you are, that you won't give up until you find her."

"I *will* find her," Marcy said forcefully.

"Absolutely, you will. No question about it. And if at any point you change your mind about wanting me to join you, if you need some help, or if you just want someone to hold your hand or scratch your back . . ."

She smiled as his fingers moved up her arm to the base of her neck, disappearing into her mop of wayward curls. "Oh, God. I must look awful. My hair—"

"Is fabulous."

She shook her head, the curls bouncing lazily across her forehead.

"Is it really possible you don't know how beautiful you are?" Vic asked.

"My mother always used to say I had way too much hair," Marcy told him.

"My mother used to say I'd be six feet tall if only I'd stand up straight."

"There's nothing wrong with your posture."

"There's nothing wrong with your hair."

Marcy laughed. "Mothers," she said.

"You said yours died when she was forty-six? That must have been very hard for you."

"Actually," Marcy admitted, "in some ways it was a relief."

"Had she been sick for long?"

"As long as I can remember."

Vic tilted his head to one side, his eyes asking her to continue.

"She threw herself off the roof of a ten-story building when I was fifteen years old," Marcy said.

"My God, I'm so sorry."

"Can you do me a favor?" Marcy asked, crawling back into bed and drawing the covers up to her chin.

"Anything."

"Can you just hold me?"

She felt his arms immediately surround her, his breath warm on the back of her neck as she pressed her backside into the concave curve of his stomach. They lay that way until eventually she felt his grip on her loosen and his breathing drift into the slower rhythms of sleep. She lay there in the dark, absorbing the reassurance of his gentle snores, then she gently extricated herself from his arms, slipped quietly out of bed, got dressed, and tiptoed from the room.

SIX

FIRST THING THE NEXT morning, Marcy checked out of her hotel.

"I notice you have a number of messages you haven't retrieved," the clerk behind the reception desk told her as she was settling up her account.

"You can just erase them."

"As you wish. If there's anything else I can help you with . . ."

"You can get me a taxi, please." Some time after she'd returned to her own room, Marcy had decided against renting a car— Lynette was right: She was unfamiliar with the roads; she wasn't used to driving on the left side of the street; she really wouldn't need a car once she arrived. Hadn't her former tour guide expressly stated that Cork was a city best experienced on foot?

"You'll be able to find one right outside the main entrance. Do you need help with your suitcase?"

"No. I can manage. Thank you."

A line of taxis waited just outside the front door. Marcy approached several before she found one willing to make the drive all the way to Cork, and even then the driver insisted on being compensated for gas and a round-trip fare. "Fine," Marcy said, climbing into the backseat. "Just get me there as fast as you can." And in one piece, she added silently as the man threw the cab into gear and the small car all but bounced away from the curb.

Luckily the driver was possibly the only man in Ireland who showed absolutely no interest in carrying on a conversation. Nor did he feel any need to show off his knowledge of Irish history and folklore. Guess he never kissed the Blarney Stone, Marcy found herself thinking as she tried to get comfortable in the cramped backseat.

It took a long time to get out of the city. For a while the taxi was stuck behind two huge dump trucks—"the new national symbol of Dublin," her guide had grunted yesterday when the bus found itself similarly trapped—each toting tons of sand and gravel. Construction was everywhere: New roads were being built, old ones widened; new apartment complexes, many of them tall, gray concrete boxes devoid of charm or character, were springing up all over the place; monstrous new homes were replacing charming old cottages. Marcy rolled down her window, then quickly rolled it back up again, the constant banging of jackhammers giving her an instant headache.

Things improved once they reached the main motorway, although only barely. Heavy traffic competed with a rapidly descending fog and patches of occasionally heavy rain to make driving conditions less than ideal. Marcy recalled having read

somewhere that Ireland was ranked the second-most dangerous country in Europe in which to drive. She couldn't remember the first. "Are we almost there?" she asked after almost two
hours had elapsed.

Are we there yet? she heard Devon's voice say, echoing her
own.

"About another hour," the driver replied from the front
seat. "People always forget how to drive in the rain."

"But it rains almost every day."

"There you go," he said, as if that answered everything. And
maybe it did, Marcy thought, leaning her head back against the
top of the seat and closing her eyes. "Where do you want me to
drop you?" he asked in what seemed like the next breath.

"What?" Marcy snapped to attention, checking her watch
to discover an hour had passed and she must have fallen asleep.
She looked out the raindrop-splattered window to find the city
of Cork.

"What hotel are you stayin' in?" the cab driver asked, navigating his way slowly through the severe congestion into the
flat of the city.

It suddenly occurred to Marcy that she had forgotten to
make hotel reservations. She pictured Lynette shaking her
head, silently berating her again for failing to think *in advance*.
"I actually don't have a room. Do you happen to know somewhere nice you could recommend?"

"Well, it's not going to be easy to find a place. It's the height
of the tourist season after all, and Cork doesn't have that many
grand hotels."

"It doesn't have to be grand. In fact, I'd prefer somewhere
simpler." Simpler meant less chance of anyone finding her. She
didn't want Judith or Peter being able to track her down as easily as they had in Dublin. Nor did she want Vic Sorvino riding

in on his white horse to rescue her, appealing as that thought might be. Experience had taught her that she couldn't depend on a man to save her. Nor should she. It wasn't fair to either of them.

Marcy opened her side window, careful not to let the rain inside the car. The bells of St. Anne's Shandon Church were sending the first eight notes of "Danny Boy" rippling down the hill and throughout the city. She smiled, a feeling of excitement filling her lungs. It didn't matter where she stayed, she thought. As long as Devon was nearby, she'd sleep on the sidewalk if she had to.

"There's Tynan's over on Western," the driver was saying. "It's a bed and breakfast, and I hear it's okay, although it might be pretty basic."

"Basic is good."

It was also fully booked. As were the next half-dozen B&Bs that sat cheek by jowl along Western Road. Good thing the rain finally stopped, Marcy thought as she dragged her suitcase up the front steps of the Doyle Cork Inn, one of the few B&Bs on the street she'd yet to try.

"Can I give you a hand with that?" a young man asked, appearing at her side to grab her suitcase. He was in his late teens, and his fair skin was scarred with the leftover remnants of a case of childhood chicken pox. There was one particularly large pockmark that sat right between his wide-set hazel eyes, like a bullet hole. A stray lock of reddish-blond hair curled into the center of his large forehead, and his mouth was filled to bursting with Chiclet-sized teeth.

A proper pair of braces would have fixed that, she heard Peter say.

"Thank you, yes." Marcy followed the young man inside to the check-in counter of the tiny lobby. "Do you have a room?"

"I believe we do, yes."

"Thank God. I was beginning to give up hope."

"Oh, you must never do that."

Marcy smiled. "I won't. Thank you. That's good advice."

"The name's Colin Doyle. My mum'll be right with you. You from America?"

"Canada," Marcy told him.

"Really? We had a guest here from Canada not too long ago. Name of Randy Sullivan, I believe it was. Do you know him?"

"No, I'm afraid I don't." She refrained from telling him that there were more than thirty-three million people in Canada. Although you never knew. It wasn't totally outside the realm of possibility that she might know this person. It was certainly no stranger than her taking off for Ireland on her erstwhile second honeymoon and finding the daughter she'd given up for dead. "Do you know this girl?" Marcy asked, pulling the latest picture of Devon out of her purse and showing it to Colin.

He took it from her hand and studied it for several seconds, his bushy eyebrows collapsing toward the bridge of his nose. "Can't say that I do," he said at last.

"You're sure? It's possible she's a student at the university. I understand it's very close to here."

"Just up the next block a bit," he concurred. Then, "No. Don't know her." He handed back the photograph. "She looks very sad, doesn't she?"

Marcy's eyes immediately filled with tears. It was her fault her daughter looked so sad.

"Sorry to have kept you," a high-pitched voice trilled as a heavy-set woman with gray-flecked, reddish-blond hair entered the small foyer. Her eyes were the same shade of hazel as her son's, although they twinkled more mischievously, as if she'd just come from something she probably shouldn't have been doing. "Name's Sadie Doyle, owner of this proud establishment." Large, surprisingly expressive hands fluttered in front of her, sweeping together the foyer, the living room to her left, and the narrow staircase to her right, the walls of which were all covered with the same garish, purple-flowered wallpaper. Marcy couldn't tell whether or not the woman was being facetious. "Mind if I have a look at that?" Sadie Doyle asked, indicating the picture of Devon. "Pretty girl. Looks a little sad though, don't she?"

Marcy felt her heart sink.

"Your daughter?"

"Yes. Do you know her, by any chance?"

"No chance at all, I'm afraid. She's here in Cork, is she?"

"Yes, she is. I'm trying to find her."

"You don't know where she is?"

Marcy felt the question sting her skin. "We've kind of lost touch."

Sadie Doyle smiled wistfully, as if she understood, although her eyes retained a hint of rebuke. "Wish I could be of help." She walked behind the counter and opened the guest register. "It's one hundred and fifty euros a night for a single room."

"That's fine." Marcy couldn't remember the exchange rate between dollars and euros but decided she'd worry about it later.

"Just how long will you be staying with us, Mrs. . . . ?"

"Taggart. Marcy Taggart. And I'll be staying a few days. Maybe a week. I'm not sure exactly how long." As long as it takes, Marcy thought. "Is that a problem?"

"No problem at all. If you could just fill this out." Sadie pushed a sheet of paper across the reception desk. "And I'll need your passport, of course. Colin here will bring it up to you in a few hours. What credit card will you be using?"

Marcy handed over her American Express card.

"You'll be in room seven, top of the stairs to your left." Sadie Doyle handed Marcy a large, elaborately carved brass key. "It's one of our nicer rooms. I think you'll be very comfortable there."

"Thank you."

"Good luck with finding your daughter."

"Thank you," Marcy said again, returning Devon's picture to her purse as she followed Colin up the stairs.

The room was small and crowded with inexpensive furniture: a double bed with an old brass headboard, a shabby-looking armoire and matching nightstand, an even shabbier-looking dresser that was missing the knobs on two of its three drawers, a high-backed chair upholstered in heavy purple brocade that was fraying along its seams, and a battered mahogany table beneath a window that looked through a slightly worn lace curtain directly into one of the upstairs windows of the B&B next door. The purple-flowered wallpaper was only slightly more muted than the wallpaper in the common areas and the carpet was a tired-looking mix of mauve and brown. No more tired-looking than I am, Marcy thought, plopping down on the bed's too-soft mattress and staring at her reflection in the frameless rectangular mirror on the opposite wall.

You're beautiful, she heard Vic whisper in her ear.

"Yeah, right," she scoffed, pushing at her hair.

"Sorry, did you say something?" Colin asked.

"What? No. Did I?" She hadn't realized the boy was still there. Probably waiting for a tip, she realized, fishing in her purse for some change.

"Is everything all right?" he asked nervously, his weight shifting from one foot to the other.

"Yes. Everything's just fine."

"Enjoy your stay," he said, his shins knocking against her suitcase as he turned toward the door.

"Oh, well. It's not so bad," Marcy exclaimed after he'd left the room, hoping to be reassured by the sound of her own voice. After all, she was used to convincing herself that things were other than the way they really were. So if she told herself enough times that the room was beautiful and that everything was fine, she would no doubt eventually come to believe it. "You pretend, therefore you are," she whispered, walking over to the window and parting the dusty lace curtains, staring into the upstairs window of the B&B next door.

It took her several seconds to realize that someone was staring back. A young woman, Marcy realized. A young woman about Devon's height with the same long brown hair. "Devon?" Marcy whispered as the woman smiled and offered a self-conscious little wave. Suddenly a man appeared at her side, holding a squirming toddler. The toddler's hands strained toward the woman, his fingers reaching for her neck as she welcomed him into her arms and smothered his face with kisses.

Not Devon, Marcy knew instantly. Devon had never been particularly fond of children. "I'm with Judith on that one," she'd said more than once.

"You have to stop imagining every girl you see is Devon," Marcy told herself, backing away from the window and retrieving her suitcase from the floor, then tossing it on the bed. Not every girl who was the same height as Devon—*A pretty girl with long dark hair and high cheekbones, who maybe walked the way Devon walked and held her cigarette the same way,* Peter had said—was her daughter. She had to stop thinking that way or she'd make herself crazy.

Too late, she thought as she unpacked her suitcase, hanging as many clothes as she could on the four hangers she found in the tiny armoire and stuffing the rest into the Salvation Army-style chest of drawers under the mirror. The bathroom was so small that when she opened the door, it hit the tub, and there was no medicine cabinet or counter for her toiletries, so she had to spread the various creams her sister had insisted she buy around the edge of the decidedly utilitarian white sink. Not that any of them did any good, she thought, unable to avoid the small mirror over the sink and staring at the fine lines that were gathering around her mouth and eyes like an unwelcome storm. "Who invited you to this party?" she wondered aloud, splashing some cold water on her face, then patting her face dry with the thin white towel hanging on a nearby hook.

Time for a little lift, she heard Judith say.

"No, thank you." Marcy backed away from the mirror, promptly hitting the bathroom door and feeling the doorknob jam into the small of her back like a fist.

Judith had had her face "done" about six years ago. "Just a little pick-me-up," she'd insisted. "So I won't look so tired."

"You wouldn't look so tired if you'd stop exercising all the time."

"I have to stay in shape."

"You're in great shape."

"Only because I exercise. You really should come with me to spin class. It would do you a world of good. And it'll do wonders for your sex life."

"There's nothing wrong with my sex life."

"Good for you. But you should come anyway. So should Devon. She's looking a little soft around the edges."

"What do you mean? Devon looks great."

"She's looking soft around the edges."

"I don't know what you're talking about."

"How's she doing these days?"

"She's doing great. What are you getting at?"

"You're not letting her eat a lot of junk food, are you?"

"She's a teenager, Judith. I really have very limited control over what she eats."

"You know the importance of a proper diet."

"There's more to life than raw fish."

"Nobody says there isn't."

"Just what *are* you saying?"

"I'm not saying anything."

"Devon's fine."

"Of course she is."

"Of course she is," Marcy repeated now, returning to the bedroom and tucking her suitcase underneath the bed, the only available space she could find. Then she changed into jeans and a fresh blouse, grabbed her purse, took a deep breath, then another, and left the room.

SHE WENT DIRECTLY back to the pub where she'd first spotted Devon. "Grogan's House," she muttered aloud as she crossed over St. Patrick's Bridge and turned left, relieved when the bright yellow sign with the bold black lettering came into view. The pub occupied the ground floor of a two-story white stucco building with a black slate roof. A couple of round, old-fashioned, ornamental lights hung amid a bunch of small, brightly colored flags that decorated the facade. Advertisements for Guinness and Beamish were etched into the glass of the large front windows. Marcy remembered none of these details from the previous afternoon. Was it possible she was mistaken about which pub she'd been in? There were so many in the area.

She approached the front door cautiously, glancing over her shoulder at the few people brave enough to be sitting on the outside patio. A second was all it took for Marcy to ascertain that Devon wasn't among them. A man was exiting the pub as she was going in, and he held the door open for her, the welcoming chatter from inside the room instantly enveloping her.

"Well, well," a voice exclaimed above the din. "Come back to finish your tea, have you?"

Marcy walked directly to the bar. "You remember me?" she asked the handsome man behind it.

"I never forget a pretty face."

Marcy felt strangely flattered. Her hand moved immediately to fidget with her hair. "I was hoping you'd be here."

If the young man was surprised by her comment, he didn't show it. His green eyes sparkled as his full lips parted in an easy grin. "Is there something I can do for you then?"

"There was a girl," Marcy said, reaching inside her purse for Devon's photograph. "Yesterday."

"Ah," he said. "A girl . . ."

"I think it was this girl." Marcy pushed the picture of Devon across the bar. "Do you know her?"

He picked up the photograph and examined it for several seconds, slowly shaking his head.

"She walked by outside and waved to you," Marcy pressed, trying to jog his memory.

His smile widened as he returned the picture to her waiting fingers. "I get lots of girls waving at me, I'm afraid."

"Our Liam's quite the ladies' man," a waitress said as she was walking past with a tray of empty beer mugs. "Shall I have a look?"

"Please." Marcy handed Devon's photo to the buxom young woman.

The waitress's loose blond curls fell toward the photograph. "Hmm," she said encouragingly.

"Do you know her?"

"She looks a bit like Audrey, don't she?" she said to the bartender.

"Audrey?" Marcy and Liam asked together.

"Yeah. You know, the girl we see hanging around with that other one, what's her name? The quiet one who works for the O'Connor family."

"I'm not sure I know who you're talkin' about," Liam said.

"Of course you do. The nanny. What's her name? Shannon, I think."

"Oh, yeah. Now I know who you mean." Liam took another look at the photograph, gazing at it for ten long seconds before shaking his head a second time. "Nah, no way that's Audrey."

"Well, I give you she's a little younger than Audrey and not so tough lookin'. . . ."

"This picture was taken a few years ago," Marcy explained.

"Well, there you go," the waitress said.

"So you think this could be Audrey?" Marcy asked, trying to fit her tongue around the new name. Devon had always loved Audrey Hepburn, she reminded herself.

"Well, I can't be sure, of course. But it could be."

Marcy stuffed the picture back inside her purse, her heart threatening to leap from her chest. "Do you know where I can find her?"

"Sorry. No idea," Liam said, turning his attention to a man at the far end of the bar.

"You might try the O'Connors," the waitress volunteered. "Shannon's their nanny. She could probably tell you where to find Audrey."

"Hey, Kelly," a customer called from his table against the wall. "How are you coming with those refills?"

"Be right there."

"Where do I find the O'Connors?" Marcy called after her.

"They live over on Adelaide Road. Don't know the exact address. But it's the biggest house on the street. You can't miss it."

Marcy walked quickly to the door. "Thank you," she called back as she stepped outside, but both Kelly and Liam were busy with customers and neither was listening.

SEVEN

ADELAIDE ROAD WAS LOCATED in the southeastern section of the city about two miles from its center. It was a surprisingly wide, winding street built up the side of a steep hill. The houses were all two stories and relatively new, making up for in square footage what they lacked in design integrity. The majority of them were painted either white or gray, with black shutters framing the front windows. Occasionally a lavender house popped up, or a set of shutters in bold fire-engine red, to relieve the monotony, bringing a small smile to Marcy's lips as she walked by. Kelly had said to look for the biggest house on the street, but so far, all the homes looked roughly the same size, the only difference being whether they had a one- or two-car garage.

A strong wind had started blowing, bringing with it the pungent scent of the harbor. Cork had the world's second-largest natural harbor after Sydney Harbor in Australia. Before coming to Cork, Marcy hadn't realized the city was a major seaport, but then she really hadn't known very much about Ireland at all.

"Ireland's the most beautiful country in the world," she heard Devon pronounce as she followed another bend in the road. "Daddy's been telling me all about it. He says we're going to go there as soon as he can get some time off."

"That's nice." Marcy decided not to tell her fourteen-year-old daughter that Peter had been making the same promise ever since they'd met and that any free time he had these days was pretty much spent on the golf course.

"He says it's got everything: mountain ranges and tall cliffs and wooded river valleys and beaches," she rattled off, as if reading from a brochure, "and that the cities are modern but the villages are quaint, and that there are huge castles and causeways made out of volcanic rock and monasteries that go all the way back to the sixth century."

"Sounds wonderful."

"He says we're going to go there real soon. Maybe even this summer."

"Don't get your hopes up, sweetie. I know Daddy means well, but . . ."

"But what?" Devon's eyes narrowed, a frown creasing her brow.

"But he's a very busy man."

"He's taking me. We're going. You don't have to come if you don't want to."

"I never said I didn't want to come."

"Why do you always have to ruin everything?" With that, Devon pushed herself off the kitchen chair and flounced from the room.

She's right, Marcy thought now, feeling the muscles in the backs of her calves cramp with exertion. I do ruin everything.

That was when she saw the house.

Bigger than all the other houses on the street by at least a third, it was further distinguished by its yellow-brick exterior, its winding flower-lined walkway, and two Juliet-style balconies off the floor-to-ceiling windows on the second floor. A pair of slender white columns stood to either side of the black double front doors, lending the house a vague—if misguided—Southern air. An enormous driveway led to a three-car garage, the doors of the garage a dark, highly polished wood. It was as if the architect hadn't been able to decide between a host of competing styles and so he'd chosen all of them.

So what now? she wondered, continuing up the street, then turning around, walking back, coming at the yellow-brick house from the opposite direction. Should she take the direct approach and simply proceed up the front walk, ring the doorbell, and ask to speak to Shannon?

"Can I tell her who wants to see her?" she heard Mrs. O'Connor ask.

Probably it wouldn't even be Mrs. O'Connor who answered the door, Marcy decided, replacing the generic young woman of her imagination with an older version. Perhaps the housekeeper, she thought, dressing the woman in a crisp gray uniform and securing her hair in a neat chignon at the back of her head. Or maybe it would be Shannon herself who opened the door. "The quiet one" was how Kelly had described her. Marcy pictured a skinny girl with fair skin and strawberry-blond hair.

In the end she settled on Mrs. O'Connor.

"She doesn't know me," Marcy imagined herself explaining to the curious owner of the house. "But I think she might know my daughter. This is her picture. Do you recognize her?"

"Why, yes. I believe that's Audrey." The imaginary Mrs. O'Connor glanced from the photograph to the interior of the house. "Shannon, can you come here a minute? There's someone here who wants to talk to you about Audrey."

"Do you know where I can find her?" Marcy demanded of the willowy apparition who approached.

"Oh, sure. She lives near the university," Shannon answered easily. "I can take you to her, if you'd like."

"I'd like that very much."

Would it really be that easy? Marcy wondered, pushing herself up the O'Connors' front walk. Or would the opposite happen? Would whoever opened the front door simply shut it in her face once she told them why she was there? Would they refuse to let her speak to Shannon, or would Shannon simply shake her head, as Liam had done earlier, and say, "No, that isn't Audrey"?

"Only one way to find out." Marcy rang the bell, then lifted the brass, leprechaun-shaped knocker and smacked it several times against the black wood, holding her breath and listening for the sound of footsteps approaching on the other side. When none were immediately forthcoming, she rang the bell again. Still nothing. "Damn it."

No one was home.

Why was it always the one thing you didn't picture, the one outcome you hadn't anticipated, that was the one you got? Marcy wondered. So now what? "I wait." What else could she do?

She looked around for a place to sit down, but there was nothing, not even a tree trunk for her to lean against. Like many new subdivisions, this one was pretty much void of trees. In modern-day Ireland, it seemed gray was the new green. Marcy glanced up at the cloud-filled sky. As long as it doesn't start raining, she thought.

It's raining, it's pouring, she heard her mother sing, her soft voice snaking up the hillside. The deceptively soothing voice continued, swirling around Marcy like a gust of autumn leaves. *The old man is snoring.*

Marcy began striding back down the hill, taking larger steps than necessary, her arms swinging purposefully at her sides, as if warning her mother to keep her distance. *Bumped his head, and he went to bed.* Her mother's stubborn voice followed after her, carried by the wind.

"It's starting again," Marcy remembered whispering to Judith. She was, what . . . all of twelve at the time?

"What's starting?"

"With Mom. It's starting again."

"How do you know?" Judith had asked. Although she was older than Marcy by two years, she was slower than her sister at sensing when disaster was imminent.

"Because I can feel it."

Judith had argued. "She's just depressed because it's raining. You know how personally she takes the weather."

"I'm telling you," Marcy said. "It's starting."

"Shit," she said now, stopping when she reached the bottom of the street. What was she doing all the way down here again? Now she'd have to climb all the way back up. She checked her watch. Almost four o'clock. Maybe she should head back into the main part of the city, grab a bite to eat, come back later.

Except it was too late for lunch and too early for dinner and she had no appetite anyway.

"You have to eat something," Judith had told her in the aftermath of Devon's accident. And then again after Peter had walked out. "You have to keep up your strength," she'd insisted, pushing a heaping spoonful of peanut butter toward Marcy's tightly pursed lips.

Marcy closed her eyes, trying to block out the myriad unpleasant memories that were flooding her brain. "Enough," she said out loud, her voice disappearing under the wheels of a passing car. A Rolls or a Bentley, she thought, opening her eyes in time to see the big black sedan disappear around the bend in the road and knowing instinctively it belonged to the O'Connors. She raced back up the street, stopping at the top of the hill to catch her breath and watching the car pull to a tentative stop in the driveway of the yellow-brick house.

From a distance of maybe fifty yards she saw a woman exit the passenger side of the car with shopping bags in each hand. As she reached the front door, she turned and called to the driver as he was about to proceed into the garage: "Don't forget the groceries in the trunk."

The woman was young, early thirties, and very pretty, with shoulder-length auburn hair and shapely, if sturdy, legs. She was wearing a navy blue skirt that covered her knees and a loose blue cardigan over a conservative print blouse. Marcy guessed from the woman's easy familiarity with her companion that this must be Mrs. O'Connor and not the nanny.

Now's your chance, she thought as the woman fished inside her designer bag for her keys. Marcy commanded herself to move, forcing one foot in front of the other, then stopping abruptly when the man emerged from the garage seconds later, his arms loaded with groceries. She saw that he was older than the woman by at least a decade and that he managed to look quite distinguished even as he struggled to keep the groceries from spilling out of the bags.

"Can you manage?" the woman asked from the doorway.

"Out of my way, woman," her husband responded with a laugh. Seconds later, still laughing, they disappeared inside the house, the door closing after them.

"Mr. and Mrs. O'Connor, I presume," Marcy said, marveling at their easy camaraderie and trying to remember the last time she and Peter had laughed that way together. About anything. Maybe in the beginning, she thought now. Before Devon. "Stop it. You're not being fair." Tempting though it was, she couldn't blame Devon for all the problems in her marriage.

Judith's unwanted and uninvited voice once again asserted itself. "You're sure you want to do this?" she'd asked when Marcy first informed her she was expecting. "You'll never have another peaceful moment, you know. You'll always be waiting, watching. . . ."

"Shut up, Judith," Marcy had said.

"Shut up, Judith," she said again now, rubbing her forehead and wondering where Shannon was. Probably with the O'Connor children, she decided. Maybe she'd taken them out for a walk. Or maybe they were playing in a nearby park. Or maybe it was the nanny's day off and the children were spending the afternoon with their grandparents.

So many maybes.

Marcy decided to give the O'Connors a few minutes to put their groceries away before ambushing them. "You can do this," she told herself, removing Devon's picture from her purse and wondering what she was so afraid of. That the O'Connors wouldn't recognize the girl in the photograph?

Or that they would?

Moments later a baby's loud wail filled the air as a young woman pushing a carriage rounded the curve at the top of the street.

Marcy found herself holding her breath as the girl came into sharper focus. She's exactly as I imagined her, Marcy thought. She marveled at the skinny girl, taking in her fair complexion and long, strawberry-blond hair. Pretty in an understated way. Not the type to draw attention to her looks with too much artifice. She was dressed in blue jeans and a light jacket, her shoulders hunched slightly forward as she pushed the carriage.

"Go on. What are you waiting for?" Marcy asked herself, speaking into the collar of her trench coat. Still, her feet refused to budge. What if this wasn't Shannon? She couldn't just go accosting every woman who walked by wheeling a baby carriage.

But the girl turned into the O'Connors' driveway, proceeding up the flower-lined walkway toward the front door. If she'd noticed Marcy standing by the side of the road, she gave no sign.

"Now," Marcy said, almost tripping over her own feet as she vaulted forward. "Excuse me, but could I talk to you for a minute?" She rehearsed it, her voice a whisper. "Excuse me," she said again, louder this time.

But the front door was already opening, Mr. O'Connor filling its frame.

"Well, hello there, my little angel," he said, lifting the crying baby into his arms. "Daddy's missed his little princess. Yes, he has. He has indeed. How was she this afternoon?" he asked Shannon. "Still colicky, I see."

Marcy couldn't hear Shannon's response. The young woman's voice was too quiet to carry the distance between them, especially since the breeze had picked up, bringing with it the renewed promise of rain. Marcy took another step forward as Mr. O'Connor carried the crying baby inside, shutting the door after him as Shannon wheeled the carriage around to the side of the house.

Marcy quickly traversed the driveway, hoping to intercept Shannon on her way back to the front door. But after several minutes passed with no sign of her, Marcy concluded that she must have used a side entrance. A glance at the side of the house confirmed a second door.

So, you ring the bell, you ask to speak to Shannon, you show her Devon's picture, Marcy instructed herself silently. How many times had she gone over this already? Shannon would either confirm the picture was her friend Audrey or she wouldn't.

Or what if she recognized the picture but refused to divulge Audrey's whereabouts? Suppose Devon had already told her all about her mother, how she'd failed her in every way possible and how she'd actually faked her own death in order to get as far away from her as she could? What then?

Would Shannon be on the phone as soon as Marcy left, calling to warn Devon that her mother was here in Cork, that she'd somehow been able to ascertain that the two of them were friends, that she was even now canvassing the city, stopping strangers on the street, showing them her picture, and that it was only a matter of time before she'd encounter someone who would point her right to Devon?

What would happen then?

Would Devon take off without a word to anyone, fly off to Spain or South America or Australia? Somewhere her mother would never be able to find her? Would she do that?

Marcy felt her shoulders slump and her knees weaken. Her daughter would do exactly that, she understood. Which was why she'd been hesitating, why she'd instinctively held back, why she couldn't confront Shannon and risk losing her daughter all over again. She had to be patient. She had to wait. Wait and watch.

You'll always be waiting, watching . . . , Judith had said.

A light rain was starting to fall. In a few more minutes, it would get stronger, heavier. She had to find a taxi, get back to the flat of the city before she was soaked to the skin. She'd return here tomorrow. And the next day. And the day after that. Eventually, Marcy told herself as she hurried down the hill, Shannon would lead her to Devon.

"WELL, WELL. CAN'T keep away, can you?" Liam said as Marcy walked through the front door of Grogan's House. His smile said he'd been expecting her. "Sit down, luv. I'll get you some tea." His hand waved toward an empty table in the far corner of the crowded room.

Barely five o'clock and already the place was almost full, Marcy observed. Did nobody ever go home?

"So, did you find Audrey?" Kelly asked, suddenly appearing at her side.

"No, but I found Shannon."

"Was she able to help you?"

"I didn't speak to her."

"Why not?"

"It's complicated," Marcy said after a pause.

"What's complicated?" Liam asked, lowering a steaming pot of tea to the table along with two mugs, then plopping into the chair across from her. "You don't mind if I join you, do you? I'm on my break, and you look in need of some company. Do you know you're soaking wet?"

Marcy quickly pulled off her coat, began patting at her hair. "I couldn't find a taxi. . . ."

"Leave your hair alone," he said. "It's quite sexy like that, you know."

Marcy laughed, flattered in spite of herself.

"That's better. So, what's complicated?"

"What isn't?"

Liam's turn to laugh. "Hunger isn't complicated," he said. "I bet you could use something to eat."

"Anything you recommend?"

"I'd try the special. Kelly, can you get the lady a special? My treat," he added.

"No, don't be silly. I can't let you do that."

"Consider it done. My way of apologizing for my rudeness earlier."

"You weren't rude."

"I was a bit abrupt. You know, about Audrey."

"Are you saying you *did* recognize her picture?"

He poured them each a mug full of tea. "Well, I might have been a little hasty in my assessment."

"Would you like to see the picture again?" Marcy was already digging inside her purse.

"Drink your tea," he instructed, taking Devon's photograph from Marcy's hand.

Marcy did as she was told, lifting the mug to her lips and taking a long sip, her eyes never leaving his. "Well?"

"I suppose it could be Audrey."

Marcy tried to swallow her growing excitement with another sip of tea. "Do you know her last name?"

Liam shook his head.

"What *do* you know about her?"

"Not very much, I'm afraid. I've only talked to her a couple of times. She moved here about a year ago. From some small town west of London, I think she said."

"She has an English accent?" Devon had always had a good ear for accents, Marcy recalled, remembering her performances in various high school plays.

"I suppose. Definitely not Irish, but I wasn't paying that

strict attention. She's not really my type. I like 'em a little older myself." A playful smile teased his lips.

Is he flirting with me? Marcy wondered, dismissing the thought as she sank back in her chair. "Can you do me a favor? Can you call me the next time you see her? I mean, immediately. And can you not say anything to her about my trying to find her?"

"Can you tell me why I should do either of those things?"

"It's complicated," Marcy said again. Could she trust him not to give her away?

"Can you at least tell me your name?"

"Marcy," she said after a pause of several seconds, deciding she had to trust someone. "Marcy Taggart. I believe the girl you know as Audrey is really my daughter, Devon."

Liam's eyes revealed a long list of questions, none of which he voiced. Instead he removed a pen from the pocket of his white shirt and slid it across the table. "Write your cell phone number on that napkin."

Marcy started to print her number along the surface of the small paper napkin, then stopped. "Oh, God, I can't. I threw it away."

"You threw away your phone?"

"I threw it in the river."

"Why on earth would you do that?"

"It's . . ."

"Complicated," Liam said, finishing for her. "Figured as much. So, just how do you propose I get in touch with you?"

"I'm staying at the Doyle Cork Inn over on Western Road," Marcy told him.

Liam nodded, retrieving his pen and scribbling his own number across the top of the napkin. "Suppose you check in with me periodically. That might be easier."

Marcy almost burst into tears. "That's really very kind of you."

"Sometimes we have to rely on the kindness of strangers," he said with a twinkle in his deep green eyes.

Marcy recognized the familiar quote from Tennessee Williams's *A Streetcar Named Desire*. She lifted her mug into the air, clicked it against his. "To the kindness of strangers."

Liam's smile was unexpectedly shy. "To finding your daughter," he said.

EIGHT

I T ALWAYS STARTED THE same way.

With soft words and a seemingly simple request.

"Darling, come lie beside me for a minute," her mother might say, welcoming Marcy into her bed, although it was almost noon. "I know you're just a little girl, but you're so wise and thoughtful. You understand so many things. Do you think you could help me out with a little problem I'm having?" Or "Sweetheart, you know how much I value your opinion. Come sit on the bed and tell me which dress you think I should wear for the party tonight—the red one or the blue?" Or "Marcy, my sweet angel. I know you're much too young to be thinking about boys, but I need your advice about what to do with your father."

Marcy turned over in her too-soft double bed in her room at the Doyle Cork Inn, wrapping the lumpy foam pillow around her ears to keep from hearing the exchange of dialogue that inevitably followed. But it was too late. Her mother was already beside her, whispering in her ear, asking for help she didn't want, opinions she quickly discounted, and advice she never took.

"I think you should wear the red one," Marcy might have answered, sitting on the end of her mother's bed and watching her mother rifle impatiently through her closet, dragging clothes off their hangers and tossing them unceremoniously to the pearl-gray broadloom at her feet.

"You really think the red is better, darling? Why is that? Do you think I look better in bright colors? Does the blue dress wash me out? Does it make me look fat?"

"You could never look fat."

The sudden threat of tears. "Do you think I've put on weight? Is that it?"

"No, I—"

"My clothes have been feeling a little tight lately, although you know, I think it's all the manufacturers' fault with their ridiculously inconsistent labeling. I mean, you buy the same size you always buy, and suddenly it doesn't fit, and I'm wondering if it's some sort of conspiracy, a conspiracy to confuse women, make them feel vulnerable and helpless, because you can never rely on sizes anymore. You have to try absolutely everything on. Which is very time-consuming and unnecessary. You shouldn't have to try everything on. It shouldn't be that way. You should be able to go into a store and pick out a pair of pants, for example, say you want a pair of pants, and you've always worn a size six or maybe an eight, there's nothing wrong about being a size eight or a ten or even a twelve or a fourteen or a sixteen. There's nothing wrong with that. What's wrong is that the manufacturers are deliberately confusing women, they're playing games with our heads, mind games, and they're making us feel insecure about our bodies, making us feel fat when we're the same size we've always been. We're not fat at all. Do you think I look fat?"

"I think you look beaut—"

"I worry about Judith. She looks as if she's put on a few pounds. She has great legs but she has a tendency to put on weight."

"No, she—"

"I'm sure she's put on a few pounds. Around the hips and thighs. And you can't dismiss it as being baby fat anymore. Not when you're almost fourteen. You're not doing her any favors by telling her she'll outgrow it. You have to tell her the truth. I told her that unfortunately she has the same body type as her grandmother, your father's mother, not *my* mother, my mother was always very slim and elegant, but the women in Daddy's family have all tended to pack on the pounds, especially around the hips, and Judith takes after them, poor thing, so she has to be especially vigilant, she can't afford to get lazy, because society is very cruel to women who don't take care of them-selves. You always have to look your best. Designers don't make clothes for fat people, I told her. And it's not easy because the manufacturers are conspiring to confuse women, and it's not fair. It's just not fair." The threat of tears became a reality. Her mother began pacing back and forth in front of Marcy.

"Mom, what is it? What's wrong? Why are you crying?"

"I'm crying because it's so sad. The world is such a cruel place. And sometimes I feel such despair. For you. For Judith. For all of us." She slammed the closet door shut, then immedi-ately opened it again, then closed it, then opened it.

"I'm going to get Daddy."

"No. Don't do that."

"But I'm scared. You're scaring me."

"Oh, sweetheart. There's nothing to be scared about. Everything's going to be just fine. I heard the most wonderful thing on TV last night. This doctor was on the news and he predicted they're *this* close to discovering a cure for cancer. And you'll see. It'll happen in your lifetime. Probably not in mine. But for sure in yours. People will live much longer than they do today. You could actually live to be two hundred years old, maybe even forever. It's not impossible. And you're such a sweet girl, Marcy. So lovely and sweet. You deserve to live forever. If only we could do something about your hair. So much hair for such a tiny face."

Marcy pushed the hair away from her forehead, sitting up in her bed at the Doyle Cork Inn, staring at the clock radio on the tiny nightstand beside her, trying not to see her mother's pained expression. Almost four a.m. Still another few hours before it got light. She flopped back down, flipped from one side to the other, then back again, hearing echoes of her mother's closet door as it opened and closed, opened and closed.

"I've made such a mess of things," her mother was saying, sobbing uncontrollably now. "I've let everybody down."

"No, you haven't."

"Yes, I have. Look at me. What have I accomplished? Nothing. I have nothing."

"You have Daddy. You have me and Judith."

Her mother stared at her as if she could see right through her, as if she didn't exist. "I had to have a Caesarian section with Judith," she said. "Did I ever tell you about that?" She continued, not waiting for a reply. "It was horrible. They gave me this horrible, big needle—they insert it right into your spine—and it's supposed to freeze you from the waist down, except they gave me too much and it froze me right up to my chest, and it felt as if I couldn't breathe, and I was crying, telling them I couldn't breathe, but the doctors insisted I was breathing just fine, even though it felt like I was dying. Can you understand? I thought I was dying. And I was so scared. I was so scared," she repeated, her shoulders shaking with the ferocity of her sobs.

And then she suddenly dropped to the floor, curled into a tight fetal ball, and fell fast asleep.

She slept for the rest of the day, and the next morning she was gone.

"Where's Mom?" Marcy remembered asking when she came downstairs for breakfast.

Judith shrugged, cutting the omelet their father had made her into tiny pieces, then lifting a forkful of the eggs to her mouth and returning it to her plate untouched. "Away."

"Where'd she go?"

"Where she usually goes," Judith replied.

Which meant nobody knew. Periodically, their mother simply disappeared. Usually for a period of several weeks. Sometimes less, occasionally more. Nobody ever knew where she went. Their father had stopped trying to find her after the first few times, stopped reporting her disappearances to the police, stopped hiring detectives to find her, stopped searching through homeless shelters and checking the dirty and raggedly dressed bodies asleep on downtown sewer grates. Once, when Marcy was in her teens and out with a group of friends from school, she thought she saw her mother rifling through a garbage bin outside a store window, but she turned away before she could be sure and quickly ushered her friends to another location.

Her father had tried to explain, using the accepted parlance of the day. "Your mother is manic-depressive. There's nothing to worry about. She's not going to die. She's not dangerous. She just gets very excited and then she gets very depressed. But as long as she takes her medication, she'll be able to function just fine."

Except she hated her medication. It made her feel as if she were, in her words, "trying to do the butterfly stroke in a vat of molasses." And so she'd stop taking it. And then the cycle would begin again: the wild mood swings, the talking too fast and interrupting too much, the unrelenting intensity that accompanied even the most mundane of acts, the hysterical fits of laughter, the terrifying crying jags, the sudden falling asleep, the eventual disappearing act.

It didn't take Marcy long to learn the signs. She got very good at predicting when her mother was about to take off. "It's happening again," she'd say to Judith. Invariably she was right.

Except once.

"Okay, enough of that," Marcy said, pushing herself out of her too-soft bed and flipping on the overhead light. She should have brought a book with her, she thought. Who goes on holiday and doesn't take a book? Something—anything—to keep her mind occupied, to keep the ghosts of the past at bay. She'd buy one as soon as the stores opened. Along with a new cell phone, she decided, walking to the window and staring through the dusty lace curtains at the closed blinds of the room across the way. She was still standing there, still staring, when the night sky began to brighten and the bells of St. Anne's Shandon Church announced the start of a new day.

AS SOON AS the stores opened, Marcy purchased a new cell phone and called Liam.

"Did I wake you?" she asked, hearing the sleep still clinging to his voice. What was the matter with her? Why had she called him so early? Why had she called him at all, for God's sake? He'd said to check in periodically, not first thing the next morning. So what was she doing? Just because he'd sat with her for the better part of twenty minutes yesterday afternoon didn't mean he was truly interested in her problems. A natural flirt, he'd only been humoring her with his attention. He didn't really care about her or her daughter. He just felt sorry for her. "I'm so sorry to bother you," she said.

"Has something happened? Have you found Audrey?"

"No. I . . . I . . . bought a cell phone," she blurted out, quickly rattling off her number. "I'm so sorry for disturbing you. I just thought this way you could call me—"

"The instant I see her," Liam said, finishing the sentence for her. "Promise," he added, as if understanding Marcy's need for reassurance. "So what are the plans for the day?"

Marcy told him about her intention to check out the university.

"Good luck," he said, hanging up before she could apologize again.

I'll need it, Marcy thought, dropping the phone into her purse and setting out for the university campus.

ACCORDING TO THE brochure the Visitors' Centre provided, University College Cork was established in 1845 and was currently one of Ireland's leading research institutes. Located on a hill overlooking the valley of the river Lee, the campus was a pleasing blend of the old and the new, an attractive quadrangle of colorful gardens and wooded grounds interspersed with old, Gothic-revival-style buildings and modern concrete-and-glass structures. More than seventeen thousand students attended the four main colleges: one college for arts, Celtic studies, and social science; one for business and law; one for medicine and health; and one for engineering, science, and food science. The university was also home to the Irish

Institute of Chinese studies, which Marcy decided probably explained the high number of Asian students she'd been seeing since setting foot on campus.

Knowing it was highly unlikely that Devon would have enrolled in anything to do with medicine, business, engineering, or law, Marcy decided to concentrate on the arts. Her daughter had always been drawn to drama. From the time she was a little girl, her dream had been to become an actress. As a teenager, she'd spoken often of going to Hollywood. Marcy had tried to dissuade her. "It's a lifetime of rejection," she'd said.

She should have been more supportive, Marcy thought now, marching along the brick and concrete pedestrian road that ran through the campus, glancing at the clusters of students dotting the white concrete benches that lined the path. Would it have killed her to be more encouraging?

"Why do you always have to be so negative?" she could hear Devon demand.

"I'm just trying to protect you."

"I don't need your protection. I need your support."

"Excuse me," Marcy said now, stilling Devon's angry voice with her own and showing her photograph to a group of young women who were walking by. "Do any of you recognize this girl?"

The three girls took turns looking at the picture. "No," the first one said, her two friends nodding in quick agreement.

"Don't know her," they said, almost in unison.

"Thank you. Excuse me." Marcy continued in the next breath, quickly approaching a young man balancing an armload of books. "Have you seen this girl? Her name is Devon. . . ."

"No, sorry."

"You may know her as Audrey."

"Sorry, no."

It was the same with everyone she asked.

"Sorry. Can't help you."

"I'm afraid not."

"Don't know her."

"No, sorry."

Marcy occasionally pressed. "Could you look at the picture again? Maybe you took an English class together?"

"I don't think so."

"Couldn't say."

"No, sorry."

"Have you tried the registrar's office?" someone suggested.

Moments later Marcy was in the office of the registrar. "She doesn't look at all familiar?" she asked the woman behind the reception desk.

"No, I can't say I recognize this one. You're sure she's a student here?"

Marcy admitted she was sure of no such thing.

The woman typed something into her computer. "Audrey, you said her name was?"

"Yes, that's right."

"Last name?"

Marcy hesitated. Which name would her daughter use? "I don't know."

The woman shook her head, her eyes seemingly focused on a spot to the left of Marcy's nose. "I'm afraid I can't help you without a last name."

"Try Taggart." Marcy spelled it. "And if there's no Audrey Taggart, try Devon."

"Audrey and Devon Taggart." The woman sighed as she typed in both names. "No, nothing for either of them. Sorry. Have you inquired at the other colleges?"

By four o'clock, Marcy had tried virtually every department on campus. She'd popped her head into every office and classroom, visited every gallery, walked down every hall, investigated every nook and cranny of every building, peeked behind every tree, asked every student she was able to corral to look at the photograph. "You already asked me," one muttered, sidestepping her as if she were a panhandler.

Marcy was just exiting the campus when she saw her.

The girl was standing on the footbridge separating Bachelor's Quay from North Mall, staring down at the water below, seemingly lost in thought. A breeze was blowing her long hair into her face, and every few seconds her hand reached up to push the pesky strands away from her mouth.

"Devon!" Marcy cried out, her voice disappearing under the wheels of a passing car. She began running up the street toward the bridge, each step bringing her closer to the daughter she feared she'd lost forever. "Oh, my God. Oh, my God." Please let her be happy to see me, she prayed as she ran. Please let her not be angry. Please let me hold her in my arms again.

Which was when she heard the shouting and turned to see the bicycle coming out of nowhere, a look of horror on the cyclist's face as he tried to avoid crashing into her. But he was traveling too fast and her reflexes were too slow, and his front wheel caught the back of her legs, spinning her around and lifting her off her feet.

In the next second, Marcy was sprawled across the pavement like a rag doll, a small crowd gathering around her. "Are you all right?" someone was asking. "Is anything broken?" "Can you stand up?"

Marcy felt hands underneath her arms, dragging her to her feet, returning her to an upright position. "I'm fine," she said, barely recognizing her own voice. What the hell had just happened?

"You're sure? Do you need to go to the hospital?" a young man asked, pushing his way to the front of the crowd.

"I don't need a hospital." What I need is to find my daughter, Marcy thought, recovering her equilibrium and deducing from the boy's ashen complexion that he was the one who'd run her down. She looked frantically toward the footbridge, but she couldn't see over the heads of those who'd stopped to help her. "Please. I have to go."

"No," the young man insisted, his strong hand on her arm preventing her from going anywhere. "You shouldn't move for a few minutes. You could have a concussion."

"I didn't hit my head. I don't have a concussion. Please, if you could all just get out of my way . . ."

"You heard the lady," the young man snapped at the small crowd. "Back off. She needs some air." The people immediately began dispersing until only Marcy and the young man remained. "I'm so sorry," he was saying, curly brown hair framing a face that was more rugged than handsome, small dark eyes skipping nervously across her features, as if checking for signs she was about to collapse.

He looked to be in his twenties, Marcy thought, her eyes straining past his head toward the footbridge. The same age as Devon. "It's okay," she said, her voice flat. "It was an accident."

"I was just goin' along, mindin' me own business, not payin' enough attention, I guess, and suddenly there you were," the boy elaborated in a strong Irish brogue. "I tried turnin' the wheel—"

"It wasn't your fault," Marcy assured him, her brain absorbing what her eyes already knew: that Devon was no longer standing on the bridge, staring absently at the water below, a breeze blowing wayward wisps of hair into her sad face.

Her daughter was gone.

She'd lost her again.

NINE

THEY GREW UP ALWAYS checking each other out, looking for signs of incipient depression, a laugh that was too loud or lingered too long, a sigh that split the air with melancholy, a smile that melted effortlessly into a frown, a mood that shifted too abruptly, cascading from high to low and then back again with unnerving speed, like the roller-coaster rides they used to enjoy when they were kids.

Except they never really had a childhood, and roller-coaster rides quickly lost their ability to thrill, especially since their daily lives proved far less predictable, and therefore far more terrifying, than anything an amusement park ride could offer.

"What's the matter? Are you upset about something?" Marcy would ask whenever she caught Judith looking even vaguely out of sorts.

"What are you still chuckling about?" Judith would demand of her sister after she'd told a moderately funny joke that had Marcy still giggling moments later. "It wasn't that funny."

"Are you all right?" Marcy.

"Is there a problem?" Judith.

"Are you depressed?" Judith.

"Is something bothering you?" Marcy.

"Marcy! For God's sake, where the hell are you?" Judith was shouting now.

Marcy held her new cell phone away from her ear, already regretting her decision to phone her sister. "I'm fine."

"I didn't ask *how* you were," Judith shot back instantly. "I already know you're nuttier than a jar of cashews. What I asked is, *where* are you? Do you know there's something wrong with your cell phone? I keep calling and getting nothing. So I called Peter and he told me the name of your hotel in Dublin, and I called them, and they told me you checked out. What are you laughing about, for God's sake?"

Marcy swallowed the few giggles still tickling her throat. Judith had always had a way with words, she was thinking, relishing the phrase "nuttier than a jar of cashews." "I've always admired your ability to express yourself."

"My ability to express myself? What on earth are you talking about?"

"You don't pull any punches," Marcy said, imagining the outraged arch of Judith's thin eyebrows, the impatient twisting of her lips. "I've always loved that about you."

"Are you high?" Judith asked.

"No, of course not." Marcy had always been too afraid to experiment with drugs.

"Where are you?" Judith repeated.

Marcy looked around her tiny bathroom in the Doyle Cork

Inn. She was sitting, naked, on the edge of the white enamel tub, steam rising like beckoning fingers from the hot water that filled it, as if inviting her to climb inside. "What difference does it make?"

"What do you mean, what difference does it make? How am I supposed to come and get you if I don't know where you are?"

"Nobody's asking you to come and get me. I don't want you to come and get me."

"Marcy, listen to me. You have to calm down. . . ."

"I *am* calm. You're the one who's all upset."

"Because *you're* in the middle of some kind of breakdown. Which, don't get me wrong, is perfectly understandable under the circumstances. Believe me, I know what you're going through," she elaborated quickly and unnecessarily. "Your daughter died, your husband left you for another woman. Not to mention our family history . . ."

"I'm not crazy, Judith."

"You're in Ireland, for God's sake. You went on a second honeymoon alone. You think that's normal?"

"It might be a little unusual, but—"

"Just like it's a little unusual to see your dead child wandering the streets of Dublin?"

Cork. Marcy almost corrected her, biting down on her lower lip to keep the word from escaping. "I didn't see her," she said instead.

"Of course you didn't see her," Judith repeated, stopping abruptly. "What do you mean, you didn't see her?"

"I didn't see her. I was wrong."

"What do you mean?" Judith asked again.

Marcy could feel her sister struggling to understand. "I realize now that the girl I thought was Devon was just a girl who maybe looked a bit like her but wasn't her. I was just seeing what I wanted to see. . . ." Marcy pictured the girl standing on the footbridge separating Bachelor's Quay from North Mall, staring absently into the water below.

"You didn't see her?"

"It wasn't Devon."

Judith's sigh of relief was almost palpable. "How do you know it wasn't her?" she asked suspiciously.

"Because Devon is dead," Marcy told her.

Judith pressed her. "You're not just saying that because you think it's what I want to hear?"

That was exactly why she was saying it, Marcy acknowledged silently. "Devon is dead," she repeated, each word cutting into her throat like a sharp knife, leaving large, gaping holes in her flesh.

She felt her sister nodding her head. "Okay," Judith said, and then again, "Okay." Another pause, another nod of her head. "So, where are you and when are you coming home?"

Marcy lied, the same lie she'd told Vic Sorvino. "I'm in Paris."

"I don't believe you."

Marcy sighed. Vic hadn't believed her either. "I'll be home by the end of next week."

"Wait. If you're really in Paris, I have a great idea," Judith said quickly. "Why don't I book the next flight and meet you there? I'm sure Terry won't mind if I go away for a few days. In fact, he'll probably be thrilled. We can go shopping and see the sights, just the two of us. Come on, say yes. It'll be fun."

Like old times, Marcy was tempted to say, except that their old times had never involved shopping or seeing the sights. Their old times had been anything but fun. "Let me think about it."

"What do you have to think about?"

"I'll call you."

"Just tell me what hotel you're in and—"

"I'll call you," Marcy said again, immediately disconnecting the phone.

She pushed herself off the side of the tub and walked naked into the bedroom, stepping over the clothes she'd left lying on the floor and tossing the cell phone onto the bed. She hated lying to her sister. But what other choice did she have?

You could have told her the truth, Marcy thought, returning to the bathroom and trying to make out her reflection in the steam-covered mirror over the sink. "Who's in there anyway?" she asked out loud, wiping the mirror clean with her forearm, only to watch it fog up again almost instantly, blending one confused feature into another before she faded from sight altogether.

The truth was that she was more convinced than ever that Devon was alive, that she'd seen her again this very afternoon, and that it was only a matter of time before they came face-to-face. After all, Cork wasn't that big a city. Tomorrow she'd go back to the O'Connor house, wait for their nanny to emerge, spend the day following her around. She was confident Shannon would lead her to Devon eventually.

If only that damn bicycle hadn't come flying out of nowhere to knock me down, Marcy was thinking as she lowered herself gingerly into the tub, we might already be together. She gasped as the hot water surrounded her, covering the fresh bruises that dotted her legs and arms.

She heard her sister admonish her: *It's not good to take such a hot bath.*

"Go away, Judith," Marcy told her impatiently, sinking down lower in the tub, the water rising to accommodate her as she stretched her feet out to their full length. She felt it creep above her chin to tease at her mouth, and she closed her eyes as the water reached her forehead, feeling her hair floating around her head like seaweed.

We have lingered in the chambers of the sea, she recited silently, recalling the last few lines of her once favorite poem by T. S. Eliot.

By sea-girls wreathed with seaweed red and brown./Till human voices wake us, and we drown.

In the aftermath of the discovery of Devon's overturned canoe, Marcy had tried to imagine what it felt like to drown. Every day for weeks she'd climbed into the tub in her master bathroom and let the water surround her, feeling it tug on her skin like an anchor, weighing her down. Then she'd slip slowly and quietly beneath the surface and open her mouth.

One time Peter had walked in on her.

He'd come into the bathroom to get ready for bed and discovered her submerged in the tub. He'd literally grabbed her by the hair and yanked her up, as if he were some goddamn caveman, she remembered thinking at the time, all the while screaming at her, "What the hell are you doing? What the hell are you doing?" Then he'd forcefully removed the door from its hinges with a wrench and a pair of pliers. The bathroom had remained doorless for the better part of eighteen months. He'd replaced it again only weeks before he moved out, as if underlining the fact that she was no longer his concern.

He needn't have worried. She couldn't have gone through with it. The feeling of panic as the water replaced the air in her body was simply too terrifying for Marcy to endure for longer than a few seconds.

Had Devon felt that same panic? she'd often wondered. Had she struggled to survive even as the icy water filled her lungs? Had she cried out for her mother one last time before she died?

Except she hadn't died, Marcy knew now.

"My baby's alive," she whispered as the water licked playfully at her ears. "She isn't dead. She isn't dead," she repeated, the pleasant sound of her words vibrating gently against her eardrums.

Except it wasn't her words that were ringing, she realized after several moments. It was her cell phone. Undoubtedly her sister, she decided, trying to ignore the persistent sound. Except it couldn't be Judith, she realized with a start. There was no way Judith could have found out her number, no way she could have traced her call. She'd blocked her number. No, the only person it could be was Liam, and if he was calling her, it meant he'd seen Devon.

Perhaps she was with him right now.

Marcy vaulted from the tub, her wet feet slipping on the tile floor and sending her crashing against the side of the bathroom door. "Damn it." She cursed, feeling new bruises already forming as she flung herself toward the bed. She'd be lucky to get out of Ireland alive, she thought, flipping open her phone. "Hello? Hello?"

"Hello?" Liam said in reply. "Marcy, is that you?"

"Liam?"

"Are you all right? You sound a little—"

"Have you seen Devon?"

"No," he said. "Have you?"

Marcy's response was to burst into tears.

"Marcy, what's the matter?"

"Nothing. It's okay. I just thought . . ."

"You thought that my calling meant I'd seen her," he said. "I'm so sorry. Of course you'd think that."

"Don't apologize. I shouldn't jump to conclusions." Marcy told him about having seen Devon earlier.

"Wait a minute," he said when she was through her story. "You're saying you got hit by a bicycle? Are you hurt?"

"I'm fine. A few bruises is all. It was my fault. I wasn't looking where I was going."

"You're sure you're all right? You could have a concussion."

"I'm fine," she repeated, sounding as tired and defeated as she felt.

"Except that by the time you got back on your feet . . ."

"She was gone," Marcy said.

"Well, I wish I was calling with some news. . . ."

"Why *are* you calling?"

She felt him smile. "There was someone here just now askin' about you."

"What? Who?"

"A man."

"What man?" Was it possible Peter had tracked her down, that he'd abandoned his new love on the golf course and flown all the way to Ireland to bring Marcy home?

"I'm pretty sure it was the man you were with the other day," she heard Liam say.

"The man I was with . . . ?" What man had she been with? "Do you mean Vic? Vic Sorvino?" Marcy asked incredulously.

"Yep, that's him. I'm starin' at his business card right now."

What was Vic doing here? "Did he say what he wanted?"

"Just that he was lookin' for you and that he thought you might have come back to the pub."

"What did you tell him?"

"Well, I wasn't sure what you'd want me to tell him, so I said no, I hadn't seen you."

Marcy couldn't tell if she was disappointed or relieved. What was Vic doing back in Cork? Hadn't she told him this was something she needed to do alone?

"Did I do the right thing?" Liam was asking.

"You did. Thank you."

"Do you want his number?"

"I have it." Marcy reached into her purse and extricated Vic's card, tearing it into a bunch of little pieces and watching them fall to the bedspread like so much confetti.

"So, what do you want me to tell him," Liam asked, "assuming he checks in with me again?"

"Tell him you haven't seen me."

"You're sure?"

Marcy felt Vic's lips brushing gently against hers, felt his fingers tracing delicate lines along her flesh, heard his soft words, *You're beautiful,* as they floated tenderly across her skin. It had felt so good to be wanted again, to have a man look at her with something other than pity or contempt. Or worse— indifference. She didn't deserve to feel so good. Not yet. Not until she'd found Devon. Not until she'd had a chance to make things right. "I'm sure."

"Good."

"Good?"

"There was just somethin' about the man that made me a bit uncomfortable," Liam said.

"Uncomfortable?"

"I don't know how else to say it. Something just seemed a little off. You know what I mean?"

Marcy shook her head. In truth, she had no idea what Liam was talking about. Vic Sorvino hadn't struck her as "off" in any way. But then she'd never been a very good judge of character when it came to men.

"Marcy?" Liam asked. "Are you still there?"

"Oh, yes. Sorry."

"I haven't insulted you, have I?"

"How could you insult me?"

"Well, if this Vic fellow is a friend of yours . . ."

"He isn't." He's just a man I met on a bus, she thought, trying not to feel Vic's warm body pressing against hers or hear his comforting snores echoing in her ear.

She didn't deserve to feel comforted.

"You hungry?" Liam was asking.

Marcy immediately felt her stomach cramp. "I am a bit, yes."

"Pick you up in half an hour," he said.

TEN

WELL, LET'S SEE. HUSBAND number one was a musician," Marcy was saying, a little voice in the back of her head telling her she probably shouldn't be discussing her sister in this way.

"You don't have to tell me," Liam said, as if sensing her reservations. "It's none of my business really. I shouldn't have asked."

"It's no big deal. Judith wouldn't care." How many times had she heard her sister boast of being "wildly indiscreet"? Besides, could any woman who'd been married five times really expect *not* to be talked about?

"I was just trying to take your mind off things."

"I know."

By "things," he meant the fact that despite taking her to

one of the most popular gathering spots for young people in all of Cork, they'd yet to spot Devon. Despite showing her daughter's picture to virtually everyone in the noisy room, they'd yet to find a single person who recognized her.

"Oh, well. It's early," he'd said as they settled into the corner booth of the crowded downscale restaurant on Grattan Street. "Maybe she'll turn up in a bit," he'd said as they'd placed their dinner orders with the pink-haired waiter. "This place stays busy all night," he'd remarked as they finished the first of their Irish coffees. "If not tonight," he'd said reassuringly as they placed their orders for a second, "then tomorrow. She'll turn up. You'll see. We'll find her."

Marcy had smiled. It felt good to be a "we."

A unit, she'd thought, feeling Peter's instant disapproval.

"You grimaced," Liam had said immediately. "Are you sorry you let me ambush you into coming out tonight?"

He notices everything, Marcy thought, looking around the brightly lit room. "No, I'm glad I came. Why *did* you ask me out?" she asked in the next breath. "I'm sure there are dozens of young women out there you could have called."

"Maybe I did. Maybe they all turned me down." Liam smiled. "Or maybe I don't find young women all that interesting."

"And you think I am?"

"I think you just might be." His smile spread to his eyes.

Marcy had blushed and turned away.

Which was when he'd asked about her family.

"I have an older sister," she'd told him, relieved to shift the focus off herself. "Judith. She's been married five times."

He laughed. "Obviously an optimist."

"That's a nice way of putting it."

Long, slender fingers played with the collar of his black

shirt before fanning out around his face, his chin resting in the palm of his hand. "And how would you put it?"

Marcy gave the question a moment's thought. "I think she's just afraid of being alone."

"My mother used to say there was nothing lonelier than an unhappy marriage."

Marcy nodded. "Your mother's a very wise woman."

"Not so sure about that," Liam said, sipping on his Irish coffee. "So . . . about those five husbands . . ."

Marcy began. "Well, let's see. Husband number one was a musician."

"You don't have to tell me. It's none of my business really. I shouldn't have asked."

"It's no big deal. Judith wouldn't care."

"I was just trying to take your mind off things."

"I know."

"In that case, what kind of musician?" he asked.

"Drummer."

"Oh, no. The worst."

Liam laughed and Marcy laughed with him, deciding to go with the flow. "He really *was* awful. But she was all of nineteen and I think the fact he made a lot of noise was very appealing to her. It kind of blocked out everything else that was going on."

"Which was?"

"Way too complicated to get into now," Marcy said. "Anyway, to absolutely no one's surprise, the marriage lasted less than a year."

"What happened?"

"The band broke up."

"Ah-ha, I see. No more noise."

Marcy agreed. "No more noise."

"And husband number two?"

"A photographer she met when she was trying to break into modeling."

"Your sister was a model?"

"For about ten minutes. Judith has a rather short attention span."

"And the marriage lasted . . . ?"

"Two weeks."

"I see what you mean about a short attention span."

"Actually, that wasn't the reason they split up," Marcy clarified. "It turned out he was gay."

Liam nodded. "Dare I ask about husband number three?"

"An advertising executive. It lasted four years."

"Well, now, that's an improvement."

"He was away a lot."

"And it broke up because . . . ?"

"He started staying home."

Again Liam laughed. "Number four?"

"A stockbroker she met at the gym. Nice enough guy until he started taking steroids."

"It lasted . . . ?"

"Eight years."

"Perfectly respectable," Liam said. "Which brings us to husband number five."

"A lawyer. Specializes in medical malpractice. Does very well indeed. They've been married almost fifteen years now."

"So, he's a keeper, is he?"

"Well, that remains to be seen."

"Any children?"

"No. Judith never wanted kids."

"Unlike you," Liam stated more than asked.

"Unlike me."

"So, how many times have you been married?"

Marcy took a deep breath, exhaled slowly. "Only once."

Liam cocked his head to one side, clearly intrigued. "So . . . widowed, divorced, happily married?"

"Separated," Marcy said. "My divorce should be final in another month or so."

"And how do you feel about that?"

"How am I supposed to feel?" Marcy could hear the sudden testiness in her voice.

"Sorry, I think that was *definitely* none of my business."

Marcy took a long sip of her Irish coffee, not because she wanted more but because it gave her time to think. "No, it's all right. It's just that I haven't really talked about it with anybody."

"Do you want to talk about it now?"

"No," she said. Then, "Maybe." Then again, "Actually yes, I think I do."

Liam looked at her expectantly.

"There's really nothing to say," Marcy told him after a pause. "I mean, what do you say? My husband left me for another woman. It's such a cliché." She took another deep breath, returned the mug of Irish coffee to her lips, then lowered it again immediately. "You asked me how I feel. I'll tell you. I'm angry. No, I'm furious. I feel betrayed. I feel abandoned. I feel embarrassed. I mean, he left me for one of the golf pros at our country club. They haven't had a scandal like this in years. And all my friends . . ." She laughed, a sharp bark that scratched at the air. "My friends. What friends? We didn't really have that many friends to begin with, and then after what happened with Devon . . ." She broke off. "I can't really blame them. It's hard for people after a tragedy. They don't know what to say. They don't know what to do. So instead of saying or doing the wrong thing, they don't say or do anything. And then pretty soon they stop calling and coming around. And then it's just the two of you. And you don't know what to say to each other either because everything you say is a potential land mine waiting to be stepped on, and it makes it hard, it makes it really hard, for a marriage to survive. Not that we didn't have problems before." Marcy continued, unable to stem the flow of words that poured from her mouth like water from a tap. "We'd been having problems for a few years, ever since it became obvious that Devon, that Devon, that Devon . . ." Her voice stuck on her daughter's name, as if it were a broken record.

"Tell me about your daughter," Liam said softly.

Marcy hesitated, trying to decide what facts to leave in and which ones to leave out. She didn't want to violate what little remained of her daughter's privacy. Unlike Judith, Devon had never willingly put herself out there for public consumption. She'd kept everything to herself, which had only contributed to her problems.

"My daughter is bipolar," Marcy began, the words somersaulting from her mouth in a series of reluctant syllables. "Do you know what that is?"

"Is it the same thing as schizophrenia?"

"No. Devon doesn't hear voices. She's not paranoid. She just has a chemical imbalance." She continued, trying to remember the exact words the doctor had used to describe the condition, then giving up in frustration. "It used to be known as manic depression."

"One minute you're happy, the next you're bawlin' your eyes out," Liam said.

"I guess that about sums it up, yes."

He apologized immediately. "Sorry. I didn't mean to sound glib."

Marcy dismissed his apology with a shake of her head. "It

tends to run in families. My mother had it as well. She committed suicide when I was fifteen."

If Liam was shocked, he didn't let on. "Is that the reason your sister opted not to have any children of her own?"

"She tried to talk me out of having any. She said I'd always be waiting, watching for signs. She was right."

"When did you first know?"

"Soon after she turned seventeen." Marcy thought back to that awful night when she'd found Devon in the kitchen, a broken flower vase at her feet, handfuls of salt at her mouth. She could see her daughter as clearly as if it were yesterday. "I'd suspected it for a while," she admitted. "Her moods were getting blacker. Her behavior was becoming increasingly erratic. There were times she'd talk so fast I could barely understand what she was saying. But after this one incident, I couldn't deny it any longer."

"What did you do?"

"Not enough. Oh, I took her to the doctor, got her started on medication and therapy, tried to comfort her as best I could. . . ."

"Nothing helped?"

"She didn't like the way the drugs made her feel." *Like doing the butterfly stroke through a vat of molasses,* her mother had said. "She hated her therapist." Marcy paused, swallowing the catch that was forming in her throat. "She hated me even more."

"I'm sure she didn't hate you."

"How can you not hate someone who looks you right in the eye and still doesn't see you?"

"I think you're being very hard on yourself."

"I lied to her, day in and day out."

"You lied to her? How?"

"I told her everything would be okay. I told her if she'd

just cooperate and take her medication, then everything would work out, that she just had to be patient, give the haloperidol a chance. . . ."

"Which is what anyone in your situation would have told her."

"No, you don't understand." Tears began falling the length of Marcy's cheeks, a few sliding between her lips to rest against her tongue. "I had no patience for any of it, for the crying jags and the craziness, for the guys she'd bring home or the trouble she'd get into. You'd have thought that after everything I went through with my mother, it would have made me more understanding. But the exact opposite was true. I didn't have the stomach for any of it. And I felt so guilty and helpless and angry all the time. I hated her for making me have to go through it all again."

"What kind of trouble?" Liam asked.

What kind of mother hates her own child? Marcy was thinking. "What?"

"You said Devon got into trouble. What kind of trouble?" he repeated.

"There were a few incidents." Marcy sighed with the memory. "One day she got into a fight with a neighbor who'd complained she was playing her radio too loud in the backyard. Devon swore at her and threw her shoe at her, just missed her head. And then she stole an expensive bracelet from one of her friends' mothers, and the woman threatened to go to the police. Another time she got involved with this guy I tried to tell her was trouble. . . ."

"But she wouldn't listen."

"And Peter was no help. He didn't know what to do or how to cope. Devon had always been a daddy's girl, and now here she was, his little angel, this child who'd worshipped him her entire life, and he couldn't get through to her. He couldn't help her. It made him feel so impotent. Which I guess explains Sarah. The other woman," Marcy clarified, and Liam nodded, as if no explanation had been necessary. "Anyway, he blamed me. He said he didn't, but I know he did. And he was right. It *was* my fault."

"How do you figure that?"

Marcy shrugged. "They were my genes."

There's no mental illness on my *side of the family,* she remembered Peter saying, although he'd apologized later.

Marcy told Liam the story of Devon's "accident," how she'd faked her own death and disappeared.

"And you thought she was dead until—"

"I never believed she was dead. Not really," Marcy insisted. "And then I saw her walk by your pub."

It was Liam's turn to shake his head. "And I thought you were a cop."

"What?"

"When you came back to Grogan's, when you showed me her picture and asked if I recognized her, I assumed you were some sort of copper or private investigator. Even after you told me she was your daughter, I didn't really believe you. I just assumed Audrey's past had caught up with her."

"Her past?"

"Well, like I said, I've only talked to her a few times. I don't know that much about her. But I've heard rumors. You know."

"I don't know. Tell me."

"Just that she'd been in some sort of trouble in London and that she'd come to Ireland to get away. Stuff like that. Nothing concrete. Like I said, just rumors. So when you showed up, askin' about her, I assumed you were with Scotland Yard or Interpol."

"And now?"

"Now I know you're tellin' me the truth." He smiled, reached across the table for her hand. "Nobody makes up a story like that."

Marcy smiled. "My husband thinks I do. He thinks I'm crazy."

"Soon-to-be-*ex*-husband," Liam corrected, "and I think *he's* crazy, letting a woman like you get away."

Marcy slowly slipped her hand away from his, placed it in her lap. "You should be careful when you say things like that. They could be taken the wrong way."

Liam's green eyes sparkled playfully. "And what way would that be?"

"Some women might think you were coming on to them."

"And what do you think?"

"I think you're just being kind."

He laughed. "First time I've ever been accused of that."

"*Are* you coming on to me?" Marcy asked, amazed she was actually asking the question out loud.

"Don't know. Haven't quite made up my mind."

Marcy smiled and shook her head. "How old are you, Liam?"

"Thirty-four on my next birthday."

"I'm fifty."

"Fifty's not old."

"It's not thirty-four."

"It's just a number. And like I said, I've never gone much for girls my own age. Lost my virginity when I was twelve to a sixteen-year-old hussy. I've had a thing for older women ever since."

Marcy rubbed her head to keep it from spinning. Surely she was imagining this entire conversation. Maybe she had a concussion after all.

"What are you thinking?" Liam asked.

"I'm thinking that for twenty-five years I had sex with only one man. My husband," Marcy told him honestly, deciding what the hell, there was no point in being anything else. "And to be truthful, in the last few years, we hardly had sex at all. At least, *I* hardly had sex. As it turned out, *he* was having plenty. But anyway, that doesn't really matter. What matters is that in all those years, no other man expressed the least interest in me, and now I'm fifty years old and I'm having hot flashes and my hair's a mess. . . ."

"Your hair is gorgeous."

"And I come to Ireland," Marcy continued, ignoring his interruption, "and suddenly, I'm like this femme fatale. I've got guys falling all over me. And I don't know, maybe it's something they put in the beer over here, or maybe I'm just putting out these vibes of not-so-quiet desperation. . . ."

"Or maybe you're just a very beautiful woman."

"You could have any woman you want," Marcy told him, doing her best to ignore the compliment.

"What if *you're* the woman I want?"

Marcy shook her head. "You don't want me."

"I don't?"

"You just feel sorry for me."

"Why would I feel sorry for you?" he asked. "You're a beautiful woman with gorgeous curls who's found the daughter she thought was dead. I'd say that's cause for celebration, not pity."

"I haven't found her yet."

"But you will."

"Maybe that's when I'll feel like celebrating."

"Well, then," Liam said, green eyes dancing with unspoken possibilities. "Looks like I'll just have to stick around and help you find her."

ELEVEN

THE NEXT MORNING MARCY returned to the house on Adelaide Road.

She was there by eight o'clock, having wolfed down the huge breakfast that Sadie Doyle prepared daily. The breakfast consisted of bacon and two eggs over medium, a bowl of oatmeal with raisins and brown sugar, and two pieces of brown toast, complete with homemade marmalade and strawberry preserves. Judith would be properly horrified, Marcy thought as she ate, knowing her sister would have ordered only a small bowl of fresh fruit along with at least three cups of black coffee. Marcy had avoided liquids altogether. Coffee had a habit of running right through her, and she wasn't sure when she'd next have a chance to go to the bathroom.

It could be a very long day, she was thinking now, checking

her watch for the third time in as many minutes. Already ten thirty and nothing had happened since Mr. O'Connor had left for work two hours earlier. At least she'd managed to find a fairly secluded spot at the side of a neighbor's house across the street from the O'Connors' from which she could stand and keep watch.

So far, there'd been nothing to see.

At least the sun was shining, she thought, purposefully ignoring the large cluster of ominous-looking clouds gathering on the horizon. Mercifully, it wasn't as cold as it had been the last several days. She thought she might actually be able to take off the trench coat that had become something of a uniform since she'd arrived in Ireland. "Going up to almost twenty-one," Sadie Doyle had remarked to one of the other guests at breakfast this morning. Marcy calculated the conversion to Fahrenheit: seventy degrees. "Positively balmy."

"Positively balmy is right," Marcy repeated now, deciding that about summed up her recent behavior. *Nuttier than a jar of cashews,* Judith had said. And she didn't know the half of it. She didn't know about either Vic or Liam, that Marcy had already slept with the former and was seriously considering jumping into bed with the latter. What was the matter with her, for heaven's sake? Had she completely lost her mind? Could she really be thinking of getting naked in front of a man more than fifteen years her junior?

Why not? she wondered in the next breath. Men did it all the time. They never seemed to worry about not measuring up to their younger counterparts. Seriously sagging butts and flaccid underused muscles never stopped them. Despite receding hairlines and straining belt buckles, they generally seemed comfortable in their own skin and assured of their attractiveness, even when such assurance was unwarranted. Wasn't Peter a prime example of this?

Not that Peter wasn't a nice-looking man, Marcy thought. He was tall, slim, and fastidious about his appearance. He was also "generously endowed," as Judith was fond of saying when referring to husbands numbers one and three. So it wasn't altogether surprising that a woman like Sarah, who was only marginally older than Liam, would have found him appealing. Although when Marcy was feeling less charitable, she wondered if Sarah would have found Peter quite so attractive if he were less *financially* endowed.

I shouldn't have eaten so much, she thought now, her stomach pressing against the top button of her jeans. If she continued to eat—and drink—the way she'd been doing these last few days, she'd put on so much weight Devon might not even recognize her.

Assuming I find her, Marcy added immediately. And then immediately after that, *Of course* I'm going to find her.

It was only a matter of time.

Maybe even today.

"Excuse me, but do you mind telling me what you're doing there?"

The voice was equal parts curiosity and indignation. Marcy spun around slowly to see a middle-aged woman in a flowered housedress standing on the front steps of the house next door, curlers in her brown hair, hands on her wide hips. All that's missing is the rolling pin, Marcy thought, smiling at the woman while silently debating whether or not to make a run for it. She took a few halting steps in the woman's direction. "I'm sorry," she told her, then stopped when she could think of nothing else to say.

"What are you doing there?" the woman asked again.

"I think I'm lost," Marcy answered weakly.

"Lost?"

"I went for a walk—"

"You American?" the woman interrupted.

"Canadian. My husband's mother was from Limerick," she added hopefully, as if that might make a difference.

The woman seemed distinctly unimpressed with Peter's lineage. "So what exactly are you doing skulking around behind the Murray house?"

"I wasn't . . . skulking."

"Looked like you were skulking to me."

"No. I just went for a walk. . . ."

"This isn't exactly a popular spot for tourists."

Marcy improvised. "Exactly. As a rule, I try to avoid the usual tourist traps."

The woman's bushy eyebrows arched skeptically. "You miss out on a lot of good stuff that way," she said.

"Yes, I probably do."

The woman tilted her head to one side, as if waiting for further explanation. Or maybe she was just waiting for Marcy to start making sense.

In which case, they could be here a very long time, Marcy thought. "It's just that I like to really explore the cities I visit, to see the way people actually live. You understand what I'm saying?"

"No, I don't think I do. It looked like you were skulking around to me."

"No, honestly. I was just resting. That hill's a real killer."

"You know what I think?" the woman asked rhetorically. "I think you were staking the place out. I think I should report you to the police."

"Please don't do that," Marcy said quickly. "There's really no need to call anyone. I'm leaving right now." Marcy started to back away. In the next instant, she was running down the hill.

"Don't ever let me catch you in this neighborhood again," the woman called after her. "You hear me? I'll call the police if I so much as see one curl on your head."

"Shit," Marcy exclaimed, doubling over when she reached the bottom of the steep hill, her breath coming in sharp painful stabs. "Damn hair," she muttered, pushing a few perspiration-soaked ringlets away from her forehead. "What am I going to do now?" she asked the ground at her feet.

Get the hell out of here, she heard Judith say. *Come home right now. Before you get yourself arrested.*

"No way," Marcy told her, turning around in a helpless circle, like a dog looking for a comfortable place to settle. She remembered seeing a small park a few blocks away. Surely inside that tiny square was a bench on which she could sit down, regroup, rethink her strategy.

You're gonna get yourself killed, Judith warned her as Marcy marched toward the impressive hedgerows of blood-red fuchsias in the distance.

Marcy dismissed her sister's nagging voice with a shake of her head, deliberately picking up her pace. Minutes later, she was sitting on a green wooden bench, surrounded by pink and blue hydrangea bushes, large patches of lacy white cow parsley, and rows of mauve foxglove spires. It really is a beautiful country, she was thinking, taking a deep breath and closing her eyes. Maybe once she found Devon, they could tour the rest of Ireland together, take the trip Devon had always dreamed of taking with her father, visiting Limerick, maybe even finding the house in which Devon's grandmother had grown up. Perhaps they'd travel to Killarney and Kilkenny, maybe even visit the famed limestone Cliffs of Moher in remote county Clare. Wherever Devon wanted to go. Whatever she wanted to do. Whatever Devon wanted, Marcy repeated silently, hearing a baby's distant cries mingling with the drone of nearby traffic.

Marcy opened her eyes to see a skinny young woman with fair skin and strawberry-blond hair pushing a baby carriage in her direction. The girl was wearing tight blue jeans and a loose white T-shirt, and her ponytail swung from side to side as she walked. Shannon, Marcy realized immediately, then immediately after that, No, it can't be. She must have fallen asleep. She was only dreaming this was happening.

"Do you mind if I have a seat?" the young woman asked shyly, waiting until Marcy nodded her consent before sitting down on the opposite end of the bench.

Marcy tried hard not to stare. Was this really Shannon?

The girl quickly removed the rubber band from around her ponytail, freeing her thick hair to fall around her shoulders. "There. That's much better. I tied it too tight. It was giving me a headache," she said, a hint of apology in her voice, as if she was afraid of offending Marcy with her unsolicited comments. She blushed, a surprisingly delicate shade of crimson. "Sorry. I didn't mean to disturb you."

"You're not. It's lovely hair." Marcy studied the girl's face, noting her almost translucent skin, her small green eyes and long, narrow nose. One of those girls who had no idea how pretty she was, probably because her mother had never told her.

Marcy immediately pictured Devon, who'd stubbornly insisted on hiding her natural beauty behind layers of concealer and heavy black eye shadow.

"Thank you," the girl said, tucking her hair behind one ear self-consciously. Inside the carriage, the baby continued to cry. "Sorry for the racket. If she doesn't settle down soon, I'll take off again." She reached out and began pushing the carriage back and forth, back and forth.

"No, that's all right. I don't mind." Marcy stood up to glance inside the carriage. "A little girl, you said?"

"A very colicky little girl, I'm afraid. She's been crying since midnight. We're half out of our minds."

"Is she your first?" Marcy asked, hoping the slight quiver in her voice wouldn't betray her.

"Oh, she's not *my* baby." The girl's blush deepened. "I'm just her nanny."

Marcy took a deep breath, trying to still her growing excitement. "What's her name?"

"Caitlin. Caitlin Danielle O'Connor."

Marcy's breath formed a small fist inside her chest, began pummeling her rib cage. "Pretty name."

" 'Tis, isn't it?"

"How old is she?"

"Almost five months."

"She's beautiful."

"Yes, she is. Even more beautiful when she's not crying."

Marcy extended her hand. "I'm Marilyn," she said, wondering if the lie was really necessary but not confident she could trust Shannon with the truth.

"Shannon," the girl said, shaking Marcy's hand and leaning back on the bench. "Are you American?"

Marcy nodded. Sometimes it was just easier to lie.

Caitlin's cries grew louder, as if protesting the deceit.

"Oh, dear." Shannon sighed, defeated.

"I could hold her for a few minutes, if you wouldn't mind," Marcy said.

"I wouldn't mind at all," Shannon said as Marcy carefully lifted the screaming baby out of her carriage. "Poor Mrs. O'Connor was up half the night walking her around. She was almost falling down from exhaustion this morning. I tried feeding her, changing her, rocking her. Nothing did any good, so I thought I might as well take her out for a walk, at least give Mrs. O'Connor a chance to catch up on her sleep."

"I'm sure she appreciates that." Marcy held the baby tightly to her breast, kissing the top of her soft head through her pink bonnet and rocking her gently. Within seconds, the crying shuddered to a halt.

"My God, would you just look at that," Shannon exclaimed wondrously. "Looks like you've got the magic touch, Marilyn. How on earth did you manage that?"

"Practice," Marcy answered, feeling a surge of pride. She'd always had a way with infants. All she'd ever had to do whenever either of her children cried was pick them up and hold them close.

Why hadn't the same magic worked as Devon grew older? When had Marcy lost the ability to soothe and comfort the child she loved more than life?

"How many children do you have?" Shannon asked.

"Three." Each lie was easier than the one before, Marcy realized. "Two boys and a girl."

"I bet the girl was the hardest."

"Yes," Marcy said, thinking, At last, the truth. "How did you know?"

"I have five brothers and two sisters. My mother said the boys were a piece of cake but the girls almost did her in."

"Are you from around here?"

"Oh, no. I'm from Glengariff. Over on Bantry Bay. On the west coast. Near the Caha Mountains. Do you know it?"

"No. I'm afraid not."

"Not surprising. It's not exactly a tourist town. I couldn't wait to get out," she confessed, glancing guiltily over her shoulder as if someone might have overheard her. "Couldn't wait to come to the big city. Soon as I turned eighteen, I was gone."

"You don't look much older than that now."

"I'll be nineteen next month," Shannon said with a blush so deep her entire face turned red.

"So you've been here almost a year?"

"Well, I started out in Dublin. But I found it a little intimidating." She blushed even harder. "It's so big. I could never get comfortable. I almost went home. But then I came here." She sighed with satisfaction. "It's much better."

"Cork's a nice size," Marcy agreed. "Very manageable."

"Yes, it is."

"Much easier to make friends here, I would think," she said, deciding to broach the subject carefully.

Shannon nodded, the blush that had been threatening to recede now back in full force. "I've always had a rather hard time making friends. I'm kind of shy, believe it or not."

"How long have you been here?" Marcy asked.

"Just over six months. I've been working for the O'Connors for four."

"Well, I'm sure you've made at least one friend during that time." Marcy pressed her, trying to keep her voice casual and light.

"I guess I have, yes."

"So that's good."

" 'Tis, yes."

Well, this is going absolutely nowhere, Marcy thought, continuing to rock the now-sleeping baby in her arms. "So, do you work around here?" she asked, deciding to circle around for a few minutes before bringing the conversation back to Shannon's friends.

"Just up the street a bit."

"It seems like a nice area."

"Oh, it's a lovely neighborhood. Definitely first-class all the way. And the O'Connor house is the biggest one on the block. Up near the top of the hill." She pointed in its general direction. "You can't miss it. It's very grand. Even my room is enormous. Almost as big as the house I grew up in. I even have my own telly and everything."

"Sounds wonderful."

She nodded enthusiastically. "I was very lucky to get this job."

"Did a friend tell you about it?" Marcy bit down on her tongue. Could she be any more obvious? she wondered.

But Shannon didn't seem to notice. "No. I went through an agency. The O'Connors had just fired their first nanny because she wasn't working out, and they needed a replacement. I was told to dress conservatively and only speak when spoken to. Apparently Mrs. O'Connor didn't take to the first girl because she was mouthy and wore her skirts too short."

Marcy could almost see the ad the O'Connors might have placed:

WANTED. LIVE-IN NANNY.
SHOULD BE SHY AND DIFFIDENT.
ATTRACTIVE BUT NONTHREATENING.
NO SOCIAL LIFE A MUST.

Shannon definitely fit the bill.

"So, what does Mr. O'Connor do?" Marcy asked.

"He's in construction. The development we live in is one of his projects."

Marcy nodded, trying to figure out a way to work Audrey into the conversation.

Shannon continued unprompted. "His father was some kind

of diplomat. He was killed by the IRA about twenty years ago, when Mr. O'Connor was a teenager."

"That's terrible."

"Those were terrible times," Shannon said.

Marcy nodded her agreement. "So, what do you do on your days off?" she asked after a moment's pause.

"Not very much. Read, look in the shops, go to the cinema."

"What kind of movies do you and your friends like?"

"All kinds."

Great, Marcy thought. Another dead end. Now what? She was running out of questions. Not to mention patience. And the baby was starting to weigh heavily in her arms. "So, do you have a boyfriend?" she asked, deciding to give it one last try.

Shannon shook her head. The motion sent her blush spreading from one ear to the other. "Audrey says I'm lucky. She says boys only bring you grief."

Marcy's breath caught in her throat at the mention of Audrey's name. "Audrey?" she repeated, her voice a whisper. Had she heard Shannon correctly?

"My friend. Well, sort of. More an acquaintance, really."

"How so?"

"Well, I haven't really known her all that long. Just a few months really. And we don't get to see each other much. My job keeps me pretty busy."

"Is Audrey a nanny, too?"

Shannon laughed. "Oh, no. Can't see Audrey as a nanny."

"Why is that?"

"Don't think she fancies children all that much, to be truthful. Although she makes a proper fuss about Caitlin whenever she sees her. Still . . ."

"Still . . . ?"

"I don't know. It's just a feeling I get." Shannon glanced at her watch.

"So what does Audrey do?"

"As little as she can get away with." Shannon's blush turned a bright tomato red, as if she'd just said the most terrible thing imaginable. "Works as a temp. That sort of thing. My goodness, would you look at the time? I really should get going."

Marcy returned Caitlin to her carriage, laying the sleeping baby gently on her back. There were so many more questions she wanted to ask Shannon: Where does Audrey live? Where is she from? Has she said anything about her past, about her mother? Where can I find her?

"Thank you so much for your help with Caitlin," Shannon was saying. "It's been really nice talking to you. Maybe we'll run into each other again sometime."

Marcy watched Shannon's skinny frame as she pushed the baby carriage out of the small park and eventually up the hill and out of sight. "Count on it," she said.

TWELVE

FOR THE NEXT THREE days, Marcy kept watch on Shannon's comings and goings. It was too risky to venture back up Adelaide Road in case the O'Connors' nosy neighbor was lying in wait, so Marcy would sit in the small park until she saw Shannon appear, pushing the baby in her pram, usually at around eleven o'clock in the morning and then again at approximately two in the afternoon, Caitlin's loud wails always preceding them, as reliable as the bells from St. Anne's Shandon Church.

In the mornings, she'd follow Shannon up and down the winding roads of the new subdivision, careful always to keep a safe distance between them, only occasionally having to duck into a nearby doorway to avoid detection. The afternoon walk was always the longer of the two outings. Yesterday Shannon had actually ventured all the way into the flat of the city, dutifully pushing the baby's carriage along the bumpy cobblestone roads while stealing wistful glances at the shop windows along the way. At three o'clock she'd stopped to have tea on the front patio of a small pub, and Marcy had watched from across the street as Shannon had tried, repeatedly and with only moderate success, to balance her hot tea while simultaneously rocking the crying baby in her arms. She'd thought of going to her rescue but ultimately decided against it. Even a girl as naive as Shannon might become suspicious of another close encounter. No, it was better to keep tabs on her from afar, to watch where she went, make note of those she spoke to.

Except she never spoke to anyone.

"I'm getting very discouraged," Marcy had confided in Liam on the phone the previous night.

"Don't be. It's not that big a city. She's bound to lead you to Audrey sooner or later."

"I need it to be sooner."

"What can I do to help?"

"You've already done more than enough."

"Would you like me to go with you tomorrow? I can arrange to take the day off work. . . ."

"No, I can't ask you to do that."

"You don't have to ask."

"No," Marcy had insisted. "It's better if you stay at Grogan's. In case Audrey walks by again."

"Okay. Whatever you think is best," he'd agreed. Then, "I could come over now. . . ."

"No," Marcy said quickly. Much as she'd wanted to see him, much as she was attracted to him, much as she wanted to believe he might actually be attracted to *her,* she couldn't afford to let herself be distracted. Not when she was so close to finding her daughter. "I'll speak to you tomorrow," she'd said.

"I'll be here."

Now Marcy watched as Shannon pushed Caitlin's carriage across the footbridge over the South Channel and continued up Mary Street toward the busy main thoroughfare that was St. Patrick's Street. Although it was overcast and familiar clouds were circling the horizon, it was actually warm, Marcy realized, feeling the weight of the trench coat she'd been carrying over her arm for the better part of an hour. Maybe tomorrow she'd actually be able to chance leaving her coat at the inn, she thought, glancing toward the weather vane on the top of St. Anne's. "Let me guess," she mumbled into the collar of her blue blouse. "Rain is in the forecast."

It was at that moment she realized that Shannon had disappeared.

Marcy spun around, her head shooting in several different directions at once. All she saw were storefronts and pedestrians. Shannon was nowhere.

Where could she have gone?

"Okay, calm down," Marcy told herself. "She'll turn up." After all, Shannon had vanished into the afternoon crowds before, only to reappear within seconds, her ponytail swinging rhythmically behind her. Now you see her, now you don't.

Besides, so what if Marcy didn't find her? It wasn't as if she didn't know where the girl lived. It wasn't as if Shannon was particularly adventurous, as if she didn't adhere to a rather rigid routine. It wasn't as if she couldn't start again tomorrow.

Start from scratch, Marcy thought, trying not to cry.

"Have you thought of going to the police?" Liam had asked last night.

But Marcy didn't want to involve the police. What if Devon were in some sort of trouble? What if by alerting them to her whereabouts, she drove her even farther underground? What if her desperate efforts to reunite with her daughter landed Devon behind bars? She couldn't take that risk.

"I could hire a private detective," she'd suggested in return.

Liam had agreed without much enthusiasm. "You could, I suppose. But it's not like in the movies. At least not here in Cork. There's not really a big demand for their services in these parts. You're probably better off on your own. At least for the time being."

Except she was as much a failure at playing detective as she'd been with most of the things in her life, Marcy was beginning to think, checking off each failing as if it were an item on a shopping list. Failure as a daughter—check. Failure as a sister—check. Failure as a wife—check. Failure as a mother—double, triple check.

She'd never even attempted a career. Yes, she'd worked in the marketing department of a small advertising agency when she first graduated college, but that job had always felt temporary and had dissolved several years later along with the company. By that time she was married and she and Peter were already planning a family. Pretty soon she was pregnant with Devon, and then with Darren, so what did she need a job for? She already had her hands full at home.

Devon's voice wafted toward her, transported from the past by the laughter of a nearby cluster of teenage girls.

"What do I have to finish college for?" Devon was demanding. She'd just informed Marcy she was going to drop out of university one semester shy of her degree.

Marcy argued with her, despite the little voice in her head warning her to back off. "Because an education is important."

"Why is it so damned important?"

"Because it is. And watch your language."

"You're upset because I said 'damned'? What's the problem with 'damned,' for fuck's sake?"

"Devon . . ."

Devon began spouting off profanities. "Shit, fuck, cock, cunt, son of a bitch."

"This is ridiculous."

"Prick, bastard, cocksucker, twat, motherfucker . . ."

"I'm not having this conversation."

"You're the one who started it."

"And I'm the one who's ending it." Marcy turned away before Devon could see her cry.

"Sure, Mommy. Walk away. That's how you deal with everything."

"This isn't about me," Marcy said, marveling at the fact that her daughter still called her "Mommy." "Motherfucker" in one breath, she thought, "Mommy" in the next.

"So I don't want to finish college. What's the big deal? It's my life, not yours."

"You only have a few courses left. Why not just get your degree and then at least you'll have options?"

"Options? What kind of options do I have? In case you haven't noticed, I'm a fucking mess. And don't you dare tell me to watch my language."

"Are you taking your medication?"

"What's that got to do with anything?"

"Because this sort of thing always happens when you go off your meds."

"What sort of thing would that be exactly?"

"The swearing, the moodiness, everything. It all gets worse."

"Worse for you, maybe. Not for me."

"Please, Devon."

"Please, Mommy," Devon mimicked.

"Okay, enough. I can't deal with this right now."

"You never could."

"I've tried."

"Like you tried with your mother?"

"What?"

"You could have stopped her, you know," Devon continued cruelly. "Stopped her from jumping off that building."

"Nothing would have stopped her," Marcy protested weakly.

"Judith told me what happened."

Marcy nodded, acknowledging defeat with a long, deep exhalation that quivered its way into the space between them. "All I've ever wanted is for you to be happy."

"All you've ever wanted is for me to be *normal*," Devon shot back.

"Yes!" Marcy shouted at her daughter, feeling the reverberations of that single word even now. "Yes, I wanted you to be normal. Is that so selfish of me? Is it so awful? Does it make me some sort of monster?"

Devon coldly watched the path of her mother's tears. "I'm the monster," she said.

"Excuse me," someone was saying now.

Marcy turned to see Devon's face dissolve into that of an elderly woman with white hair. The woman was using a wooden cane to navigate the busy street.

"I can't get around you," the woman said, her gentle smile producing a series of wrinkles that ran up from her mouth to circle her watery blue eyes.

"Oh. Sorry." Marcy immediately moved out of the way so that the old woman could pass. How long had she been standing in the middle of the street like that? she wondered, glancing down at her watch. Long enough for Shannon to disappear completely, she acknowledged, deciding to call it a day. In the morning she'd return to Adelaide Road. If Shannon didn't lead her to Audrey by the end of the week, she'd bite the bullet and confront her directly. Tell her that the girl she knew as Audrey was actually her daughter, Devon. Ask for her help in locating her.

Probably she should have done that right from the beginning, she thought. What had she been thinking?

Judith would undoubtedly tell her she hadn't been thinking at all, that she'd stopped thinking clearly the day Devon disappeared into the icy waters of Georgian Bay. "Why won't you take the medication the doctor prescribed?" she'd pleaded weeks, even months after the event.

"Because I don't need antidepressants."

"You're trying to tell me you're not seriously depressed?"

"Of course I'm depressed. I'm *seriously* depressed. But I'm depressed *for a reason*. I *should* be depressed. Why mask it? It'll only prolong the misery."

"Take the pills. At least for a little while. To get you over the hump."

"Okay, fine." Marcy had finally acquiesced.

Except the pills had replaced her depression with a stupefying numbness that was far worse, and she'd eventually stopped taking them. Her mother had been right—the drugs *did* make you feel as if you were doing the butterfly stroke through a vat of molasses—she'd realized when she felt her head starting to clear and her senses, touch, taste, sight, gradually returning to something approaching normalcy.

For the first time she'd understood Devon's preference for despair over indifference.

Of course, by then such understanding was of little consequence. Another unfortunate example of too little, too late.

Devon had been right, too, she acknowledged now, taking a final look up and down St. Patrick's Street. She could have stopped her mother from leaping to her death. Judith knew it. They all knew it.

Marcy was turning around when she saw a baby carriage emerge from inside a shop near the corner. Seconds later, Shannon popped into view, one hand pushing the carriage, the other holding a bottle of soda. She maneuvered the carriage into the street, sipping her soda from a straw as she continued in the direction of Merchant's Quay.

"Okay, you've wasted enough time," Marcy said out loud, glancing around self-consciously in case someone had overheard her. But if anyone had, they'd probably assumed she was talking on her cell phone. It was much easier to be crazy in public these days. "You'll just tell her the truth," Marcy continued aloud, finding comfort in the sound of her voice. "Tell her who you are. Ask for her help. Beg for mercy."

She was within half a block of Shannon when she saw a young man ride up on a bicycle. She saw Shannon smile as he approached, her blush as strong as a red traffic light. The boy stopped and dismounted, touching her arm as he dutifully admired the baby in her charge. That's kind of sweet, Marcy thought, as she wormed her way between two slow-moving pedestrians. It wasn't until she was almost on top of them that Marcy realized she was staring at the same young man whose bicycle had sent her flying a few days ago.

"No, that's impossible," she exclaimed, stopping abruptly, causing the man behind her to crash into her.

"I'm so sorry. I didn't realize . . . ," he began.

"My fault," Marcy told him. "I thought I . . . It was my fault." Surely she was imagining things. This couldn't be the same boy who'd run her down.

Could it?

She moved closer.

"So, does she ever stop cryin'?" the young man was asking Shannon over the sound of Caitlin's constant wails.

"The doctor says she has colic," Shannon explained.

"Does he say how long it's gonna last?"

"He says he doesn't think it should go on much longer, but I don't think he knows, to be honest."

"God, it must get on your nerves. Is there nothing you can do?"

"Believe me, we've tried everything. Holding her, taking her for long walks, going for rides in the car. She won't take a pacifier. Nothing works. Except for this one woman I met in the park the other day. All she had to do was pick her up and Caitlin went dead quiet. It was like some kind of miracle, I tell you."

"Sounds more like witchcraft," the boy said, and laughed, then spit on the sidewalk, as if to ward off the evil eye. "You're sure she wasn't a witch?"

I've been called worse, Marcy thought, edging closer still. "It's him," she whispered.

What did it mean? Was it a simple coincidence or something more sinister? What was his connection to Shannon? And if he *was* connected to Shannon, did it necessarily follow that he was connected to Devon as well? "Okay, calm down. Think this through. Don't go jumping to conclusions." Except how could she help it? She'd been searching for Devon, had just miraculously spotted her standing on the footbridge over Bachelor's Quay, was in fact racing toward her, when at that exact moment his bicycle had appeared from out of nowhere, barreling toward her and sending her sprawling. His prolonged solicitations had delayed things even further, and by the time she'd extricated herself from his clumsy concern, Devon was gone. Marcy had assumed it was a combination of bad timing and worse luck. But maybe something more deliberate had been at play. Maybe her accident hadn't been an accident at all. Maybe the boy had purposely knocked her down, alerting Devon to her presence and giving her time to get away.

Which meant what? That Devon knew she was here?

Was it possible?

Or was she reading too much into things? After all, Cork wasn't that big a city. It made perfect sense that Shannon and the boy might know each other, that their relationship—if you could call stopping to chat on a busy street corner a relationship—was as innocent as it was innocuous. Just because Shannon was also friends with the girl she knew as Audrey didn't necessarily mean anything. The boy might not know Audrey at all.

Or he might.

Which meant what?

"What does it mean?" Marcy demanded of the concrete at her feet. "Damn it, what does this mean?"

"Marilyn?" she heard someone calling from a distance. Then closer, "Marilyn? Yoo-hoo."

Marcy looked up to see Shannon crossing the street, waving furiously and heading in her direction.

"It's me. Shannon. From the park," she announced over Caitlin's loud cries. "I thought I recognized you."

Marcy fought hard to control her emotions. She wanted to grab hold of Shannon's elbows and demand answers: Who is that boy you were just talking to? What is his connection to Audrey? Is there one? How much can you tell me about my daughter? Instead she said, "Shannon, of course. It's nice to see you again."

"What an amazing coincidence! I was just talking about you, and suddenly here you are."

"You were talking about me?"

"Yes, to this friend of mine. Well, more an acquaintance really. I was telling him how amazing you were with the baby." She looked to the now vacant spot where she and the boy had been standing, then back to Marcy. "Are you feeling all right? You look a little pale."

"Just tired, I guess." Marcy suddenly realized how true that statement was. "I've been doing a lot of walking."

"Busy sightseeing, are you?"

"I hadn't realized Cork was such an exciting city."

"People are always amazed by how much there is to do here. Do you fancy a spot of tea?"

"Tea sounds wonderful."

Shannon checked her watch. "I still have time before I have to head back. Why don't we head over to Grogan's?"

"Grogan's?" Marcy felt the name stick to the roof of her mouth, like an unwieldy piece of bubblegum.

"It's just up the way a bit, across St. Patrick's Bridge. It has a nice outdoor patio. Makes it easier with the carriage and all."

Marcy smiled, trying to collect all her conflicting thoughts into one place, make them more manageable. She gave up when that proved impossible. Instead she smiled even wider, revealing the two rows of perfectly straight white teeth Peter had once found so irresistible, and said, "Lead the way."

THIRTEEN

I F LIAM WAS SURPRISED to see her, he didn't show it. Nor did he let on that he recognized either of them.

"And how are you today, ladies?" he asked, approaching their tiny round table on the small outside patio. There were perhaps a dozen people crowded into the makeshift space, the sun throwing a circle of light, like a giant floodlight, on the wild pink rhododendrons and flirty bluebells that lined the black wrought iron enclosure.

Marcy marveled at how she'd failed to notice such magnificent flowers on any of her previous visits. Had she always been so unaware of her surroundings? "We're good, thank you."

"Lovely afternoon, isn't it?" he continued.

"'Tis," Shannon agreed shyly. "So warm."

"Nice change." Marcy felt her heart flutter inside her chest and wondered whether it was her proximity to Shannon or Liam that was the cause.

Inside her carriage, Caitlin started howling.

"Unfortunately, some things never change," whispered Shannon, glancing apologetically toward the other patrons, most of whom seemed oblivious to the baby's wails.

"And what do we have here?" Liam peered inside the baby's carriage. "Somebody doesn't care much for the sun, I see."

"Somebody doesn't care much for anything," Shannon said.

"Think she'd fancy a bottle of Beamish?"

The blush that accompanied Shannon's laugh almost matched the surrounding rhododendrons. "I know *I* would."

"Two Beamishes?" He looked toward Marcy for confirmation.

"I think I'd better stick with tea," she told him.

"Make that two," Shannon concurred quickly. "Mrs. O'Connor would have a right fit if I came home with beer on my breath. She says that Ireland is paying dearly for its drinking culture, that in the last twenty years alcohol consumption has increased by almost fifty percent and that binge drinking is assuming epic-like proportions among teenagers and young adults."

"She says all that, does she?" Liam asked.

"She says that according to a recent survey, more than half of Ireland's youth experiment with alcohol before the age of twelve, and that by the time they reach their mid-teens, half the girls and two-thirds of the boys are drinkers."

"Shocking." An amused grin played with the corners of Liam's lips. "So, you work for the O'Connor clan over on Adelaide, do you?"

"Yes. Do you know them?" A look of apprehension suddenly clouded Shannon's small green eyes.

"I know *of* them," Liam clarified. "Who doesn't? One of the richest families in Cork," he explained to Marcy. "Wasn't his father murdered by the Sinn Fein?"

"Shot and killed while on a visit to Belfast in 1986," Shannon said quietly.

"Guess we were all pretty crazy back then," Liam said.

Marcy thought of reminding him he would have been just a child *back then* but quickly thought better of it. What was the point of reminding him again of the difference in their ages?

"So, two teas and some warm milk?"

"I have a bottle of apple juice with me, thanks," Shannon said before Liam hurried off. "Not that she'll take it. Unless you'd like to try?" she asked Marcy hopefully.

In response, Marcy held out her arms, and Shannon quickly scooped up the crying baby and handed her to Marcy, along with her bottle.

"Hello, sweetheart," Marcy cooed, kissing the tears from Caitlin's wet cheeks and smoothing a few delicate wisps of reddish-yellow hair away from her forehead. "Who's my sweet girl?" In the next instant, the baby was lying still against Marcy's breast, suckling contentedly on her bottle.

"Bloody amazing," Shannon marveled. "I don't know how you do it."

Marcy shrugged, wondering when her power to comfort her own children had deserted her. Not that her son had ever required much comforting. A spectacularly easy baby who'd matured into an independent, easygoing young adult, Darren was his sister's opposite in almost every respect. Marcy had always wondered if Darren's temperament was innate or if he'd somehow sensed his mother could handle only so much. She searched her memory for the last time her son had come to her with a problem. Had he ever? And had she been too preoccupied with Devon to notice?

"You should come over to our house," Shannon was saying, "give Mrs. O'Connor a lesson."

"From what little you've told me about Mrs. O'Connor," Marcy said as thoughts of Darren retreated to the far corner of her brain, "I don't think that would go over very well." She watched a young man in the corner of the patio throw his head back and laugh out loud. How nice to be able to laugh with such unrestrained abandon, she thought, suddenly picturing the young man she'd seen laughing earlier with Shannon. There must be a way to inject him into the conversation, a way to bring him up without arousing undue suspicion.

Shannon demurred, looking uneasily from side to side, as if checking for spies in their midst. "She's not so bad really. She tries really hard with Caitlin."

"I'm sure she does."

"I think she just thought it would be easier."

Marcy nodded. We all do, she thought, watching Liam approach with their teas.

"I see somebody has the gift," he remarked, putting their ceramic teapot in the middle of the table, followed by a pair of sturdy, all-white cups and saucers.

"Isn't she amazing?" Shannon asked.

"And beautiful to boot," Liam said with a smile. "Can I get you anything else? Some biscuits perhaps?"

"No, thank you," Shannon said.

"I'd love something sweet," Marcy said at the same time.

Liam winked. "Sweets for the sweet."

Shannon leaned forward conspiratorially. "I think he likes you," she said as he left the table.

Marcy felt her cheeks grow pink.

"You're blushing," Shannon exclaimed with a laugh.

Marcy corrected her. "It's a hot flash."

"What's that?"

"It's when . . . nothing." She didn't have the patience to explain the joys of menopause to the curious young woman. "You're right. I'm blushing."

"Glad to see I'm not the only one. I blush all the time. I hate it."

"It's very charming on you."

Shannon's face turned almost fuchsia. "Do you really think so?"

"Absolutely. And I'm sure that the young man you were talking to earlier would agree with me." What the hell—it was as good an opening as she was likely to get.

A look of confusion caused Shannon's blush to spread toward her ears. She cocked her head to one side like a curious cocker spaniel.

Was it possible she'd imagined the whole episode? Marcy wondered. It wouldn't be the first time she'd seen things that weren't there. At least according to Peter and Judith.

"Oh. Oh, yes, of course," Shannon said. "You mean Jackson."

"Jackson?"

Shannon lifted the teapot from the table. "Shall I pour us a cup?"

"Thank you."

"Smells delicious. I love a good cup of tea, don't you?"

"Yes, I do. Interesting name . . . Jackson," Marcy remarked.

"Calls himself Jax. With an X." Shannon giggled. "He says it's the way they do things in America."

Marcy felt her pulse quicken. "He's American?"

"No. Just watches a lot of American telly." She took a sip of her tea. "Mmmn. This is delicious. Have some."

Marcy immediately lifted her cup to her lips, feeling the

hot and soothing tea as it filled her mouth and trickled down her throat. "Do you get a lot of American television shows over here?"

"Some. Mrs. O'Connor isn't a fan. She says American television is too violent and a return to violence is the last thing Ireland needs."

"Mrs. O'Connor is a woman of strong opinions."

"Yes, she is that. Nice, though," Shannon added quickly, stealing another glance around.

"So is this Jackson someone special?" Marcy asked after a pause. A smile accompanied the slight shrug of her shoulders, as if to suggest the question was innocent and of little consequence.

Shannon almost choked on her tea. "Oh, no. No. I barely know him."

"More like a friend of a friend, is he?" Marcy pressed, straining to keep her voice light.

Shannon looked a little confused, her green eyes narrowing, almost disappearing, and then suddenly widening again. "Oh, look. Here come your biscuits."

"Brought you a few extra," Liam said, laying the plate of sugar-dusted cookies on the table, the back of his hand brushing up against Marcy's, sending gentle spasms of electricity up her arm to the base of her neck. "My treat."

"I told you he likes you," Shannon whispered as he made his retreat. "Oh, shortbread. My favorite."

"Have one."

"Can't. Mrs. O'Connor doesn't approve of eating between meals. She's always going on about how slovenly and undisciplined young people are these days, says there's an epidemic of obesity in the world, that it's all a matter of self-control and that a person's character is revealed by what they eat."

"Mrs. O'Connor sounds like a bundle of laughs." No wonder her baby is always crying, Marcy thought. Then, in the next breath, Sure. Blame the mother.

Shannon's face looked as if it was about to burst into flames. She put her hand to her heart, as if preparing to take an oath. "I'm afraid I've given you the totally wrong impression about Mrs. O'Connor."

"You didn't."

"She's really a very nice woman."

"I'm sure she is. Have a cookie."

Shannon quickly grabbed one off the plate, nervously bit off its end.

"So, are Jax and Audrey friends?" Marcy asked, throwing caution to the wind. The subtle approach was clearly getting her nowhere.

"How did you know that?" Shannon took another bite of her cookie, washing it down with a sip of her tea. "Are you psychic?"

Marcy shrugged, as if to say, Lucky guess. "Isn't she the one who said boys only bring you grief?"

Shannon giggled. "She does say that, yes."

"Sounds like she's speaking from experience."

"They used to be an item."

Marcy felt the hot tea in her throat turn to ice, forming a cube that wedged in her larynx. She practically had to scrape the next words out. "Used to be?"

"Over and done. She said I could have him, if I wanted." Shannon's cheeks went from red to purple.

"And do you?"

Shannon waved away the suggestion with a nervous flutter of her fingers. "Oh, I don't think Mrs. O'Connor would approve of someone like Jax."

"Why is that?"

"He's a bit on the wild side."

"How wild?" Marcy asked.

"He's got a bit of a reputation. Nothing awful, mind you, but not exactly the kind of young man you bring home to mother."

Marcy shuddered, recalling the man Devon had been involved with in the months prior to her supposed drowning. "You don't know what you're getting yourself into," she'd warned her daughter.

"You don't know what you're talking about," was Devon's instant retort.

"Not that he fancies me or anything," Shannon was saying, a fresh wave of blood washing across her cheeks.

"Why wouldn't he?"

Another nervous giggle. "Well, you don't see the boys exactly lining up, now, do you?"

"I think any boy would be lucky to have you," Marcy offered, her frazzled brain working a mile a minute. If Audrey and Jax knew each other, she was thinking, if they'd once been lovers, surely that meant there was no way his running into her with his bicycle could have been coincidental. It had to have been deliberate.

Which meant what?

That Devon knew her mother was here? Or that someone was trying desperately to keep her from finding out?

"You really think so?" Shannon asked hopefully.

"I absolutely do." Marcy smiled at the baby in her arms. "She's falling asleep," Marcy commented, and in the same breath, "So, how long have you known Audrey?"

"I met her just after I started working for the O'Connors."

"Is she from around here?"

"No. I think she's from London originally." Shannon suddenly started to laugh.

"What's so funny?"

"You should hear her impression of Mrs. O'Connor. It's hilarious. She has the accent down pat."

Marcy cleared her throat in an effort to keep a scream from emerging. "Does she do other accents as well?"

"Oh, yes. German, Italian. American. She's quite amazing, really. Do you think I could have another cookie?"

"Help yourself."

Shannon took another cookie from the plate, broke it into two equal halves, then stuffed one half inside her mouth. "Guess it'll come in handy when she goes to California."

"She's going to California?"

Shannon nodded, scooping up some wayward crumbs from around her lips with her tongue. "So she says."

"Does she say when?"

"Pretty soon, I think." She returned the uneaten half of her cookie to her plate, staring at Marcy with wary eyes. "Why are you so interested in Audrey?"

Marcy shrugged. "Just making small talk. These cookies are the best. Here, you have the last one."

"No. I really should be getting home." Shannon pushed back her chair, started to stand up.

"Do you think it's a good idea to disturb the baby?" Marcy asked quickly.

Shannon acknowledged the sleeping baby in Marcy's arms with a deep sigh. "You *do* have a way with her."

"I'm sorry if I ask too many questions," Marcy apologized. "It just gets a little lonely," she added for good measure, "traveling by myself."

"Oh, I know how you feel," Shannon said, softening immediately and reaching for the other half of her cookie. "When I first moved to Dublin, I was so lonely. I didn't know anyone.

Even after I came to Cork, it was so hard at first. I had no one to talk to. I can't tell you how many nights I cried myself to sleep."

And then you met Audrey, Marcy wanted to say. Instead she said, "And then you got a job with the O'Connors."

"Yes. And then I met Audrey," Shannon volunteered on her own.

"And Jax."

"And Jax," Shannon agreed. "Not that I get to see them very often. Mrs. O'Connor keeps me pretty busy."

"I'm sure she does."

"Don't get me wrong. She's a lovely woman. Very fair and generous."

"I'm sure she is."

"I hope I haven't given you the wrong impression."

"I'm sure you haven't."

"I'm very lucky to have this job." Shannon looked toward the tavern's front door. "You fancy some more tea?" She waved toward the window.

"Sounds good." More tea meant more time for questions.

The tavern's front door opened. Footsteps approached their table.

"Could we have another pot of tea, please?" Shannon asked politely.

Marcy looked up and smiled, expecting to see Liam. Instead she saw Kelly.

"Well, hello, there," the waitress said, recognizing Marcy immediately. "I see you found Shannon all right."

The blush instantly drained from Shannon's face. "What?"

"I'll be right back with your tea," Kelly said, spinning around on her heel and returning to the inside of the pub.

Shannon was already half out of her chair, the red in her

cheeks having returned with a vengeance, spreading down her neck and disappearing into the top of her T-shirt. "What did she mean, 'I see you found Shannon all right?' Have you been asking about me?"

"No, of course not. She must be confusing me with someone else."

"And you must be confusing me with an idiot. Do you think I'm stupid?"

"Please sit down. I can explain."

"Asking all these questions about me and my friends! Did Mrs. O'Connor put you up to this?" Shannon demanded, tears filling her eyes.

"What?"

"She sent you, didn't she? To check up on me. Find out who my friends are, who I see and what I do. You're going to report back to her all the nasty things I said. . . ."

"You didn't say anything—"

"I'll lose my job. . . ."

"I have no intention of saying anything to Mrs. O'Connor."

"What do you want then? Who are you?"

Marcy noted Shannon's outrage was beginning to attract the attention of some of the other patrons and kept her voice purposefully low, hoping to encourage Shannon to do the same. "My name is Marcy—"

"It's not Marilyn?" Shannon demanded in outrage, as if lying about her name was the worst of Marcy's transgressions. "Give me the baby," she ordered, a note of hysteria creeping into her voice. "Give her to me straightaway."

A portly, middle-aged man got up from his seat at a nearby table. "Is there a problem here?"

"She won't give me back my baby."

As if on cue, Caitlin opened her eyes and started to whimper, the whimper quickly becoming a cry, the cry metastasizing into a howl.

"Give the girl back her baby, ma'am," the man instructed, as others on the patio rose from their seats.

"Of course I'll give her back the baby," Marcy protested. "I'm not trying to steal her baby, for heaven's sake."

Caitlin's screams filled the air as Shannon lunged toward Marcy and the crowd closed in. A brawl broke out between two would-be Sir Galahads. Punches were thrown. An errant fist connected with Marcy's cheek.

In the next instant, all was chaos.

FOURTEEN

D O YOU WANT TO tell us what happened?" the police officer was asking.

"I've already told you."

"Tell us again."

Marcy lowered her head, the left side of her face still throbbing as she stared at the gray concrete floor. Could she really go
through the whole sad story again? What more could she say?
That it was all a huge mistake? That she was sorry? That they
were wasting precious time? That Shannon had undoubtedly
contacted Audrey by now, told her that some crazy woman
named Marcy had been asking questions about her and was
currently being detained at the Garda station along the South
Mall? "I wasn't trying to steal the baby," she said instead, sure
that Devon was packing her bags at this very minute and pre-

paring to leave the city. She raised her head toward the two men and one woman, all dressed in neat, dark blue uniforms, then turned quickly away. She hated uniforms.

"We know that," the older of the two men admitted after a pause. His name was Christopher Murphy and he was about forty, with close-cropped blond hair and a wide nose that had been broken at least once and not properly reset, so that it veered sharply to the right. He sat on the edge of the wide oak desk that occupied most of the room and smiled at her indulgently.

His teeth could use a good cleaning, she heard Peter say.

"You know that?" Marcy repeated.

"The girl, Shannon Farrell, gave us a statement, said she'd just as soon forget the whole incident."

"Then what am I doing here?" Marcy was already beginning to rise from her chair. "If you'd just give me back my passport . . ." She nodded toward the stack of papers on his desk. Her passport was lying open on the top.

"Please sit down, Mrs. Taggart."

Marcy took a cursory glance around the windowless room, surprised by how familiar it seemed. Why was it that wherever you went in the world, police stations always looked the same? Did they all use the same interior decorator? she wondered. Was there a special handbook that prison authorities gave out to potential designers? Not that she'd seen the insides of many police stations, other than in the movies and on TV.

Just one, Marcy thought with a shudder, stifling the memory before it could take root.

Still, she'd expected something more colorful from a country like Ireland, with its deep sense of history and innate flair for melodrama. The old Cork City Gaol she'd visited with her tour group had been suitably majestic, a three-story castle-like building whose cell walls still boasted their original graffiti, even though its prisoners were now made of wax. In contrast, the new Bridewell Garda Station, on the line of the old city wall on the north channel of the river Lee, was relatively modern in structure and appearance. Unfortunately the station where she was currently being detained was an uninspired combination of the two—ancient without being imposing, modern without being sleek, a muddle of conflicting styles whose end result was no style at all. It was dreary, tired looking, and smelled of body odor and disillusionment.

"I don't understand. If you already have Shannon's statement . . . ," Marcy told the officer, or "garda," as policemen in Ireland were called. She shifted her gaze toward the female garda standing against the dull green wall. Her name was Colleen Donnelly—lots of Ls, lots of Ns, lots of Es, Marcy had thought when the young woman introduced herself—and she was maybe twenty-five. Surprisingly delicate in appearance, she had pale skin that was liberally sprinkled with freckles and a mouthful of tiny, niblet-like teeth.

Some good veneers would do wonders, Peter observed from behind Marcy's eyes.

The remaining garda gave his name as John Sweeny, although Marcy noted that his colleagues always referred to him as Johnny. He was about thirty and of average height and weight, although his gut was surprisingly prominent for someone so young. His ruddy complexion gave weight to otherwise bland features, and his mercifully ordinary teeth drew no unsolicited comments from the dark recesses of Marcy's brain.

As with almost all law enforcement officers in Ireland, none of them was armed. For one giddy moment, Marcy considered making a run for it.

"We can still charge you with disturbing the peace," Christopher Murphy told her.

"Disturbing the peace? You've got to be kidding."

"A table was overturned, a teapot was smashed, some dishes were broken."

"I'm the one with the black eye."

"A regrettable accident."

"Exactly."

"What were you doing with the baby, Mrs. Taggart?" Christopher Murphy asked.

"I've already told you. . . ."

He referred to his notes. "Shannon asked you to hold her."

"Yes. The baby has colic. For some reason, when I hold her, she stops crying."

"And how do you know Shannon Farrell?" Colleen Donnelly asked.

"I met her in the park a few days ago. We happened to bump into each other again today on St. Patrick's Street. She asked me if I'd like to go somewhere for a cup of tea. Like an idiot, I said yes."

"Like an idiot?" Christopher Murphy repeated.

"In light of what happened, yes."

"What are you doing in Ireland?" asked John Sweeny.

"What?"

"What brings you to Ireland?" he said again, as if they were just two people having an innocently pleasant conversation.

"How is that relevant?"

"Indulge me."

"It's a long story."

"We have lots of time."

Marcy sighed her resignation. "I'm here on holiday."

"Alone?"

"Yes, alone. Is that a crime?" She noted the look that passed between the two men. The look warned her to watch her tone. "Sorry. I just don't understand the point of these questions."

"Your husband didn't come with you?" the older garda asked, more statement than question.

"No."

"May I ask why?"

"No, you may not."

Another shared glance.

"We're getting a divorce," Marcy finally offered, sensing that this information diminished her even further in their eyes. Now she was not only a troublemaking foreigner, she was pathetic as well, a woman whose wild, unpredictable ways had no doubt cost her the love of a stable orthodontist. She felt the sudden threat of tears and raised her hand to her cheek, as if to ward them off.

"Cheek still sore?" Colleen Donnelly asked. "Would you like more ice?"

"No, thank you. I'm fine." It *did* hurt and she *wasn't* fine, but what the hell. She'd tend to her black eye later. She'd wasted enough time. All she wanted was to get out of there as soon as possible.

"You're Canadian, I see."

"Yes."

"Toronto's a lovely city."

"Yes, it is."

"When are you going back?"

Marcy almost laughed. The Irish were many things, she was discovering, but subtle wasn't one of them. "I'm booked to go home at the end of next week." Another shared glance between the two men. "Is that it? Are we finished? Can I go now?"

"Who's Audrey?" Christopher Murphy asked, as if Marcy hadn't spoken.

"What?"

"Miss Farrell said you seemed awfully interested in a friend of hers named Audrey."

Marcy shrugged, lifting her hands into the air and opening her palms toward the recessed ceiling, then bringing them back together in her lap. "Shannon mentioned her. I was just making conversation."

"She said you asked a lot of questions about Audrey and a young man named Jackson." Again, he checked his notes. "Jax," he stated, putting particular emphasis on the X.

"You say that name as if you know him," Marcy said hopefully, trying to keep her voice as neutral as possible. Hadn't Shannon told her that Jax had something of a reputation? Was it possible he'd ever gotten into trouble with the law, that these officers were familiar with him?

"Can't say the name rings any bells," Christopher Murphy said, answering her silent question. "What about you, Johnny? You know anyone named Jax?"

The younger garda shook his head.

"My cousin just named her baby Jax," Colleen Donnelly said.

"Like I said," Marcy told them, "I was just making conversation, trying to be polite."

Officer Murphy waved his hand in the direction of her bruised face. "This is you trying to be polite?"

"Look. None of this is my fault. I'm the victim here. I was the one who was attacked."

"And we can press charges, if you'd like."

"I don't want to press charges. I told you that. I just want to get out of here."

"Then tell us what's really going on, Mrs. Taggart," Colleen Donnelly said. "Maybe we can help you."

Marcy looked from one garda's face to the next, all three of the officers staring back at her with varying degrees of compassion and curiosity. Could they help her? she wondered. Could she trust them with the truth?

"Audrey is my daughter," she said after a lengthy pause, deciding she had no other choice *but* to trust them.

"Your daughter," all three repeated, their voices overlapping.

"She disappeared almost two years ago."

They waited for her to continue. Christopher Murphy raised one thin eyebrow and brought his lips together, as if he were about to whistle.

How much could she tell them? "We thought she was dead—"

"Why would you think that?" John Sweeny interjected.

"Because that's what she wanted us to think. Because she was confused and depressed." Marcy answered their next question before they could ask it. She told them about Devon going up to their cottage and the subsequent discovery of her overturned canoe in the middle of the bay. She told them of her marriage's disintegration and her husband's desertion. She told them of coming to Ireland and seeing Devon walk by Grogan's House, of Liam and Kelly identifying her daughter's picture as the girl they knew as Audrey, and their revelation that Audrey was friendly with a girl named Shannon who worked as a nanny for a wealthy local family.

"So, let me get this straight," Christopher Murphy said when she was through. "You're saying you spied on the O'Connor house, that you followed Shannon to the park—"

"I didn't follow her to the park. I was already there—"

"But you *had* followed her previous to that meeting in the park?"

"I was hoping she'd lead me to my daughter."

"Why didn't you just ask Shannon where to find her?" was the next logical question.

How many times had she asked herself the same thing? "Because I was afraid that if Devon knew I was here, if she knew I'd seen her, then she'd disappear again. And I couldn't take that chance."

"Who's Devon?" Johnny asked, his unlined brow wrinkling in confusion.

"My daughter."

"I'm sorry, I thought you said your daughter's name is Audrey."

"Audrey is the name she's using."

"Why would she be using an alias?"

"Obviously because she doesn't want to be found," Marcy replied testily.

"You don't think she'd be happy to see you?" Colleen asked.

"No."

"Why is that, Mrs. Taggart?"

"Because there were issues. . . ."

"What kind of issues?"

"It's complicated. Our relationship was . . ."

"Complicated," Johnny repeated.

"Yes. Devon was having a hard time. She blamed me for a lot of her problems—"

"Such as?"

"I'd really rather not get into that."

"If you want our help, isn't it best we know all the facts?"

"I'm not asking for your help," Marcy said.

"Why not?"

"What?"

Christopher Murphy reasserted his position as leader. "I assume you have pictures of your daughter. Can I see them, please?"

Marcy reached inside her purse and pulled out the photographs of Devon, placing them in his outstretched hand. The other two officers immediately pressed against his side, passing the pictures back and forth across his midriff.

"Pretty girl," Johnny remarked.

"Can't say she looks familiar," Colleen said.

"No. Don't know her," Officer Murphy agreed. "Tell me, why didn't you come to us when you first saw her?"

Marcy stared at him blankly. Another question for which she had no satisfactory response.

"I mean, I think I understand your not wanting to confront Shannon," he continued gently, "but we might have been able to help you find Audrey."

"How could you have helped me?"

"Well, that *is* our job, Mrs. Taggart. We help people. Or try to anyway. We could have circulated her picture, talked to Shannon in an official capacity, asked around, found out about Audrey, made sure she really is your daughter."

"What are you saying? That you don't believe me?"

"I'm not saying that at all. It's just that you only saw her for half a second through the front window of Grogan's House," the senior garda reminded Marcy. "If I'm not mistaken, those windows are covered with advertisements."

"I know what I saw."

"I don't doubt it's what you *think* you saw."

"Now you're starting to sound like my husband," Marcy said with a sneer, instantly regretting voicing this thought out loud.

"Your husband thinks you might be mistaken?"

"My husband's thoughts are no longer my concern."

"Have you spoken to him about this?"

"Yes, as a matter of fact, I have."

"And?"

Marcy swallowed her growing frustration. "He prefers to believe our daughter is dead."

"Why would any father want to believe his daughter is dead?"

"Because sometimes it's just easier that way. And Peter has always preferred to take the easy way out."

"Always?" Christopher Murphy asked, his eyebrows moving toward the bridge of his nose. "You're saying this has happened before?"

"No, that's not what I'm saying."

"*Has* it happened before, Mrs. Taggart?"

"Has *what* happened?" Marcy demanded. Then, before he could answer, "Look. I've had enough of this. I appreciate your wanting to help, I really do, but it's not necessary. So if you'll just give me back my passport, I'll be out of your hair." Instinctively Marcy's hand reached for her head, her fingers disappearing into a mass of frenzied curls. I must look like a lunatic, Marcy thought. No wonder they think I'm deranged.

Officer Murphy pressed her. "This isn't the first time you've thought you've seen your daughter, is it, Mrs. Taggart?"

"I don't understand how any of this is relevant." How many times had she said that already? Maybe it was she who was irrelevant.

"Has this happened before, Mrs. Taggart?" he repeated a fourth time.

If he asks me that again, Marcy thought, I'm going to punch him right in the mouth. She closed her eyes, shook her head. "Yes, it's happened before." She reopened her eyes in time to catch the knowing look that passed among all three officers. Just what is it you think you know? Marcy demanded silently. Trust me, you know nothing.

"So, it's possible you could be mistaken this time as well, is it not?"

"No, it's not poss— Yes, I guess it could be possible," she said in the next breath, deciding she might as well tell them what they wanted to hear. She'd been a fool for thinking she could trust them or that they might be able to help her. Tears filled her eyes and fell the length of her cheeks. They stung where her flesh was bruised and tender, and she brushed them away with the back of her hand. "Is that all?"

"Yes," Christopher Murphy said with a sigh. "I believe it is."

"Good. Then I can go?"

"You can go." He reached toward the pile of paperwork on his desk, retrieved Marcy's passport, and handed it to her along with the pictures of Devon.

Marcy tucked them into her purse as she rose to her feet. "Thank you."

"Would you like us to call someone for you, Mrs. Taggart?" Colleen asked gently.

Marcy thought of Liam. She could use a friendly face about now, she thought, shaking her head. "No. There's no one."

"Actually, I believe there's someone waiting for you in the hall," Christopher Murphy said, reaching for the old-fashioned black rotary phone on his desk. "Jenny, is that gentleman still waiting for Mrs. Taggart?" he asked. "He is? Good. Tell him she'll be out straightaway."

Marcy made an effort to smooth down her hair as John Sweeny opened the door to the hall. Thank God for Liam, she was thinking, hoping he wouldn't get in trouble for taking off work or that he wouldn't be held responsible for the damage she'd caused. Mostly she hoped she didn't look too awful.

She stepped into the dust-lined, narrow hallway, her head turning from side to side, looking for Liam.

She saw the blue eyes first, the rest of him only gradually coming into focus as he pushed himself off one of the folding chairs lining the wall.

"Marcy," Vic Sorvino said, rushing to her side. "My God, look at you."

FIFTEEN

W HAT HAPPENED?" HE ASKED, his eyes darting from her black eye and bruised cheek to the tops of her scuffed shoes and then back again. "Are you all right?"

"Vic! What are you doing here?"

A sheepish grin crept onto his sweet mouth. "You left without saying good-bye."

"What?" Was he serious? What was he saying?

"I was worried about you. The way you just took off . . ." He paused, took a long, deep breath. "I couldn't stop thinking about you."

"How did you know where to find me?"

"Then they told me you'd been in a fight—"

"Who told you? I don't understand. What are you doing here?" Marcy asked again.

"I stopped by Grogan's House. The waitress told me what happ—" He looked around. Officers Sweeny and Donnelly were listening to their exchange from the open doorway. "Look, why don't we go somewhere more private?"

Marcy wasn't sure this was such a great idea in light of what had happened the last time they'd gone somewhere more private. Still she allowed him to lead her by the elbow out of the station and onto the busy South Mall.

"Take care," Colleen Donnelly called after her.

"Did they hurt you?" Vic was asking. "Because if they laid a hand on you, we can contact the American embassy—"

"I'm Canadian," Marcy said, reminding him. "And no, the police were really very kind. I don't understand. What are you doing here?" she asked a third time, stopping in the middle of the busy street. "Aren't you supposed to be in Italy?"

"I decided Italy could wait a few more days."

"But why?"

A flush of embarrassment stained Vic's cheeks, visible even in the growing darkness of the early evening. "I would have thought that was pretty obvious."

What was he saying? "I've never been very good with the obvious," Marcy admitted as pedestrians surged by them on both sides. "I'm afraid you'll have to spell it out."

Vic took a quick glance over both shoulders. "Look. Why don't we go grab a beer or get something to eat? It's almost six o'clock."

As if on cue, the bells of St. Anne's Shandon Church began ringing out the hours.

"I'm really awfully tired," Marcy said. "It's been one hell of a day."

"Where are you staying?"

Should I tell him? Marcy wondered. Vic Sorvino was a

thoughtful, decent guy who'd been nothing but nice to her. So why was she hesitating? She tried not to recall the tenderness of his touch, the way his hands had gently caressed her body. Yes, they'd been good together. Maybe even great. Still, a one-night stand was a one-night stand. What was he doing still hanging around? "At a little bed and breakfast over on Western Road," she told him.

"Lead the way."

SHE WAS FIFTEEN years old the day she walked into her parents' bedroom and found the now-familiar scene of her mother standing naked in the middle of the room, the contents of her closets strewn across her bed, the drawers of her dresser open and empty, dozens of delicate lace bras and panties thrown on the carpet like so much debris. Every necklace she owned appeared to be hanging from the wrists of her outstretched hands. Her eyes were swollen and red from crying.

"What are you doing?" Marcy asked, although she knew the answer well enough to mouth the response along with her mother.

"I have nothing to wear."

Marcy shrugged and turned away. So it was starting again, she thought, her stomach twisting into a series of tight little knots. Why had she come up here? She could have simply eaten her breakfast and left for school with nothing more than a casual shout of good-bye up the stairs, as Judith had done, as her sister did every morning. No way Judith was ever going to find herself in this position—standing in the doorway of her parents' bedroom, her mother naked in front of her, at least a dozen beaded necklaces dangling from her arms like tinsel on a dried-out Christmas tree.

It had been almost a year since the last occurrence, a year in which her mother had dutifully followed her doctor's orders and stayed on her medication, a year without major incident, a year of relative calm. A year in which Marcy had allowed herself to be lulled into a false sense of security. A year in which she'd permitted herself the fantasy that they were a normal family, that they could actually be happy, that she might be able to relax her guard.

Which was all it took for everything to go to rat shit, she realized when she saw her mother standing naked in the middle of the room—one moment when you weren't looking.

"Maybe you could help me, darling," her mother was saying, several long beaded necklaces falling from her wrist to the floor as she beckoned Marcy forward. The necklaces slithered across the carpet and came to rest at Marcy's feet, where they coiled in on themselves like brightly colored snakes.

Venomous snakes, Marcy thought, taking a step back. "I'll be late for school."

"This will only take a minute."

"You should get dressed." Marcy stared just past her mother at the orange-and-black Calder lithograph on the far wall. It embarrassed her to see her mother in the nude, her once slender body now flaccid and lined with unflattering veins. "You'll catch cold."

Her mother laughed, incongruous tears streaming down her face. "You don't catch cold from being naked, silly girl. You catch cold from a virus. Everybody knows that."

"I have to go."

"No. Please don't leave me."

"I'll call Dad."

"No, you can't do that. He's in court all day today. A very important case. We can't disturb him."

"Then I'll call your doctor."

"He's on holiday." A note of triumph crept into her mother's voice, as if she'd been planning this for some time.

Marcy crossed the room toward the en suite bathroom, opened the medicine cabinet above the sink, and began rifling through the various creams and lotions for her mother's medication. "Where are your pills, Mom?"

"Gone."

"What do you mean, gone?"

"I flushed them down the toilet." Again, that disturbing note of triumph.

"Please tell me you're joking," Marcy said, lifting the cover off the toilet and staring into the empty bowl. The joke's on me, she thought.

"I stopped taking them weeks ago. I don't need them anymore, darling. They were just making me sick."

"They were making you *well*."

"Then I'd rather be sick," her mother said stubbornly.

"I have to go." Marcy walked briskly out of the bathroom, heading for the door. "I'm going to be late."

Her mother's hand on her arm stopped her. Another necklace rolled off her wrist and dropped to the floor, coming apart on impact, its delicate orange beads scattering in all directions. "Why don't you wear any makeup, sweetheart? A little blush or mascara would do wonders for you, take some of the emphasis away from your hair."

In response, Marcy grabbed a pair of shapeless gray sweatpants from the bed and thrust them against her mother's chest. "Get dressed, Mom."

"Please, won't you stay with me a little longer?"

"I can't. I'll see you later."

"There's so much cruelty in the world," her mother said,

triggering the start of another crying jag. "All those poor abused children and animals, all those people dying in poverty." She sank to the floor. "Sometimes I feel such despair."

I don't have the patience for your despair, Marcy thought. "I have to go. I have a French test first period."

"Then you should run along," her mother said, abruptly shifting gears, both hands waving Marcy out of the room. The remaining necklaces hanging from her wrists tumbled to the floor.

Marcy turned and fled the room.

"Good luck on your test," her mother called after her.

"You just left her like that?" Judith demanded when they passed each other in the school corridor later that morning.

"What was I supposed to do? I didn't see you sticking around."

"Whatever. Did you call Dad?"

"He was in court. I left him a message."

"She'll be all right," Judith said. "She always is."

"Yeah," Marcy agreed, thinking that maybe at lunch she'd go home to make sure.

Except that when it came time for lunch, she chose to go out with a bunch of friends to a nearby greasy spoon instead. If the experience of the past fifteen years had taught her anything, she reasoned, it was that nothing she could do would make any difference. Her mother would spend the next few weeks in a progressive downward spiral of crying jags and incoherent babbling, and then she'd likely disappear for a few days, maybe even weeks, living on the streets and sifting through garbage bins until somebody recognized her and brought her home.

And then the cycle would start all over again.

Except it didn't.

At two o'clock that afternoon she and Judith were summoned into the principal's office, where two uniformed officers were waiting to inform them that their mother had committed suicide by jumping off the roof of a ten-story office building near the busy intersection of Yonge and St. Clair.

"Don't feel guilty," Judith told her as they waited for their father to pick them up from school and take them home.

Marcy nodded. She didn't feel guilty about her mother's death. She felt relieved.

And for that, she'd felt guilty ever since.

"MARCY?" VIC CALLED softly from the bed. "What are you doing?"

Good question, Marcy thought, turning from the window where she'd been staring out at the closed curtains of the upstairs window of the bed and breakfast next door, trying to make sense of everything that had happened in the last twenty-four hours. Hell, why stop there? she wondered. How about the last twenty-four years? The last fifty? When had her life ever made any kind of sense? "What time is it?" she asked, wrapping her pink cotton bathrobe tighter around her. What was Vic Sorvino doing in her bed? How the hell had she let this happen? *Again*. What was the matter with her? Yes, he was an attractive man, and yes, he made her feel wanted and desirable and even beautiful. But she was hardly a teenager, for God's sake, easily seduced by a few well-chosen words. Had she no self-control whatsoever?

Vic reached for his watch on the tiny nightstand beside the bed. "A little after nine," he said, laying the watch back down and sitting up, the sheet falling across his naked torso. "You hungry?"

Marcy shook her head no. "You?"

"Not really. How's the cheek?"

"Okay."

"Think that eye could use some more ice?"

"No. I hear the raccoon look is very big for fall."

Vic chuckled, patted the space beside him. "Come back to bed."

"I don't think that's such a good idea."

"Why not?"

"I don't know." Marcy shrugged. "I don't know what I'm doing anymore." How did this happen? she wanted to shout. How did you end up in my bed?

Except she already knew the answer. This was all her doing. They'd barely made it up the stairs before her lips were reaching hungrily for his. She was tearing at his shirt before she'd even closed the door to her room. "I don't know what's the matter with me."

"There's absolutely nothing the matter with you," Vic said.

"I practically attacked you, for God's sake."

"I don't recall any protests on my part."

"I normally don't act that way." She laughed. "Except, of course, for the last time we were together."

"And you asked me what I'm doing here?" he said, sardonically.

"What *are* you doing here, Vic?"

The air turned suddenly serious. "I told you. I was worried about you."

"Don't be."

"Can't help it. It seems I've grown quite attached."

"That's probably not a very good idea."

"On the contrary, I think it's the best idea I've had in years."

"Why?"

"*Why?*" he repeated, shaking his head. "I'm not sure I can answer that. I don't know. Maybe I sense a kindred soul."

"Or maybe you just feel sorry for me."

"I feel many things for you," he shot back quickly. "Sorry isn't one of them."

Marcy smiled in spite of her attempt not to.

"Come back to bed," he said again.

What the hell? Marcy thought. Why not? It wasn't as if she had anything better to do. It was after nine, it was dark, everything hurt, she had a black eye and a sore cheek, and the odds of her finding Devon if she went out again tonight were almost nil. Plus she was exhausted. She lay down on the bed, Vic's arms immediately encircling her, his body fitting neatly around hers, as if it belonged there.

"We can go out again, if you'd like. Make the rounds of all the pubs," he said, as if reading her mind. "Maybe we'll see her."

Marcy shook her head, feeling Vic's breath warm against the back of her neck. "We won't see her."

"We might."

"No. She knows I'm here. She doesn't want me to find her."

"You don't know that for sure."

"I don't know much, that's for sure."

"Tell me what kind of trouble she was in," Vic said.

"What?"

"You told me in Dublin that Devon was in some sort of trouble."

"Yes," Marcy said. Had she told him that?

"With the police?"

"She'd gotten mixed up with some guy who was into cocaine, which of course was the last thing Devon needed. It just made her more depressed."

"What happened?"

"They went to a party one night. It got kind of loud. A neighbor called the police. They found drugs. Devon was charged along with everyone else. Our lawyer scheduled a meeting with the Crown attorney. He thought that because of Devon's condition, we might be able to persuade him to drop the charges if she'd agree to get help."

"And?"

"The weekend before that meeting was supposed to take place, Devon went up to our cottage." Marcy's voice caught in her throat. "She never came back."

"You'll find her, Marcy. You'll bring her home."

There was a long silence. "What if it's not her?" Marcy asked, the question she hadn't permitted herself even to contemplate until now. "What if Peter and Judith and the police are right? I only saw her for half a second through a window that was covered with beer ads. Maybe it wasn't her. Maybe she wasn't the girl I saw standing on the bridge. Maybe I'm as crazy as everyone thinks I am."

"I don't think you're crazy."

"You married your realtor," Marcy reminded him.

Vic laughed. "I guess sometimes we just want so badly to stop hurting, we do crazy things."

"Is that what I'm doing?"

"I don't know," he said. "But I'd like to be here when you find out."

Marcy flipped over onto her back, her eyes seeking his. "You really are the nicest man," she said as she reached for him again.

SHE AWOKE TO the sound of bells ringing.

Except they weren't bells, she realized, sitting up and looking toward her purse on the floor next to the bed. The ringing was coming from inside her bag. It was her phone.

Careful not to disturb the man still sleeping beside her, Marcy grabbed her purse, taking it with her into the bathroom and closing the door behind her, perching on the side of the tub, feeling the enamel cold against her bare skin. "Hello?" she whispered.

"I think I might have found her," Liam said without further preamble.

"What?" Was she dreaming? "How?"

"Well, I've been asking around, as you know, and it looks like it's finally paid off. I just got a call from an acquaintance of mine. He says that a girl matching your daughter's description recently rented a small house just down the way from his ex-wife. He saw her yesterday when he went to visit his kids."

"There are a lot of girls matching my daughter's description," Marcy told him.

"This one's named Audrey."

Marcy gasped, quickly covering her mouth with her hand and trying to contain her budding excitement. "Where is she?"

"A tiny village very close to here, called Youghal."

"Yawl?" Marcy repeated, pronouncing it as he had.

"I'll pick you up in twenty minutes," he said.

SIXTEEN

M ARCY WAS HALFWAY DOWN the main staircase of the Doyle Cork Inn when Vic's voice stopped her. She froze, looking back to see him standing at the top of the stairs, her pink cotton bathrobe draped carelessly across his shoulders and tied haphazardly around his waist, his legs and feet bare. He'd been sleeping so soundly, she hadn't wanted to disturb him. Or at least that's what she'd told herself as she was rushing to get dressed.

"Marcy, what's happening?"

"I have to go." Why hadn't she woken him up? she wondered now. Why hadn't she told him where she was going? Surely she owed him that much.

"Where? It's not even seven thirty." He looked around, as if despite his serious state of undress, he was considering coming after her.

"We might have found Devon," she said again, hurrying down the remaining stairs toward the front door.

"Who's 'we'?"

Was that the reason she hadn't told Vic where she was going? Because she didn't want him to see her with Liam? Or was it because she didn't want Liam to see her with Vic?

Sadie Doyle suddenly appeared in the small foyer, a bright green apron completely covering the front of her blue, flower-print dress, a large wooden spoon in her hand. "Good morning, Mrs. Taggart. Lovely day out there this morning. Will you be joining us for breakfast?" Her glance drifted toward the stairs, her face registering both surprise and amusement at the sight of a half-naked Vic Sorvino. "Oh. Hello."

"Give me a minute to get dressed," Vic urged Marcy, ignoring Sadie Doyle's salacious gaze. "I'll come with you."

"No. Please. I don't know if there's room."

"You understand that there's an extra charge for overnight guests," Sadie Doyle said to Marcy, her eyes remaining firmly on Vic.

"Fine. Whatever." Marcy's hand was already reaching for the door.

"Marcy, wait."

"I can't," Marcy said. "I'll call you later." Then she opened the door and rushed out onto the street.

"Marcy . . . ," she heard him call after her.

The street was already congested with heavy morning traffic. She didn't even know what kind of car Liam drove, Marcy realized, peering into the front window of each passing automobile. "Where are you, Liam?" she cried, looking up and down the busy street. Damn it, where was everybody going so early?

She checked her watch. Not quite twenty minutes had passed since Liam's surprise phone call. In that time she'd

washed, brushed her teeth, pulled on a pair of jeans and a gray
sweater, and tucked her uncombed hair into a jeweled clip at
the back. Stubborn tresses were now pushing against the clasp,
rebelling against their confinement. Several maverick curls had
already wormed their way to freedom, shooting off in a number
of different directions, like a fireworks display. There'd been no
time for makeup, just a hastily applied streak of lipstick as she
was tiptoeing from the room.

What difference did any of that make? Marcy told herself.
They'd found Devon. She was less than an hour away from seeing her daughter again.

She wondered again why she hadn't told Vic about Liam's
phone call and where she was going. What had stopped her?
She'd felt so safe, so comfortable, so secure in his arms. Her
breath had come freely and without pain for the first time in
months, maybe years. Despite everything that had happened,
despite everything experience had taught her, she'd actually
found herself starting to relax her guard.

And wasn't that when disaster always struck?

Maybe that was why she hadn't told him.

"Come on, Liam," she muttered now. Every minute counted.
A minute could mean the difference between finding her
daughter and losing her again. They couldn't afford to waste
any time.

I could call him, Marcy thought, reaching into her purse for
her cell phone, then deciding against it. She was overreacting.
She had to calm down. If there was a problem, Liam would phone.

In the months after Devon's supposed drowning, Marcy had
often dreamed her daughter had phoned and asked to meet her
somewhere—at Starbucks in the Spadina Village, beside the
Carole Tanenbaum vintage jewelry collection at Holt's, at the
ferryboat entrance to the Toronto Island. And always some-

thing kept coming up that stopped them from reuniting. Marcy would wake up day after day in a pool of frustrated tears. Eventually Peter stopped asking what her dreams were about. He soon gave up trying to comfort her altogether.

And he *had* tried, Marcy realized, pacing back and forth in front of the Doyle Cork Inn. At least for a little while. Until her pain had proved too much for him to bear. Until her grief had threatened to overwhelm them both.

And then he'd run.

Like I'm doing now, she thought, hearing a door open behind her and turning to see Vic, now fully dressed, step outside onto the inn's front landing, his blue eyes searching out hers, his kind face full of questions. "Marcy," he said, and she felt herself swaying toward him.

A series of loud, staccato honks filled the air as a small black car suddenly pulled to a stop beside her, its passenger door opening, a hand beckoning her inside. A handsome face with sleepy green eyes suddenly filled her frame of vision. "Get in," Liam said, taking off before she was fully seated, before she'd even had time to close the door.

Marcy turned back for a final glance in Vic's direction. What he must think of me, she thought, immediately chasing such thoughts from her mind. She had other more important things to think about now than Vic's hurt feelings. There would be plenty of time for explanations and amends after she was reunited with her daughter.

Devon, she thought, watching as Vic grew smaller, less distinct with each passing block. They'd found Devon.

How would Devon react when she found herself face-to-face with her mother? Would she fall into her arms or run screaming in the opposite direction?

"Sorry I'm late," Liam was saying, pulling Marcy from the

future back into the here and now. "The traffic's been fierce. My God, that's some shiner you've got."

Marcy's hand immediately shot to her face.

"Does it hurt?"

"No. Not too much anymore. I put ice on it." She pulled the seat belt around her and snapped it into place, then stole another quick glance behind her. Vic was no longer standing on the doorstep of the Doyle Cork Inn.

"I brought coffee," Liam said, handing Marcy a large paper cup as she settled back into her seat and tried to make herself comfortable. "Double cream, double sugar, which is the way I like it. Is that all right? I wasn't sure how you took it."

"Sounds great," she said, her hand shaking as she removed the dome-shaped lid from the cup and raised the steaming hot coffee to her lips.

"You nervous?" Liam asked.

Marcy nodded.

"Don't be. We should be in Youghal in about half an hour, depending on how long it takes to get out of the city. So take a deep breath, try to relax, and drink up."

Marcy did as instructed, inhaling deeply before taking a long swallow. The sugar immediately glommed onto her tongue.

"Too sweet?"

"It's fine," Marcy said, grimacing.

Liam laughed. "You're not a very good liar, are you?"

"Apparently not," she said, shuddering, and he laughed again.

"You don't have to lie to me, you know. And you don't have to drink coffee you don't like. In fact, you don't have to do anything you don't like."

He's so young, Marcy thought. "It's really not so bad," she said.

"And you really are a very bad liar."

"Okay. This is possibly the worst cup of coffee I've ever had in my entire life. How can you stand it so sweet? It's like glue."

"See? That was much better, wasn't it?"

"You're right. You should never lie. It takes up way too much energy." She took a deep breath, released it slowly. "Why do people lie anyway?"

Liam regarded her quizzically. "You're sure you want to have this discussion so early in the morning?"

"Why not? It doesn't look like we're going anywhere very fast." She glanced out the windshield at the cars piling up in front of them. Try to relax, she told herself in Liam's voice. They'd be in the village of Youghal soon enough. And after that she'd be with Devon. "I guess sometimes it's just easier to lie than to tell the truth," she said, answering her own question.

"Tell it or face it?" he asked.

She smiled in recognition of the subtle distinction. "Both."

"Is the truth really that difficult to deal with?"

"It can be."

"So you're saying that we use lies as a means of protection?"

"Sometimes."

"Protection or delusion?"

"Both," she said, as she'd said earlier. "Sometimes it's nicer to be lied to."

"Do you think we lie more to others or to ourselves?" he asked.

"I have no idea." Marcy shook her head. "You're right—it's too early in the morning to be having this conversation."

"I think you lied about liking the coffee because you didn't want to hurt my feelings," Liam said.

Marcy nodded. It was true. She'd spent her life being afraid of people's feelings.

"You don't have to worry about that," he told her.

"I don't?"

"No. Don't have any feelings."

Marcy laughed, the tension of the morning finally starting to dissipate. She tried not to stare at the pronounced curl of his eyelashes while noting that the black of his tousled hair was a perfect match for the black of his V-neck sweater. She wondered if this was accidental or deliberate. "I had no idea you were such a student of human nature."

"I'm a bartender," he said. "Same thing."

Marcy smiled, the smile stretching into her sore cheek, causing her to wince and bring her hand to her face.

"Cheek still hurts?"

"Just when I smile."

"It hurts when you're happy?" he asked, rephrasing her answer.

Yes, Marcy thought, although she said nothing. That's it exactly.

"I'm sorry I couldn't get down to the station yesterday," Liam apologized. "I wanted to, but Mr. Grogan was pretty upset about what happened, so I thought it best that I stay and help get things cleaned up. Then word got around about the fight and naturally we got real busy, so then it was impossible to get away. . . ."

"You don't owe me any explanations."

"I would have come if I could."

"Believe me, you've done more than enough."

"Were you able to get any sleep last night?" he asked.

"A bit." Marcy felt an involuntary stirring between her legs.

"I see he found you," Liam said, as if he'd felt it, too.

"What? Who?"

"That guy who's been asking about you. Vic something-or-other. He stopped by Grogan's again yesterday, asking more questions. Kelly told him about the altercation before I could stop her."

"Yes. He found me." Marcy swiveled around in her seat, stared out the rear window at the wall of cars and taxis behind them. Was Vic in one of them? she wondered. Was he following them?

"Stayed the night, did he?"

Marcy hesitated.

"Not that it's any of my business," he added.

"It's not what you think," she said.

A mischievous smile curled through Liam's lips. "Thought we were through lyin' to each other."

Marcy sighed. "Okay, it's *exactly* what you think."

He laughed. "Well, good for you."

"I'm not so sure about that."

"Why not? He's a nice-looking man, rich, obviously madly in love with you."

"What? No. That's ridiculous. We barely know each other. We just met last week. On a bus, for God's sake."

"Nothin' wrong with buses," Liam said. "I once had a fabulous affair with a woman I met on a bus."

"You did?"

He nodded. "I was just sittin' there, mindin' me own business, when this very attractive older woman gets on, takes the seat directly across from me, starts giving me the once-over. I ignored her at first. But then I realized I was just being rude, so I smiled. Just tryin' to be polite, you understand."

"I think I'm getting the picture," Marcy said, relieved the focus had shifted to him.

"And she smiled back. And next thing you know she's getting up out of her seat and coming over to sit next to me. And pretty soon we're talking and joking around, and her hand is on my knee and she's inviting me over to her house for a bite to eat, which suits me just fine since I've already missed my stop and I'm starvin'. And the whole thing just took off from there. Lasted almost a year."

"Why did it end?"

"Her husband gave her an ultimatum."

"She was married?"

"With six kids. You look shocked."

"I'm shocked that anyone with six children would have time for an affair," Marcy said. I'm shocked that anyone would have six children, she thought.

"People tend to make time for things that are important to them." He turned onto South Main Street, continuing east at a snail's pace through the flat of the city. "You never cheated on your husband?"

"No. Never."

"But he cheated on you."

"Yes."

"Not very smart, was he?"

Marcy smiled appreciatively.

"Anyway, I don't think he's the man for you."

"Well, clearly he didn't either."

"No, I don't mean your husband," Liam clarified. "I mean this other guy. Vic. I don't think he's right for you."

"What makes you say that?"

"Just a feeling I have."

"I thought you said you don't have feelings."

He laughed. "I have them. I just don't keep 'em."

It was Marcy's turn to laugh.

"I like it when you laugh," Liam said.

"So do I."

"You're really very beautiful, you know. Although . . ."

"Although?"

One hand left the wheel to reach behind her head and undo the clasp in her hair. "There. That's much better. Shake your head."

"What?"

"Shake your head. Let the curls loose."

"You're crazy." Marcy protested, but she did as she was told.

"Doesn't that feel much better?"

Marcy had to admit that it did, despite the renewed throbbing of her cheek from all the shaking of her head. "How do you know he's rich?" she asked.

"What?"

"You said that Vic was rich. How do you know that?"

Liam shrugged. "Well, when he came by the pub looking for you, he said he was staying at the Hayfield Manor Hotel, and you pretty much have to sell the farm to stay at that place. Did you tell him where you were goin' this morning?"

"No."

"Why not?"

"I don't know."

"I do."

Marcy stared at him without speaking. Enlighten me, her eyes said.

"I don't think you fully trust him."

"What?" Was he right? Was that the real reason she hadn't told him?

"You want to know what else I think?" Liam asked.

"What?"

"I think I'm jealous."

He laughed and Marcy laughed with him.

"I'm serious," he said, the laughter coming to an abrupt halt. "I'm jealous."

"Why would you be jealous?"

"Because it should have been me last night," he said simply.

Marcy said nothing, although her heart was beating so fast it threatened to burst from her chest.

"He really doesn't mean anything to you?" Liam asked.

Marcy shook her head, turning away from him to observe the slowly passing scenery in a concerted effort to calm down. Would they never get out of this damn city?

"We should be on the coast road in a few more minutes," Liam said, as if reading her mind. "Why don't you try to catch a bit of sleep before we get there?"

"I *am* kind of tired," Marcy admitted, her head spinning.

"Lean back, close your eyes, think pleasant thoughts," he instructed her, and for the second time that morning, Marcy did as she was told, leaning back against the black leather seat and allowing her eyes to shut.

Almost immediately she saw Devon walking toward her, her long, thin arms extended. In the next instant, she was caught in her daughter's surprisingly strong embrace, Devon's smooth skin a soothing balm against her sore cheek. "Mommy," her daughter whispered lovingly in her ear, the word a soft caress.

My baby.

"Marcy."

"Hmm?"

"Marcy," Liam said again as Devon evaporated in her arms. "Marcy, wake up."

Marcy opened her eyes to see Liam's smiling face looming above hers. It took her a second to realize the car had stopped and they were no longer moving.

"We're here," Liam said.

SEVENTEEN

W E'RE IN YOUGHAL?"

"Yes. Are you okay?"

"I'm fine. I can't believe I fell asleep."

"You were exhausted."

"What time is it?"

"Eight forty-five. The traffic was absolutely brutal. Over an hour to go twenty miles. Bloody ridiculous."

Marcy looked at the vast expanse of majestic beach stretched out in front of her, trying to get her bearings. "Where are we exactly?"

"Just outside the town walls, which, incidentally, date back to the thirteenth century. That's the Blackwater River straight ahead." Liam pointed toward the breathtaking expanse of water. A wide laneway of grass and a pedestrian walkway, along which an impressive number of would-be bathers were already walking, separated them from the river. "It flows into St. George's Channel to the east and the Celtic Sea to the south. This here's Green Park Beach, which is just minutes from the center of Youghal." He smiled sheepishly. "Inside every Irishman is a tour guide just waiting to get out."

Marcy smiled, thinking that it wasn't all that surprising that Devon might have found refuge here. It was an undeniably beautiful spot, unspoiled and serene. Even a cursory glance around was enough to reveal a plethora of boating activities— already powerboats were disturbing the water's smooth surface, leaving a couple of dinghies to bob up and down in their wake. In the distance a yacht was cruising slowly by. Across the way, Marcy noticed a sign advertising whale watching, another touting the joys of wreck diving. Lots for Devon to do, she thought. Or she could rent a canoe and paddle for hours in quiet solitude up and down the coast.

Except that Devon was essentially a city girl at heart. Could she really have found the happiness she craved in a tiny fishing port on the edge of nowhere? "Where does my daughter live?" she asked Liam.

"Marcy . . ."

"Don't say it."

"You have to be prepared," he said anyway. "There's a chance it might not be her."

"You said she was here," Marcy insisted.

"I said I was told that a girl matching your daughter's description had been spotted here in Youghal—"

"A girl named Audrey."

"Yes. But I don't want you to get your hopes up too high. You need to be prepared in case we're wrong."

"We're not wrong."

"Hopefully, no."

"Where is she, Liam?"

"Within walking distance."

"Then what are we waiting for? Let's go." Marcy pushed open the car's passenger door and stepped onto the pavement, a strong wind almost flattening her against the side of the car, blowing her hair into her eyes and mouth. She was still trying to remove some errant strands from between her teeth when Liam came around to her side of the car and took her by the elbow, guiding her away from the river and across the street toward the town.

"It won't be so windy once we get away from the water."

"So, tell me more about Youghal," she said as they walked toward the town's center. Not that she was particularly curious about the place itself, but she knew it was important to keep her mind occupied and her heart rate steady. She was already almost giddy with anticipation, her knees all but knocking together with suppressed joy. It was important to steady her nerves, to stay as calm as she could. The last thing she wanted to do was come face-to-face with her daughter, only to pass out.

"Really?" Liam's green eyes sparkled. "You want the guided tour?"

"Knock yourself out."

"Okay. But it'll cost you."

Marcy smiled as Liam cleared his throat and pushed back his shoulders.

"Youghal is the county's major coastal town and leading beach resort," he began. "Basically, it's a fishing and market village whose main claim to fame is that Sir Walter Raleigh was once its mayor, way back in 1588. Supposedly he planted Ireland's first potatoes here, as well as introducing tobacco to the locals." They turned a corner. "We are now entering the city center," Liam continued in his most sonorous voice. "Like many coastal villages, Youghal residents are quite fond of brightly colored houses, like the ones you'll see lining the quaint, narrow streets leading down to the water." He directed her around a line of compact cars that were parked along the sidewalk. "Straight ahead of you is the famous clock tower, which was built in 1777 as a jail to imprison renegade Catholics. It was routinely used as a torture chamber and was long regarded as a symbol of terror and tyranny."

Marcy stared at the beautiful, gray stone, five-story structure with well-stocked flower boxes adorning its eight small windows. A high arch allowed cars to pass right through the clock tower's center.

"Not so scary anymore, is it?" Liam said.

"It's very beautiful."

"Yes, I guess it is. This way," he said, leading her past a series of shops and sandwich bars painted a host of garish colors—green trim on blue stucco; orange shutters in the middle of canary-yellow walls; bright, butterscotch-colored door panels and turquoise columns surrounding tomato-red front doors. "See that sign?" He pointed to a sign in the shape of an arrow that said SHOPPING in large bold letters. Directly beneath it was the Irish word "*Siopadóireacht.*"

"What's that?" Marcy asked.

"I believe you would call that a return to our roots," he told her, explaining that while most people in Ireland still preferred to speak English, there had been an enthusiastic revival of the Irish language in recent years.

Marcy thought of the time she and Peter had taken their kids on a short holiday to Quebec City, where French was the predominant language and all storefronts and street signs were written solely in French. Her son, Darren, had taken it all in stride. Devon, however, was indignant. "Aren't we in Canada anymore?" she'd demanded impatiently, struggling to understand where she was. "What happened to English?" Marcy wondered how her daughter was managing here in this small coastal village, where ancient Gaelic was enjoying a hardy comeback.

They veered off the main street, immediately finding themselves on a street so narrow they could barely walk side by side. Still, cars somehow managed to squeeze by them at impressive speeds. "Watch yourself," Liam said, cautioning her, on more than one occasion.

"Are we almost there?"

"Almost."

Tiny row houses lined the cobblestone street, each a different vibrant hue. Most were one-story homes containing a single upstairs bedroom above the front door. "Charming" was probably the word most often used to describe them, Marcy thought. Still, Devon had grown up in a spacious house in Hogg's Hollow, a decidedly upscale residential area of Toronto. Her bedroom alone was probably the same square footage as most of these homes. Even then, she was always complaining about not having enough room, enough space, enough privacy. Could she really be content in such confined quarters?

One narrow, ancient street twisted effortlessly into the next. Occasionally someone opened a window to yell something across the street at a neighbor. Bicycles frequently whizzed by, ducking between cars both moving and parked right up against the houses. "Careful," Liam warned again.

"Which way?" Marcy asked when they stopped for traffic at a busy intersection.

"Down this street." Liam pointed to his right.

"Amazing how much traffic there is."

"You don't have traffic in Toronto?"

"Oh, we have plenty of traffic. Just that the streets are wider."

"And paved with gold?" Liam asked playfully.

"Yes, absolutely. All Toronto streets are paved with gold."

"I think I'd like to see that," Liam stated. "Would you be my tour guide when I come to Toronto?"

When, Marcy noted. Not *if.*

"Okay, here we are," he was saying in the next breath, stopping in front of a pale blue, two-story house at the corner.

"This is it?"

"No. That one over there." Liam pointed with his chin across the street at a pink house with green trim and a purple front door.

"That's where she lives?" Pink was Devon's least-favorite color. Too girly, she'd always proclaimed, even as a child refusing to wear the pink dresses Marcy had bought her.

"Fifteen Goat Street," Liam said, pulling a scrap of paper out of his pocket and checking the address. "That's what I've got written down."

Marcy took a deep breath, feeling her legs grow weak.

"Are you all right?"

"I just can't imagine Devon living in a pink house on a street named Goat."

"Well, there's only one way to find out." He stepped off the curb.

"Wait. What if she's not home?"

"Then we'll go somewhere for a cup of tea and come back later."

"What if she won't see me?"

"We won't give her that choice. Marcy," he said patiently, "what is it? What's the matter?"

"I'm scared."

"Don't be." He took her hand, led her across the street to the red front door. "Do you want to knock or shall I?"

"I'll do it." Marcy lifted the shamrock-shaped brass knocker and banged it against the door.

No response.

"She's not home," Marcy whispered, fighting back tears.

"Try again. I thought I heard something."

Marcy put her ear to the door. "I don't hear anything."

"Try again."

Marcy knocked louder.

Still no response.

"What if she looked out the window and saw me?" Marcy asked. "What if she saw it was me and now she won't answer the door?"

In response, Liam took the knocker from her hand and banged it adamantly against the wood.

"She's not here," Marcy said, deflated.

"Wait," Liam said. "I'm sure I hear someone moving around."

"She won't answer. She won't see me."

"Just a minute," a woman's voice suddenly called from inside. "I'll be right there. Hold your horses."

"Oh, God," Marcy said, holding her breath as the door fell open.

A young woman with short blond hair and wide, questioning eyes stood on the other side. She looked from Marcy to Liam and then back to Marcy. "Can I help you?" she asked.

Marcy opened her mouth to speak, but no words came out.

"We're looking for Audrey," Liam said in her stead.

"She in some sort of trouble?" the young woman asked.

"No," he replied. "We just want to talk to her."

"What about?"

"Who are you?" Liam asked.

"Who are *you*?" the girl asked in return.

"My name's Liam. This is Marcy Taggart, Audrey's mother."

The young woman's eyes shot to Marcy. "Audrey's mother, is it?"

"Yes," Marcy said, more a sigh than a word. Then stronger, "I'm Dev— Audrey's mother."

"Well, fancy that. Audrey," she called toward the dark center of the house. "You better get over here. There's someone to see you."

"Yeah? Who is it? I'm a little busy at the moment, trying to rescue your muffins."

"Been cooking," the girl explained sheepishly, her eyes never leaving Marcy. "The muffins can wait," she called back. "You've got a visitor."

"Who is it?" Cautious footsteps approached.

"See for yourself."

A young woman stepped out of the dark hall into a warm spotlight of sun.

Marcy took one look at the girl's long brown hair and sad dark eyes. Then she fainted in Liam's arms.

"WE NEED TO talk," Marcy said to her daughter.

She was standing in the doorway to Devon's bedroom. Outside, a cold rain was coming down in sheets and a strong October wind was blowing the remaining orange and red leaves off the tall maple tree on the front lawn and splattering them across the windows of Devon's room.

"I don't want to talk," Devon said, plopping down on her unmade bed.

"Then you don't have to," Marcy said, stepping gingerly into the room and navigating her way carefully around the discarded clothes covering the beige carpet. Marcy recognized some of the items as recent purchases from a shopping trip she'd taken Devon on, hoping to cheer her up. The clothes now lay crumpled on the floor, their price tags still in place. "I'll talk. You listen."

Devon shrugged. She was wearing a pair of yellow flannel pajamas that Marcy had bought her the previous Christmas. The clerk had forgotten to remove the plastic tag filled with dye that stores often affixed to clothes in an effort to cut down on shoplifting, but Marcy had somehow made it out of the store without setting off any bells and whistles. The tag now clung to the cuff of Devon's pajama bottoms. Devon had never bothered taking them back to the store and asking someone to remove it. Marcy had once remarked that it looked like one of those electronic ankle bracelets the courts sometimes made people wear when they were placed under house arrest, which seemed prophetic, even appropriate, she thought, under the circumstances.

"You're in a lot of trouble, Devon."

"I'm not in trouble." Devon leaned back against her pillows, her eyes already glazing over with boredom. "Our lawyer's going to get me off."

"We don't know that for sure."

"He got me out on bail, didn't he?"

"That's different."

"It wasn't my fault. I didn't know about the drugs."

"I don't believe you," Marcy told her.

"Naturally." Devon sniffed dismissively.

"Even if I did believe you, it's irrelevant. The fact is you were there. You were with a man the police have identified as a known drug dealer—"

"His name is Tony and he's not a drug dealer."

"I don't care what he is. You're not to see him again."

"What?"

"This is not up for discussion."

"The hell it isn't."

"I'm talking. You're listening. Remember?" Marcy told her.

"I'm over twenty-one. You can't tell me what to do."

"As long as you live in this house, I can and I will."

Devon jumped off the bed, flew toward her mother, arms flailing. "Then I guess I'll just have to move out."

Marcy didn't flinch, her toes digging into the bottoms of her shoes as if to root her in place. "I remind you that one of the conditions of your bail is that you continue to live at home."

"So now you're my jailer?"

"I'm your mother."

"Yeah. Great job of that you're doing."

"This is not about me."

"No? This is your fault, you know. It's your rotten genes I inherited."

"And I'm sorry for that. I really am. Yes, you got dealt a rotten hand. Believe me, I wish I could wave some sort of magic wand and have all your pain disappear. But I can't. And you're not a child anymore, Devon. You're an adult. At some point you have to play the cards you were given, you have to start taking responsibility for your own life."

"Which is exactly what I'm trying to do."

"How? By hanging around with losers, by getting arrested, by doing drugs?"

"I thought you wanted me to take drugs."

"Taking your medication is hardly the same thing."

"You're right. Your drugs make me feel bad. My drugs make me feel good."

"Devon, this is ridiculous. You're acting like a twelve-year-old."

"I *am* twelve years old! Like it or not, Mommy, that's all I am."

"Well, I don't like it!" Marcy shot back, her patience spent. "I don't like it one damn bit. I'm tired of being the mother of a twelve-year-old child. I want to be the mother of a twenty-one-year-old woman. Do you hear me, Devon? Do you understand? I'm tired of parenting." She burst into a flood of angry, bitter tears. "I've been a parent since I was a child, and I'm sick of it. I can't do it anymore. I don't *want* to do it anymore. Do you hear me?"

She braced herself for Devon's fiery response, another war of words she'd inevitably lose, leaving her limp and exhausted, her body covered with invisible scars and bruises. Instead Devon wrapped her arms around her mother and held her close. "I hear you, Mommy," she said softly.

"CAN YOU HEAR me?" a voice was asking from somewhere in the distance. "Marcy, can you hear me?"

Marcy opened her eyes to find two worried faces staring down at her. She pushed herself up onto her elbows and looked around. She was lying on a small, brown velvet sofa in the middle of a tiny room. There was a fireplace on the opposite wall and a faded orange chair in the far corner. A standing lamp with a pleated shade and a water-stained coffee table completed the decor. The walls were covered in beige-flowered wallpaper. Matching curtains covered the front window. "What happened?" she asked warily.

"You fainted," Liam told her.

Marcy swung her feet onto the worn wool carpet of the

floor. "Where's Audrey?" she asked the young blond woman
standing beside Liam.

Audrey suddenly appeared in the doorway, the tray in her
hands holding a steaming pot of tea, four mugs, and a plate of
freshly baked muffins. "I'm right here," she said.

EIGHTEEN

"S O, HOW LONG HAVE you been living in Youghal?" Liam asked as they sipped their tea. He was sitting on the sofa beside Marcy. The blond girl, who was about thirty and whose name was Claire, had pulled the orange chair closer to the coffee table and was curled up inside it. Audrey sat on the floor at her feet.

"Just a few months," Claire answered. "There's still a lot we want to do with the place—get rid of this awful wallpaper for a start—but we'll just have to take it one step at a time. How are the muffins? They any good?"

"Delicious," Liam said.

"We still haven't quite got the hang of the oven. It's very temperamental. Isn't it, Audrey?"

Audrey nodded. "It's a right pain," she said, tucking some

hair behind her right ear and staring at Marcy. "You haven't touched anything."

"I'm sorry," Marcy said, pushing the reluctant words from her mouth. Her throat was so dry, it hurt to speak, let alone eat.

"Don't like cranberries?" Claire asked.

"No, I love cranberries."

"Course, they're frozen. But that's all right. Can't have everything fresh. Especially in this part of the world." Claire took a big bite of her muffin, followed by a sip of her tea. "How's the tea?" she asked.

"Perfect," Liam said.

Were they really talking about tea and cranberries? Marcy wondered, lifting her steaming mug to her lips and forcing herself to take a sip. The hot liquid raced down her throat as if someone had taken a match to a fuse. I'm on fire, she thought. Any second now, I'm going to implode.

"So, you like to cook, do you?" Liam asked, seemingly determined to keep the inane conversation going.

"Well, *I* do," Claire answered, reaching over to give Audrey an affectionate cuff on the side of her head. "Can't say the same for this one here."

"Hey, watch it there," Audrey said, grabbing Claire's hand and holding it.

Marcy felt her eyes widen and she tried to look away. But it was too late. Audrey had already taken note of her response.

"Something wrong?" she asked.

Marcy shrugged, as if to say, *No, of course not. Anything you choose to do is fine with me.*

"A few of the neighbors got their noses out of joint when we first moved in," Audrey said with a laugh. "Afraid we'd turn all their daughters into raving lesbos."

"Yeah, but they've more or less all come around."

"Claire won them over with her muffins," Audrey said, beaming.

"Guess you've got to expect that sort of thing in a town the size of Youghal," Claire said.

"What made you settle here?" Liam asked.

Both women sighed. "Don't know, really," Claire answered for both of them. "I was working in a bakery in Dublin. Audrey was a teller in a bank."

"Which I hated," Audrey interjected.

"We came here on a holiday about a year ago, decided we liked the look of the place, thought we'd give it a go."

"Thought we might be able to save some money, open up a bakery of our own one day." Audrey twisted her head around to smile at Claire.

"It'll happen," Claire said. "You'll see."

"Well, your muffins really are delicious." Liam motioned toward the tray on the coffee table. "Do you mind if I have another?"

"Please, help yourself."

What's he doing? Marcy wondered. Why are we prolonging this agony? Haven't we made enough small talk for one afternoon? Can't we just get out of here?

"So, what made you think my Audrey might be your daughter?" Claire asked, as if sensing Marcy's restlessness.

Tears immediately filled Marcy's eyes and she bit into her muffin to muffle the sob that was building in her throat.

"I'm afraid that was my fault," Liam said.

"It's nobody's fault," Marcy told him.

"We were acting on my information."

"You were told a young woman matching Devon's description lived here and that her name was Audrey." Marcy took a deep breath, turning her attention back to the two young women, both of whom had been watching their exchange with unsuppressed curiosity. "My daughter disappeared about two years ago," she explained. "Liam has been kind enough to help me look for her. We thought we might have found her."

"That's why you fainted when you saw me?" Audrey asked.

"Liam warned me not to get my hopes up," Marcy said. "He said I should be prepared you might not be Devon, but I . . ."

"You couldn't help it," Claire said with obvious sympathy.

"I couldn't help it," Marcy agreed. I couldn't help so many things, she thought.

"Do I look like her at all?" Audrey asked.

"Superficially, yes, I guess so. You're about the same age, same height, same long, brown hair."

"There's a lot of girls with long brown hair."

"Yes, there are."

"Not all named Audrey, though," Liam said.

"You must be horribly disappointed," Claire said.

"I'm getting used to it," Marcy told her.

"What happened to her?" Audrey asked. "Your daughter, I mean. She just wandered off one day?"

"Something like that," Marcy told her, not wanting to get into the particulars.

"You have a fight or something?" Audrey pressed her, not willing to let it go so easily.

"Or something," Marcy whispered.

"Audrey"—Claire chastised her—"it's really none of our business."

"Sorry. It's just that it's a bit like what happened with my mum and me, isn't it?"

"You didn't just wander off," Claire said.

"No, but I haven't spoken to her in six months."

"Audrey's parents weren't my biggest fans," Claire explained.

"It wasn't you. It would have been anyone."

"They couldn't accept the fact that their daughter . . ."

"I come from a very traditional Catholic family," Audrey clarified. "I have four brothers, all big, strapping men. . . ." She giggled. "They'd keep trying to fix me up with their friends, but I just wasn't interested. Naturally I assumed something must be wrong with me."

"Then she met me," Claire said proudly.

"Well, no. First I met Janice."

Claire made a face. "Oh, yes, Janice. But that wasn't serious."

"No, but it *was* an eye-opener. I tried to tell my parents, but they weren't having any of it. They said it was a phase, that it would pass, that I had to go to church and beg God for forgiveness, ask Him for guidance."

"And He guided her straight to me," Claire said with a laugh.

"Yes." Audrey's smile stretched from ear to ear. "My mum had asked me to pick up some pastries on my way home from work. Someone at the bank recommended this great little bakery that had just opened up around the corner. . . ."

Her face was wider than Devon's, her jaw more pronounced, Marcy was thinking as Audrey spoke. She'd known the second she saw her that Audrey wasn't her child.

"Her parents were furious," Claire said.

"They refused to even meet Claire."

"They'd hang up on me when I called."

"They told me I was going straight to hell."

"Instead we came to Youghal," Claire said happily.

"Does your mother know where you are?" Marcy asked.

Audrey's face immediately clouded over. "I told her we were leaving town, that I'd call her when we settled in."

"And have you?"

Audrey shook her head, her brown hair coming loose from

her ear to obscure the entire lower half of her face. "Don't really see much point in it," she mumbled. "They're never going to change."

"When you said you were Audrey's mum, I almost wet my pants," Claire said.

"They've never actually met," Audrey explained.

"It's so weird, the way things work out, isn't it?" Claire commented.

"That it is," Liam said, rising to his feet. "And now I think we should probably go, let these two charming women get on with things. . . ."

"I think you should call her," Marcy said, remaining seated. "Tell her where you are. At least let her know you're safe."

"She doesn't care."

"She's your mother," Marcy said forcefully. "She cares."

There was silence.

"We really should go," Liam said.

Marcy pushed herself to her feet. "Thank you for all your kindness."

"Not to mention the fabulous muffins."

"Wait. Let me give you some to take home." Claire ran toward the kitchen at the back of the house.

"No, really, that's not necessary. You've done more than enough."

"Sorry it didn't work out the way you hoped," Audrey said as Claire returned with a bag of muffins and handed it to Liam.

"Call your mother," Marcy said before following Liam out the door.

"WHEN DEVON WAS little, about two, maybe three," Marcy was telling Liam as they neared the outskirts of Cork, "she took her

Magic Markers and drew all over the living room walls. I'd just had them painted. I mean, the workers had literally just finished up the day before. And I was on the phone with Judith. I think she was between husbands at the time. At any rate, there was some sort of major trauma going on in her life, and I was trying to calm her down, get her to see it wasn't the end of the world. Whatever. It doesn't matter. The point is that I was on the phone and not paying enough attention to Devon, who'd been quietly drawing at the kitchen table with her Magic Markers, and at some point she got up and went into the living room without my noticing. And then suddenly she was back, grinning from ear to ear. And she said, 'Mommy, come see what I did.' She always called me 'Mommy.' Even when she was all grown-up. I always loved that." Tears filled her eyes. "Anyway, she grabbed my hand and led me into my freshly painted living room and showed me, very proudly—oh, she was so proud— what she'd done." Marcy took a deep breath, not sure whether or not she could continue. She'd never told this story to anyone. She'd been too ashamed. "And I saw all these black and red and green swirls all over my new, eggshell-colored walls. I mean, she'd scribbled over every spot of wall she could reach. And I'm looking from this happy little face to these graffiti-covered walls, and I'm thinking of all the money I've just spent, and I feel this anger rising inside me like lava from a volcano, and this little voice in my head is telling me to stay calm, not to overreact, that I might be able to wash it off, and that even if I can't, I can get the painters to come back and redo it, it's not the end of the world, all the things I'd just been saying to Judith. And I could see how thrilled Devon was, and that she was waiting for me to tell her how beautiful her drawings were, and I knew, *I knew,* that's what I should do, that I could wait till later to explain that we don't draw on walls, that sort of thing, what all the advice books tell you to do. But even as I was thinking those things, I could feel my anger building and the muscles in my face starting to twitch with rage, and I watched Devon's face, that beautiful little face filled with so much pride and happiness, I watched it literally dissolve in front of my eyes, like it was melting. And I heard this awful voice, *my* voice, screaming, 'What have you done? My God, what have you done?' And Devon was crying, begging me to stop yelling. But I couldn't. And I marched into the dining room and saw she'd done the same thing in there, which just set me off again. I'm screaming and carrying on. And suddenly she stopped dead and grabbed her stomach, like she'd been punched, and then she turned around so that her back was to me, and doubled over, as if I'd physically assaulted her, and she let out a wail, God, this awful wail, I'll never forget it, like a wounded animal. It was horrible. It was so horrible."

"Marcy," Liam said gently, reaching for her hand, "Devon didn't run away because you yelled at her when she was two years old for scribbling on the walls."

"She was only a baby. I was the adult. I didn't have to yell. . . ."

"No, you didn't. But you did. So what? It was two decades ago. Devon probably doesn't even remember it."

"There were other times."

"What—that you yelled at her? That you were less than perfect? You're a human being, for God's sake. Human beings make mistakes. We yell when we shouldn't, and we probably *don't* yell when we *should*. I'm sure there were plenty of times you more than made it up to her."

Marcy refused to allow herself to be comforted by his words. "When Devon was about eight, I decided it would be a good idea for her to take piano lessons. We had this baby grand piano that Peter had inherited from his mother, which just sat there in the corner gathering dust, and occasionally Devon would go over and bang on it, so I thought it would be a good idea for her to learn to play. She seemed keen, so we hired this guy to come over and give her lessons. She was a natural. Except I noticed that when her teacher wasn't there, when he wasn't actually sitting beside her, she was hopeless. I'd tell her to practice and she'd just sit there and bang at the keyboard. And I'd get so frustrated—"

Liam interrupted. "Marcy, why are you doing this?"

"That's exactly what I'd say to Devon. *Why are you doing this? You know the right notes. They're right there in front of you. Just read the music.* Well, of course, it turned out she *didn't* know the right notes. She *couldn't* read the music. Her teacher had never taught her the basic fundamentals, like how to tell one note from the next, so she'd just watch what he played and copy his fingers. And of course by the next day, she couldn't remember anymore and that's why she'd just flail away. . . ."

"When I was five, my mother caught me in the kitchen, eating the pie she'd baked for company that night, and she came at me with a meat cleaver," Liam said.

"What?"

"Well, she insists it was a wooden spoon, but I'm sure it was a meat cleaver. And once she gave me a spanking for putting salt in the sugar bowl and ruinin' her morning coffee. And another time she hollered at me—and let me tell you, nobody could holler like my mother—just because I told her I'd like to throw my baby brother under the wheels of a bus. Not because I did it, mind you, just because I said I'd like to. How's that for a miserable excuse for a human being? I tell you, I'm scarred for life."

"You're minimizing what I did," Marcy said.

"And you're blowin' it all out of proportion. For God's sake, Marcy. How do you get out of bed in the mornin' with the weight of all that guilt on your shoulders?"

It's not easy, Marcy thought. "I expected too much from her."

"So what? Big deal. You expected too much. What about your son? Do you expect too much from him, too?"

The mention of her son caught Marcy off guard, as it always did. Devon had a way of taking up every inch of space in her brain, crowding her brother out. "Darren is different." Marcy pictured her son's cherubic little face as it passed through awkward adolescence on its way to handsome young man. "He was always smiling, always happy when he was little. He never gave me any trouble." I neglected him terribly, she realized. "Devon took all my energy." She frowned. "What is it they say about the squeaky wheel?"

"Haven't a clue. But I *do* know that what's done is done. The past is over and there isn't a damn thing we can do about it. So what's the point of beatin' yourself up about something you can't change? Unless, of course, that *is* the point."

"What's that supposed to mean?"

"Well, maybe you like wallowin' in all that guilt because it allows you to stay stuck in the past, prevents you from movin' forward. Maybe that's what you want."

Marcy felt a twinge of outrage poking at her side. "You think I want to be miserable?"

"Don't know," he said again, his voice deliberately provocative. "Do you?"

"I just want things to be normal," Marcy said, burying her face in her hands. That was all she'd ever wanted. "Maybe if I'd—"

"No," Liam said, suddenly pulling to the side of the road

and shutting off the car's engine. "No more maybes." He kissed her before she could say another word.

The kiss was passionate and grew even more urgent as it progressed. Marcy felt strong hands at her waist, on her cheeks, in her hair. So different from the way Vic had kissed her just last night, she found herself thinking.

What's happening? she wondered, feeling dizzy and out of breath as she pulled away from Liam's embrace.

Liam apologized immediately.

"Why did you do that?"

"I've been wanting to kiss you since the first minute I laid eyes on you."

"You have? Why?"

Liam looked as confused as she felt. "God, Marcy. Do you really have to ask?"

Marcy's head was spinning. She stared at the empty field by the side of the road in order to steady it. "Where are we?" she asked, realizing she had absolutely no idea where they were.

"Just outside the city limits. I'm really sorry," he said again.

"No, it's my fault."

Liam smiled. "Not everything is your fault, Marcy." Then, tenderly, "Things will work out in the end, you'll see."

"And if they don't?"

"Then it's not the end."

Marcy laughed through her tears. "How'd you get to be so smart?" She reached out to touch his hand, then thought better of it. As comforting as his arms were, as thrilling as his embrace was, Marcy realized they weren't the arms she wanted around her. She pictured Vic standing outside the door of the Doyle Cork Inn, his wounded eyes following Liam's car down the busy street. Would he be waiting for her when she got back?

As if he sensed what she was thinking, Liam took a deep

breath, straightened his shoulders, and restarted the car's engine, waiting for a break in the traffic before pulling back onto the main road. Within minutes, they were mired in traffic, the sound of jackhammers pounding against the sides of their heads.

"Damn construction," Liam muttered.

"There's certainly enough of it going on."

"My father used to work in construction," he said, obviously straining for conversation as they crawled toward Western Road. "He was killed twelve years ago when a building he was working on collapsed. Never knew what hit him, as they say."

"I'm so sorry."

"The company claimed it was his own damn fault. He should have been wearin' a helmet, that sort of thing. They paid the funeral expenses, but other than that, we got nothin'." He shook his head. "Oh, well. What's done is done, right? Think I remember a very wise man once saying that there's no point beatin' yourself up over things you can't change."

"He *is* a very wise man," Marcy said.

"Just not the man you want." Liam pulled to a stop in front of the Doyle Cork Inn.

"Liam . . ."

"It's all right. It'll all work out in the end," he said, green eyes twinkling. "And if it doesn't . . ."

Marcy got out of the car. It's not the end, she finished silently.

NINETEEN

SADIE DOYLE WAS WAITING for her in the inn's small reception area, hands on her wide hips. "That'll be an extra fifty euros for your guest," she announced before Marcy was through the door.

"Is he still here?" Marcy asked hopefully, her eyes running up the stairs toward her room.

Sadie shook her head, the tightly set curls of her gray-flecked, reddish-blond hair barely moving. "Nah. He left hours ago. Got tired of waitin' around, I guess."

Marcy tried to mask her disappointment with a smile. What did I expect? she wondered. "Did he leave a message?" she asked hopefully.

Another vigorous shake of Sadie's head, the motion dislodging the stale scent of too much hair spray. "I'll just tack that extra charge onto your bill, shall I?"

"Yes." Marcy walked toward the stairs.

"Where'd you run off to in such a hurry anyway?" Sadie asked, disguising the question she'd obviously been dying to ask as an afterthought. "You find your daughter?"

This time it was Marcy's turn to shake her head. She proceeded up the stairs in silence, deciding to call Vic as soon as she got to her room. Liam had said he was staying at the posh Hayfield Manor Hotel, which was relatively close by. She'd ring his room, apologize profusely for running out on him again, and tell him about what had happened in Youghal. He'd understand and forgive her without a second's hesitation. They'd arrange to meet for dinner. He'd stay the night, or maybe this time she'd stay with him, spend the night in the warmth of his arms, surrounded by luxury. And this time she wouldn't skip out in the wee hours of the morning or abandon him without so much as a word of good-bye. She'd been wrong to treat him in such a cavalier fashion, wrong to exclude him when all he wanted was to help. She'd make it up to him tonight, she was thinking as she strode purposefully down the hall toward her room, key in hand, her hand reaching for the door.

It took several twists of the key until she succeeded in unlocking the door, and then it suddenly swung open, as if pushed. Marcy froze, thinking for an instant that she must have the wrong room. This couldn't be hers. "Oh, my God," she gasped, slowly stepping over the threshold, her eyes flying from one corner of the room to the next, trying to absorb what they were seeing. "Oh, my God," she said again, louder this time. Then, "No. No."

The room looked as if a terrible storm had swept through it. Everything was in violent disarray. The sheets had been ripped from the bed, the mattress dislodged and left dangling precariously across the bed frame. It had been slashed down its center, and its stuffing sprouted across its surface like weeds. Every drawer in the place had been opened and upended. The closet had been emptied, her clothes ripped from their hangers and left in a crumpled heap on the carpet. Even her toiletries hadn't been spared, she noted, glancing into the bathroom, the bottles smashed, the tubes emptied, her toothbrush snapped in half. "What the—" Her words froze in her throat as she approached the bed, her shaking hand reaching for a pair of panties whose crotch had been slashed repeatedly with either scissors or a knife. "Oh, God," she exclaimed in mounting horror, realizing that every item of her clothing had been violated in some way: her underwear, her nightgown, her blouses, her sweaters, her black slacks, even her trench coat. Nothing had escaped mutilation. Everything had been slashed, shredded, gutted. "No!" she shouted at the flowered walls. "No, no, no, no!"

She heard heavy footsteps on the stairs, followed by a shrill scream. Then more footsteps, faster, nimbler than the ones before. A whoosh of air behind her. A sharp intake of breath.

"My God. What have you done?"

Marcy spun around to see both Sadie and Colin Doyle standing in the doorway, their eyes reflecting the horror of what was before them, their faces red with indignation and disgust. "What have *I* done?" Marcy sputtered. "You think I did this? I just got back, for God's sake. You saw me walk through the door no more than a minute ago. You think I had time to do this?"

Sadie Doyle said nothing, her face absorbing the damage to the room.

"Would I do this to my own things?" Marcy waved her slashed underwear in Sadie's face.

Sadie held firm, stubbornly folding her arms across her chest. "You're responsible nonetheless."

"*I'm* responsible? How do you figure that?"

"Looks like your friend didn't appreciate your runnin' off the way you did this mornin'," Sadie said.

Tears filled Marcy's eyes. "He didn't do this," she said, her voice shaking. He couldn't have, she thought.

"Who then?"

"You tell me."

"You accusin' *me* of somethin'?"

Marcy looked from Sadie to her son.

"You think Colin did this?"

"Who else had access to this room?" Marcy asked.

"Aside from your gentleman friend, you mean? The one you ran out on this mornin', the one who sat here half the day waitin' for you to come back, the one who snuck out when he thought no one was lookin'?"

"What are you talking about?"

"I'm talkin' about the fact your boyfriend was still sittin' here waitin' when I came to make up your bed this mornin', asked if I'd mind him hangin' around awhile, 'til you got back. I said it was no skin off my nose, but I was gonna have to charge you extra. He said, no problem, he'd take care of it later. Then I saw him sneakin' out of here about an hour or so later without so much as a fare-thee-well. I guess now we know why."

"That can't be," Marcy muttered impotently. "He would never—"

Sadie scoffed, the harsh sound sweeping through the air like a broom.

"Where do you keep your keys?" Marcy asked suddenly.

"What?"

"The keys to the rooms. You obviously have a master set. . . ."

"They're in a safe place."

"Where? Behind the reception desk?"

The look that passed through Sadie's eyes told Marcy her guess was correct.

"And you're not always at that desk, are you, Mrs. Doyle?"

"It's either me or Colin."

"But sometimes you're both busy with other things. It's possible someone could have come in, taken those keys, and—"

"And what? Decided to ransack your room? Why would anybody want to do that?"

"I don't know." Marcy felt her knees grow weak and fought to stay upright. "I don't know."

"Yeah? Well, this is what *I* know. I know my room's been trashed. That's what I know. And I know somebody's got to pay for the damage. Now, I don't know how well you know that guy who spent the night, but frankly, he looked a little shifty to me. Maybe he was lookin' for somethin', maybe he thought you had some money lyin' around. Any jewelry missin'?"

Marcy looked through her tears toward the empty drawer where she'd put her earrings. "My gold earrings are gone," she said dully, glancing back at Colin.

"What are you lookin' at me for? I didn't take 'em."

"I'm not accusing you of anything. I'm just trying to figure out what happened."

"What happened is that my property got smashed up, and you're on the hook for the damages," Sadie Doyle said again.

"Let me get this straight," Marcy said angrily, her patience exhausted, her head on the verge of exploding. "*My* room got broken into, *my* belongings were destroyed, *my* earrings are missing, it's *your* hotel, and yet *you* expect *me* to reimburse *you*? You guys are nuts!" she added for good measure.

"Call the gardai," Sadie instructed her son.

"WELL, HELLO THERE, Mrs. Taggart," Christopher Murphy said in greeting, running his hand through the stubble of his short blond hair. He closed the door behind him, walked toward her chair. "It's so nice to see you again."

"Do you think we could dispense with the sarcasm?" Marcy asked, concentrating her attention on the messy stack of papers on the garda's desk. It seemed to have grown substantially since she was there yesterday.

"How's the eye?"

"Better, thank you."

"Let's have a look." He tilted her chin gently toward his face. "Suppose you tell me what happened this time," Murphy said as the door opened again and Colleen Donnelly entered the room, immediately followed by John Sweeny and his overhanging gut. Marcy felt her heart quicken at the sight of their neat, dark blue uniforms and immediately brought her eyes to her lap. "Is there a problem, Mrs. Taggart?" Christopher Murphy asked.

"The problem is that I've done nothing wrong and yet, here I am."

"Again," Murphy added.

"Yes. Again."

"Would you mind looking at me, Mrs. Taggart?"

Reluctantly, Marcy brought her head up.

"If you've done nothing wrong, why do you have such trouble looking me in the eye?"

"I have no trouble looking you in the eye."

"And yet you've been staring at the floor, at my desk, at the wall, at anything *but* me since I walked in."

"It's not you," Marcy said after a pause. Then, when that clearly didn't satisfy him, "It's just that uniforms have always made me a little nervous." I shouldn't have told him that, she thought immediately, catching the startled expressions on the faces of all three gardai. "There's no rational reason for it. I've just always been that way. My sister says I'm worse than her poodle," she added, trying to laugh, to show them she understood just how silly it all was.

"Your sister?" Sweeny asked. "Is she here in Cork?"

"No. She's in Toronto."

"Would you like us to call her?" Colleen Donnelly asked.

"Why would I want you to do that?"

"I thought you might appreciate some support."

"It's not every tourist who gets hauled into the garda station two days in a row," Murphy added.

"Believe me, it wasn't my idea."

"You're the victim," Sweeny said, although his tone said otherwise.

"Yes. That's right."

"Tell us what happened, Mrs. Taggart," Murphy said.

Marcy sighed. From her experience the day before, she knew they weren't going to let her leave until she provided them with a plausible version of the events. Might as well get this over with, she decided. "I came back to the inn—"

"You'd been out all day?" Murphy said, interrupting.

"Yes."

"Mind my asking where?"

"I went to Youghal."

"Youghal? Sightseeing, were you?"

"I was looking for my daughter."

The three officers exchanged glances. "Did you find her?" Sweeny asked.

"No."

"What made you think she'd be in Youghal?"

"What difference does it make?" Marcy asked testily. "I thought you wanted to know about what happened when I got back."

"You ever think they might be connected?"

"What?" Was it possible? Marcy thought. "What do you mean?"

"Go on then," Murphy said without answering her question. "You returned to the inn. . . ."

"I went up to my room and discovered that someone had torn it apart. Everything I owned had been slashed or destroyed."

"Sounds like the work of a scorned lover," Sweeny stated.

"Mrs. Doyle said you had company last night," Murphy added.

"Was it the man who was here yesterday?" Colleen Donnelly asked.

"He never would have done something like this," Marcy insisted.

"Know him well, do you?"

"Well enough to know he didn't do this." Did she? Marcy wondered. The truth was she barely knew Vic Sorvino at all.

"Mrs. Doyle said you ran out early this morning like a bat out of hell."

"I'd hardly describe it as a bat out of hell."

"But you *were* in a hurry."

"Yes, I guess so."

"Meeting someone, were you?"

"Yes."

"Mind telling us who that was, Mrs. Taggart?"

"Yes, I do mind."

"Mrs. Taggart," Murphy said imploringly.

"His name is Liam. I . . . I don't know his last name," she admitted, her face flushing with embarrassment. At the very least, she should have asked Liam his last name, she thought. "He works at Grogan's House." Out of the corner of her eye, Marcy saw Colleen Donnelly scribble down this latest piece of information.

"The scene of yesterday's altercation," Sweeny remarked, barely suppressing a smirk.

"Yes."

"Okay, so you ran out on one man to go meet another," Murphy said, summing it up.

"It's not the way you're making it sound."

"Sounds like a motive to me," Sweeny said. "What's this other guy's name? The one who spent the night," he added unnecessarily.

This is ridiculous, Marcy thought. There was no way Vic had had anything to do with the trashing of her room. She might not know him well, but surely she was a good enough judge of character to know that. She thought suddenly of Peter, his carefully constructed smile beaming at her through the reflection in the glass covering a framed diploma on the far wall. She'd had no inkling of his affair with Sarah, never would have suspected he was capable of betraying her in such a cavalier fashion. So much for her ability to judge character. "His name is Vic Sorvino," she said. "He's staying at the Hayfield Manor Hotel."

Christopher Murphy nodded toward Colleen Donnelly, who nodded back almost imperceptibly before leaving the room. "Did Vic Sorvino know you were meeting Liam?"

"No."

"Did he know of your plans to visit Youghal?"

"No."

"I understand that after you ran out on him, he pursued you into the hall."

"Yes."

"Almost naked, from what I understand."

"That's a slight exaggeration."

"And then he followed you onto the street."

"He was fully dressed at that point."

"And he returned to your room again after you left."

"According to Mrs. Doyle."

"Who claims he was in your room waiting for you when she went in to make up the bed," Murphy stated.

"Yes, that's what she says."

"You don't believe her?"

"I don't know what to believe. For all I know, it could have been Mrs. Doyle who trashed my things."

"And destroyed her own property? Why would she do that?"

"You'd have to ask her."

"We already have. Frankly, it seems highly unlikely."

"What about her son?"

"It appears Colin was out for most of the morning."

"Which left the front desk largely unattended," Marcy said, pouncing. "Which means anybody could have wandered in off the street and taken the master key and gone up to my room. . . ."

"But why, Mrs. Taggart?" Murphy asked logically. "Why would someone do that?"

"I don't know."

"That would mean someone had been watching the inn and seen you go out, waited until Mr. Sorvino exited the premises hours later, and noted the reception desk had been left unattended, none of which makes any sense unless . . ."

"Unless?" Marcy hung on the word as if she were suspended from a clothesline.

"Unless it has something to do with your daughter," Murphy said.

Marcy tried to digest what he was saying. "You think there's a connection between my search for Devon and someone breaking into my room and trashing my things?" Marcy asked.

"You said yesterday there'd been issues with your daughter," Murphy explained, "that there were problems between the two of you, that perhaps she might not want to be found. . . ."

"You think it was Devon who did this?"

"I'm simply suggesting it's a possibility."

"But why?"

"Perhaps she was looking for something."

Marcy hugged her purse close to her chest. Was it possible?

"Or maybe that was her way of telling you to go home, to leave her alone."

"Or maybe it was someone else," Marcy said. "Someone who doesn't want me to find her."

Murphy shrugged as Colleen Donnelly reentered the room. "We've just checked with Hayfield Manor. Apparently Mr. Sorvino checked out at noon."

Disappointment stabbed at Marcy's chest. "Can I go now?" she asked.

"Where exactly is it you plan to go, Mrs. Taggart?" Murphy asked.

He was right, Marcy realized. She couldn't very well go back to the Doyle Cork Inn. She smiled. "It looks as if Hayfield Manor has an unexpected vacancy," she said.

TWENTY

I'M SORRY. HOW MUCH did you say?" Marcy asked the bright-eyed, dark-haired receptionist, who didn't look a day over twelve.

"Six hundred and fifty euros," the girl repeated with a smile that exposed her entire upper gum.

I could do something about that, Peter said from the dark recesses of Marcy's brain.

Six hundred and fifty euros translated into around a thousand dollars, Marcy calculated silently, thinking that Peter would have a fit when he saw this month's credit card bills, whose charges he'd agreed to cover for two years—"within reason," he'd stressed—when she'd agreed not to contest their divorce. Silly man, she thought now. Had he really expected a crazy woman to act reasonably?

"Is that all right?" the receptionist asked, small clouds of worry disturbing the sky blue of her eyes. "It's a deluxe room. I'm afraid there's nothing else available at the moment."

"It's fine." Marcy pushed her credit card across the black-and-gold-flecked marble counter. She could use a little deluxe treatment about now, she was thinking, wondering if the room she was getting was the same one Vic had abandoned earlier.

"Do you need help with your luggage?"

"Don't have any." Marcy surveyed the soft peach-and-gold-colored foyer with its marble columns and magnificent mahogany staircase. The hotel resembled an elegant, if large, manor home of the type that was common at the turn of the century, but the truth was that it had been built in 1996 and expanded to its current eighty-eight rooms in 1999. Nothing is what it seems, Marcy thought, returning her credit card to her wallet. "Is there somewhere I can buy a toothbrush and toothpaste?"

"Housekeeping can provide you with that, and we have a wonderful spa that sells all sorts of beauty and hair products," the receptionist told her without further prompting.

Marcy's hand went immediately to her hair, tucking it behind her ears and feeling it instantly bounce back to its former position as the receptionist handed her the key card to her room. "You're in room 212. The elevator is straight ahead. Or you can take the stairs." She pointed with her chin toward the elegant staircase.

Two small children suddenly came crashing against Marcy's legs, a sweet-faced girl of about eight, followed by her more rambunctious, towheaded younger brother, triggering memories of Devon and Darren when they were little. The girl apologized immediately and profusely, her big eyes shooting toward the front door, her little face growing tense as she waited for her mother, who was struggling with a bunch of shopping bags, to catch up. Her brother, oblivious to everything but his own fevered imagination, continued running in increasingly ragged circles around them.

She's so serious, Marcy thought, aching to reach out and stroke the young girl's cheek, to reassure her that everything would be all right. Except how could she offer such assurances when she was sure of no such thing? Hadn't she offered the same empty promises to Devon?

Marcy moved slowly toward the elevator. It had been an exhausting, frustrating day, full of surprises—first the trip to Youghal and the meeting with Claire and Audrey, followed by the drive back to Cork, the kiss in the car, the discovery of the ransacking of her room, and the indignity of her repeat visit to the garda station. The last eight hours had been a veritable roller-coaster ride of anticipation, disappointment, accusations, and despair. Was this how Devon had felt most of the time? Marcy wondered, feeling utterly drained both physically and emotionally. It required all her strength to push one foot in front of the other.

"Hold the lift," a voice called out in crisp British tones. Seconds later, the woman with the shopping bags ushered her two children into the elevator, inadvertently forcing Marcy against the back wall of the tiny space. "Sorry," the woman said. "Simon, settle down," she instructed her son, who was still spinning around in circles like a top. "Jillian, what's wrong, pumpkin?"

The little girl said nothing, her lower lip quivering.

"What is it? Don't you like the new dress we bought you?"

"That's just it. The dress is perfect," the child said, gazing imploringly at her mother.

"I don't understand," the woman responded.

"Where will we ever find a pair of shoes to match it?" the young girl wailed.

Her mother laughed. She was still laughing as the elevator doors opened onto the second floor.

Had Marcy ever felt the freedom to laugh at her daughter in such a casual way? Or had she interpreted Devon's every frown as a potential harbinger of impending doom, an intimation of coming disaster? And had she unconsciously transferred those fears onto Devon, creating doubt and turmoil where none had previously existed? Had she read too much into things . . . or not enough? "Excuse me." Marcy wiggled her way around the still-spinning boy, touching the top of his blond head as she made her exit.

"Mummy," she heard the boy exclaim as the elevator doors shut behind her, "she touched me."

Mommy! she heard Devon cry, her voice cutting through the past like a hook to grab at Marcy's heart. She spun around, already knowing there was no one there.

Her room was only steps from the elevator. Marcy opened the door to find a wall of leaded windows overlooking a private garden, and a beautiful marble bathroom with a large tub and separate shower stall. The bed was king size, the sheets crisp and white, the walls a pale apricot. A fluffy white bathrobe hung in the closet. "I think I'll stay here forever," she said, lying down on top of the bedspread and gazing up at a portrait of two young women that hung over her head. She closed her eyes, picturing Vic lying beside her, imagining his arms tight around her. Seconds later, she was asleep.

She dreamed she was in the shoe department of a large store, her feet bare, piles of discarded shoes spread out on the floor around her. "I need something to match my dress," she told the hapless salesclerk, pulling on the sides of the emerald-green apron covering her blue, flower-print dress.

"There's nothing here," the clerk told her. "You should go home."

"I'm not leaving. Not until I find my shoes."

"You're being ridiculous," the clerk told her in John Sweeny's voice.

A man came running toward her, holding out a pair of black stilettos, their leather scratched, their heels broken. "How about these?"

It was Vic Sorvino.

"Vic!" Marcy exclaimed, her arms reaching for him.

"Don't touch him," Liam cautioned, appearing out of nowhere to snatch the shoes from Vic's hands. "I don't trust him." Liam tossed the shoes to the floor. They ricocheted off the wood and bounced toward the wall.

Marcy woke up with a start, the sound of shoes hitting the floor continuing to reverberate in the distance.

"Housekeeping," she heard someone say from outside the door to her room, accompanied by a gentle knocking. Not shoes, she realized, sitting up in bed and glancing at the clock. It was after five. She'd been asleep the better part of two hours.

The door opened and a uniformed maid entered the room. Both women gasped. "Oh, I'm so sorry," the maid said, backing toward the door. "I didn't realize anyone was here. I knocked and knocked. I'll come back later."

"No, that's all right." Marcy jumped off the bed, crossing toward the large windows. "I must have fallen asleep. Please, go ahead. Do . . . whatever."

"I'll just be a minute."

Marcy watched the young woman, whose long dark hair was twisted into a braid at the back of her head, turn down the bed and fold up its ochre-colored bedspread, then lay it across the top shelf in the closet. If the maid was surprised not to see any clothes on the hangers, she didn't let on.

"Will there be anythin' else I can do for you?" she asked.

Marcy shook her head. Then, "Wait!" She reached for her purse, quickly extricating the envelope containing her daughter's pictures and holding out the most recent one. "Do you recognize this girl, by any chance?"

The maid took the photograph from Marcy's trembling fingers, bringing it so close to her face that she was almost touching it with her short, upturned nose. "No, can't say that I do," she said.

Marcy pressed. "Are you sure? You don't sound sure."

"It's just that I can't see so good without my glasses."

"So you *might* know her?"

"No. Don't think so," the girl said.

"But without your glasses . . ."

"I squinted. That's almost as good." The maid smiled as she returned the picture to Marcy's hand.

"Damn it," Marcy muttered when she was gone. Had she really expected her to recognize the photograph? She shook her head, no longer knowing what she expected. She plopped back down on the side of the bed, understanding she was no farther ahead than she'd been when she first arrived back in Cork. If anything, she was in worse shape. She had no leads, no clothes, not even a toothbrush.

As if on cue, there was another knock on the door. "Housekeeping," a woman's voice announced.

Had the maid realized she was mistaken, that she recognized Devon after all? Marcy threw open the door to find a big-bosomed, gray-haired woman of around sixty holding a toothbrush in one hand and a small tube of toothpaste in the other. "I understand you're in need of these," she said brightly.

"Thank you," Marcy said, the hand holding Devon's picture reaching for the items.

"Oh, who's this now?" the woman from housekeeping asked.

"Do you know her?" Marcy asked in return.

The woman studied the picture for several seconds. "I thought for a minute it might be Katie."

"Katie?" Marcy could barely fit the word around the sudden pounding of her heart.

"My neighbor's daughter."

"Her name is Katie?"

"Yeah, but it's not her."

"You're sure?"

The woman nodded. "Now that I have a good look, I can see they're quite different around the eyes."

"You're sure?" Marcy asked again. "Have you known Katie long?"

"Only all her life," the woman said, and laughed. "She's a handful, that one. Always has been. Who's this, then?"

"My daughter," Marcy told her. "Also a handful."

The woman smiled. "Yes, well. I guess they all are at that age. I better be off. Enjoy your stay. If you need anything else, just ring."

I need my daughter, Marcy thought. "Thank you," she said. Then, "This girl, Katie . . ." she began, not sure what she was going to say next.

"Yes?" The woman waited, a puzzled wrinkle disturbing the otherwise serene line of her smile.

"Do you know the sort of places she likes to go? A favorite pub or hangout? My daughter will be joining me soon," she added when she saw the puzzled expression on the woman's mouth spread to her eyes. "I thought it would be nice to take her to a few places where there are lots of young people."

"Oh, there's no shortage of those." The woman laughed. "There's Dingles, over on Oliver Plunkett Street. I understand it's pretty popular. And there's Mulcahy's on Corn Market. It's a bit rough, but the kids all love it."

"Thank you." Corn Market Street was in the flat of the city. No doubt she'd walked past Mulcahy's many times in the last few days and failed to notice it. It might be worth another look, she thought, deciding to shower first.

Hopefully a blast of hot water will wake me up, she thought as she stepped under the shower's oversized nozzle. Emptying the tiny bottle of shampoo the hotel provided on her head, she scrubbed her scalp until it tingled, wishing she could clean out the inside of her brain as thoroughly, free it of all the cobwebs of the past, the doubts and recriminations she carried with her everywhere. And now there were questions as well: Could Vic Sorvino really have had anything to do with the trashing of her room at the Doyle Cork Inn? Was he really capable of such a vicious act? And if so, why?

She unwrapped a small, round bar of lilac-scented soap and began vigorously rubbing it across her naked torso, grateful for the amount of lather it produced. The questions continued: Was Vic angry with her for running off? Was he jealous at seeing her drive off with another man? Was he a psychopath?

Did he know something about Devon? Something he didn't want her to find out?

The thought shot through Marcy like an electric shock, her arms shooting into the air, the bar of soap flying from her hands. It bounced to the tile floor, slid into a corner. Marcy froze.

Was it possible?

No, she told herself, regaining her composure and equilibrium and retrieving the soap from the floor, the water from the overhead nozzle continuing to spill down her cheeks, carrying the bitter taste of lilacs into her mouth. It wasn't possible. It didn't make sense.

But then, what did?

She heard her cell phone ringing as she was getting out of the shower.

"Marcy, are you all right?" Liam asked as soon as she said hello. "The gardai were just at Grogan's, askin' all sorts of questions. What the hell happened?"

Marcy balanced the phone against her ear as she struggled into the terry-cloth bathrobe and gathered both sides around her, throwing a towel over her wet head. "The police were there?"

"They just left. They said your room had been ransacked. . . ."

Marcy quickly explained everything that had happened since Liam had dropped her off in front of the Doyle Cork Inn.

He made a sound that was halfway between a laugh and a snort of disbelief. "What—I can't leave you alone for a second?"

"Apparently not."

"The police think it was that guy you was with. Is it true he destroyed all your things?"

"Somebody did," Marcy said, still reluctant to conclude it was Vic. "What did the police say exactly?"

"Exactly not very much indeed. Just asked a lot of questions, mostly about you. And your daughter."

"What sort of questions?"

"How long I'd known you, your background and stuff like that, if I thought you were unstable," he added after a brief pause.

Marcy held her breath. "And do you?" she asked with a sad smile, hoping Liam wouldn't take offense.

A second's silence, then, "What I think is you're not safe."

"What are you talking about? Of course I'm safe. Why wouldn't I be safe?" Until this very minute, the thought that she might actually be in danger had never occurred to her.

"Some lunatic just trashed your room and tore up all your things," Liam said forcefully. "He could come back, Marcy. I really think you should think about goin' back to Toronto."

"I'm not going anywhere."

"You're just bein' stubborn. All right, look. We'll talk about this tomorrow."

"There's nothing to talk about. I'm not going anywhere until I find Devon."

Another pause. "All right. I have to go. Grogan's givin' me the evil eye. Will you do me a favor and just stay put for the rest of the night?"

"I don't know. I was thinking of going over to Mulcahy's."

"Mulcahy's over on Corn Market? Have you taken total leave of your senses? It's a dive. No way you're goin' there alone. No, you're goin' to order room service and get into bed, and that's the end of the story."

"Okay," she said, agreeing reluctantly.

"You promise?"

Marcy smiled. "You don't have to worry about me, Liam."

"Can't seem to help it."

"I'll talk to you tomorrow." Marcy was still smiling as she disconnected the line and tossed the phone to the bed. She wondered idly if it was the same bed Vic had slept in and pondered again if there could be any connection between the soft-spoken, middle-aged man from Chicago and her daughter. She mulled over each encounter, replayed their previous conversations, reconstructing each one in as much detail as she could remember. Had his interest in her been more than a simple combination of attraction and opportunity? Was there something sinister behind his seemingly innocent facade? Was he really a recently divorced, retired widget salesman from Chicago, still grieving the death of his first wife, or had that all been a clever ruse, calculated to charm and disarm her? Was there even such a thing as a widget? Marcy wondered, almost laughing out loud. Had anything he'd told her been the truth?

Liam is right, she decided, drying her hair with the towel around her neck. Her head was spinning; her eye had resumed throbbing. She was in no condition to go out again tonight. She should just stay put, order room service, and get to bed early. She'd go out first thing in the morning and buy some new clothes.

At least my photographs of Devon escaped unharmed, she thought gratefully, grabbing her purse from the desk near the wall of windows and hugging it tightly to her breast. Everything valuable, everything she really needed, was in this bag— her money, her passport, her memories. She opened it and withdrew the by-now-tattered envelope containing Devon's pictures. "My baby," she whispered, gently laying the photographs along the desk's smooth surface, watching as Devon grew up before her bewildered eyes. "My beautiful baby."

My beautiful mommy, Devon whispered back.

Marcy removed the picture of her own mother from the envelope. "My beautiful mommy," she repeated, laying her picture down beside Devon's, breathing in their uncanny resemblance. Slowly, reluctantly, her fingers trembling, she reached back inside the envelope and removed the second, smaller envelope, the one marked "MOMMY," carefully withdrawing the single sheet of lined paper that was folded neatly inside it. She turned the piece of paper over in her hands several times before unwrapping it, lifting it to her tear-filled eyes.

My beautiful mommy, she read, Devon's awkward scrawl playing hide-and-seek with her tears. *I don't expect you to understand what I'm about to do.*

Marcy trembled. When had she ever understood anything her daughter had tried to tell her?

Please don't be mad, and understand that this is not a decision I've made lightly. I know how much pain I've caused you. Believe me when I say I have no desire to cause you any more. Marcy lowered her head, unable to continue. When she looked up again, her tears blinded her to everything except the letter's last paragraph. *"Please know how much I love you,"* she read out loud, desperately trying to match her daughter's voice with the words she'd never heard her say.

Her hands shaking, Marcy refolded the tearstained paper and returned it, along with the photographs, to her purse. Minutes later, her damp curls framing her head like a wreath, she crawled back into the jeans and gray sweater she'd been wearing all day and headed out the door.

TWENTY-ONE

MARCY HAD TO WALK up and down both sides of Corn Market Street twice before she spotted the sign for Mulcahy's. No wonder she'd missed it, she thought, staring at the ragged piece of scrap metal with MULCAHY's hand-painted in black across it, accompanied by a wobbly arrow pointing toward a narrow flight of stairs at the side of an ancient dry-cleaning shop. "This can't be right," she muttered, glancing over her shoulder. But the normally busy street was relatively quiet. Only a few people were out walking, most having run for cover when the skies had opened in a sudden violent cloud-burst half an hour earlier. Marcy had taken temporary refuge under the green-and-white-striped awning of a nearby butcher shop, listening to the thunder's furious roar as she watched impressive streaks of lightning catapult across the dark sky.

Her sneakers and socks were soaked right through to her skin, and the odor of damp denim and wet wool mingled with the fragrance of leftover lilac from her shower. I'll be lucky if I don't catch pneumonia, she thought, thinking again that Liam was right. She should have stayed at the hotel, ordered up a nice meal and a glass of red wine, and gone to bed early. What was she doing standing alone on the corner of a deserted street, shivering with the cold and damp, and staring at a square piece of crumpled metal with the word MULCAHY'S hand-painted in black across it, next to an arrow pointing down?

Straight into hell, she thought dramatically, and might have laughed had she not been so altogether miserable. This is crazy, she thought as she descended the concrete steps, stopping at the closed basement door. She tried the handle. It didn't budge. She knocked. Nobody answered. "Hello," she called out stubbornly, already knowing the place was deserted. "Is anybody there?"

Of course nobody's here, she told herself, continuing to knock regardless. The place, such as it was, *whatever* it was, was obviously closed. Sealed up tighter than a drum, she thought, wondering what night it was and realizing she'd lost all track of time. Since she'd come to Cork, one day had pretty much blended into the next. "Hello," she called again, refusing to give up.

"Excuse me," she heard someone call from somewhere above her head.

Marcy backed away from the door, looked up toward the street. She saw an enormous pair of legs, stretching for the sky. The legs were attached to a man whose head seemed disproportionately small for the rest of him, probably due to the angle from which she was viewing him. Drops of rain clung to his handlebar mustache, glistening under the glow of a nearby streetlamp. Marcy wondered for an instant whether she might be hallucinating.

"Can I help you with somethin'?" he asked.

"I'm looking for Mulcahy's," Marcy said.

"It would appear you've found it." The man nodded toward the sign.

"It seems to be closed."

"Don't think it opens 'til after ten," the man said.

"Ten?" Marcy repeated, glancing at her watch but unable to read the time in the dim light. Still, how late could it be? Seven o'clock at most, she calculated, listening as the bells of St. Anne's Shandon Church confirmed her estimate with seven loud peals. What was she supposed to do for the next three hours? "Are you sure?" she asked the man, but there was no answer, and Marcy realized he'd already left. Guess I could head over to Grogan's, she thought, then quickly dismissed the idea. Mr. Grogan wouldn't be too happy to see her again, and she didn't want to get Liam in trouble. He'd already put himself out for her more than enough. Besides, he'd only try to talk her into returning to her hotel and catching the first available flight to Toronto. Did he really believe she was in actual danger? She dismissed the uncomfortable thought as she returned to street level and turned north toward Kyrl's Quay, a smattering of raindrops falling on her already wet shoulders.

The water in the North Channel of the river Lee was dark and moving swiftly. Marcy hurried along beside it until she found a pleasant-enough-looking pub, the sound of traditional Irish music escaping its walls to beckon her inside. She pushed open the door and immediately found herself in a bright and crowded room. There was a raised podium at the front where three young men were finishing up their last song. "We'll just take a wee break and be back with you in a quarter hour," the

leader of the band said into the microphone, this announce-
ment followed by a smattering of applause and a few good-
natured boos.

"Sing 'Danny Boy,'" someone shouted.

"Sing it yerself," one of the band members shouted back.

"Oh, Danny Boy," half the pub immediately responded,
miraculously in tune, as Marcy's eyes searched the room for an
empty table.

"Lookin' for me?" a man asked, pushing an empty chair
toward her with the heel of his brown leather boot.

Marcy smiled at the man, who was probably in his early for-
ties, and balding, although his eyebrows were dark and bushy.
A cursory glance around the room revealed there were no other
free seats. "Thank you, but I wouldn't want to put you out."

The man motioned for her to sit down. "What are you
drinkin'?" he asked.

What the hell, Marcy decided, sitting down at the small
table. He looked pleasant enough, and she had three hours to
kill. "A beer, maybe?"

"Two Beamishes," the man shouted at the waitress. "Name's
Kieran." He extended his hand across the table.

"Marcy." She shook his hand, noting his firm grip, which
lingered perhaps a beat too long.

"Where you from, Marcy?" he asked. "You're not from
around here, I know that much."

"I'm from Toronto."

"Canada, is it, then?"

"It is." She laughed, although she wasn't sure why.

"You have a nice laugh," Kieran remarked.

"Thank you. You're from Cork, I take it."

"Lived here all my life. Best city in the world."

"It's lovely."

"All the lovelier since you got here." Brown eyes twinkled mischievously.

Marcy laughed again. "Someone's been kissing the Blarney Stone."

"Every chance I get. You hungry?" he asked when the waitress appeared with their beers.

"I'd love a sandwich."

"Ham and cheese?"

"Perfect."

"Two ham and cheese sandwiches," Kieran told the waitress.

"Thank you," Marcy said. "That's really very kind of you."

"I see you got caught in the rain."

Marcy's hand flew self-consciously to her hair. "I must look like a drowned rat."

"The most glorious drowned rat I've ever seen." Kieran smiled, revealing a substantial overbite.

His mother should be shot for not getting that fixed when he was a child, she heard Peter say.

"A euro for your thoughts," Kieran said playfully.

"Do you know a place called Mulcahy's?" Marcy asked.

"Over on Corn Market?"

"Yes."

"It's not your kind of place, that's for sure."

"Why not?"

"Well, it's a wee bit raunchy. Loud music, drugs, loose women. Or so I'm told." He laughed. "What makes you ask about Mulcahy's?"

"Someone suggested it was a place young people liked to gather," she explained. Then, "I'm looking for my daughter." She quickly reached inside her purse and withdrew her daughter's photograph. "Do you know her, by any chance?" What was she doing? There was no way he'd recognize Devon's picture.

Kieran took the photo from her hand, studied it for several seconds, his thick eyebrows meeting at the bridge of his strong nose, his brown eyes growing dark. He looked back at her, his eyes burrowing deep into hers, as if he were trying to see inside her head. "I might," he said, dropping the picture to the table as Marcy felt her heartbeat quicken. "Mind my askin' why you're lookin' for her?"

"It's a long story. Please . . . you know her?"

"I love long stories," he said stubbornly.

The waitress approached with their beers. "Your sandwiches'll be out in a few minutes."

"Drink up," Kieran said, clinking his beer mug against Marcy's. "You were sayin'. . . ."

Marcy did as she was told, chugging back a mouthful of beer and feeling her eyes sting as the liquid reached the back of her throat. She swallowed. "My daughter and I haven't spoken in several years," she told him, deciding to stick to the most salient points. "I heard she was in Cork. That's why I'm here. Please, if you know anything . . . I need to see her."

"What'd you say her name was?"

"I didn't. Devon," she added quickly, not wanting to antagonize him. "But she might be calling herself Audrey."

"Audrey, yes." He tapped the photograph with the index finger of his right hand. "That's her all right. Lovely girl, she is. Quiet, respectful, always a smile and a kind word."

"You've talked to her?"

"Just 'Hello,' 'Good-bye,' 'Nice day.' That sort of thing."

Marcy's eyes welled up with tears. "And you're sure this is her?"

"Well, now, that depends. What are you gonna do when you find her?" He took another sip of his beer.

"Nothing. I just want to talk to her."

"She's not in any trouble, is she?"

"No."

"I wouldn't want to get her in trouble."

"You wouldn't be. Please. How do you know her?"

"She works for the old lady who lives across the street from me mum. I've seen her a few times when I go to visit."

Was it possible that after all her frantic efforts, a chance run-in with a stranger in a pub was going to lead her to her daughter? "What sort of work does she do?"

"She's like a companion, I guess you'd say. Does Mrs. Crocker's grocery shoppin', her laundry, tends the garden, takes her for walks, stuff like that. In exchange, she gets a place to stay, rent-free."

"Where does Mrs. Crocker live?"

"Over in Montenotte, up in the Cork hills," Kieran said.

"Is that far from here?"

"It's a bit of a drive."

Marcy reached into her purse for her cell phone.

"What are you doin'?" Kieran asked.

"If you'd give me Mrs. Crocker's exact address, I'll call a cab. . . ."

"You're gonna go there right now?"

"Please. I've already wasted so much time."

Kieran quickly downed the last of his beer. "No need for that," he said, pushing himself away from the table. "Come on. I'll take you there."

"I DON'T KNOW this part of the city," Marcy said, staring out the car window through the light rain that continued to fall at the commercial thoroughfare that was MacCurtain Street. It felt as if they'd been driving for hours, although less than twenty minutes had passed since they'd left the pub.

"What about yer sandwiches?" the waitress had called after them.

"Give 'em to Stanley," Kieran had called back, waving at a man watching them from the bar.

"Who's Stanley?" Marcy had asked.

"A friend of mine. You took his seat."

"What?"

"Happens all the time," Kieran had said with a laugh. "Almost there," he said now as he turned the car onto Summerhill Road and continued up into the Cork hills.

Marcy tried to control her growing excitement. It was so amazing, the way things worked out, she thought again. If she hadn't ignored Liam's advice, if she hadn't gone out, if Mulcahy's hadn't been closed, if it hadn't been raining, if she hadn't ducked into that particular pub on that particular street at that particular time, if Stanley had been sitting in his seat, if she hadn't met Kieran, then none of this would be happening. She wouldn't be on her way to see Devon. After all her careful planning, it all boiled down to a simple coincidence, to being in the right place at the right time. Was it really possible?

She glanced at Kieran, marveling at his willingness to put himself out this way for her. The kindness of strangers, she heard Liam say. And he was right. In barely a week, she'd lucked into an amazing trio of men, Vic, Liam, and now Kieran, all willing and even eager to aid in her search for her daughter. After the last two loveless years of her marriage to Peter— longer, if she was being really honest—she'd pretty much given up on men. And then she'd met Vic, who had made her feel beautiful and worth loving again, and Liam, who had made her feel young and desirable. And now Kieran was driving miles in the rain when he could have been enjoying another pint of beer with his friend Stanley in a nice dry pub.

Why? Marcy wondered, brushing aside a sudden unpleasant twinge of doubt.

Was it the kindness of strangers or something else entirely?

They drove through the residential district of St. Luke's, continuing on toward Montenotte. "Almost there," Kieran said again.

What had possessed her to get in a car with a total stranger and drive miles into the Cork hills on a dark and rainy night? I should have taken a cab, Marcy thought, admonishing herself. Except if she'd refused Kieran's offer, he might have been insulted enough not to tell her where she could find Audrey. And that was a chance she couldn't take. She would risk everything to find her daughter.

Minutes later, they pulled into the driveway of a small, two-story, semidetached house. "That's Mrs. Crocker's place over there." He pointed to a similar house directly across the street.

"It looks awfully dark."

"Probably at the movies. Mrs. Crocker loves movies. Audrey takes her at least twice a week. Let's have a look, shall we?" He jumped out of the car, sprinting through the rain to Marcy's side and opening her door. Grabbing her elbow, he guided her quickly across the street toward Mrs. Crocker's house.

Please let her be home, Marcy prayed, taking shelter under the front awning as Kieran knocked on the door. Please let her be glad to see me.

But after several seconds, it became obvious that her prayers would go unanswered. Marcy tried to peer inside the front window, but its old lace curtains were closed and the flower box on the outside of the window prevented her from getting too close.

"Should be back soon," Kieran said with assurance. "Come on. You're gettin' soaked. We can wait over at me mum's."

"Your mother won't mind?" Marcy asked as they recrossed the street.

Kieran removed a key from his pocket and opened the front door. "Not at all," he said, flipping on the overhead light and shaking the rainwater from his hair like a dog. "Mum?" he called as he led Marcy into the living room. "You home?" No answer. "Probably gone to the movies with Mrs. Crocker and Audrey. You fancy another beer?"

Marcy looked around the room, which was comfortably furnished with an overstuffed gold-and-brown-striped sofa and matching chair. A large-screen TV on a low table took up most of the opposite wall. "I don't think so, no."

"Oh, come on," he said, walking into the tiny kitchen off the living room and returning with a beer in each hand. "It'll take the chill off."

Before she could refuse, he popped the caps off the bottles and handed her one. Then he plopped down on the sofa, patting the pillow beside him. "Sit down, luv. Take a load off."

"I'm too anxious," she told him honestly, recognizing that her unease had little to do with seeing Devon again and everything to do with her growing apprehension at the fact that she was in the middle of nowhere, in a strange house with a man she barely knew. "And wet," she added, afraid of offending him. "I wouldn't want to ruin your mother's nice things."

"I wouldn't worry about that," he said, taking a swig of his beer directly from the bottle. "Come on, luv. Relax a little." Again, he patted the cushion beside him.

Marcy ignored his invitation, walking to the window beside the TV, setting her beer on the low table on which it sat, and pulling back the brown-and-mustard printed curtains to stare at the house across the street. It looks as deserted as Mulcahy's, she thought, concentrating on the pattern of the curtains in an effort to control the growing panic spreading through her veins. What had she done? How stupid could she be? "This isn't your mother's house, is it?" she said when she could find her voice, carefully measuring out each word.

He laughed. "Guess you got me there."

"Whose house is it?"

"It's mine," he admitted sheepishly, as if he were a small boy who'd been caught with his hand in the cookie jar.

It was then that Marcy noticed a silver-framed photograph beside her untouched bottle of beer. It was of an attractive, middle-aged woman with a square jaw and short brown hair, her arms wrapped around two young boys, both wearing Kieran's vaguely guilty grin. "I take it this is your wife and sons."

"Charles and Walter," he said easily. If he was embarrassed, he gave no sign of it.

"You have a very handsome family."

Kieran acknowledged her compliment with an almost imperceptible nod of his head. "Sit down, luv," he urged.

"Where are they?"

"In Kilkenny for the week, havin' a bit of a holiday."

Marcy released a deep breath of air. "Is there really a Mrs. Crocker who lives across the street?"

Kieran rose to his feet, crossing toward her in two giant steps. "Of course there's a Mrs. Crocker. And a lovely, understandin' woman she is, too. Married to me friend Stanley, so she'd kind of have to be. She's in Kilkenny with me wife. Stanley and me'll be joinin' up with them in a couple of days."

"Stanley was the man at the bar," Marcy stated.

Kieran laughed. "Some nights he gets lucky; some nights it's me."

"And Audrey?" Marcy asked, already knowing the answer but needing to hear the words out loud.

"Can't say I've had the pleasure." Kieran's hands reached out to stroke her arms.

"You said you knew her. Why would you say that?"

"It was what you wanted me to say, wasn't it, luv? And a man should always tell a woman the things she wants to hear."

"So this whole thing was a ruse to get me up here."

His response was to lean forward, kiss the side of Marcy's neck.

"You didn't recognize my daughter's picture."

His lips moved to the side of her mouth, his hands to her breasts.

"This is all a big game to you."

"Ah, come on, darlin'. You looked like you could use a little fun." One hand crawled underneath her sweater; the other slid toward her buttocks.

In the next second, Marcy brought the bottle of beer crashing against the side of his skull.

Kieran staggered back, blood dripping from the gash at the side of his head. "What the . . . ?"

Marcy stared at the now broken bottle in her hand, no clear memory of how it got there. Beer was dripping down Kieran's face, mingling with the blood inside his hairline. "If you touch me again, I swear I'll kill you," Marcy heard someone say, then recoiled, recognizing the voice as hers.

"Are you crazy? What—you think I'm gonna force you? Need I remind you that you came here of your own accord? Shit, I'm bleedin' all over the bloomin' carpet."

"I want to go home."

"There's the door, you crazy bitch."

"How am I supposed to get back to the city?"

"Try flyin' there on your broomstick, why don't you? Shit, my wife's gonna have a right fit when she sees this mess."

Marcy bolted toward the front door, opening it and quickly fleeing into the night, outraged cries of "Crazy bitch" pursuing her down the twisting curves of the rain-soaked streets. More than an hour later, the sharp slope of St. Patrick's Hill mercifully popping into view, she heard a car pull up beside her. A door opened, blocking her path, forcing her to a stop. A man got out, his firm hand on her arm preventing her from continuing.

"Excuse me, ma'am," the uniformed garda said. "I think you need to come with me."

TWENTY-TWO

I T WAS ALMOST ELEVEN o'clock by the time Marcy made it
back to the flat of the city. She was exhausted; her clothes
reeked of her spilt beer; there was a bloodstain on her sleeve
she doubted would wash out; her feet ached; her head ached
more. What the hell is the matter with me? She berated herself,
picking an errant chip of broken beer bottle from the silver
threads of her sweater and flicking it to the road. Had the garda
seen it? she wondered. Probably not, she decided in the next
breath. If he had, he never would have let her go. "When did I
get this stupid?" she asked out loud.

You were always naive, she heard Judith say.

"I'm not the one who got married five times," Marcy
reminded her. Then, "Great. Now I'm talking to myself." She
shook her head. Beats talking to the police, she thought, grate-

ful to be out of the officer's car, more grateful he hadn't hauled her off to the station for further questioning. What was it with the Irish police force anyway? Did they have nothing better to do with their time than harass innocent tourists?

Okay, maybe not so innocent. And the young garda had seemed genuinely concerned with her welfare. Was there a problem? he'd asked solicitously. Was she hurt? Had she been accosted? What was she doing wandering the streets of Cork alone, in the dark, in the rain? Just how much alcohol had she consumed?

He'd made her sit in the front seat of his car for the better part of an hour, making small talk as the rain continued to pour down, asking politely whether he could see her passport, examining it closely as he talked about having a cousin in Hamilton named Dalton O'Malley, and did she know him, by any chance?

Marcy had explained that Hamilton was approximately an hour's drive from Toronto and no, she didn't know his cousin, although she was sure he was a very nice man, and could she please go now? The rain was tapering off, she'd sobered up, and she was anxious to get back to her hotel.

"What hotel?" he'd inquired.

"Hayfield Manor."

"Nice hotel," he'd remarked, obviously impressed. "I'll take you there." Except within seconds after he started his engine, a call had come in about a suspected break-in in the area.

"You go," she'd told him, as if he required her permission. "I'll be fine."

Still he'd hesitated. "You'll go straight back to your hotel?"

"I swear," she said, then as soon as he was gone, "Goddamn it." She shrugged. "Well, I swore," she said, watching him drive away. Then, taking tiny baby steps, her weight on her heels, she approached the steep incline of St. Patrick's Hill, feeling the strain on the back of her calves as she made her descent and recalling the words of her former tour guide: "Americans say it rivals the notorious streets of San Francisco."

"They're right," she said now, skidding across a damp patch of concrete and pitching forward, her hands instinctively lifting into the air to prevent her from falling on her face. She continued in that posture for the rest of the way, her hands raised and wobbling at her sides, as if she were walking a tightrope. Which maybe I am, she thought, seeing St. Patrick's Bridge in the near distance and continuing purposefully toward it, thinking she'd never been so happy to see a damn bridge in her entire life.

Judith used to be afraid of bridges, she suddenly remembered. For years her sister had refused to drive across them, which made getting places occasionally awkward and time-consuming. She couldn't remember when this had ceased to be an issue, if indeed it had. Luckily for Judith, Toronto didn't have that many bridges.

Grogan's House was only blocks away and Marcy fought the almost unbearable urge to head toward it, continuing down St. Patrick's Street toward Corn Market instead. What am I doing now? she wondered. I really *am* crazy.

Crazy bitch, she heard Kieran shout from somewhere behind her.

This is crazy, Judith said after him. *You can't keep doing this to yourself. You have to accept reality.*

"It's *your* reality, not mine," Marcy told her.

The reality is that Devon is dead.

"We don't know that for a fact."

Yes, Judith insisted. *"We do."*

Judith had always been so sure Devon had killed herself. Was that why Marcy had never shown her Devon's letter?

"Studies have shown that suicide frequently runs in families, that one suicide validates another," Peter had pronounced, echoing the opinion of the psychiatrist he'd insisted she see.

"You think that just because my mother killed herself, that means our daughter did, too?"

"She paddled her canoe into the middle of the damn bay in the middle of bloody October. She wasn't wearing a life jacket. She was depressed. . . ."

"She was happier than she'd been in months. You even commented that she seemed calmer, more peaceful. . . ."

"Studies have shown that people who have decided to kill themselves are often happier in the days leading up to their suicide," he'd insisted.

"Have you always been such a pompous ass?" had been Marcy's blistering retort.

Why hadn't she shown Peter the letter?

She'd told herself that it had been addressed to her and her alone. "MOMMY," Devon had written across its clean surface. But she'd always known such rationalizations were a lie. Peter was her husband. He'd deserved to see what Devon had written. Not sharing Devon's letter with him had been the final nail in the coffin their marriage had become.

"It's my fault he ran off with the stupid golf pro," she said now, the sudden realization stopping her in her tracks.

Don't be ridiculous, she heard her sister say, her voice emanating from a naked mannequin in the window of a nearby dress shop. *Nobody forced him to have an affair.*

"I shut him out."

Big deal. Stop making excuses. You were right the first time— he's a pompous ass.

"Which doesn't make it any less my fault."

Oh, please. Everything's always your fault. Excuse me, but I think I prefer the crazy lady to the martyr.

"Excuse me," the voice said again.

"What?" Marcy turned to see a couple of teenagers dressed entirely in black, tattoos covering the boy's neck and creeping up into his tall mohawk, assorted piercings disturbing his girlfriend's powdery complexion, both sets of lips working furiously, chewing gum as if their lives depended on it.

"Are you goin' in or what?" the girl asked, transferring her weight from one foot to the other. Marcy noted her black fishnet stockings had holes in both knees.

"What?"

"You're blockin' the stairway," the boy said.

"Oh, sorry." Marcy stepped aside. It was only then she noticed the metal, hand-painted sign that said MULCAHY'S, its black arrow pointing toward the ground.

The basement door opened to admit the young couple and a jolt of loud rap music shot toward the street, causing Marcy to take a step back, as if she'd been pushed. Cigarette smoke blasted from the room as if from a furnace, the distinctive smell of marijuana racing up the steps to tease at Marcy's nostrils. How many nights had Devon come home, that same sickly-sweet smell clinging to her clothes?

Was she here? Marcy wondered. Was her daughter somewhere in that dark, smoky basement right now, taking hits off clumsily hand-rolled cigarettes and gyrating to the murderously relentless hip-hop beat, her voice raised in unmelodious song, shouting hostile lyrics toward the dank, indifferent walls? Was she locked in a new lover's arms, her hips grinding suggestively against his, her eyes glued to the door, waiting . . . watching . . . ?

Well, hello there, Mommy. What took you so long?

It was just the sort of place Devon would be drawn to, Marcy was thinking as the door opened again and another wave of noisy exuberance rushed toward her on a cloying cloud of odoriferous smoke. So what am I waiting for? she wondered, starting down the steps and almost colliding with a blue-haired young woman who was staggering up, the girl's heavily shadowed eyes frantically searching for a place to be sick.

The heavy steel door opened just as Marcy was reaching for it, dispensing two skinny young toughs whose long hair was plastered to their scalps with perspiration. "Tessa, you cow," one of them shouted, "you're not throwin' up again, are you?"

"Excuse me," Marcy said to the accompaniment of Tessa's violent retching. She quickly pushed past the boys into the dark, pulsating room.

It took a few seconds for Marcy's eyes to adjust to the almost total blackness, even longer before her lungs stopped stinging and she was able to breathe. There had to be at least a hundred people crowded into a space that comfortably held maybe forty at best. In the far corner of the room, a ghoulish-looking DJ was spinning records, combining rock and hip-hop, rap and the Rolling Stones. Everywhere people were dancing to the merciless beat. Others were merely jumping up and down in place, as if in the throes of an epileptic fit. There was a smattering of girls dancing with other girls, their boyfriends encouraging them from the sidelines while they swayed spastically and passed joints between them, everyone laughing and letting off steam, the steam rising and forming poisonous clouds around Marcy's head, threatening to cut off her supply of air.

And then she saw them. They were standing against the back wall, their faces only intermittently visible above the wildly bobbing heads, their bodies so close together their flesh seemed to be joined. The boy was whispering something in the girl's ear, and she was giggling, bringing the back of her hand to her mouth in an effort to contain her laughter, her eyes lifting coyly toward his and then quickly returning to the floor.

Marcy felt her heartbeat quicken as she skirted the wall, feeling like a sand crab as she sidled closer, her head down, trying not to draw any unwarranted attention to herself. She was almost beside them when she felt a hand clamp down on her shoulder.

"Excuse me," a man said rudely, "but where do you think you're goin'?"

Marcy reluctantly turned toward the powerful voice, praying it wasn't another garda. She was careful to keep her chin low, her eyes downcast, her voice soft. Even from this submissive position she could see the man was massive, his chest muscular and expansive inside his black T-shirt, his biceps the size of boulders. "I'm sorry, I—"

"There's a ten-euro cover charge," the man said, holding out his large, sweaty palm.

Marcy quickly reached inside her purse and dropped ten euros into his hand. He promptly stamped the back of her hand and disappeared into the crowd. Marcy glanced around the room self-consciously, wondering if anyone had been watching their exchange and noting that she was at least two decades older than everyone else in the room. Had anyone noticed?

Pretending to be smoothing down her hair while covering her face with her fingers, Marcy raised her eyes and held her breath. Please let them still be here, she prayed, almost afraid to look. If the commotion had alerted them to her presence, if they'd recognized her and immediately taken off . . . "Please," she whispered, the word escaping her lips and free-falling toward the floor.

They hadn't moved.

Thank God, Marcy thought, drawing closer.

"I said, what do you think of all this?" she heard the boy shout toward his companion.

Marcy was suddenly grateful for the noisy crowd because it meant the boy had to yell to be heard. She just had to get close enough to eavesdrop without being detected.

"Never seen anything like it," the girl shouted back.

"They don't have places like this in Glengariff?"

"They don't have much of anything in Glengariff."

The boy continued after several seconds had elapsed. "So, Shannon, are you glad you came?"

"You know I am."

"I know *I'm* glad," Jax said.

Shannon lowered her head, her long, strawberry-blond hair falling across her thin nose. Jax's hand immediately moved to tuck the hair behind her ear. Marcy's gold earring glinted at her through the darkness.

Marcy gasped, bringing her hand to her mouth to block the sound. So it had been Jax, after all, who'd broken into her hotel room. Why? Stealing her earrings could only have been an afterthought, an opportunity he chose not to waste. What else had he been hoping to find? The photos? Devon's letter? Or had the trashing of her room been a warning, a way of telling her to back off, leave town, leave her daughter alone?

"I thought Audrey was supposed to be joinin' us," she heard Shannon say.

"Guess she changed her mind. Are you disappointed?"

Shannon giggled. "No. Are you?"

"Nah. Kinda glad, actually."

Marcy felt her eyes sting with tears. Audrey was supposed

to he here, but she'd changed her mind. Once again she'd come so close, only to fall short.

Was there any chance her daughter might still show up?

"Do you think she's got a fella?" Shannon asked.

"Audrey's always got a fella," was Jax's terse reply.

"Do you know who he is?"

"Nah. She don't say much about him. I think he's older."

"Older? Mr. O'Connor's age, you mean?"

"Don't know. She keeps talkin' about how mature he is, that sort of shit. Anyway, who gives a fuck? You're here. That's all I care about."

Even in the dark, Marcy could see Shannon blush.

"It was a lucky thing you called when you did," Shannon said.

"Yeah, I'm a lucky bugger all right."

"I mean it was lucky you called *today*. Tomorrow, you'da missed me."

"Are you goin' somewhere then?"

"Over to Kinsale for a few days. Mrs. O'Connor's got an aunt who's not well."

"What's the matter with her?"

"Cancer."

"My granddad died of cancer."

"Mine, too. It's so sad really."

"So when will you be back?"

"Sunday night."

"Oh, not so long then."

"No. Only three days."

"Still, I'll miss you."

"You will not. You're just sayin' that."

"It's the God's honest truth. I like you a lot. What—you don't believe me?"

Shannon giggled. "I don't know."

"You think I'd have given you those earrings if I didn't?" Jax asked.

Another involuntary cry escaped Marcy's lips. Jax's head immediately twisted in her direction. Was it possible he'd heard her, despite all the noise? Marcy quickly turned away, brought her hand up to hide her face.

"Hold on a minute," Jax said.

"What is it?"

Oh, shit, thought Marcy, feeling him advance. Had he seen her? What was he going to do? She had to get out of there, get out now.

Except she couldn't move. She was trapped, as if she were mired in quicksand, squeezed between dozens of sweating, undulating bodies, unable to feel her feet or even wiggle her toes. She felt a scream rise in her throat as Jax began shouldering his way through the throng.

It took Marcy a few seconds to realize that he wasn't moving toward her, that he was, in fact, taking off in the opposite direction.

"Jax, wait. Where you goin'?" Shannon called after him.

"Be right back," he yelled, fighting his way toward the door.

Marcy immediately began worming her way through the stubborn wall of revelers after him, elbowing past groups of teenage girls, stepping on their boyfriends' boots—"Hey, watch it!" "What's yer hurry, granny?"—till she reached the door and escaped into the cold night air, her ears ringing, her eyes shooting up and down the street.

Where did he go? she wondered, running up the steps and stopping suddenly, realizing how exposed she was. Had that been his plan all along? Had he known she was watching and bided his time, baited his trap, knowing she'd follow him? No way he could confront her in a room full of people. No, if he'd been smart enough to break into her hotel room without anyone noticing, he was smart enough to realize he had to wait until he had her alone.

She heard him before she saw him, his voice coming at her in waves from around the side of the building. "I'm tellin' you," he was saying, "that's what she just said."

Who's he talking to? Marcy wondered, tiptoeing closer, head down, shoulders slumped forward, body hugging the brick wall as she strained to make out his words. Who else was there?

"Okay, I'll go over the whole thing from the beginnin'," he said, and Marcy realized he was talking on his cell phone. "We're at Mulcahy's. She's like a bleedin' alien, all googly eyed and full of wonder, never seen anythin' like it in her life. You'd think she was from bloody Mars, for fuck's sake. Yes, I gave her the earrings. Yes, she loved 'em. Just like you said she would. So I got the stupid girl eatin' out of the palm of me hand. Everything's movin' accordin' to plan. I'm startin' to feel like fuckin' James Bond. Hey, we should call this 'Operation Babycakes.'" He laughed. "Anyway, that's when the dumb twat lowers the boom. Says she's goin' away for a few days. Tomorrow. 'Til bloody Sunday. To fuckin' Kinsale. The whole bleedin' family's goin'. Apparently, Mrs. O'Connor's got a sick aunt. Fuckin' cancer," he sneered.

He paused to catch his breath, allowing Marcy a few seconds to try to make sense of what she'd just heard. *Yes, I gave her the earrings.* Judith had given her those earrings for her fiftieth birthday. *Yes, she loved 'em. Just like you said she would.* Just like *who* said she would? *I'm startin' to feel like fuckin' James Bond. Hey, we should call this "Operation Babycakes."* What were they planning? Who else was involved? *She's goin' away for a few days. . . . The whole bleedin' family's goin'*. What did it mean? Was Devon somehow involved? Involved in what exactly?

Good God. What had her daughter gotten herself into now?

"Yeah, I know it's only three days, but I can already taste that money. . . ."

Marcy's cell phone suddenly began ringing in her purse. Shit, she thought, frantically trying to muzzle the sound by stuffing her purse under her sweater and pressing down on it with her arms. Had Jax heard it?

"Hold on a sec," he said, the heels of his boots clicking against the cobblestone. "Thought I heard somethin'."

Marcy immediately ducked inside the doorway of a nearby store, almost overwhelmed by the smell of nearby vomit. Tessa, you cow, she thought, recalling the laughter of Tessa's friends. Her phone continued to ring, the sound mercifully fainter now. Would Jax still be able to hear it? Would he find her? What would he do when he did?

A sudden burst of noise, the angry sound of Mick Jagger directing someone to get off his cloud, laughter, coughing, a girl's voice rising above everything else: "Jax, are you out here?"

"Comin', luv," he answered immediately.

Marcy heard heavy footsteps descending the steps.

"I was worried about you. Is everything all right?" Shannon asked as the door closed behind them.

Marcy immediately extricated her purse from her sweater and her cell phone from her purse. But it had stopped ringing. She tossed the phone back into her purse, deciding it had likely been Liam calling to check up on her. Should she call him back? And tell him what? That instead of staying put and ordering room service as he'd wisely suggested, she'd spent the night going from one disaster to another? That her amateur sleuthing had almost gotten her raped? That she'd come this close to spending another night in a garda station? That she'd stumbled upon Jax with Shannon in a notorious after-hours club? That she may or may not have uncovered some possibly nefarious plot that may or may not involve her daughter?

Shielding her head from a fresh onslaught of raindrops, she began the long walk back to her hotel.

TWENTY-THREE

S HE DREAMED OF CAKE. Double-layer vanilla cake with rich vanilla icing and lots of gooey red flowers. The kind of cake that Devon always requested for her birthday. "She has such a sweet tooth," Marcy explained to the smattering of guests around the long dining room table.

"Sweets for the sweet," Shannon said, blushing the same color as the roses on the cake and adjusting the party hat on her head.

"Sugar and spice and everything nice," Judith added. She was dressed all in black. Her well-toned arms were covered with tattoos.

"That's what little girls are made of," Jax said, entering the room, a crying baby in his arms.

"Oh, let me see," Devon gushed, running toward them.

"Take her." Jax transferred the baby to Devon's eager arms. "She weighs a right ton."

"She's so cute."

"If you like babies," Jax said dismissively.

And suddenly Marcy and Liam were strolling down the cobbled roads of Youghal. "Where are we going?" she asked him.

"Haven't you heard? Claire and Audrey have opened a bakery. They make the best cakes in all of Ireland."

"What's their secret?" Marcy asked.

"Cranbabies," Liam said.

Somewhere in the distance, a baby started crying.

"Please, can't somebody do something about that incessant racket?" Vic Sorvino asked, walking quickly past, clearly in a hurry.

"Vic?" Marcy called after him. "Wait. Where are you going?"

"Kinsale," he answered. "I have a date with Devon."

"But you're too old for Devon." Marcy glanced toward the ground, watching the cobblestones at her feet become autumn leaves as a cool wind pushed at her back. She entered a clearing, seeing Georgian Bay stretched out before her, an empty canoe drifting aimlessly in the middle of its rough waters. Devon was sitting on a blood-splattered, gray cashmere blanket at the water's edge, Shannon beside her, a baby crying in her arms.

"Did you bring the cake?" Shannon asked.

Marcy held out a large wicker picnic basket.

Devon stood up, took the shrieking infant from Shannon, and walked toward Marcy, her mouth twisting into a cruel smile. "Here's the girl you've always wanted," she said. Then she opened her arms and let the baby fall.

Marcy bolted upright in her bed, frantically grabbing for the child before she hit the cold earth. "No!" she cried, the sound of her protest piercing her subconscious like a pin through a balloon. She woke up, gasping for air, her hands pulling help-lessly at her sheets. "Damn it," she said with a sigh, coming fully awake and flopping back down on her pillow. Pushing her hair away from her face with her still trembling fingers, she glanced at her bedside clock, amazed to see it was almost eight a.m. She was so exhausted from the events of last night, she probably would have slept 'til noon had her nightmare not jolted her awake. "Stupid dream," she muttered as its details began to fade and break up, like a bad telephone connection. Cakes and babies, she thought, shaking her head at the ridicu-lousness of it all.

Babycakes.

"Operation Babycakes," she remembered Jax saying jok-ingly. Marcy's brain suddenly scrambled to retrieve the few fragments of her dream that remained in an effort to corral them and bring them into sharper focus. She saw Devon walk-ing toward her, a demonic smile on her lips, a howling baby in her arms.

The O'Connor baby, Marcy realized, finding it difficult to breathe. "Caitlin," she whispered, sitting up again, her whole body growing ice-cold.

What was she thinking? Was it possible?

"No," she answered immediately. "You're being silly and melodramatic."

Was she? What was she thinking?

Everything's movin' accordin' to plan, she heard Jax say.

What plan? What did it mean?

"Absolutely nothing," Marcy told herself, repeating the words again in an effort to give them greater weight.

Except . . .

Except what if it did?

What if it meant something after all? Something of consequence. Something even sinister. Something almost too terrible to contemplate.

Yes, I gave her the earrings. Yes, she loved 'em. Just like you said she would.

Like who said?

Audrey? Marcy thought.

Had he been talking to her daughter?

Were Jax and Devon involved in some crazy scheme regarding the O'Connor baby? And did that crazy scheme include winning over the baby's hapless and naive nanny?

Bleedin' alien, Jax had called her. *Stupid girl. Dumb twat.*

Hardly the words of an infatuated suitor.

Yeah, I know it's only three days, but I can already taste that money.

And if Jax *had* been talking to Devon, exactly what were they talking about?

Was it possible that there was a plan to kidnap Caitlin O'Connor and hold her for ransom? And was Shannon an active participant in the carrying out of that plan or was she simply an unwitting dupe?

Could Devon really be involved?

Marcy jumped out of bed, ran into the bathroom, threw some cold water at her face, and brushed her teeth with the toothbrush the hotel had provided. There was no time for a shower, she decided as she pulled on the same clothes she'd been wearing the day before. No time to go shopping. No time to eat breakfast. No time for anything except finding her daughter and stopping this insanity once and for all.

She might not have known where to find Devon, but Marcy

knew exactly where the O'Connors lived. She'd go there now. Go there and warn them that their baby was in danger. Tell them everything she'd overheard at the club last night. It was still early. Hopefully they hadn't left for Kinsale yet. After all, it took time to get organized when you traveled anywhere with a baby, especially one as colicky as Caitlin. With any luck, they'd still be home. There'd be time to catch them before they left, to warn them.

What would Shannon say? Would she support Marcy's story, risk incurring Mrs. O'Connor's wrath by admitting the truth of where she'd been and with whom? Or would she deny it, afraid of losing her job? Would she laugh derisively and dismiss Marcy's ravings as those of a seriously deranged individual who'd been pestering her for days, an obviously deluded and unbalanced woman who was well-known to the local gardai?

Which was exactly why she couldn't call officers Murphy, Donnelly, and Sweeny, Marcy understood. What could she tell them, after all? That she'd eavesdropped on a phone call outside a seedy after-hours club, a one-sided conversation at that, a *vague* and one-sided conversation, and from that brief, vague, and one-sided conversation, she'd magically deduced that the O'Connor baby was in danger and that her daughter, yes, the same daughter who was missing, the same daughter she was searching for, the same daughter everyone else was convinced had drowned almost two years earlier, might be involved. Yes, of course they'd believe her. Why wouldn't they?

"It doesn't matter," Marcy told herself.

It didn't matter if the O'Connors believed her or not. It didn't matter if anybody believed her. What mattered was that by warning the O'Connors, by alerting them to a potential threat, they would be all the more vigilant regarding their daughter, and Marcy would have put an end to this harebrained scheme that was sure to bring disaster down on the heads of all those involved. She would have succeeded where she'd failed so often in the past: in protecting her daughter from herself.

Assuming Devon was involved.

Was she?

Marcy took a few seconds before running out the door to run a comb through her hair and apply a hint of lipstick. It would help if she didn't look too crazy, she thought. What she was about to tell the O'Connors was crazy enough.

She decided to take a taxi, a mistake, she decided once she was firmly ensconced in the cab's backseat. The traffic was especially awful and the cab driver particularly garrulous. "Is there any way we can get there faster?" she asked him, sitting forward in her seat and giving him the O'Connors' address. "I'm in a huge hurry."

"A *huge* hurry, are you?"

"It's just that I'm running late."

"Americans are always in a hurry."

"Actually, I'm not American." Marcy corrected him, an automatic reflex, then wished she hadn't.

"What *are* you then?"

"Canadian."

He scoffed. "What's the difference?"

Marcy had no desire to go into the various cultural differences that distinguished the two countries. "What's the difference between north and south Ireland?" she asked in return, then bit down on her lip. She really *was* crazy, she thought. What was the point in being so provocative?

"Are you kiddin' me?" the cabbie sputtered. "The difference between the north and the south of Ireland?"

"Forget it," Marcy said. "I'm sorry. I didn't mean—"

"Have you no knowledge of history?" he demanded.

"It was a silly thing to say."

"I'll give you a wee refresher course."

"That's really not necessary."

"In 8000 BC, the earliest known human settlers arrived in Ireland," he said, clearing his throat with a flourish.

Dear God, thought Marcy.

"In 2000 BC, the first metalworkers arrived. In 700 BC, the Celtic settlement of Ireland began. The Gaels arrived in 100 AD. About three hundred years later, St. Patrick returned to Ireland as a Christian missionary." The taxi drove over a large pothole, sending Marcy bouncing a good foot into the air.

"Do you think you can concentrate on the road?" she asked the driver.

"The years between 500 and 800 AD are often referred to as the golden age," he said, ignoring her plea. "Ireland became one of the largest centers of Christianity in Europe."

"Look. I'm really sorry if you took offense—"

"Then the Vikings invaded, then the Danes, then the English. In 1204, Dublin Castle was founded as the center of English power. By the 1500s, Henry VIII declared himself king of all Ireland and began the suppression of the Catholic Church. Queen Elizabeth I subsequently proclaimed Ireland an Anglican country."

Marcy sank back in her seat, deciding it was pointless to argue further. What the hell? The history lesson would help to pass the time, keep her mind occupied and her blood pressure down. And she might even learn something.

The cabbie continued. "In 1641, an Irish Catholic revolt in Ulster ended in defeat. Eight years later, Oliver Cromwell invaded. In 1690, the armies of King James the second, a Catholic, were defeated, consolidating the Protestant order in England. In 1782, the Irish parliament was granted independence. In 1801, it dissolved, becoming part of the United Kingdom. Then, 1845," he pronounced ominously. "Surely you know what happened then."

Marcy returned to an upright position, her mind searching for an answer, like an errant student caught not paying attention in class. "I-I'm not sure," she stammered.

"The start of the Great Famine," he said with a disapproving shake of his suitably red hair. "Lasted over three years. Almost two million people either died or emigrated, mostly to America."

"Yes, that was terrible. . . ."

"In 1886 and again in 1894, bills for home rule were defeated in parliament," he said, dismissing her pity with a wave of his hand. "In 1905 came the founding of Sinn Fein. You know what that means?"

"Trouble?" Marcy asked, catching the driver's glare in the rearview mirror.

"Sinn Fein means 'We Ourselves,' and in 1918 they won a landslide victory against the Irish Parliamentary Party. From 1919 through 1921 was the Irish War of Independence led by Michael Collins, which led to the Anglo-Irish Treaty whereby Ireland was partitioned into twenty-six counties forming the Free State and six that remained part of the UK."

Marcy leaned forward again. Despite herself, she found herself growing increasingly interested in this impromptu history lesson. "Did you used to be a teacher?"

He shook his head. "Every Irishman could tell you as much. Couldn't you? About Canada?"

"I was never very good in history," Marcy replied. What *had* she been good at?

"In 1922 and '23—the Irish civil war," the cabbie declared, "between the government of the Free State and those who opposed the Anglo-Irish Treaty. Michael Collins was assassinated by the IRA, who considered the treaty a sellout. In 1937 the Free State adopted a new constitution and abandoned its membership in the British Commonwealth. The country changed its name to Eire. In 1948, the Republic of Ireland severed its last constitutional links to Britain."

"You left out the Second World War," Marcy said, admonishing him.

"Ireland was neutral."

"You prefer to fight among yourselves," Marcy remarked, and was grateful when he laughed.

"I guess we do." He stopped the car. "Well, here we are, 117 Adelaide Road."

Marcy looked out the side window at the large yellow-brick house with its flower-lined front walk and three-car garage. Hopefully Mr. O'Connor's car was still inside it.

"That didn't take too long, now, did it?" the cabbie asked.

"You did great," Marcy told him, including a generous tip along with the fare. "Thank you. And for the history lesson, too. I learned a lot."

"Next time I see you, there'll be a quiz," he said before pulling away from the curb.

Marcy watched the cab disappear around the bend in the road, then she turned on her heel and ran up the O'Connors' front walk, ringing the bell and pounding on the black double doors. "Please be home," she prayed. "Please don't let me be too late."

But after several seconds, it became obvious that no one was there.

"Damn it," Marcy exclaimed, walking around to the side of the house, knowing there was little point in knocking on the side door but doing it anyway. She approached the garage and jumped up, trying to see inside the sliver of glass that ran along the top of all three garage doors. But the glass was too high and the inside of the garage too dark, and what difference did it make if their car was inside anyway? If the O'Connors had a three-car garage, there was a good chance they had more than one car. Besides, they could have taken the train or even a taxi to Kinsale, she thought, wishing she'd had the foresight to ask her driver to wait until she'd known whether anyone was home. Now what was she supposed to do?

"I could leave them a note," she said out loud, returning to the front of the house and seeing curtains move in the window of the house across the road. She dug inside her purse for a piece of paper but found nothing but a few crumpled pieces of Kleenex. "Naturally." What had she been planning to say anyway? *Hi, you don't know me, but I think someone is planning to kidnap your baby!* "Yeah, right," she said as her cell phone started ringing. She retrieved it from her purse, flipped it open.

"Where are you?" Liam asked before she had time to say hello.

Marcy told him.

"What?" he barked. "What are you doing over there?"

Marcy told him about her trip to Mulcahy's, about seeing Jax with Shannon, about overhearing his phone conversation and her subsequent suspicions.

"Wait a minute," he interrupted. "You're saying you think there's a plot to kidnap the O'Connors' baby?"

"You think I'm crazy," Marcy said. Of course he'd think she was crazy. What other option had she left him?

He surprised her by saying, "I think you should call the gardai."

"What?"

"Call the police, Marcy," he translated. "Now."

"I can't."

"Why not?"

"*They'll* think I'm crazy," she said.

"They *already* think you're crazy," he said, reminding her. She smiled.

"Look, Marcy. You're in way over your head. You've done everything you can. Now let the police handle it."

"I'm afraid Devon might be involved. I don't want to get her in trouble."

"If your suspicions are correct, it's too late for that."

"But what if I'm wrong?"

"What if you're right?" he asked in return. "What if you're right and something happens to the O'Connor baby, and you could have stopped it? You'll never forgive yourself."

"I know," Marcy said. "I just don't know if I can."

The sound of sirens in the distance, getting louder, drawing nearer.

"Call the gardai, Marcy," Liam urged.

Marcy watched a police car tear up the street and pull to a stop in front of the O'Connors' driveway, watched as the nosy neighbor emerged from her house across the street and conferred with one of the gardai, while another garda walked purposefully up the path of the O'Connors' front lawn toward her.

"Call the police," Liam said again.

"That won't be necessary," Marcy said.

TWENTY-FOUR

R EALLY, MRS. TAGGART," CHRISTOPHER Murphy was saying, leaning back in the chair behind his desk and cup-
ping his hands behind his head. "We have to stop meeting this
way."

Marcy smiled, appreciating the senior garda's attempt at
levity, however strained. She knew what he probably wanted
to do was lock her in a holding cell until she was due to leave
Ireland, or better yet, personally escort her to the airport and
strap her into her seat on the Air Canada jet back to Toronto
himself. Despite his outwardly calm demeanor, she recognized
the look of contained fury in his eyes that said he was this close
to leaping across the desk and wrapping his fingers around her
throat. She'd seen that same look in Peter's eyes many times in
the months leading up to his eventual desertion.

"I'm truly sorry for all the trouble I've caused," Marcy told him.

Murphy waited, as if he'd already heard the "but" that was about to follow.

"But I haven't done anything wrong," Marcy said obligingly.

"Not much you've done right either," was Murphy's instant retort.

"That's true," Marcy was forced to concede. "But, as far as I know, I haven't broken any laws."

"Don't know about that. I think a good case might be made for being a public nuisance."

"A public nuisance? That's ridiculous."

"This is your third visit to this station in as many days," he said. "Not to mention the little stunt you pulled last night."

"The stunt . . . ?" Dear God, had that bastard Kieran filed a formal complaint?

"I understand you spent some quality time with one of our boys in the front seat of his patrol car," Christopher Murphy said, nodding toward the open folder on his desk.

Marcy felt her shoulders slump. "You know about that," she stated more than asked.

"Marcy Taggart, Canadian citizen, found wandering the Cork hills at around ten p.m.," he recited from memory, "a little wobbly on her feet, smelling of alcohol, likely inebriated . . ."

"I was not drunk."

"No? What were you then?"

"I just needed some air."

"At ten o'clock at night? In the pouring rain? Far from your hotel?" Murphy nodded, then shook his head, as if arguing with himself over how best to proceed. "Is that what you were doing this morning as well then? Just getting some air?"

Another weary shake of his head when Marcy failed to respond. "Mrs. Leary said it wasn't the first time she caught you snoopin' around the O'Connors' house."

"I wasn't *snoopin'*," Marcy replied pointedly, then immediately wished she hadn't. Christopher Murphy wasn't the enemy. What was the point in antagonizing him? "If anybody's a snoop, it's that damn Mrs. Leary."

"She saw you peeking in her neighbor's windows, tiptoeing around the side of their house, looking in their garage," Murphy rattled off, carefully enunciating the final G of each verb.

"I was just trying to see if the O'Connors were still home."

Murphy nodded. "The fact that nobody answered when you knocked or rang their bell wasn't enough of a clue?"

"I already told the other officers—"

"You were trying to warn them," the garda stated as the door to his office opened and Officer Sweeny stepped inside. He walked around the side of Christopher Murphy's desk and whispered something in his ear, his pronounced belly brushing up against the sleeve of Murphy's uniform. Murphy nodded several times, and Sweeny left the room with a knowing smile in Colleen Donnelly's direction. The female garda was standing in a far corner of the room, one thin ankle crossed over the other, her shoulder leaning against the off-white wall, so quiet that Marcy had all but forgotten she was there.

"Yes, that's right," Marcy said.

"That there's a plot afoot to kidnap their baby."

"Right again," Marcy said, trying to ignore the tired note of skepticism she heard in the policeman's voice.

"And you think this because . . . ?"

"I've already explained."

"Explain it again."

Marcy sighed, understanding the drill. Might as well

cooperate, she thought, knowing there was no point in arguing. She wasn't going to get out of here until she went over
every last detail of her story again. And, very likely, again
after that.

"I overheard a phone conversation," she said, folding her
arms across her chest and speaking to the floor.

"Back up a minute," Murphy barked, his tone forcing her
eyes up to his. "Where was this?"

"Outside Mulcahy's." Marcy glanced at the temporary black
tattoo on the back of her hand. It had faded only slightly from
the night before, despite repeated attempts to remove it.

"And what, pray tell, possessed you to go to a place like
Mulcahy's?"

"I was looking for my daughter—"

"That would be Audrey?"

"Devon," Marcy said, correcting him.

"Yes, right. She's just calling herself Audrey these days.
Who told you about Mulcahy's?"

"I asked one of the housekeeping staff at my hotel if she
knew a popular spot for young people. . . ."

"And she mentioned Mulcahy's."

"Yes."

"And so you went there."

"Yes."

"Alone?"

"Yes."

"What time was that?"

"I'm not sure. Around seven, I think."

"Mulcahy's is an after-hours club. It doesn't open until ten."

"So I discovered."

"So you decided to go for a long walk," he said.

"No. First I went to a pub."

"Which one?"

"I don't remember."

"You don't remember?"

"It was on the North Channel. There was a band playing Irish music. I don't know its name. Why? What difference does it make? It was just a pub in the area."

"What did you eat?"

"I don't understand. Why are you asking me this?" Her eyes appealed to Colleen Donnelly for assistance. Colleen Donnelly's eyes remained stubbornly blank and unhelpful.

"Just trying to get a feel for things, Mrs. Taggart. Surely you remember what you ate for dinner last night."

"It was a ham and cheese sandwich," Marcy said, recalling the meal she'd never had the chance to eat.

"And how was it?"

"Fine."

"Glad to hear it."

"Have a beer with it?"

"Yes."

"How many?"

"Just one."

"You're sure about that?"

"Quite sure."

Murphy stretched his arms high above his head before leaning forward and resting his elbows on his desk, his chin balancing on the backs of his hands. "Okay, so how long would you say you were in the pub? An hour? Two, maybe? Just trying to establish a timeline," he explained before Marcy had a chance to protest.

She cleared her throat. Had that idiot Kieran actually had the gall to report her to the police? Was Murphy trying to trick her with this parade of seemingly innocent questions? "I don't think I was there all that long," she said. "I ate my sandwich, drank my beer, then I left."

"And did what?"

"Nothing. Just walked."

"In the rain?"

"It's usually raining," she told him.

"Yes, that's unfortunately true," Murphy said with a laugh.

Marcy sat back in her chair, trying to appear relaxed, to will the stiffness from her lips so that her smile wouldn't appear as forced as she suspected it looked. She crossed her legs at the knees and then brought her hand up to tuck her hair behind her ear.

"What's that on your sleeve?" Murphy asked immediately.

"What?" Marcy quickly lowered her arm, taking only a cursory glance at the dried blood that stained her sweater.

"Looks like blood."

"Blood?" Marcy pretended to take a closer look. "No. Of course not. It's ketchup, that's all."

"Take ketchup on your ham and cheese sandwich, do you?"

"It's not blood," Marcy said, louder than she'd intended.

"Ketchup it is then. All right." He returned to his original line of questioning. "So, you walked around for a couple of hours in the rain until you were stopped by Officer Reagan. . . ."

"Yes."

"And you sat and chatted with him awhile, until he received a call about a burglary. . . ."

"Yes."

"And then instead of going back to your hotel, as I believe you promised him you would do, you headed straight back to Mulcahy's."

"Yes," Marcy said guiltily. Did the Irish consider it a crime to break your promise?

"And at Mulcahy's, you just happened to see the lad you say ran you down with his bicycle some days back."

"Yes."

"And he was with Shannon, the girl you fought with at Grogan's House the other day."

"You're twisting what happened. . . ."

"And you overheard them plotting to kidnap—"

"No," Marcy interrupted, understanding this was no careless mistake on his part. "I overheard Jax on his cell phone."

"When you followed him outside," Murphy stated.

"Yes."

"And he was talking about kidnapping the O'Connor baby?"

"Not exactly."

"What exactly?"

"He said that everything had been moving according to plan," Marcy told him. "He made a joke about 'Operation Baby-cakes'—"

"Operation Babycakes?" the garda repeated incredulously.

"I know it sounds ridiculous."

"And you naturally assumed he was referring to the O'Connor baby."

Marcy decided to ignore the inherent sarcasm of the word "naturally." "Not right away, no. I had no idea what he was talking about at the time."

"When did you figure it out?"

Marcy hesitated. This was the part she'd been dreading, the moment she went from nuisance to nutcase. "Later."

"Later? What happened . . . later?"

"I had a dream." She admitted it reluctantly, already picturing the bemused looks of condescension on the faces of the two gardai.

"So this epiphany came to you in a dream, did it?" Christopher Murphy asked as Colleen Donnelly pushed herself away from the wall and buried her growing smile behind the fingers of her left hand.

"That's not what I said."

"I'm sorry. I thought you did."

"The dream just helped me put the pieces together."

"Perhaps you'd be good enough to explain how."

"Jax said that everything had been moving according to plan," Marcy repeated yet again, her voice rising. "He said he was starting to feel like James Bond and that maybe they should call their plan—"

"Operation Babycakes," both gardai said together.

"Yes. That's right. But now everything was going to have to be delayed because the O'Connors were going away for a few days, and he was upset because he could already taste the money."

"The money they were going to collect as ransom?"

"Yes."

"Did he actually ever use the word 'ransom'?"

Marcy shook her head. "No."

"You just assumed that's what he meant?"

"Bit of a leap, don't you think?" Colleen Donnelly interjected.

Marcy glared in her direction. "What else could it mean?"

"If you thought there was a plot to kidnap the O'Connor baby," Murphy asked logically, "why didn't you call us?"

Marcy took a deep breath, pausing for several seconds before answering. "Because I was afraid that Devon might be involved. I didn't want to get her in trouble, and I thought if I could just talk to the O'Connors—"

"So, you rushed right over to their house to warn them?" Murphy asked probingly, his tone indicating that he already knew the answer to his question.

Shit, Marcy thought. Shit, shit, shit. "No."

"You didn't try to warn them?"

"Not right away, no."

"You waited 'til this morning?"

Marcy nodded.

"And why is that, Mrs. Taggart?"

"I already told you. I needed time to figure things out."

"Because you weren't sure."

"I was tired. . . ."

"Tired and confused," Murphy added.

"I just needed some time. . . ."

"To sleep on it."

"Yes."

"So you went to sleep and had a dream. . . ."

"It's not as simple as you're making it out to be," Marcy insisted. "My subconscious was obviously trying to piece everything together."

"So it was your subconscious that told you this Jax person had been possibly conspiring with your daughter, Devon or Audrey or whatever she's calling herself these days, that same daughter who everyone else, including your ex-husband, insists is dead, that these two people conspired to seduce the O'Connor nanny in order to kidnap their baby. . . ."

"Believe me, I know how crazy this must sound," Marcy said.

"It does sound a trifle far-fetched," Colleen Donnelly said.

"I'm not crazy," Marcy told them.

Crazy bitch! she heard Kieran shout.

This is crazy, she heard Judith mutter.

"I'm not crazy," Marcy repeated, tears falling the length of her cheeks.

Christopher Murphy came around the front of his desk,

perched against its side, and leaned in toward her. "Mrs. Taggart, I don't doubt for a minute that you believe everything you've told us. I also believe your intentions are honorable and pure."

"It's just that you don't think what I'm saying has any merit," Marcy said.

"Can you try to look at it from our perspective?" He took a deep breath before continuing. "You've suffered two terrible losses in as many years: Your daughter was presumed drowned almost two years ago in a tragic accident, and your husband left you. You're alone in a strange country; your imagination is working overtime; even *you* have to admit you're not behaving rationally. You've already been hauled down here twice before for creating a disturbance; you've been tossed out of your hotel and picked up for wandering the streets; you've been sleeping with virtual strangers—"

"Excuse me?"

"I'm sorry. I don't mean to sound judgmental. Of course you're free to sleep with whomever you like."

"I've slept with exactly two men in the last quarter of a century," Marcy said. "My husband and—"

"A man you met on a bus." Murphy finished for her. "We spoke to Vic Sorvino," he added before Marcy could muster up any further cries of indignation.

"You did? When?"

"We intercepted him at the airport yesterday afternoon as he was about to board a plane for Rome. He denied trashing your hotel room, said that when he left, everything was in order. He made no objections to our searching his luggage or his pockets for your earrings. Our search revealed nothing."

"Oh, God. Poor Vic." Of course he'd had nothing to do with the trashing of her hotel room. It had been Jax. He'd stolen her earrings, given them to Shannon.

"And Liam Flaherty?" Colleen Donnelly asked.

"Liam?" The sudden mention of his name—his last name was Flaherty?—startled Marcy. "I'm not sleeping with Liam."

"What exactly *is* your relationship with Mr. Flaherty?" Murphy asked.

It seemed strange to hear the police refer to Liam as Mr. Flaherty, Marcy thought. It gave him a weight, a substance, she'd formerly denied him. "He's a friend. I told you, he's been helping me look for Devon. You can ask him, if you'd like."

"Think I just might do that. He's waiting in the next room."

"What?"

"Sweeny said he showed up about half an hour ago, very concerned about you."

"He begged me to call you," Marcy told them.

"Should have listened to him."

About a lot of things, she thought.

"If you'll excuse me a minute," Murphy said, leaving the room before Marcy could think of a reason to object.

"He's a very handsome man," Colleen Donnelly remarked as Christopher Murphy closed the door after him.

"Officer Murphy?"

Colleen laughed. "Liam Flaherty."

"Oh. Yes, I guess he is."

"That Sorvino fellow isn't half-bad either. And much more age appropriate, if you ask me."

Marcy shrugged, tuning Colleen Donnelly out and thinking of how humiliated Vic must have been to be "intercepted" at the airport by the police, to be questioned and searched. He must hate me, she thought.

". . . Can't imagine what it's like to be married to the same man for twenty-five years," Colleen was saying as Marcy tuned back in.

She agreed. "It's a long time."

"My parents separated when I was two. Never really knew my dad. My mother burned all his pictures, so I never even knew what he looked like. I used to imagine he was this big, tall, handsome bloke with red hair and a full beard. Sometimes I'd see a stranger walkin' down the street and I'd pretend it was him, and I'd follow him around, sometimes for hours. One time I had myself absolutely convinced. . . ."

Marcy sighed, recognizing that Colleen was trying to gain her confidence and trust with her probably made-up story. "You think that's what I'm doing?"

"Sometimes we just want something so bad. . . ."

"You think I want my daughter to be involved in a kidnapping plot?"

"I think you want your daughter back," Colleen said simply.

"I think we're through talking," Marcy told her sharply. Then she sat back in her chair and closed her eyes. She didn't open them again until she heard the door open and Christopher Murphy announce she was free to go.

TWENTY-FIVE

WHAT TIME IS IT?" Marcy asked Liam, shielding her eyes from an unexpected burst of sunlight as they exited the garda station.

"A little before noon."

"What!" She glanced at her own watch for confirmation. "How is that possible?"

"You've been at the station all morning."

Marcy shook her head. Half a day gone already. Hours of her life disappearing without warning. Her daughter no closer to being found. "They think I'm crazy," she said morosely.

"Yeah," Liam said with a smile. "I think they might." He raised his hand to flag down a passing cab. "Hayfield Manor Hotel," he told the driver as they climbed into the backseat.

"Thanks for coming down."

"No thanks necessary."

"Did they give you a hard time?"

"Nah. I'm tough."

Marcy settled back against the taxi's black leather seat, trying to ignore the awful gnawing sensation in her stomach that reminded her she hadn't had anything to eat in almost twenty-four hours. "What sort of questions did they ask you?"

"Same as last time. How we met, why I'm helping you, whether I believe you, what I know about last night . . ."

"What did you tell them?"

"The truth."

"Which is?"

"That I don't know a damn thing about last night, that we met in the pub where I work, that you're convinced you saw your daughter, and that I'm trying to help you find her because a) I like you, and b) yes, I *do* believe you."

Marcy smiled. "Thank you for that."

"No thanks necessary," he said, as he'd said earlier. "Why didn't you tell me what you were plannin' to do last night?"

"Because you'd already told me not to do it."

"Fat lot of good that did."

"It was stupid." Marcy admitted it. "Although not quite as stupid as going to the O'Connor house this morning."

"True."

She shook her head. "I've lost all credibility as far as the police are concerned."

Liam nodded. "I think that last bit about the plan to kidnap the O'Connor baby might have tipped the scales."

"I guess it sounded pretty weird."

"Did you have to tell them the idea came to you in a dream?"

Marcy expelled a deep breath through barely parted lips. *I'm an idiot,* she thought. "So what do I do now?"

"You?" Liam asked, raising his voice loud enough to attract the attention of the taxi driver, whose eyebrows arched noticeably higher in his rearview mirror. "*You* do nothin'. Do you hear me? Not a bleedin' thing. Unless you want them to lock you up and throw away the key."

"But what if I'm right? What if something happens . . . ?"

"Then it happens. They certainly can't say they weren't warned."

"Do you think they'll at least talk to the O'Connors?" Marcy asked hopefully.

Liam shrugged. "Don't think it's high on their list of priorities."

"Would *you* talk to them?" Marcy asked after a moment's pause.

"Me?"

"*Somebody* has to warn them." Marcy saw the look of resignation that flitted across Liam's wondrous green eyes, the look that told her she might have lost her credibility with him, too. "Unless, of course, you don't believe me . . ."

"It's not a question of whether or not I believe you."

"What *is* it a question of?"

"I believe you saw your daughter. . . ."

"But?"

"But to go from that to thinking she might be involved in some kind of nefarious plot . . ."

"Kind of tipped the scales for you, too, did it?" Marcy asked, throwing his earlier words back at him.

Liam sighed. "These are the facts, Marcy: You overheard a one-sided conversation on a rainy night outside a noisy after-hours club, and then you had a crazy dream. . . ."

"Which explained everything," she said vehemently, then stopped. She was too tired to have this conversation again.

Besides, he was right. Just as Christopher Murphy was right. And Colleen Donnelly. And John Sweeny. And Judith. And Peter. Hell, everyone was right. She really *was* crazy.

"Okay, look," Liam was saying. "What the hell? In for a penny, in for a pound, as they say. If it'll make you feel better, I'll talk to the O'Connors."

"Really?"

"As soon as they get back. Nothing's going to happen 'til then, right?"

"They had to delay their plans," Marcy concurred. "What will you say to them?"

"Don't know. Guess I'll have to think of somethin'."

"I'll go with you," Marcy said eagerly.

"No. You'll stay put. Do you understand? You've done quite enough. You won't budge from your hotel room. Are we agreed?"

"Agreed," Marcy said reluctantly.

"Is that blood?" he asked suddenly, staring at her sleeve.

"What? No." Marcy pretended to be noticing the blood-stains on her sweater for the first time. "I don't know what that is."

"It looks a lot like blood to me."

"Well, it isn't. I must have brushed up against something." Marcy hated herself for lying to the one true friend she had. But admitting it was blood meant explaining what had happened with Kieran, and there was only so much stupidity one man could be expected to stomach without running, scream-ing, for the nearest exit. "I've been wearing the same clothes for two days now. I really should stop and pick up some new things," she said, realizing they'd just passed the Merchant's Quay Shopping Centre. "Can you stop here?" she asked, tap-ping the driver on his shoulder.

"Marcy, for God's sake, what are you doing?" Liam asked as she opened the door and jumped out of the cab. "Marcy, wait up!"

"I'm fine, Liam. Really," she called back at him, knowing how insane she must appear. "I just need some new clothes," she added, watching as he scrambled to pay the driver. "You don't have to babysit me," she told him when he finally caught up to her inside the entrance to Marks and Spencer.

"Actually, I do," he told her.

"What do you mean?"

"I promised the gardai I'd keep an eye on you," Liam said sheepishly. "It was the only way they'd agree to your release."

"Oh."

"Is it so awful," he asked, "havin' me around?"

Marcy studied his beautifully chiseled face, losing herself momentarily in the unabashed intensity of his gaze. "Why are you being so nice to me?"

"I think you already know the answer to that," he said, tilting his head, his lips moving slowly toward hers.

Marcy realized he was going to kiss her again. In the middle of the day, in the middle of a crowded shopping mall, in the middle of this stupid, awful mess, a beautiful young man fifteen years her junior was going to kiss her.

And this time she was going to kiss him back.

Maybe she wasn't as crazy as everyone thought.

"Hold on a minute," Liam said, his soft breath teasing her newly closed eyes.

Instantly she felt him pulling away from her side and she opened her eyes to see him moving toward the tall glass doors of the entrance. What was he doing? Where was he going? What was he looking at? she wondered, her eyes racing after his. "What is it?"

"I thought I saw . . ."

"Audrey?" Marcy felt the color drain from her face as her body began to sway, preparing to take off running in any direction with a simple nod of his head.

"No," Liam said quickly, putting his hand on her arm, as if to steady her. "I'm sorry. I wasn't thinking."

"Who did you see?"

"I thought it was that man you were with, the one I saw at your hotel. . . ."

"Vic Sorvino?" Marcy pushed open the heavy door, her eyes pummeling their way through the crowded flock of Saturday afternoon shoppers. "You saw Vic?"

Liam backtracked. "I don't know for sure it was him. Shit. Now you've got *me* seeing things."

Was it possible Vic was still in Ireland, Marcy wondered, that he hadn't caught the next flight to Rome after his brush with the police? And if he *was* still in Ireland, if he was still right there in Cork, if he was, in fact, at this very minute, in the Merchant's Quay Shopping Centre, then the next logical question was why. What was he doing there? Was he following her? *Why?*

"I don't see him," Liam said as Marcy's eyes continued to sweep the mall.

Marcy agreed seconds later. "No." She took a series of deep breaths in an effort to control the too-rapid thumping of her heart, stopping when they made her feel dizzy and lightheaded.

"Are you all right?" Liam asked. "You look a little pale."

"Excuse me," a woman said, pushing past them into the store.

"I really need to find some new clothes," Marcy heard herself say, her voice coming from somewhere outside her body, as if she were a ventriloquist's doll, unable to function without someone pulling her strings.

"What do you need?" Liam asked, taking a final look around before guiding her past the rows of confectionery treats toward the women's-wear section at the back of the large store.

I need to have my head examined, Marcy thought. "Everything," she said.

Twenty minutes later, casting wary glances over her shoulder for any sign of Vic Sorvino, she approached the sales counter, her arms loaded with two pairs of pants, one black, one khaki; two T-shirts, one white and one beige; a blue-and-white-striped cotton blouse; a navy peacoat; some socks; a new bra; a pair of pink-and-white-flowered flannel pajamas; and half a dozen pairs of Calvin Klein panties. "That should do me," she said, handing the items to the flame-haired, gum-chewing salesclerk.

"You don't want to try any of them things on?" the girl, whose name tag identified her as Sissy, asked.

"No. I'm sure they're fine."

Sissy cracked her gum, as if to say, "Suit yourself," then began ringing up the items. "There's no tag on this one," she said accusingly.

"Oh, sorry," Marcy apologized, accepting that this was somehow her fault.

"Hey, Adeline," Sissy called to a young woman who was walking by. "Can you do a price check for me? This lady lost her tag."

Marcy protested. "I actually don't think there was one."

"There's always a tag," Sissy said with a roll of her bored brown eyes.

"Eighty-eight euros," Adeline shouted back several long minutes later.

Sissy entered the appropriate numbers into the computer. "That's six hundred and forty-four euros in total," she announced between snaps of her gum. Marcy handed over her credit card to be swiped. "There seems to be a problem with your card," Sissy said seconds later.

"What?"

"It's not going through."

"That's impossible. Try again."

Sissy dutifully ran the card through again. "Nah. It's not acceptin' it. Sorry."

"I don't understand," Marcy mumbled, her dizziness returning.

"Is it possible you forgot to pay your bill?" Liam asked.

"No. Peter takes care of that. And he's always on time. He's positively anal about it. Not a day early, not a day late. It's like a mantra with him. He says that the credit card companies charge interest from the first second you're late, so there's no way he's going to let them make interest on his money by paying them early. Just as there's no way he'll let them earn interest by being late. So he's always exactly on time," she said, feeling her knees grow weak. She understood she was babbling but was unable to stop, as if it was only the sound of her voice that was keeping her upright.

"Marcy," Liam said, "are you okay?"

"Do you have another card?" Sissy was asking. "Otherwise, I'll have to ask you to step aside. There's other customers waitin'."

"Here." Liam handed his card to the salesclerk. "Use this."

"No." Marcy protested over the sudden ringing in her ears. The bells of St. Anne's Shandon Church, she thought, amazed at their power. "I can't ask you to do that."

"You'll pay me back as soon as you get this straightened out."

Get what straightened out? Marcy wondered as the ringing grew louder. My credit? My daughter? My life?

"If you'll just sign here," Sissy told Liam. Marcy noticed the salesgirl's hand brush up against his as she pushed the itemized bill across the counter.

"I don't understand," Marcy was muttering as he signed it. Except she did understand. She understood all too well. Peter, alarmed by her recent actions, had cut off her access to her credit cards. The ringing in her ears grew more intense. "Can't somebody please turn off those damn bells," she cried as the ringing reached a crescendo and the room began spinning out of control. In the next instant, her knees gave out. The last thing she saw before she fainted was Liam reaching out to grab her before she hit the floor.

SHE WOKE UP to the sound of knocking.

"Who is it?" Marcy sat up in bed, quickly orienting herself to her surroundings. The leaded windows and delicate, apricot-colored walls told her she was back in her room at the Hay-field Manor Hotel. The clock on her bedside table announced it was almost six o'clock, although she wasn't sure if this meant six in the morning or six at night until she looked closer and saw the p.m. in bold red letters in the bottom right corner of the clock's square face. Okay, so early evening. Which might account for the stiff, vaguely familiar pink-and-white pajamas she was wearing. Where had they come from? And six p.m. seemed rather early to be in bed. Was she sick? What had happened to the rest of the day?

"Room service," called a voice from outside the door.

Marcy threw on the white terry-cloth robe that lay stretched across the foot of her bed and stepped tentatively onto the ivory carpet, her bare toes gripping its thick-piled surface with the intensity of a woman clinging to the side of a mountain. I don't remember ordering anything from room service, she thought.

"Where would you like me to set this up?" a man asked as she opened the door, then wheeled the cart into the center of the room before she had a chance to respond. He was about thirty, with auburn hair, a nose that was thin and long, and lips that were surprisingly thick. His white jacket was at least a size too big for him.

"I think there's been a mistake," Marcy said.

The young man quickly checked the bill. "Room 211?"

"Yes, but—"

"Steak, medium rare; baked potato, butter and sour cream; mashed carrots," he said, lifting the silver covers from their platters with such a dramatic flourish that Marcy found herself taking an involuntary step back. "Plus a Caesar salad to start and some sticky toffee pudding for dessert. Also bottled sparkling water."

Marcy was about to protest that she hadn't ordered any of those things, but the delicious aroma of the steak plus the very thought of sticky toffee pudding made her reconsider. "You can set it up right here." She indicated the side of the bed.

"If you'll just sign this chit," he told her.

If you'll just sign here, she heard Sissy say to Liam.

When was that? How long ago?

Marcy scribbled her name on the appropriate line, adding a generous tip. Let's see Peter try to do something about that, she thought as the young man headed for the door. "Peter," she whispered, a vague memory rubbing itself tantalizingly against her brain, like a cat against a bare leg.

"I'm sorry?" the young man asked, stopping. "Did you say something?"

"No. I just remembered . . ." Peter had cut off her access to her credit cards. When? Why? "It's nothing."

"Would you like me to send someone up to close the curtains?"

"No, that won't be necessary."

He nodded. "Just wheel the cart into the hall when you're done."

"I'll do that."

"Enjoy your meal and have a good night."

Marcy closed the door after him, then plopped down on the bed and tore hungrily into her steak. When was the last time she'd eaten?

When was the last time you had something to eat? she heard Liam ask, his face looming above hers. When? Where?

Marks and Spencer, she remembered, the hours she'd misplaced suddenly returning to her in a frenzied rush: the morning taxi ride to Adelaide Road; the empty O'Connor house; the nosy neighbor; the police; the garda station; Liam; the visit to the mall; Vic Sorvino; shopping for clothes; the mix-up with her credit card; the awful ringing in her ears; losing consciousness; waking up to the sound of Liam's voice. *When was the last time you had something to eat?*

He'd insisted she have a bowl of soup before escorting her back to her hotel and tucking her into bed. "Here," he'd told her, handing her a small white pill.

"I can't believe I fainted—again."

"Put this under your tongue," he told her.

"What is it?"

"It'll help you sleep."

"I don't need to sleep," she'd argued, her voice weak and unconvincing.

"The hell you don't. Look, I have to go to work and I don't

want to spend the rest of the day worryin' about you. I'll have room service send up something for your dinner. In the meantime, get some rest. You don't want to be half-dead when we find your daughter, do you, now? So do us all a favor and take the damn pill."

"I took the damn pill," Marcy said now, remembering.

Then she wolfed down her steak, her baked potato and mashed carrots, her salad and her sticky pudding, drank the entire bottle of sparkling water, and finally wheeled the cart into the hall, climbed back into bed, and fell sound asleep until morning.

TWENTY-SIX

I T WAS RAINING WHEN she woke up.

Marcy glanced at the clock through lids that refused to open more than a quarter of the way. "That can't be right," she muttered, pushing her face right up against the clock's clear plastic face. Could it really be almost ten o'clock? Was it possible?

She reached for the phone, punched the "0" for the front desk, and listened to the receptionist's cheery, "Good mornin', Mrs. Taggart. How can I help you?"

"You can tell me what time it is." Marcy's voice was so husky she didn't recognize it. She almost looked over her shoulder to make sure no one was beside her.

"Certainly. It's just comin' on ten o'clock."

"In the morning?"

A slight pause. "Are you all right, Mrs. Taggart?"

"I'm fine. Thank you. I must have slept in."

"Well, you couldn't have picked a better day for it," the receptionist informed her. "It's rainin' somethin' fierce out there. You don't want to be out in that if you can help it."

Marcy looked toward the window. The heavy salmon-colored drapes were still open, revealing a morning so dark and dreary it might as well have been night. Rain was pelting the leaded windows like an army of small stones. "Crap," Marcy said, forgetting about the phone still in her hand.

"Yes, I guess that about sums it up," the receptionist said. "Can I do anything else for you, Mrs. Taggart?"

"Coffee?"

"I'll have room service bring you up a pot. Anything you'd like with that? Juice? Eggs? Toast?"

"Juice. And eggs. And toast. Orange, over-medium, rye," she added before hanging up. Then she lay back down, closed her eyes, and fell asleep again until room service arrived half an hour later with her breakfast.

LIAM'S PHONE CALL woke her up again at two that afternoon.

"Thank God," he said when she answered in the middle of the third ring. "When you didn't call, I started to worry you'd gone out."

Marcy looked toward the window. It was still pouring, the sky even darker than it had been earlier. She looked at the clock. "Please tell me it's not two o'clock."

"Did I wake you up?" he asked incredulously.

Marcy pushed herself into a sitting position. "I can't seem to keep my eyes open. What kind of pill was that you gave me last night anyway?"

"Just a Valium. Shouldn't make you this dozy. Maybe you're

coming down with something. Do you want me to call a doctor?"

"No, I'm fine. I guess I was just more exhausted than I realized."

"No kidding," Liam said. "You've been operating on all eight cylinders since you got here. I'm amazed you're still breathing, to be perfectly frank."

"I've wasted the whole day," she said sadly.

"You haven't wasted a damn thing. Have you not seen what's doin' out there? Believe me, the only people steppin' outside today are the tourists who don't know any better. It's a sign, Marcy," he told her.

"A sign?"

"A sign to take a day off and get some rest."

"Doesn't look like I have much choice," Marcy said, sleep tugging at her eyelids, forcing her head back onto her pillow.

"I'll swing by on my way to work."

"No. You don't have to do that."

"I never do anything I *have* to," he told her. "Anyway, I'm off to visit my mum. She's been complainin' she don't see enough of me lately."

"Didn't you just say you never do anything you *have* to?" she asked him.

He laughed. "Guess the rules don't apply to mothers," he said before saying good-bye.

"Guess not." Marcy thought of her own mother as she hung up the phone. Certainly rules of any kind had never applied to her.

She's a world unto herself, Judith had once remarked, although Marcy could no longer remember whether her sister had been referring to their mother or to Devon.

Marcy climbed out of bed, discarding her flannel pajamas on the bathroom floor as she stepped into the peach-grained white marble shower, letting the hot water pour down on her head and wondering, not for the first time, what she could have done differently, what she *should* have done differently, if there was one thing she could have changed, one thing she could go back in time and redo, one thing that would have altered the course of all their lives, brought her anywhere but here.

You think too much, Judith had once said, chastising her.

The key is to stop thinking, Sarah had similarly told her during one of Marcy's early golf lessons. *That's the problem with golfers today. They're a bunch of overeducated control freaks trying to play a game you can't control. So don't think. Just swing.*

Marcy wondered exactly when Sarah had stopped thinking and started swinging with her husband. "Don't think," she told herself now, stepping from the shower and wrapping herself in two luxurious bath towels, then rifling through her bag of recent purchases, selecting the khaki pants and beige T-shirt to go over her new underwear. The pants were a little big, the T-shirt a trifle snug, but not so big or snug that anyone would notice. She combed her wet hair, feeling it drip onto her shoulders as she reached for the phone. She read the instructions for making a long-distance call, understanding it was still morning in Toronto, although definitely late enough to call, then punching in Peter's number without further thought. "Just swing," she repeated out loud.

The phone rang four times before voice mail picked it up. "Hi," said Sarah's annoyingly peppy voice. "You've reached Sarah Harris . . ."

". . . and Peter Taggart." Peter's voice chimed in, almost alarming in its enthusiasm for being who he was.

Sarah continued. "We're unavailable to take the call at the moment."

"Oh, God," Marcy moaned, suddenly remembering that this was the weekend Peter would likely be visiting their son at camp, where he was a counselor for the summer. Naturally Sarah would be right beside him, smiling and chirpy and as nauseatingly supportive as always—the mother Marcy should have been. No wonder Darren had been making noises about moving into his father's new house when he got back home.

"So, if you'll leave your name and number and a short message after the beep," Peter said, "we'll get back to you as soon as we can."

"Bye for now and have a wonderful day," Sarah added just before the beep.

"I'd love to," Marcy told them. "But it seems that someone has cut off my credit, so if the man with the nice smile and straight teeth would be kind enough to straighten this mess out as soon as possible, I'll be generous enough not to put the kibosh on this whole divorce thing as soon as *I* return. With your daughter," she added for good measure. And then, because she still wasn't satisfied, "Bye for now, and go fuck yourself." She slammed down the receiver.

They were right, she thought, laughing out loud. It felt good not to think, to just come out swinging. Hell, it felt great.

For about ten seconds.

And then it felt like shit.

"God, what have I done?" She groaned. Peter would hit the roof when he heard her message. He'd be more convinced than ever he was dealing with a lunatic. No way he'd restore her credit. "Shit." What was she going to do now?

She quickly pressed in another number. "Please be home. Please be home."

Marcy pictured her sister, back from her morning workout and relaxing with a giant cup of black coffee at her white stone kitchen table, the Sunday *Star* spread out around her, her nose buried in the pages of obituaries. In the years since their mother's death, Judith had taken to reading these notices religiously, carefully noting the age of each deceased. "I just feel better when I see one or two who are younger than me," she'd admitted rather sheepishly. "I know it sounds a little ghoulish but it makes me feel like I've accomplished something."

"Hello," her sister said now, answering after the first ring.

"Judith, hi."

"Marcy! Where the hell are you?"

"Still in Ireland."

"Shit."

"Judith, listen to me, I need your help."

"You need help all right."

"Judith . . ."

"All right. What can I do?"

"I need money."

"What?"

"I don't have any money. Peter canceled my credit cards."

"Then come home."

"I need you to send me a money order," Marcy said, continuing as if Judith hadn't spoken. "Not much. Three thousand dollars should be enough. I wouldn't ask you, but I didn't bring my bank card, and I'm running out of cash. . . ."

"Three thousand dollars?" Judith repeated incredulously.

"I'll pay you back."

"What do you need three thousand dollars for?"

"I had to buy a few things. It's a long story."

"I'm listening."

"Trust me, you don't want to hear this one."

"Are you in some kind of trouble?"

"No. Honestly. Listen, if it's the money you're worried about, I'll pay you back as soon as I get home."

"And when will that be?"

"Soon."

"How soon?"

"As soon as I find Devon," Marcy said, picturing her sister's head drop toward her chest in dismay.

"You said you'd come to terms with that. You told me—"

"She was happy, wasn't she?" Marcy said, interrupting. "I mean, it wasn't all misery and gloom. There were times when Devon was happy. Weren't there?"

Judith's voice instantly softened. "Of course there were."

Marcy thought of the weeks immediately preceding Devon's disappearance, times when her daughter had seemed not only happy but almost serene, her smile genuine and steady, her voice soft and calm. Had she already solidified her plans to flee the country?

Of course, Judith would argue, as Peter had, that there was another reason for Devon's apparent serenity: that people on the verge of suicide were often at peace once they'd actually made the decision to end their lives.

"Will you or will you not send me the money?" Marcy pleaded, trying to block out the unpleasant thought. Don't think, she told herself.

"Where do you want it sent?" Judith asked after a pause of several seconds.

It was Marcy's turn to hesitate. She was reluctant to reveal her exact address. But what choice did she have? "Send it to the Hayfield Manor Hotel in Cork." Marcy grabbed the notepad beside the phone and read Judith the hotel's address. She pictured her sister scribbling the information across the top of the columns listing Toronto's recently deceased.

"You're in Cork? I thought you were in Dublin."

"You'll courier me the money order overnight?" Marcy said, more demand than question.

"I'll go to the bank first thing tomorrow morning. You should have the money by Tuesday."

"Thank you."

"Marcy, please—"

"I have to go," Marcy told her sister before hanging up the phone. She sat for several minutes in silence, feeling her heart ticking down the seconds like a metronome, her mind purposely blank. Then, accompanied by her new mantra—Don't think; don't think; don't think—she jumped up, took one final look at the rain pummeling her window, grabbed her new peacoat and purse, and headed out the door.

SHE SAW HIM as soon as she reached the lobby.

He was standing, half-hidden, behind a pillar near the grand mahogany staircase and she might have missed him had she not stopped to ask the concierge whether she might borrow an umbrella.

"You're not thinkin' of goin' out in that, are you?" the concierge asked incredulously.

But Marcy was already walking away from him and toward the man behind the pillar. Clearly sensing her presence, the man took several steps back, as if trying to disappear into his surroundings, his eyes staring resolutely at the floor even as she stopped directly in front of him. "What are you doing here?" she asked without preamble.

Vic Sorvino raised his eyes to hers with obvious reluctance, clearly embarrassed at having been discovered. "Marcy," he said, the sound of her name on his lips causing her to go immediately weak in the knees.

What is the matter with me, for God's sake? she wondered impatiently. "What are you doing here?" she asked again.

"That's a good question."

"What's the answer?"

Vic suddenly looked as confused as she felt. "I don't know."

"I don't understand."

"Neither do I."

They stood this way for several seconds, Marcy unable to turn away. It wasn't that he was all that much to look at, she tried to tell herself. Liam was far more handsome; hell, even Peter was better looking. There was just something about Vic. Maybe it was the way he looked at her, the blistering intensity of his blue eyes, the way they latched on to her own and refused to let go, burning into the secrets in her brain. The threat of real intimacy. Was that why she was being so mean to him? Because she knew that once he saw her—*really* saw her— the yearning on his face would be replaced by disgust and he'd run screaming for the nearest exit?

As had almost everyone she'd ever loved.

Her mother.

Peter.

Devon.

Don't look at me, she wanted to tell him. Some secrets are best left undisturbed. "Have you been following me?" she said instead, suddenly reminded of yesterday's sighting at the mall.

"Not exactly."

"What exactly? Was that you yesterday, at the mall?"

"Maybe we should sit down." He led her toward a nearby sofa, sinking into the overstuffed, apricot-colored velvet seat beside her, taking her hand in his.

"Was that you or not?" she asked again, trying to ignore the tingling in her arm.

"Yes."

She quickly brought her hand back to her lap. "I don't understand. Why?"

He shook his head, a deep whoosh of air escaping his lungs, then shook his head again, as if he himself didn't quite believe what he was about to say. "After I was questioned by the gardai regarding the break-in at your hotel room, I decided to stick around for a few more days. I asked Detective Murphy to keep me informed." Vic cleared his throat, shook his head a third time. "He called me yesterday, said you were being brought to the station. I went right over, hoping to get a chance to talk to you, convince you that I had nothing to do with the trashing of your room—"

"I never believed it was you," Marcy said, interrupting.

"Well, thank you for that anyway."

"Nobody told me you were there."

"It doesn't matter," he continued. "You left with that young man from the pub, and I don't know, I just decided to follow you. Don't ask me why."

"Why?" she asked anyway.

"I guess because I was worried about you. I'm still worried about you."

"You don't have to be."

"Somebody breaks into your hotel room and trashes your things, I'd say that's cause for concern."

"But not *your* concern."

Vic sat very still for several very long seconds. Then he took a deep breath, as if inhaling the full import of what she was telling him. "No, I guess not." A hint of a wry smile tugged at the corners of his mouth. "Okay. I admit I'm a little dense about these things, but even I see the light eventually." He rose to his feet. "I'm sorry. I won't pester you again."

"Do you know my daughter?" Marcy asked suddenly, surprising herself with the question she hadn't meant to ask.

He looked startled. "What?"

"My daughter. Do you know her?"

Vic looked around uneasily. "No. Of course not. How would I know Devon?"

Again, the easy, almost casual use of her daughter's name. "You've never met?"

"Marcy, you're not making any sense. You're from Toronto. I live in Chicago. When could I possibly have met your daughter?"

"You're right. I'm sorry. Of course you don't know her." Marcy apologized immediately, watching as Vic's eyes wandered toward the lobby's front entrance. "What is it?"

"Looks like you have a visitor," Vic said.

She followed the direction of his gaze to see Liam walk through the front doors, shaking the rain from his shoulders with an exaggerated shrug. "Liam," she stated, pushing off the sofa and rushing toward him. "What are you doing here?"

"I was just about to ask you the same thing. You weren't thinking of going out in this mess, were you?" he asked accusingly, as if he already knew the answer.

"I thought you were going to see your mother."

"Decided to come see you first," he said. "Good thing, too, by the looks of it." Then he leaned forward and kissed her full on the mouth. "I've got news."

"What kind of news?" Marcy asked, feeling the imprint of his lips on hers. She glanced over her shoulder toward Vic, knowing he'd felt it, too.

But there was no longer anyone sitting on the overstuffed velvet sofa by the stairs.

Vic was gone.

TWENTY-SEVEN

IT WAS ALMOST SIX in the morning when Marcy finally abandoned the idea of sleep. She'd been up all night, tossing and turning, trying to sort through the events of the last twenty-four hours. Hell, why stop there? How about the last twenty-four years?

"I've got news," Liam had announced.

"What kind of news?"

"I drove by the O'Connor house. Don't ask me why."

"Why?" Marcy asked now. Why? she repeated silently, sitting up in bed and staring at the window, her arms wrapped around her bent knees. Sometime in the last few hours, the rain had finally stopped. Was that a sign?

It's a sign, Marcy, Liam told her. *A sign to take the day off and get some rest.*

I was worried about you, Vic said. *I'm still worried about you.*

You can stop worrying about me, Devon whispered from the gray early morning mist outside the window. *I'm fine, Mommy. I'm happy.*

We haven't been happy in such a long time, Peter said.

"The lights in the house were all on," Liam had told her yesterday afternoon.

I admit I'm a little dense about these things, but even I see the light eventually.

"They must have come home early."

It's gotten to the point where I hate coming home, Peter said.

"They're home?"

Maybe if you tried it more often.

That's not the point.

What is *the point?*

The point is I'm not happy. We're *not happy.*

"Happy," Marcy repeated now. Such a ridiculous word. What did it mean?

I'm fine, Mommy. I'm happy.

"So, I decided, what the hell," Liam told her. "I'll just phone them."

"You phoned the O'Connors?"

"They were in the phone book. It was easy."

You're not making this very easy for me.

"What did you say to them?"

What are you trying to say?

"Well, it was Shannon who answered the phone."

I'm in love with someone else.

"Which was perfect, because it was Shannon I wanted to speak to anyway."

You're in love with another woman? Who, for God's sake?

Sarah.

Sarah? Our golf instructor?

You say that like it's a dirty word.

How long has this been going on?

Not long. A few months . . .

We've been married almost twenty-five years. We're going to Ireland for our twenty-fifth anniversary.

I was married to my first wife for almost thirty-three years, Vic interjected, reasserting his presence in her head.

"I explained who I was," Liam said, "and assured her I wasn't trying to get her in any trouble but that it was very important she listen to me."

"What did she say?"

One day Kathy said she was feeling kind of funny.

"She didn't say anything. She just listened."

Three months later, she was dead.

Sit down, girls, the school principal told Marcy and her sister, ushering them inside his brightly lit office. *I'm afraid I have some very bad news.*

"And what did you say?"

We have lingered in the chambers of the sea . . .

"That I knew she'd been out with Jax on Friday night and that he'd given her a pair of earrings, earrings he'd stolen from your hotel room. . . ."

By sea-girls wreathed with seaweed red and brown . . .

"She got all flustered, said she knew nothing about it, that she'd had no idea the earrings had been stolen. She begged me not to tell the O'Connors or go to the gardai."

Marcy, the police are here.

"I told her that I had good reason to suspect that Jax and Audrey were using her to get to the O'Connor baby. . . ."

We've found an overturned canoe. . . .

"My God, how did she react to that?"

"Well, naturally, she got very upset. . . ."

Has your daughter been depressed lately?

"What did she say?"

No, you're wrong. There has to be some mistake. . . .

"That she was sure I was mistaken, that it wasn't possible . . ."

Till human voices wake us . . .

"Somehow I managed to convince her. Or maybe she was just afraid of getting into trouble and losing her job."

Our daughter is dead, Marcy.

Devon is dead, Marcy.

"At any rate, she agreed to help us."

"What?"

"Shannon has agreed to help us find your daughter," Liam said, temporarily silencing the other voices in Marcy's head.

"How?"

"By talking to Audrey, setting up a meeting . . ."

Marcy held her breath, waiting for the rest of the sentence.

"Except it won't be Shannon who goes to meet her. . . ." Liam said.

"It'll be me," Marcy whispered now, as she had the day before.

"It'll be you," he repeated.

"Do you really think Shannon will go through with it?"

"I think she's too scared not to. Afraid we'll go to the gardai about the earrings, or worse, blab to the O'Connors about Jax, and she'll be out of a job. Nah, Shannon will come through for us, you'll see."

Marcy pushed herself out of bed and walked to the window, stared beyond the rain-soaked garden into the blank screen of the early morning horizon, watching it fill with images of yesterday. The garden became the hotel lobby, its shrubs morphing into sofas, a series of trees at the garden's periphery melding into the mahogany staircase, the wet grass weaving into an elegant area rug.

"How soon do you think this meeting will take place?" Marcy recalled asking Liam.

"Could be as early as tomorrow."

"Tomorrow?"

Today, Marcy realized, shivering despite her warm pajamas.

"Shannon said she was gonna call Audrey as soon as the O'Connors went to bed, try to set somethin' up."

"Do you think Audrey will get suspicious?"

"Nah. Why would she? They're friends, aren't they? Friends arrange get-togethers."

"I guess."

"What's the matter?" Liam asked. "Not getting cold feet, are you?"

Was she? "It's just that after everything that's happened, it seems almost too easy. . . ."

"It's not a question of being easy," he told her. "It's a question of greed."

"Greed?"

"If our boy Jax hadn't gotten greedy, if he hadn't seen your earrings when he went to trash your hotel room and decided to pinch them, we wouldn't have had any leverage. Shannon would probably have told me to sod off the minute I told her why I was calling. It was them earrings that made her stop and think twice." He laughed. "I told you that things have a way of working out in the end."

And if they don't . . . , Marcy thought now.

We have lingered in the chambers of the sea/By sea-girls wreathed with seaweed red and brown. . . .

"It's not the end," she said out loud.

Till human voices wake us . . .

"It's not the end."

And we drown.

"It's not the end."

Our daughter is dead, Marcy.

Devon hadn't drowned.

"It's not the end."

So this is it? Marcy asked her husband of almost twenty-five years, noticing his image lingering by the garden gate. *You're really leaving?*

It's better this way, Marcy. You know it is. We'll just end up hating each other if I stay.

Too late, she told him. *I already hate you.*

That's too bad. I was really hoping we could be friends. We still have a son together.

I don't need to be reminded I have a son.

Are you sure of that?

Damn you, Peter, Marcy thought, watching his image evaporate and the garden return to normal. Damn you for saying that.

Damn you even more for being right.

She returned to the bed and picked up the phone, quickly punching in the number for Darren's cell. It was picked up after three rings, although there was no voice on the other end, only muffled sounds and heavy breathing. "Hello?" Marcy said. "Hello, Darren? Darren, are you there?"

"Mom?" a sleepy voice whispered.

"Oh, my God," Marcy said, realizing she'd forgotten about the time difference. "I'm so sorry. Did I wake you?"

She pictured her son huddled beneath the covers of his narrow bed in the old log cabin he shared with the eight ten-year-old boys in his charge and understood he was keeping his voice purposely low so as not to wake them. The curly brown hair he'd inherited from her was no doubt coiled into a comical assortment of hirsute twists and turns, and the serious hazel eyes he'd inherited from his father would be struggling to stay open.

"It's okay," he told her. Then, with growing panic, "Is something wrong? Did something happen to Dad? Did he have an accident on his way home?" The questions spilled out one on top of the other, each one more urgent than the last.

"There was no accident," Marcy assured her son, feeling a pang of jealousy at his concern.

"He didn't have a heart attack or anything, did he? He seemed okay this afternoon."

"Your father is fine," Marcy told him.

"I don't understand," Darren said, the last remnants of sleep falling from his voice. "Why are you calling?"

"I just wanted to talk to you."

"At one in the morning?"

"I'm really sorry about that. I forgot about the time difference."

"Time difference? What are you talking about?" Darren asked.

"Didn't Dad tell you?"

"Tell me what?"

"I'm in Ireland."

"You're in Ireland?" her son asked incredulously.

Marcy heard the silent *Are you crazy?* that followed. "I'm sorry I couldn't be there today," she told him.

"Why? You never come to visitors' day."

"That's not true." Marcy started to protest, stopping when she realized that it was true. She had always found some excuse not to make the trip to Maine: Devon wasn't feeling well; Devon didn't want to go and Marcy didn't think it was a good idea to leave her alone; Devon had been acting out again, refusing to take her meds. And then after Devon's overturned canoe was found floating in the middle of Georgian Bay, Marcy had been too consumed with grief to go anywhere. It was all she could do to get out of bed. "How's the weather up there?" she asked.

"You're asking me about the weather?"

"It rains here almost every day."

"What the hell are you doing there?" Darren asked.

"I don't know," Marcy admitted.

"Weren't you supposed to go there with Dad, like a second honeymoon kind of thing?"

"Yeah, well, that didn't exactly work out as planned, did it?"

"Is Aunt Judith with you?"

"No."

"You're alone?"

"Yeah. It's kind of nice, actually. I've never really spent any time alone before."

"What's going on, Mom?"

"Nothing's going on."

"Are you having a nervous breakdown?"

"What? No, of course not."

"You're in Ireland," her son told her. "You're calling me at camp at one o'clock in the morning."

"I'm not having a nervous breakdown."

"You're not thinking of doing anything crazy, are you?" He immediately qualified his statement. "Crazier than what you've been doing, I mean."

"I'm not thinking of killing myself, Darren."

"Are you sure? Because it kind of runs in the family."

"Your sister didn't kill herself."

"Dad says she did."

"Your father is wrong."

"Mom . . ."

"Look, I really should get going, let you get back to sleep."

There was a second's silence, then, "Sure," Darren said. "Whatever."

"I love you," Marcy said.

"Yeah. Good night, Mom."

Marcy hung up the phone. So, she thought. Her son couldn't say "I love you," even when he feared she was on the verge of suicide. Could she blame him? She hadn't been an active presence in his life in years. Devon had sucked up all her energy, drained her motherly juices dry. And even then, Marcy had managed to fail her. I'm an awful mother, she thought.

Oh, please, Judith said impatiently, appearing without warning. *Enough with the self-flagellation. You weren't an awful mother. Do I really have to remind you what a truly awful mother looks like?*

She tried her best, Marcy argued silently.

So did you.

My son hates me. My daughter is . . .

Is what? her sister asked, as clearly as if she were standing right beside her. *Your daughter is what, Marcy?*

What have I done? Marcy wondered. What am I doing?

Slowly, as if her feet were encased in cement, Marcy walked to the desk across from the bed and retrieved her purse. Then she sank to the carpet and opened it, pulling out the by-now-tattered envelope inside and placing the pictures of Devon in a semicircle around the lone picture of her mother, running her fingers lovingly across their cheeks.

Then she withdrew the second envelope, unfolded the letter inside it, and began to read.

My beautiful Mommy, she began, then stopped. Could she really do this? Did she have any choice?

Marcy began again, hearing Devon's voice filtering through each word. *My beautiful Mommy, I don't expect you to understand what I'm about to do. Please don't be mad, and understand that this is not a decision I've made lightly. I know how much pain I've caused you. Believe me when I say I have no desire to cause you any more.*

Marcy pictured herself racing down the hall to Devon's bedroom right after the police had left, finding the letter addressed to her that her daughter had placed carefully on her pillow, and quickly pocketing it before Peter could arrive and demand to see what it was. "No note?" he'd asked, standing ashen-faced in the doorway moments later.

"No note," she'd lied, waiting until later when she was alone to open it again. Those first awful lines, lines that seemed to suggest . . .

"No," Marcy told herself now, as she'd told herself then, returning the letter to its envelope, then pulling it out again with her next breath, forcing herself to continue.

These last few years have been a mix of heartache, pain, and despair. I wish with all my heart it was otherwise. I know how hard it's been for you. I hope you know how hard it's been for me, too. Sometimes it has taken every ounce of strength I have just to put one foot in front of the other, to make it through each endless day. It's gotten to the point where even saying good morning hurts because I see the hope in your eyes that simple greeting elicits. Then I have to watch that hope die as the day drags on and on and on. One day bleeds its poison into the next. Each day is worse than the day before. Nights are the worst time of all.

I feel as if I've descended into a bottomless pit of sadness, and there's no way I can climb out, no matter how far down your hands reach, no matter how desperately they try to pull me up. The well is too deep, the water too cold. I feel myself sinking farther and farther below the surface. I now realize that giving in is the only way out.

I can honestly say I feel better, lighter, more energized, than I have in years. I'm actually happy, strange as that must sound. Knowing what I have to do has freed me to remember all the good times we shared: the mornings we spent drawing at the kitchen ta-ble, the nights you spent patiently sitting beside my bed, waiting until I fell asleep, the afternoons we spent curled up together on the sofa watching Sesame Street, *and then later,* The Young and the Restless. *How grown-up that made me feel! I remember the time you took me to the ballet when I was barely four years old and let me dance in the aisle as the Sugar Plum Fairy danced on the stage, and how you clapped so proudly when I was done. I remember shop-ping for shoes when I was fifteen and you bought me a pair of boots that were more expensive than the ones you bought for yourself be-cause you saw how much I loved them. I remember you sitting in the audience of every painful high school play I was in, cheering me on at each and every swim competition, the pride I saw in your face whether I won or placed a distant fourth.*

Most of all, I remember our wonderful summers at the cottage, the days spent canoeing and lying in the sun, the long walks through the woods, the barbecues at sunset, the mother-daughter confidences we shared before the darkness in my soul made such confidences impossible. You were always so wise, so patient, so loving. How I wished I could be just like you.

Please forgive the awful things I said to you. I know there was nothing you could have done to save your mother. Just as there's nothing you can do for me now. You did everything you could. This isn't your fault.

Please know how much I love you, how much I've always loved you, and how much I always will.

And know that I'm finally at peace.

Devon.

"Oh, God," Marcy whispered, tears pouring from her eyes and streaming down her face. What did it mean? That her daughter had indeed paddled her canoe into the middle of Georgian Bay that cold October morning almost two years ago and purposely disappeared beneath its frigid surface? That no matter how hard she'd tried to convince herself otherwise, nothing could distill the terrible clarity of Devon's words? Was that why she'd stubbornly refused to show the letter to anyone else? Because then she'd have been forced to acknowledge that Peter and Judith were right, that Devon had taken her own life?

I now realize that giving in is the only way out.

"Oh, God," she said again as the phone beside her bed began to ring. She stared at it without moving. Her daughter was dead. Marcy couldn't deny it any longer.

In truth, she'd known it all along.

The ringing stopped in the middle of the fifth ring, only to start up again seconds later, as if whoever was calling knew she was there.

Exhausted by the sound, Marcy crawled toward the phone and picked it up. "Hello," she said.

"Hello, Mommy," the voice announced curtly. "I understand you've been looking for me."

TWENTY-EIGHT

I T WAS ALMOST NOON when Marcy left Hayfield Manor and headed toward the grounds of St. Fin Barre's Cathedral, located in the city's South Bank. She'd spent the morning in a state of restless anticipation, unable to eat or sleep, pacing back and forth for a full half hour only to sit resolutely still for the next, afraid to leave her room until the appointed hour, jumping each time the phone rang, going over the conversation with her daughter again and again and again, hanging on her every word.

"These instructions must be followed to the letter," Devon had told her in an angry whisper. "One slip, one misstep, and I swear you'll never see me again."

"There won't be any missteps. I promise," Marcy had said.

Devon continued. "You don't go anywhere; you don't talk to anyone; you don't tell anyone where you're going."

"I won't."

"Don't even think of calling the police."

"Of course not. I wouldn't—"

"And not a word to that sexy young boyfriend of yours."

"What? No. He's not my . . . Devon, please . . ."

"Be in front of St. Fin Barre's Cathedral at one o'clock."

"St. Fin Barre's Cathedral," Marcy repeated, trying to place its exact location in her mind. "One o'clock."

"And remember—we're watching you."

And then nothing.

"Devon? Devon, hello? Are you still there? Wait. Don't go. Devon? Devon?" Marcy sat on her bed, staring blankly out the window toward the garden, knowing their connection had been severed but waiting nonetheless, the phone poised at her ear for the next twenty minutes on the off chance there was something wrong with the line and her daughter was also waiting patiently on the other end. She'd remained in this posture—waiting, hoping, praying for the sound of her daughter's voice.

We're watching you, Devon had told her.

Who was watching her? Were they out there even now?

In response to this disturbing thought, Marcy dropped the phone into its carriage and jumped from her bed, pulling the curtains closed, then returning to the bed, then quickly returning to the window and reopening the curtains, staring into the shifting gray mist.

Was anyone out there?

"Who's watching me?"

She'd showered and dressed in her new black pants and crisp, blue-and-white-striped cotton blouse, taking extra time and care with her hair and makeup, wanting to look beautiful for Devon. She'd even ordered room service so that she wouldn't run the risk of fainting again when she saw her, but when breakfast arrived, she'd been unable to swallow anything but the coffee.

Liam had called her cell phone several times to tell her he'd yet to hear from Shannon and to ask how she was holding up. Did she want company? He had a few hours before he had to be at work, he'd suggested hopefully. Desperate as Marcy was to tell him about her daughter's phone call, she'd said nothing.

And not a word to that sexy young boyfriend of yours.

"I was up most of the night," she'd told him instead. "I should probably try to get a little sleep. In case Shannon calls later."

"Good. Now you're starting to take care of yourself," he'd said enthusiastically. "I'll phone you as soon as I hear any-thing."

"Liam . . ."

"Yes?"

I spoke to Devon. She called. We're meeting at one o'clock. "I hope you know how much I appreciate everything you've done."

"I know," he'd said, a smile in his voice. "Now get some rest. I'll talk to you later."

I hate lying to him, but what other choice did I have? she wondered now, walking purposefully toward the South Bank, pushing her way through the still-dense fog that draped the sides of College Road like dusty old curtains. Located south of the river Lee, the South Bank encompassed not only St. Fin Barre's Cathedral but also the city's seventeenth-century city walls, the remains of Elizabeth Fort, and the relatively new city hall, built in 1936. Despite the distance from her hotel to the magnificent church, she'd decided to walk rather than take a cab and risk getting stuck in traffic. She'd been hoping some fresh air would clear her head and calm her nerves, but the air was heavy and stale, and she jumped each time she heard a car horn, making her more nervous than ever.

Marcy continued along College Street, feeling the damp air seep underneath her new navy peacoat and trying to ignore the dull ache spreading through her fingers. She should have bought gloves, she was thinking, burying her cold hands inside her pockets. Although who thinks of buying gloves in July?

"For God's sake, what were you thinking?" Peter had shouted in her ear less than an hour ago.

Marcy had been just about to leave her room when the hotel phone rang. Thinking it might be Devon, she'd flung herself toward it, answering it before it completed its first ring.

"Peter," she'd sputtered when she could find her voice. It was barely seven o'clock in the morning, Toronto time. "How did you find me?"

"Your sister phoned. As did our son. You scared him half to death, you know. How could you call him like that, in the middle of the night? For God's sake, what were you thinking?" His fury had grown stronger, louder, with each word. "And how could you leave that ridiculous message on my answering machine? Have you completely lost your mind?"

"I can't talk to you now," she'd said in response, dropping the receiver back into its carriage as if it had suddenly burst into flames. She'd glanced out the hotel window, searching for faceless shadows in the fog as, seconds later, the phone began ringing again.

"Did you just hang up on me?" Peter demanded as Marcy lifted the phone to her ear.

Her response was to hang up again. She had neither the time nor the energy for his outrage. Nor could she tell him the truth—that Devon had contacted her, that she was an hour away from meeting up with their daughter. Not that he'd believe her in any event. But you will, she thought as the phone began ringing again. Then she'd grabbed her purse and her new jacket and fled the room, the phone's persistent ring following her out the door and down the stairs into the lobby.

It was half an hour later when Marcy finally turned onto Bishop Street, the three giant spires of the French Gothic cathedral rising out of the fog to impose themselves on the skyline. Four large tour buses were parked across the street. "The current building, which sits on the exact spot St. Fin Barre selected for his church and school in 600 AD, dates from 1870 and is especially noteworthy for the highly orna-mental mosaic of its interior," Marcy heard one tour guide expound as he tried to herd those in his charge toward the main entrance.

Marcy's eyes shot through the crowds jostling for prior-ity position, searching for any sign of Devon. She saw lots of young women, many with long brown hair, a few with sad eyes and prominent cheekbones, but none with the specific combination of features and attitude that defined her daugh-ter. She checked her watch. It was still early. Devon had told her to be here at one o'clock—"Be in front of St. Fin Barre's Cathedral at one o'clock," had been her precise words—and one o'clock was still twenty minutes from now. Which meant Devon probably wasn't here yet, Marcy decided, her eyes con-tinuing to flit from face to face as she pushed her way through the throng of tourists toward the massive front doors of the church. Devon was rarely on time for anything. How many times had she kept Marcy waiting to drive her to school while she dawdled in the bathroom? How many dinner reservations had they forfeited because Devon couldn't decide what to wear? What about the time they'd missed the entire opening act of *Swan Lake* because Devon had decided to take a shower at the last minute?

Marcy understood that Devon's almost pathological tardiness had been due to her insecurity and was part and parcel of her illness. When Marcy and her daughter were finally reunited—not long, not long!—she'd make sure Devon got the help she needed. They'd find a doctor her daughter liked and trusted, one who would see to it she received the proper dosage of her medication. It was just a chemical imbalance after all, and once that balance had been corrected . . .

"Mother!" someone called, and Marcy spun around to see a young woman with long brown hair running toward her. "For heaven's sake, Ma, how many times have I told you not to go wanderin' off?" the young woman asked breathlessly, grabbing the elbow of an elderly woman to Marcy's right.

Marcy saw that the woman wasn't so young after all, that she was, in fact, probably closer to Marcy's age than to Devon's and that her mother looked frightened and confused, as if she wasn't at all sure who this angry woman was.

"She's not all there, I'm afraid," the woman explained sheepishly in answer to Marcy's stare. "Alzheimer's." She sighed. "The doctors keep encouragin' us to take her to her favorite places, but every time we do, she just goes wanderin' off. You've gotta watch her every damn second. She's worse than my twelve-year-old."

"Are we goin' to meet your father now?" the older woman asked.

"No, Ma. Da's been gone for more than ten years. You know that."

"Gone for ten years? Where'd he go?"

"Don't worry, Ma. I'm sure he'll be home for supper." She leaned toward Marcy. "He's dead," she whispered.

"He'll be home for supper?" the woman's mother asked hopefully.

"Yes, Ma. He'll be home at six o'clock sharp." The woman confided to Marcy in her next breath. "It's weird lyin' to your ma about stuff like this, but what the hell? It makes her feel good, and she won't remember any of it later anyway." She shrugged, leading her mother back into the crowd.

Marcy followed after them with her eyes until they were no longer visible. She checked her watch again. Still ten minutes to go, she thought, wondering if she was waiting in the right spot.

Be in front of St. Fin Barre's Cathedral at one o'clock, Devon had told her.

But the church was enormous and "in front" could mean just about anywhere. Was she supposed to stand by the entrance or to either side of the imposing wooden doors? Should she stand close to the building or a comfortable distance away? Had Devon taken into account the sheer volume of visitors? Would she be able to spot her in the middle of all these people? What if Devon didn't see her? What if she got tired trying to fight her way through the crowds? Devon had never been very good with crowds. What if she panicked and took off without making contact? Or what if she failed to recognize her mother? It had been almost two years since they'd last seen each other after all. I should have worn something brighter, Marcy thought, something that would make me stand out. She quickly removed her jacket, hoping the blue and white stripes of her shirt would be sufficient to capture her daughter's attention. "I'm freezing," she muttered into her collar moments later, putting her jacket back on. Again her eyes searched through the dense pockets of tourists that were almost as thick as the fog.

She was checking her watch again when her phone rang. Marcy reached inside her purse, retrieved her cell, brought it to her ear. "Hello?" she asked warily.

"Marcy?" Liam's voice sliced through the dull mist like a warm knife through butter.

"Did you hear from Shannon?" Marcy asked, sneaking a worried glance over her shoulder. What if Devon saw her talking on her phone? What if she assumed Marcy was talking to the police?

"Not a word. I was thinking maybe I should give her a call—"

"No. Please don't do that."

"Just to see if she's managed to contact Audrey."

"I don't think we should pressure her."

"I wasn't going to pressure her. I was just going to . . . Where are you?"

"What?" Marcy pressed the phone tightly against her ear in an effort to keep the persistent buzz of tourists at bay.

"Have you gone out somewhere?"

"No. I'm just in the lobby. There was another mix-up with my credit card," she lied.

"Sounds like there's quite the crowd there."

"A bus full of tourists just arrived," Marcy said, watching as a tour bus pulled into a parking spot across the street. Not quite a lie, she thought.

"So, the Hayfield Manor's takin' in tour groups now, is it?" Liam asked incredulously. "Guess the economy's affectin' everyone."

"I have to go," Marcy told him. "They're waiting to talk to me."

"You sure you don't want me to come over, give you a hand?"

"Positive. Everything's under control, and I don't want to be responsible for you getting fired."

"Thinkin' of me then, are you?"

"I have to go," she said again, trying not to sound too impatient.

"Okay, but if I don't hear from Shannon in the next hour, I'm gonna call her," he said.

"Fine."

"Maybe even pay her a visit."

"I really don't think that will be necessary."

"Yeah? You know somethin' I don't?"

"No, of course not. I'm just trying to think positively."

"Okay, then. Positive thoughts it is."

"Positive thoughts," she repeated.

"I'll call you later."

"Okay." She quickly returned the phone to her purse, slowly executing a 360-degree turn. "Positive thoughts," she whispered.

No sign of her daughter.

And remember—we're watching you, Devon had warned.

Was someone watching her now? Reporting on her every move? Had that someone seen her on the phone, warned Devon to stay away?

"Positive thoughts. Positive thoughts."

And not a word to that sexy young boyfriend of yours.

Had whoever was watching her been close enough to overhear her conversation? Did they know she'd told Liam nothing?

Maybe I should have, Marcy thought. Maybe I should have told him everything. Then he wouldn't be sweating out the fact that Shannon still hasn't phoned. He wouldn't be thinking of calling me again, possibly even paying me an unnecessary

visit. Oh, God. If I'm not careful, he's liable to screw everything up.

Positive thoughts. Positive thoughts.

"Excuse me," a woman said from somewhere beside her.
The accent was distinctly North American.

"Devon?" Marcy said as she turned toward the voice.

"Excuse me," the woman repeated with a flip of her
shoulder-length blond hair, "but we're trying to get through."

"Oh, I'm sorry. I didn't realize. . . ."

"Some people are just oblivious," Marcy heard the woman's
male companion mutter as they pushed past.

Marcy felt tears forming behind her eyes. "Not yet," she
whispered. There was still more than enough time for tears.
Always plenty of time for tears, she thought, hearing the distant bells of St. Anne's Shandon Church strike one.

"Don't turn around," a familiar male voice suddenly whispered in her ear.

Marcy's breath caught instantly in her lungs.

"Start walking," the voice instructed.

"Where's Devon?"

"Keep walking. Straight ahead. Don't look back."

"Where are we going?"

"To see your daughter."

"Why isn't she here?"

"Keep walking." A strong hand on the back of her elbow
guided her through the crowd.

"Where is she?"

"Not far. You tell anyone where you were going?"

"No. No one."

"Good. Keep walking. Head toward Sullivan's Quay."

"Will Devon be there?"

"Don't ask so many questions."

"I just want to see my daughter."

"You will."

They walked for several minutes in silence, a thousand thoughts swirling inside Marcy's brain, like clothes in a dryer. Where was he taking her? Were they really going to see Devon, or was this some sort of trap?

A sudden pressure on Marcy's elbow directed her to stop.

"Let me have your phone," her escort directed.

"My phone? Why?"

"Just give it here."

Marcy reached inside her purse and took out her cell phone. It was pulled from her hand before she had a chance to object.

"Don't think you'll be needing this anymore," he said, tossing the phone into the nearest trash bin.

"But—"

"Keep walking."

"Is all this intrigue really necessary?" Marcy asked as they approached Sullivan's Quay.

"Probably not. But it's kind of fun, don't you think? Turn left at this next street."

"And then what?"

"You'll see when we get there."

"Are you really taking me to Devon?"

"What else would I be doin'?" he asked.

"I don't know. What were you doing that afternoon you ran me down with your bicycle?" Marcy spun around on her heel to look the young man directly in the eye.

"Tryin' to get you to mind your own business," Jax said with a sneer. "Obviously it didn't work."

"Devon *is* my business."

The boy shrugged, causing audible crinkles in his bomber-style black leather jacket. They continued walking for several more blocks. "Get in the car," he said, stopping suddenly.

"What?"

He reached for the door handle of a small black car parked along the side of the street. "You want to see your daughter, don't you?"

"Yes. Of course I do."

He pulled open the door. "Then get inside. She's waitin' for you."

TWENTY-NINE

THEY'D BEEN ON THE road for almost an hour, Marcy continuing to pepper him with questions, Jax continuing to ignore her, when he finally broke his self-imposed silence. "Stop lookin' at me," he said. "You're givin' me a headache."

Immediately Marcy brought her eyes to her lap. "Sorry. I didn't mean to stare." Truthfully, Marcy hadn't even realized she was staring. But her eyes had grown weary of peering through the fog trying to determine where they were, and she was starting to feel vaguely nauseous due to the constant twists in the road and the boy's constant shifting of the car's gears to accommodate them. She'd merely focused on the closest animate object she could find.

"Like what you see?" Jax asked, lips curling smugly toward a smile.

"Not really."

He laughed. "I heard you had quite the sense of humor."

"Really? Who told you that?"

"Who d'you think?"

Not Devon, Marcy thought, trying to remember the last time she'd made her daughter laugh. Their relationship had been defined by tears, not laughter. "Where are we going?" she asked.

"You'll see soon enough."

"Is it far?"

"Far enough."

"Will it take long?"

"Long enough."

Marcy sighed with frustration. This is ridiculous, she thought.

"Might as well sit back and enjoy the ride," Jax said, turning on the radio and then turning it off again when the accompanying static proved more loud and unruly than the traditional Irish music.

Marcy sat dutifully back in her seat and leaned her head against the headrest, returning her attention to the narrow road outside. They'd left the main highway about ten minutes earlier and were now winding their way south along the rugged coastline toward . . . what exactly? Where was he taking her?

She glanced surreptitiously in his direction, pretending to be rubbing her still-sore cheek. Surprisingly, the boy was handsomer in profile than he was face-on, the inherent laziness of his features less obvious, his nose and chin more clearly defined. Even his small dark eyes seemed less vacant, although maybe that was because he was concentrating so hard on the road ahead. Rain was now mixing with the fog, making the visibility almost nil.

"How long have you known my daughter?" Marcy ventured to ask as they drove through a welcome dry stretch of road some ten minutes later.

"About a year," he answered, just as she'd given up hope of his doing so.

"How did you meet?"

"What difference does it make?"

"No difference, I guess. I was just curious."

Another lengthy silence. Marcy noted a sign for Clonakilty, then another for Galley Head farther down the road.

"We met at this club called Mulcahy's," he said finally.

Marcy suppressed a gasp, wondering if he was toying with her, if his reference to Mulcahy's had been deliberate, meant to provoke her.

"Understand you were there the other night," he remarked, answering her silent question.

"Yes," she said, not sure what, if anything, he expected her to say next.

"What'd you think of the place?"

"Interesting," Marcy answered.

Jax laughed. "It is that." He laughed again. "Not exactly your cup of tea, I would imagine."

"Not exactly my demographic, no," Marcy said, then wished she hadn't when she saw the angry narrowing of Jax's eyes.

"What the hell's that supposed to mean?"

"Demographic? It refers to your age, marital status, profession . . . where you fit in socially and statistically, that sort of thing," she said, trying to explain. The look on his face told her she was only making things worse.

"Think you're really smart, don't you? Think you're so superior."

"No, I—"

"You're no better than anybody else."

"I never said I was."

"No, but you think it."

"No, I really don't."

"I'm not stupid, you know."

"I didn't say you were."

"You don't have to say it."

"I don't think you're stupid."

"Do you think I'm smart then?"

"I don't think my daughter would be interested in you if you weren't," Marcy said, trying to bring the focus of the conversation back to Devon.

Jax smiled. "I guess she does think I'm pretty smart."

Another lengthy pause, another interlude of heavy rain.

"Do you mind my asking what your relationship is with my daughter?" Marcy strained to sound casual, as if she were asking only as a way to pass the time.

"Yeah, I mind."

More silence, interrupted only by the sound of the wipers working furiously across the front windshield.

"Are you askin' if we're lovers?" Jax said as they passed a sign announcing they were within twenty kilometers of the town of Skibbereen. "Is that what you're wantin' to know?"

"Are you?" Marcy obliged him by asking, a sick sensation in the pit of her stomach.

"We were once. Not so much anymore."

"Why is that? Is she with someone else?"

Jax shrugged, his leather jacket crinkling noisily around his ears. "You'd have to ask Audrey."

"I'm asking you."

"And I'm not tellin'," he said, sounding all of six years old.

More silence as the small car twisted along the narrow

single-lane road, speeding beside rivers and around mountains, through valleys and tiny fishing villages. Where the hell was he taking her?

"The day you ran me down with your bicycle," she said, watching his jaw tighten and fingers stiffen on the wheel, "you had to know where I was, you had to have been following me."

"You should have seen yourself. You were so pathetic. 'Excuse me,'" he said mockingly, raising his voice at least an octave while his eyes remained resolutely on the road ahead, 'but do any of you recognize this picture? It's my daughter. Do you recognize her? Can you help me?'" He snickered.

"Who told you to follow me?"

He said nothing.

"Whose idea was it to trash my hotel room?"

Still nothing.

"Who told you to destroy my things?"

He shook his head, as if trying to rid himself of a pesky fly.

"Why did you do those things?" Marcy asked.

He glanced over in her direction, lowering his chin and lifting his eyebrows. "We were kinda hopin' it would be enough to convince you to go back home."

"And stealing my earrings?"

"Oh, that one was all my idea," Jax said proudly. "Saw 'em lyin' there. Couldn't resist."

"You gave them to Shannon," Marcy stated.

"And didn't she look lovely in 'em?" He pulled the car to a sudden stop in the middle of the narrow roadway.

Marcy's first thought was that he was going to kill her and throw her body off the side of one of the surrounding cliffs. No one will ever know what happened to me. I'll simply disappear.

Like Devon, she thought.

She looked frantically out her side window, seeing nothing but fog. "Why did you stop? Where are we? Is Devon here?"

To her surprise, Jax burst out laughing. "Can't quite picture your daughter out gallivantin' with a bunch of sheep. Can you?" He motioned out the front window at the herd of sheep slowly emerging from the fog to cross at the unmarked rural intersection. "Not exactly her 'demographic,'" he added pointedly as Marcy watched the sheep disappear down an almost invisible country lane.

Ten minutes later, the last of the sheep gone, he threw the car back into gear, shifting clumsily from first to fourth in seconds, the car jerking its displeasure as it picked up speed.

"Is it much farther?" Marcy asked, her bladder pushing at her side. "I could use a bathroom."

She expected to be either ignored or rebuked. Instead he said, "There's a place a few kilometers down where we can stop."

"I'd appreciate it, thank you."

"I do like to be appreciated. You're welcome." He laughed.

He was still chuckling when they pulled up in front of an old turquoise-painted alehouse that materialized from out of nowhere on the side of the road, its windowsills lined with flower boxes, the flowers all but collapsing under the steady downpour. Smoke was rising from its stone chimney, mingling with the fog. "You got two minutes," Jax told her, grabbing Marcy's arm as she was about to open her car door. "I'll be standin' right outside the door. Don't do anything stupid."

"Like what?" Marcy asked incredulously. What was he expecting her to do? Make a run for it?

"Like try to call anyone."

"You threw away my phone, remember?"

"Any funny business, you'll never see your daughter again."

"You've been watching too much television," she told him, exiting the car.

"Yes, Mommy," he sneered, following after her. "I've been a very bad boy, Mommy. You going to spank me?"

Marcy's response was to run for the entrance. Even though the distance was less than six feet from car to pub, she was thoroughly soaked by the time she got inside. The first thing she saw was a roaring fireplace, and she fought the urge to collapse into one of two rickety-looking rocking chairs in front of it. Her legs were weak from sitting in the cramped front seat of Jax's car for so long, her knees threatening to buckle under her. How much farther did they have to go? Was he really taking her to see her daughter?

"Would you just look at you," a pretty red-haired waitress exclaimed. "You look frozen to death. Go stand by the fire, luv. Get warm."

"Don't have time," Jax said, coming up behind Marcy and resting a heavy hand on her shoulder. "Me mum's in need of a toilet," he announced to the six men gathered at the bar. Marcy winced, then followed the waitress's raised finger toward the washroom at the back of the dimly lit room. "I'll have a Guinness," she heard Jax say.

"Should you be drinking?" Marcy asked when they were back in the car, the open bottle of beer planted firmly between Jax's sturdy thighs. "I would have thought the driving's tough enough—"

"Don't think."

Don't think, she heard Sarah say. *Just swing.*

"I just meant—"

"Not interested in what you meant." He took a long sip of

his beer, and then another, as if to underscore his point. "Uh-oh. I'm forgettin' me manners," he said, waving the bottle under her nose. "You want a sip? Don't be shy, now."

Marcy turned her head aside, the smell of the beer causing her stomach to lurch. "How much longer?" she asked after another few minutes. It felt as if they'd been driving forever.

"Not much." He turned down a narrow side road, tossing the now-empty beer bottle into some high grass as he edged the car up the side of a steep cliff. "Too bad it's so wet and miserable out there. You can't appreciate the view. It's pretty spectacular once you reach the top."

Even with the wind and the rain, Marcy could hear the waves of the Celtic Sea hitting the rocks below. Where the hell was he taking her? "Where are we?" she asked.

He surprised her by answering, "Roaringwater Bay. Good name, eh?"

What was Devon doing in a place called Roaringwater Bay?

She isn't here, Marcy realized with a certitude that almost took her breath away. The boy had never had any intention of taking her to her daughter. In all likelihood, he was spiriting her as far away from Devon as possible. On Devon's instructions? she wondered. Had this whole elaborate charade been Devon's idea? Was everything? Does she hate me that much? Marcy wondered.

Please know how much I love you, how much I've always loved you, and how much I always will.

"Did she ever talk about me?" Marcy asked, the question falling from her mouth before she even realized it was forming.

"Audrey?" Jax asked, as if Marcy might have been referring to someone else.

"Her name is Devon," Marcy said, correcting him.

"She's Audrey to me."

"Did she ever talk about . . . when she was Devon?" Marcy asked tentatively.

"Nah." The boy shrugged. "Said there wasn't much to talk about."

"She never mentioned her brother?"

"Didn't know she had one."

"Or her father, or her aunt?"

"The one who was married six times?"

"Five," Marcy corrected him absently, feeling a stab of unexpected jealousy.

"Said she had a grandma who killed herself."

"My mother."

"Know what happened to *my* ma?" Jax asked, almost proudly.

Marcy shook her head.

"My da killed her."

"What?"

"It's the God's honest truth. He came home drunk one night," Jax stated casually, as if he were talking about the inclement weather. "And my ma started in on him, accusin' him of stealin' the money she had hidden away, money she made from cleanin' other people's houses, and they got into it, as rip-roarin' a fight as any of us eight kids could remember, and she's yellin' and carryin' on somethin' fierce, and so he starts pushin' her around, business as usual when he's drunk, which is pretty much all the time, except suddenly he's got this big butcher knife in his hand, and next thing you know, my ma's lyin' dead on the floor, her throat slit from ear to ear, blood gushin' out everywhere, like he'd struck oil or somethin'."

"Good God."

"Yeah, well, He was certainly nowhere around that night. Although the place was soon crawlin' with gardai. They were everywhere. And they're slippin' around in all the blood. You should have seen 'em. One of 'em goes crashin' against the wall, almost breaks a leg. It was pretty funny, I tell you." He laughed. "So, a few months later, there's a trial, my da goes to jail, us kids get put in a bunch of foster homes. Big fuckin' mess."

"How awful for you. I'm so sorry."

Jax glanced warily in her direction. "What are you sorry for? You didn't do it."

"I'm sorry you had to go through that."

"No big deal."

"Your father killed your mother right in front of you. I'd say that's a very big deal."

"Yeah, well, nobody's askin' you, are they?"

"I'm sorry," Marcy said, apologizing again.

"I don't need your pity."

"It's not pity."

"Well, whatever the hell it is, I don't need it." He punched angrily at the dashboard with his right hand, causing him to lose control of the wheel. The car veered sharply to the left, bouncing between rocks and crevices and coming dangerously close to the side of the cliff before spinning to a stop. "Shit! Look what you made me do," Jax cried, his face ashen, his voice a full octave higher than normal. "Are you tryin' to get us killed?"

"I'm sorry," Marcy said.

"Jesus, is that all you ever say?"

Marcy was about to apologize again and had to bite down on her tongue to keep the words from escaping.

"It's bloody irritatin', you know that?" The color was slowly returning to his cheeks. "You'd think you were responsible for every bad thing that ever happened."

"Sometimes that's the way I feel."

"You really think you're so bloody powerful?"

Marcy almost smiled. She'd always felt the exact opposite, as if she had no power at all. But maybe he was right.

"Talk about feelin' superior." He returned the car to the road without so much as a glance in either direction. "You asked before if she ever talked about you," he said as they continued up the side of the steep hill.

Marcy saw the outline of an old farmhouse in the distance. Was that where he was taking her? "Did she?"

"She told me about this one time when she was a little girl and you yelled at her for scribblin' on the walls."

Marcy felt her stomach cramp. "She remembered that?"

"Said it was her earliest memory. Said she can still hear you screamin'."

Tears flooded Marcy's eyes, began streaming down her cheeks. This was worse than flying off the side of the cliff, she thought, worse than crashing into the sea below.

"You used to yell at her a lot, didn't you, Marcy?" Jax continued, warming to his subject and clearly enjoying the sight of Marcy's tears. "Audrey said you did. She told me you made her take piano lessons and then you'd yell at her when she'd make a mistake."

So she remembered that, too.

"Don't feel quite so superior now, do you, Marcy?"

Marcy said nothing.

"What's the matter? Cat got your tongue?"

They continued in silence, the single-story farmhouse at the top of the cliff becoming larger, more dilapidated-looking the closer they got, resembling more a sprawling old ruin than a place where anybody actually lived. Marcy noted that its gray bricks were a seemingly haphazard compilation of varying shapes and sizes and that its windows had been boarded up with weathered strips of wood. No one had lived here for a very long time, she understood as Jax pulled up to the side of the house and stopped the car, although smoke was rising from the crumbling stone chimney.

"Looks like somebody's lit a fire," he announced, opening his car door.

Immediately the sound of a baby's cries filled the air, competing with the howling of the wind.

Marcy's head shot toward the sound.

"Ah, the dulcet tones of Miss Caitlin O'Connor," Jax said with a laugh.

"She's here?"

"In the flesh."

"And Devon?"

"Where else would she be?" Jax came around to Marcy's side of the car, opened her door, and grabbed hold of her elbow. "You can leave your purse in the car," he told her. "You're not gonna be needin' it."

THIRTY

THE OLD HOUSE WAS dark and smelled of abandonment. Thin streaks of light slithered through the cracks in the thick planks of wood covering the windows, competing with the dull glow radiating from a fireplace in one of the interior rooms, the normally comforting odor of burning wood wrestling with the pervasive stench of decay. A baby's cries permeated the dank air, seeping through the walls like a slow leak and beckoning Marcy to come closer. She felt Jax's hands on her back, pushing her forward.

There was no furniture, no appliances, nothing to differentiate one room from the next. Just a series of stone walls and dirt-covered floors. "Follow the screams," Jax said ominously as Marcy passed through one doorway and then another, the baby's cries growing louder with each step, the smell of smoke heavier and more acrid, the light from the fireplace flashing like a dying disco ball, illuminating nothing. "Duck your head," Jax said, his hand in her hair, pushing her into the next room.

The first thing Marcy saw was the shadowy figure of a young woman sitting in a high-backed chair in the middle of an otherwise empty room. The second thing she saw was a flash of strawberry-blond hair falling into small, terrified eyes. The third thing was the gag in her mouth, followed almost immediately by the gnarled rope that was wound tightly around her torso, securing her to the chair.

"Oh, my God. Shannon!"

"Shut up," Jax said, silencing Marcy with another push.

Which was when she saw the baby lying in a cardboard box between Shannon's tethered feet and the fireplace. The baby's face was awash with tears, glistening like a shiny red balloon in the indifferent flicker of a fire that was now more ashes than flame. It supplied little light, even less heat.

"God, that's one noisy little fucker," Jax exclaimed, shaking his head in dismay and scratching his curly brown hair.

"Took you long enough," a voice announced from the shadows.

Marcy's eyes shot toward the sound, her heart pounding, her legs threatening to buckle under her. She saw nothing. "Devon?" she whispered, the word trampled beneath the baby's piercing cries.

"I was expecting you an hour ago."

"Yeah, well, have you seen what's doin' out there? Besides, your ma had to make a pit stop," Jax said with a sneer, and Marcy had to grip the floor with her toes to keep from falling over.

"Devon," Marcy said, louder this time.

"She prefers Audrey," Jax said.

"What's the matter, Mommy?" the voice asked provocatively. "You don't look very happy to be here."

Marcy spun around in a helpless circle. "Where are you?" she pleaded, her eyes skirting the bare gray walls. "Please, baby, let me see you."

"I'm not your baby." The voice was flat, full of all-too-familiar disdain.

Marcy's eyes grew slowly accustomed to the dim light, like a camera lens subtly adjusting its focus. She could see Shannon more clearly now, the frightened girl securely fastened to her high-backed chair. She noted the almost imperceptible movement of Shannon's feet as they struggled to loosen the rope at her ankles and saw her shoulders straining against the ties that bound her torso to the chair. She read the plea in the girl's terror-filled eyes as Shannon glanced toward the large iron poker leaning against the jagged, irregular stones of the fireplace, then followed those eyes to a back door at the opposite end of the room.

"Please, won't you let me see you?" Marcy begged softly, her whole body aching to take her daughter in her arms. Even now, she thought. Despite the almost surreal tableau in front of her. Despite Devon's part in it. Despite everything.

"You'll see me when I'm ready to be seen."

"I just want to hold you."

"I don't think that's a very good idea."

"Why not? What's going on? What are you mixed up in?"

"Oh, I think you already know the answer to that one. Don't you, Mommy? Understand you gave the gardai quite an earful. Understand they think you're as mad as the proverbial hatter." She laughed. "Which fits into our plans rather nicely, actually."

"What plans?" Marcy saw a shadow flicker on the wall, a shake of long dark hair.

"You want details? You're not going to like them."

"I think you owe me at least that much."

"I don't owe you a damn thing."

"Look," Jax said impatiently. "We're wastin' time, Audrey. We've got the money. Let's just shoot 'em and get out of here."

A muffled scream escaped the gag at Shannon's mouth. Her struggles became more obvious and desperate. She began furiously rocking her chair back and forth, back and forth.

A distant memory echoed through Marcy's brain—a closet door being opened, then closed, opened, then closed, opened, then closed—as Audrey suddenly emerged from the shadows and walked purposefully into the center of the room, her long dark hair obscuring most of her face, although a gun was clearly visible in her right hand.

"Relax," she said to Shannon, laying her free hand forcefully on Shannon's shoulder, bringing the girl's wild rocking to an abrupt halt. "We're not going to shoot you." She glanced toward Marcy, an unexpected spark from the fireplace dancing across her face, illuminating her cruel smile. "My mother is."

Marcy gasped and fell back, as if she'd been struck. Shannon resumed her frantic struggles with her restraints. The baby continued howling at her feet.

"It's really very simple, Mommy. You had most of it figured out already. Except your part in it, of course." Audrey's smile widened as she warmed to her subject, clearly pleased for this opportunity to show off. "You see, the original plan was to kidnap cranky little Caitlin here, hold her for ransom, and make it look as if Shannon was responsible. But then you entered the picture, showing your stupid photographs to half the populace and telling your ridiculous sob story to anyone who'd listen, so we had to improvise. I mean, your timing really sucked. We'd been planning this for months, and the last thing we wanted was to draw attention to ourselves just when we were ready to make a move. At first we thought we could just ignore you, and maybe you'd go away. But you wouldn't be ignored and you wouldn't go away. Then we tried to distract you, but you're rather single-minded in your focus, aren't you, Mommy? Then we thought we'd scare you. Turns out you don't scare all that easily either. We thought of killing you, but then we realized we could actually use you to our advantage, that you could be our—what's the word for it? Scapegoat? Yeah, that's it. Poor Marcy, undone by grief over her daughter's untimely death, fixates on dumb, naive Shannon, and when Shannon rebuffs her pathetic attempts at friendship, she goes off the deep end and hires someone to kidnap her and the baby. Increasingly desperate and delusional, she kills them both, and then, overwhelmed with guilt and remorse, turns the gun on herself. Meanwhile her accomplice disappears with the ransom money."

"That would be me," Jax said, an audible swagger in his voice.

"Well, not exactly," Audrey said sweetly, raising the gun in her hand and pointing it directly at Jax's head.

"What the hell are you doin'?" Jax asked, all traces of swagger suddenly gone.

"It's just so much easier to divide five hundred thousand euros by two than by three, don't you think?" she asked.

Then she pulled the trigger.

Caitlin's screams filled the air as the bullet lifted Jax off his feet and propelled him backward, his arms shooting up and over his head, his legs extending straight in front of him, blood gushing from the gaping hole in the middle of his forehead as he came crashing to the floor. In the next second Shannon was hurling herself in Audrey's direction, the chair to which she was tied catching the side of Audrey's hip and knocking them both to the floor, the gun flying from Audrey's hand. Marcy grabbed it just as Audrey was about to, their fingers brushing up against each other, sending shockwaves up Marcy's arm, directly to her heart.

"Don't move," she warned Audrey, pulling back and away, one hand fighting with the other to steady the gun.

"Could you really shoot me, Mommy?" Audrey asked plaintively as the baby's cries miraculously shuddered to a halt.

Marcy stared deep into the young woman's eyes. "Don't call me Mommy," she said forcefully. "I don't know who the hell you are, but you're not my daughter."

"Marcy!" a man shouted, his voice resonating throughout the room, her name bouncing off the walls like a stray bullet.

Marcy didn't have to turn around to know who it was. She'd been expecting him. "Liam," she said, her head angling toward him while she still kept Audrey firmly in her sights.

"It's okay, Marcy," Liam said soothingly, emerging from the doorway. "I've been right on your tail all afternoon. The gardai are on their way." He moved closer. "You can give me the gun. It's okay now."

"Stay back," she warned, steadying her hand on the weapon.

He laughed. "Marcy, what are you doin'? It's me, Liam. I'm on *your* side, remember?"

"You're not on my side."

"What are you talkin' about?"

"It was you all along. You planned this whole thing."

How else could Audrey have known about her visits to the garda station, that the gardai had dismissed her as delusional with grief, unless Liam had told her? How else could Jax have

known about her mother's suicide and her sister's many mar-
riages? Or that Devon always called her Mommy? All confidences she'd shared with Liam. Just as she'd told him about her
guilt at having yelled at Devon for scribbling on the walls and
not practicing her piano lessons correctly. Things she'd never
told anyone else.

"You think this was my idea?" His eyes swept the room.
"You think I'm the big criminal mastermind here? You really
think I'm that smart?" He took another step forward. "Come
on, Marcy. Give me the gun."

"You really think I'm that stupid?" Marcy asked in return.

"Marcy—"

"Please don't make me shoot you."

"Shoot me? Come on. You're talkin' crazy."

"Yeah, I'm sure you did a great job of convincing the gardai
that I'm nuttier than a jar of cashews." She laughed, thinking
of Judith.

"A jar of cashews? Do you hear yourself?" Liam asked, as
if she'd taken total leave of her senses. Marcy could almost
close her eyes and hear Peter. The only difference was the Irish
accent. "Come on, Marcy. Put down the gun. You're hysterical.
You don't know what you're sayin'."

Which was when they heard the sound of sirens approaching in the distance.

My God, Marcy thought, momentarily distracted by the
siren's abrasive wail. Could she be wrong? Had Liam called the
police after all?

Liam suddenly shot toward her, wresting the gun from her
hand and pushing her roughly to the floor. She tripped over
Jax's body and rolled toward the fireplace. "Get the baby," she
heard Liam shout.

Marcy watched Audrey snatch Caitlin from her box and

bolt for the back door, Liam right behind her. Struggling to her feet, Marcy grabbed the poker from beside the fireplace. What the hell am I going to do with this? she wondered.

She heard Sarah admonish her. *Don't think. Just swing.*

Don't think, she repeated silently. And then, aloud, "Just swing."

She raised her arm, heard the whoosh of the poker as it sliced through the air, absorbed the echo of steel impacting on bone as it connected with Liam's back, then watched him pitch forward, the gun dropping from his hand as he crumpled to the floor. Marcy grabbed the gun and jumped over his unconscious body, the outside wind snapping at her face like a damp towel as she chased after Audrey. The police sirens were getting closer, filling the air with their caterwauling and harmonizing with Caitlin's angry screams. Marcy searched frantically through the fog for Audrey, finally spotting her running down the side of the steep hill. Marcy struggled to catch up to her, stumbling repeatedly over the uneven terrain and falling twice. In the distance, she could make out at least half a dozen police cars making their way up the winding road. "Audrey," she shouted toward the fleeing woman. "Stop! The gardai are here. You can't get away."

Audrey's response was to edge even closer to the side of the cliff, the wind causing her long hair to dance wildly around her face, highlighting her superficial resemblance to Devon.

"There's nowhere to go," Marcy told her over the sound of the waves crashing against the rocks below. Although they were standing no more than ten feet apart, they had to shout to be heard.

"One more step and it's bye-bye, baby." Audrey extended the arm holding Caitlin, dangling the infant over the side of the cliff.

Marcy pictured her mother in the seconds before she took her fatal plunge, imagined her flying through the air to the concrete below. "Just give her to me, Audrey," Marcy pleaded. "That way at least you'll have a chance of getting away."

"And what are the odds of that, do you think?" Audrey said. "Think I can just disappear into thin air?"

"Maybe."

"Like your daughter?"

Tears stung Marcy's eyes. "My daughter didn't disappear," she said, acknowledging the truth aloud for the very first time. Her mother and her daughter, she thought, flip sides of the same tragic coin. "She's dead."

"Thought you didn't believe that."

"I didn't want to believe it."

"Yeah? Well, I'll tell you what," Audrey said as somewhere behind them cars screeched to a halt and doors slammed shut. "I'll make you a trade—the baby for the gun. What do you say?"

"It's a deal," Marcy agreed quickly.

"You first," Audrey directed. "Toss the gun over here." She pointed with her free hand to a patch of grass near her feet. "No funny stuff or I swear the kid takes a very nasty tumble."

"No funny stuff." Marcy gently pitched the gun in the appointed direction, watched it disappear into the tall, wet grass next to Audrey's feet. "Now give me the baby."

Audrey stared at Marcy for several long seconds, as if debating her next move. Then she advanced slowly forward, extending the baby toward Marcy.

Just like my dream, Marcy thought, holding her breath. *Here's the girl you've always wanted,* Devon had said, just before releasing the baby in her arms and letting her fall.

My baby is dead, Marcy thought. I couldn't save her.

"She's all yours," Audrey said now, dropping the crying baby into Marcy's grateful hands.

"Marcy!" a voice shouted as Vic Sorvino emerged from the fog and ran toward them.

Audrey jumped at the sound of his voice. She lunged toward the gun in the grass, tripping over her feet and losing her tenuous grip on the bumpy ground. Marcy watched helplessly as she stumbled backward, unable to control the muscles in her legs, her arms flailing wildly at her sides as her feet lost contact with the earth and she plunged off the side of the steep hill, her screams echoing in the wind, accompanying her into the frigid waves of Roaringwater Bay below.

THIRTY-ONE

WHEN DID YOU REALIZE she wasn't your daughter?" Vic was asking, holding on tightly to Marcy's still-shaking hands.

They were sitting side by side in front of the messy desk in Christopher Murphy's office at the garda station. Murphy had just excused himself to confer with Donnelly and Sweeny in another room.

"Not right away," Marcy answered. "It was dark in the farmhouse, so when I first saw her I couldn't be sure. Her hair was the same as Devon's; she looked to be the same height and build. The shape of her face was similar, although her voice was different, even when she whispered. But she kept calling me Mommy, and so I kept telling myself that it had been a few years since the last time I'd heard her speak, and that she was older now and she'd been experimenting with various accents, that her voice could have changed. The usual rationalizations. I've gotten pretty good at them lately." She sighed, deciding that "rationalizations" was something of an understatement. "Anyway, like I said, it was pretty dark, and at first she kept her head down. Her hair was hiding most of her face. And then Jax said they should just shoot us and get the hell out of there, and Audrey walked over to Shannon and said, cold as ice, 'We're not going to shoot you. My mother is.' And suddenly, there was this spark from the fireplace that lit up her whole face. She was smiling, and I heard Peter say, 'That girl needs a good set of braces.'" Marcy shook her head. "And that just knocked the wind right out of me. I mean, you remember the picture of Devon with her porcelain braces. Her teeth were perfect, and this girl's teeth were crooked. They weren't Devon's teeth!" She released a long, audible breath. "The truth is I probably knew all along." She reached into the purse on her lap and withdrew the tattered envelope containing Devon's photographs and the note her daughter had written, handing it over to Vic. "You can read it," she said as Vic gently unfolded the piece of paper. "I think I knew it was a suicide note all along. I just didn't want to accept it. I kept telling myself that she could have changed her mind at the last second. Or that she just wanted us to think she was dead."

Vic read the letter, then quietly returned it to Marcy's purse. "She obviously loved you very much."

Marcy nodded. "I loved her, too. But it wasn't enough to save her."

"I loved my wife," Vic said. "It wasn't enough to save her either."

"Your wife had cancer. It's not the same thing."

"Isn't it? They were both sick. Sick with something they couldn't control. You have nothing to feel guilty for, Marcy."

"Don't I? I told her I was tired of parenting. What kind of mother does that make me?"

"A pretty normal one."

Marcy thought again of the times she'd berated Devon for not concentrating on her piano studies, of that awful afternoon when she'd hollered at the proud toddler for scribbling on the walls, the way the child had turned and clutched her stomach, as if she'd been mortally wounded.

Except that Devon's note hadn't mentioned any of those things, Marcy realized. Instead she'd written about all the wonderful times they'd shared, the happy memories of watching TV together, of going to the ballet and relaxing at the cottage. She'd talked only of love.

"I loved her so much," Marcy said, crying softly.

"I know you did. And more important, Devon knew it."

Marcy swiped at the tears falling down her cheeks with the back of her hand as the door opened and Christopher Murphy reentered the room, followed by John Sweeny and Colleen Donnelly.

"Apparently Mr. Flaherty has supplied us with a full confession," Murphy said, coming around to his side of the desk and plopping down in his swivel chair.

It took Marcy a few seconds to comprehend that Liam was the Mr. Flaherty in question, a little longer to digest the rest of what Murphy was saying.

"It seems that Liam's father used to work for the O'Connors' construction company. He was killed in an accident at work some years back, and according to Liam, his family was denied proper compensation. Liam decided to rectify that by kidnapping the O'Connor baby and holding her for ransom. He met

Audrey when Jax brought her 'round to Grogan's House one night. Audrey was new in town, from London originally, in and out of trouble most of her life. Together, the three of them hatched this plan to seduce Shannon and kidnap Caitlin, all stuff you pretty much had figured out," Murphy said with an admiring nod in Marcy's direction. He leaned forward, resting his elbows uneasily on the mounds of paperwork. "Then you showed up, convinced you'd seen your daughter, and started showing Devon's picture around, and apparently a nosy waitress decided she thought the picture looked like Audrey. Things just sort of mushroomed from there."

"When did they kidnap the baby?" Marcy asked, trying to assign an order to the day's events, as if that might help explain them.

"This morning, when Shannon took her for a walk. The ransom demand was made within minutes of her being spirited off. Mr. O'Connor had three hours to come up with the money and was warned not to contact us or Caitlin would die."

Marcy absorbed this information with a nod of her head, still trying to sort out fanciful fiction from hard, cold fact. Liam had been lying to her from the very beginning; the only truthful thing he'd ever said to her was when he claimed not to recognize Devon's picture. But she'd preferred to believe his lies, to flatter herself into thinking he might be genuinely interested in her when his attempts at seduction had been nothing but an elaborate ruse, calculated to elicit information, to keep her off balance and in line. The times he'd urged her to call the police, he'd done so not only with the knowledge of how ridiculous she'd sound, but also to keep suspicion off himself. He hadn't called the O'Connor house last night; he hadn't spoken to Shannon; Shannon had never agreed to get in touch with Audrey. His calls to the hotel last night and this morning had been nothing but a way of checking up on her. Likewise his phone call when she was at St. Fin Barre's Cathedral—just a way of ensuring that she was following Audrey's instructions, that she'd told no one where she was going or what she was up to.

"And now Audrey is dead," Marcy said out loud.

"I'm afraid so, yes," Sweeny stated. "Her body washed up on some rocks near Bear Island about an hour ago."

"I don't understand—how did you know where to find me?"

"You can thank Mr. Sorvino for that," Colleen Donnelly said.

Marcy looked to Vic for an explanation.

"Check your purse," he said.

Marcy opened her purse and began rummaging around inside it. She withdrew her wallet, her passport, the envelope with Devon's pictures and suicide note, a tube of lipstick and a pair of sunglasses, some errant breath mints scattered along the bottom of the bag, and . . . something else, she realized, her fingers surrounding a small metal object and holding it up to the light. "What is this? Is this a widget?" she asked accusingly.

"A what?" Murphy asked. The three gardai exchanged puzzled looks.

Vic laughed. "Not exactly."

"It's a tracking device," Sweeny explained, taking it from Marcy's hand and turning it over in his own.

"We planted it in your purse at Mr. Sorvino's rather insistent suggestion," Murphy said.

"I believe he threatened to sue us for the indignity he suffered at the airport if we didn't comply," Donnelly added.

"Clearly an empty threat," Vic demurred.

"Clearly. Still, he was so convinced you were in danger. . . ."

"And he was threatening to camp out in our lobby. . . ."

"And go to the American embassy . . ."

"Despite the fact you're Canadian," Murphy said, interjecting.

"So we decided to humor him."

"We were with you from the moment you left your hotel room this morning," Sweeny stated.

"Even let this one tag along," Donnelly said, nodding toward Vic. "Still not quite sure how that happened. Never realized you were such a softie," she said to Murphy.

Murphy acknowledged her remark with an embarrassed clearing of his throat. "Let's just say it was the least I could do for a man whose three sons are all police officers."

The sound of a baby's wails shot through the halls, like a steel ball from a cannon. It was followed by a timid knocking on the door. A young woman with short, dark hair poked her head inside the room. "Mr. and Mrs. O'Connor are waiting in the next room," Marcy heard her whisper. "They'd like to see Mrs. Taggart, if that's all right."

Seconds later, the O'Connors were ushered into the room. Marcy rose to greet them.

"Mrs. Taggart, we can't thank you enough," Mr. O'Connor said, striding toward her and furiously pumping her hand.

Mrs. O'Connor was standing beside him, her normally attractive face pale and blotchy from crying, her arms wrapped protectively around her screaming infant. "I don't seem to know how to comfort her," she whispered tearfully. "Shannon says you have quite the way with her. Perhaps you'll share the secrets of your success," she added shyly.

Marcy smiled, acknowledging the sometimes painful

truth—that there were no such secrets. "Sometimes you just get lucky," she said.

IT WAS DARK by the time Marcy and Vic returned to the Hayfield Manor. The intermittent rain had finally stopped; the wind had ceased blowing. According to the taxi driver who drove them back to the hotel, tomorrow was expected to be a beautiful day, full of warmth and sunshine. Already it felt more temperate than it had all day, although Marcy was doubtful she'd ever feel truly warm again. She was looking forward to a hot meal, followed by a hot bath, then climbing into bed. Tomorrow she'd see what she could do about changing her flight.

"You're sure I can't convince you to come to Italy with me?" Vic asked as they lingered in each other's arms beside the hotel's front entrance.

"I'd really love to," Marcy said, fighting the almost overwhelming urge to invite him up to her room, to lose herself in the comforting passion of his embrace. Except she'd been lost for far too long already. "I just don't think it's a very good idea right now. I need time to get my head on straight. Maybe I've been having a delayed nervous breakdown. Maybe I'm as crazy as Peter thinks I am. I don't know. I *do* know that I haven't been normal, that I haven't been behaving rationally, for almost two years. Since Devon died," she said, forcing the words from her mouth. "I need to go back home, find a good therapist, make things right with my son, get my house in order. Then maybe in a while, if you're still available . . ."

"I'm available," Vic said quickly.

Marcy smiled. "You didn't tell me your three sons are policemen."

"They aren't." He gave her a sly grin. "I made it up."

"You lied to the gardai? Why?"

"I had to say something to persuade them to let me go with them, didn't I?"

"You lied?" She marveled at him.

He shrugged. Then he kissed her, a soft, gentle kiss she felt lingering on her lips long after they said good-bye. Marcy stood watching from the doorway as Vic climbed back into the waiting taxi and disappeared into the night.

"Marcy?" a voice called from somewhere behind her.

Marcy turned to see a tall, thin woman with blond hair and well-defined biceps pushing herself off the sofa beside the mahogany staircase and walking steadily toward her. Was it possible? Or was she still seeing things that weren't there? "Judith? What are you doing here?"

"Did you think I was just going to wait around for you to regain your sanity and come home?" her sister asked in return. "I've been sitting here all afternoon. Where the hell have you been? Who was that man?" she said in the same breath.

"A friend."

"You don't have any friends."

Marcy smiled, drawing her sister into her arms and holding her tight. "I have you."

Judith threw her long, powerful arms around Marcy's neck. "Yes, you do." They remained in that posture for some time, each reluctant to relinquish her hold on the other.

"You know I love you, don't you?" Marcy asked.

"I love you, too." Judith pulled slowly out of their embrace, looked nervously around. "What about . . . ? Did you find . . . ? Is Devon . . . ?"

"Devon is dead," Marcy said, her voice steady. She took a deep breath, released it slowly. "She killed herself. Just like our mother."

Tears filled Judith's eyes, eyes that Marcy realized were the same exact shade of brown as Devon's. Why had she never noticed that before? "It wasn't your fault," Judith said.

"I know."

"There was nothing you could have done—for either of them."

"I know."

"I'm sorry I wasn't more supportive."

"You don't have to apologize," Marcy told her. "I'm just so glad you're here now."

"Yeah, well, I'm not so sure *I* am," Judith said with a nervous chuckle. "Do you have any idea how many damn bridges this city has?"

Marcy laughed. "I think I have a rough idea."

"I really do love you, you know."

"I know."

"You're sure you're all right?" Judith asked.

Marcy smiled. "I will be," she said.